# ECHOES IN TIME

JULIE MCELWAIN

Echoes in Time
A Kendra Donovan Mystery

Julie McElwain
Seshat Books

In Time book series

*A Murder in Time*
*A Twist in Time*
*Caught in Time*
*Betrayal in Time*
*Shadows in Time*
*Ripples in Time*

Echoes in Time
Copyright 2025 Julie McElwain

Interior Design by Lorna Reid



Hardcover ISBN: 979-8-9873810-4-5
Paperback ISBN: 979-8-9873810-5-2
Ebook ISBN: 979-8-9873810-6-9

To Bostyn and Kenzie,
You are both growing up too fast

# ONE

*Sunday, September 8, 1816*

"*No—!*"

Edwina looked up at the faint cry. The Bowden Theater had been designed so that you could hear a whisper on stage even if you were sitting on the other side of the auditorium. Here, in the small area near the backstage door, sound carried like a faraway echo, indistinct enough to make Edwina wonder if she'd heard anything at all.

Her fingers, chilled from her recent trip to the baker, tensed on the handle of the wicker basket. She held her breath, listening intently.

*Nothing.* Not even the normal creaks and groans often heard in the old building.

Maybe she'd imagined it. She'd always had a vivid imagination. *Get yer bloomin' head out of the clouds, girl, ye've got chores to do!* Her mum's voice rang across the years, making her stomach twist. *Stop wool-gathering, Edwina, and milk that cow!*

It was that imagination—and the stubborn belief that she was meant for greater things than languishing on her family's small farm in Dorset—that led her to run away at the age of fourteen. For a time, she hadn't regretted her decision. She'd been a bright-eyed, pretty child, and had found a home in one of the smaller theater companies on Drury Lane. Oh, not as one of the performers. But she hadn't expected that, had she? Leastwise, not right away.

The theater's owner, Old Man Bolling, had allowed her to sleep in one of the playhouse's dusty cubbyholes, and gave her a shilling a week to fetch and carry whatever the company required. Bottles of gin and goblets of wine for after-performance toasts—or to drown their sorrows for poorly received shows. Shawls for chilled shoulders. Tubs of hot water for aching feet. Not exactly what she'd envision when she'd come to London, but it was less work than churning butter or picking weeds out of her mum's garden patch. And there was always a chance, shimmering in front of her like a golden dream, that she'd bewitch someone enough to allow her on stage.

Everything had been going fine until the night she'd woken to Old Man Bolling crawling on top of her, his hands sliding up her skirts.

Even now Edwina shuddered at the memory of his fetid breath and rough, roaming fingers. Afterwards, no one had been particularly interested in her tale of woe. Not the watchmen or local constable, who'd leered at her and offered to look into her claim—*if* she was friendly to them. Not the actresses, who'd studied her with hard eyes and wondered what the bloody hell had she thought would happen when she fluttered her eyelashes so prettily at Old Man Bolling, no doubt hoping that he'd send one of them packing and give her *their* role. Best to get used to such things, they told her. And, if she had more than fluff betwixt her ears, she'd find a protector among the randy bucks who flooded the theater each night. At least she'd be able to earn a few coins and trinkets, because, heaven knew, she wouldn't get one more tuppence out of that bastard Bolling when he tumbled her.

Certain she would never be free of Old Man Bolling's lechery, Edwina bolted for another theater in Covent Garden. It hadn't taken her long, though, to learn that the actresses had been telling her the truth, to realize that Old Man Bolling wasn't the only libertine in town.

She should have run back home then, except for the sickening sense of shame. After three years in London, she was no longer an innocent, and, God save her soul, she'd even occasionally bartered her body for money to eat, her wages barely affording her a bowl of jellied eels sold by a costermonger who worked the lane.

Maybe she would have eventually returned home, if her fortunes hadn't changed.

Now her breath hitched, a lump lodging painfully in her throat. This was another memory that she preferred to avoid, much as she shied away from the looking glasses stationed in the dressing rooms and hallways.

But the fire haunted her dreams.

She couldn't remember how the blaze started, but the speed— oh, Lord, the *speed*—of the flames had been terrifying. Her skirts had become engulfed by the time she'd fled the theater. She should have perished. She *wished* she'd perished, wished her flesh and bones had turned to ash along with the theater's walls and roof. However, the eel costermonger who'd set up his cart outside the theater saved her.

Edwina would never forgive him.

In an odd quirk, the right side of her body remained relatively unscathed, while her left side . . . *oh, God.* Her flesh was scorched and scarred from ankle to brow.

Her visions of sharing the stage with the likes of Edmund Kean and Maria Davison were shattered that night. So was her half-formed idea of returning to her family. *Not now.* Not when she'd become this hideous creature with her twisted, pitted flesh. She couldn't bear having her siblings stare at her with fear, or her mum and pa looking at her with pity. Or, worse—scorn. *Ye always thought ye were better than us, didn't ye, girl? Now look at ye!*

Tears gathered in Edwina's right eye, blurring her vision. Her left eye, with its puckered skin around the orb, remained dry. The fire had made it impossible for tears to ever form in that eye.

Determinedly, she blinked away the moisture. The fire was two years ago. She was seventeen now, no longer a baby. She'd learned, hadn't she? A Quaker family had taken her in, tended her wounds until she was strong enough to leave. She'd found work at the Bowden Theater. Again, she fetched and carried, but it was her skill with needle and thread that had become her greatest asset. She assisted Old Beatrice, the company's seamstress, in creating new costumes and patching up old. It was a job done mostly in the shadows. She'd merged into the background, much like the props and timber cutouts wheeled on stage for each act. No one wanted to look too closely at her scarred face.

A mirthless smile twisted her mouth. At least she could sleep unmolested in one of the theater's cubbyholes.

Still, Edwina had her peepers, even if her left eye was deformed and dry. She'd become a keen observer, noticing things others did not.

*Like the two gentlemen.*

Oh, they were dapper, all right, with their expensively tailored topcoats and curly brimmed beaver hats, blending in with the other swells. But they were . . . *different.* Like the other bucks, they would smile, their expressions affable, but their eyes were always cold. Lust didn't drive them as it did the others, but something else, something that made Edwina back away whisper-soft, deeper into the theater's gloom, so as not to attract their attention.

Still, she hadn't given them a thought until yesterday, when the lady had come asking about Clarice.

Clarice had been cast in the coveted role of Portia for the upcoming production of *The Merchant of Venice.* For one week, she'd reveled in her new status, strutting around the stage like she was a bloody duchess.

Then, a week ago, she'd vanished.

When Edwina had overheard the lady quizzing Mr. Myott, the theater manager, about Clarice, her mind had instantly flashed to the two gentlemen. They'd been part of Clarice's circle of admirers.

Unfortunately, the lady's timing had been poor—less than an hour before Saturday evening's opening act, and the troupe was scurrying to and fro across the stage in their final preparations. Tempers were short and anxiety high. Normally, Mr. Myott treated Quality with a toad-eating deference, but stress had made him snap at the gentry mort, ordering her to leave.

Edwina had waited until Mr. Myott ran off to scream at the

jugglers for wearing incorrect costumes for the opening act, then approached the woman. Ignoring the lady's start of surprise and the way her eyes darted across Edwina's scarred face, Edwina had offered to share what she knew if the lady returned to the theater at ten o'clock on the morrow. She only asked for a few coins in return.

"*Stop! No!... PLEASE!*"

Edwina came back to the present in a rush. *That* wasn't a figment of her imagination. Pulse accelerating, she gathered her skirts to hurry down the long, shadowy corridor connecting the theater's backstage to the auditorium.

The scent of linseed oil, greasepaint, sawdust, and melted tallow assailed her nostrils. The morning's cold, gray light streamed through skylights and windows, an architectural necessity to save on candles during rehearsals and when sceneries were being built. The playhouse was small by Covent Garden standards, seating a mere three hundred. Four balcony tiers with private boxes flanked the stage. Iron spikes bordered the audience pit. Auditorium seats fanned out in three sections from the pit and stage.

Edwina stepped into the auditorium and froze when a scream shattered the silence. Movement caught her eye and she looked upward, to the top balcony on the right side of the stage. Her good eye widened in horror as a winged creature rose up and soared over the railing. Instead of flapping its wings to take flight, the creature let out an unearthly shriek as it plummeted down... down... *down.* The shriek was abruptly cut off as it hit the back of the seats with a startling crack.

Edwina's hand flew to her mouth to stifle her own scream. The silence that followed was so dark and vast that she had the dizzying sensation that she'd dropped into a bottomless well. Her gaze locked on the figure bent at an awkward angle over two seats. Not a supernatural bird of prey, but the lady she was supposed to meet. The black velvet cape she wore spread around her like broken raven wings.

Slowly, Edwina raised her gaze from the unnaturally still form to the top balcony and the man leaning over the balustrade. His face was partially hidden by his wide-brimmed hat and the collar of his greatcoat, but she knew who he was. For a brief moment, she met his eyes. They seemed to scorch her like the fire she'd survived.

Then he was gone.

Edwina didn't know how long she stood there transfixed until her inner voice screeched: *Don't stand there, you stupid cow—run!*

Drawing in a shuddering breath, she yanked her skirts past her knees and pelted down the hallway. In the distance, she heard the pounding of boots as he raced down the stairs. Terror speared her as she launched herself against the backstage door—and nearly screamed when it didn't budge. *Trapped,* she thought wildly. It took her a second to realize she hadn't unlatched it. *Stupid, stupid girl!*

The running footsteps behind her sounded like thunder. Slick with sweat, her hand fumbled with the latch. She threw open the door. Stumbled. Righted herself, then bolted down the alley. Heart hammering, she ran like the devil was chasing her.

*Because he is. And if he catches me, I'm as good as dead.*

# TWO

*Tuesday, September 10, 1816*

Kendra could honestly say that in her twenty-seven years, she'd never once imagined her wedding day. She had never been one of those girls who giggled over boys and dreamed about walking down the aisle to some shadowy figure waiting for her at the altar. And even if she had, never in a million years could she have imagined *this* wedding day. How could she? It wasn't so much a matter of where she was currently sitting—Aldridge Castle's formal dining room— but *when*. She'd been born in the late twentieth century—more than two hundred years in the future.

Time traveler.

*Freak.*

Her fingers tightened on the delicate crystal flute she held. It had been more than a year since she'd found herself unexpectedly transported through a vortex or wormhole, but there were still moments when her head swam and she wondered if she'd wake up one morning to discover that it all had been a dream.

A chill raced down her arms. A year ago, she would've given anything for that to happen, to wake up in her own bed in her apartment in Maryland. To push a button to light up the room, and jump in a shower with hot, pulsating water. To drive herself to her job as a special agent in the FBI's the Behavioral Science Division. But now . . .

*Now* the idea of returning to her own timeline made her stomach churn with anxiety.

Slowly she sipped the champagne, easing her dry throat. She let her gaze roam over the guests seated at the long, linen-covered table. There were more chairs than people this morning, but that was fine with Kendra. She'd feared that the wedding, which had taken place forty-five minutes ago in the small village church, would be an elaborate affair, with the attendees sporting more titles than the Library of Congress. Such things were expected when you married the Marquis of Sutcliffe, the nephew—and heir—to the powerful Duke of Aldridge. She'd been pleasantly surprised to discover that weddings in this era—unless you were royalty—tended to be small, private affairs, limited to family and close friends.

She had no family. Her parents, Dr. Carl Donovan and Dr. Eleanor Jahnke, hadn't been born yet.

The crowd had mostly been made up of villagers, who'd gathered outside the ancient stone church, lining the cobblestone streets of Aldridge Village while Kendra and Alec exchanged vows inside. Then they'd cheered the small wedding party as they made their way back to the castle for breakfast.

The guests themselves were an odd consortium. Even Kendra recognized their peculiarity. Occupying one side of the table was the Duke of Aldridge's sister, Lady Carolyn Atwood, and her daughter, Lady Mary Ballinger. Lady Mary had traveled from her home in Cumbria at her mother's behest. Kendra suspected she had been invited solely to hold the smelling salts in case the countess fainted from the sheer horror of having to accept Kendra—an American with no pedigree or social graces—into their prestigious family. God knew, Lady Carolyn had warned her nephew enough to reconsider his proposal.

Next to them was Lady Rebecca and her parents, Lord and Lady Blackburn. Most people noticed Rebecca's beautiful auburn hair, but they quickly became distracted by the pockmarks that marred her face, the result of a childhood bout of smallpox. Certainly, they never saw the cleverness in the cornflower blue eyes or the spirit that lifted her chin and squared her shoulders. An ardent supporter of the early feminist Mary Wollstonecraft, Rebecca had been quick to accept

Kendra's unorthodox behavior. Although Kendra hadn't told Rebecca her most carefully guarded secret—the fact that she was a time traveler—she considered the other woman a friend. Really one of her only friends, regardless of century.

On the other side of the table were Kendra's guests: Dr. Ethan Munroe, Sam Kelly, and Phineas "Finn" Muldoon. Only Dr. Munroe blended in with the aristocrats' silks and superfines. He was a distinguished-looking man in his early fifties, with a silvery mane that he tied into an old-fashioned queue and contrasting black eyebrows. His eyes were gray and intelligent behind round gold spectacles that he pinched on his hawklike nose. It wasn't his person, but his profession—a former doctor who now operated an anatomy school in London—that had made him an outcast in society.

Sam and Muldoon, on the other hand, were wearing their Sunday best, but there was no mistaking their working-class roots in the rougher wools and tweeds. Both men sat a little closer to one another, as though they'd each subconsciously sought comfort in the other's presence.

Kendra had to suppress a smile. Their camaraderie was ironic, given Sam was a Bow Street Runner (this era's version of a police detective) and Muldoon was a reporter for the *Morning Chronicle*. Like the relationship between the police and the press in her own timeline, their relationship was, more often than not, contentious.

"My lady? Ah . . . my lady?"

"I believe Harding is referring to you, my dear," the Duke of Aldridge whispered, amusement glinting in his blue eyes as he leaned toward her.

Kendra realized that the Duke's stoic butler was standing at her elbow, holding a champagne bottle.

"Oh." *I am no longer Kendra Donovan; I'm now the Marchioness of Sutcliffe. Holy God.*

"Would you care for more champagne, my lady?" Harding repeated.

Kendra looked at the delicate flute in her hand. It was empty. "Uh . . . yes, thank you."

The butler kept a poker face as he poured the champagne, but Kendra recognized her blunder. Thanking a servant for doing their duty was simply not done when you were a marchioness.

Kendra watched the champagne bubbles froth to the lip of the flute. She'd made the decision to stay here, in this time—assuming the vortex that had opened a month ago hadn't just been her imagination. Still, she knew that she'd never really fit in here, with the rigid rules and class system.

"We shall leave soon, my sweet."

Kendra glanced at the green-eyed man on her other side. Alec, the Marquis of Sutcliffe. Her husband. And the reason she'd chosen to stay in an era where she didn't belong—because living without this man had become too painful to contemplate. Love had been unexpected, not always welcome, but too big to deny. And it still amazed her, not only that she'd fallen in love with him, but that the love had been reciprocated.

The gold flecks in his forest-green eyes were more pronounced this morning, gleaming like molten embers, shadowed by spikey black lashes. The sensual mouth in the lean, handsome face curved in a slow smile. Kendra could feel her face grow warm under her husband's regard, her blood quickening.

In her former life, she'd been a child prodigy, a product of her parents' experiment in eugenics, and an FBI agent. She did *not* blush. Or, rather, she'd never met anyone who'd made her blush before. Alec was more potent than the alcohol she was drinking.

She raised an eyebrow, although her breath wasn't quite steady. "Are you trying to reassure me?"

His smile widened. "Perhaps." He took her hand and raised it to his lips, brushing a butterfly-soft kiss over her knuckles. "Or mayhap I'm reminding myself that I need to be patient. Soon, I shall have you all to myself. You've made me the luckiest of men."

"I chose you," she whispered, leaning toward him to stare into his eyes. She saw them darken at the memory of the night she'd said those words. The moment she'd finally made the decision to let the past—the *future*—go. To trust in their love and build a life together in the here and now.

"We chose each other," he returned softly.

"Sutcliffe, what are your future plans?" Lady Mary asked loudly, breaking the spell that bound Kendra to Alec. She suspected that had been Lady Mary's intention. Public affection, even between a bride and groom on their wedding day, was frowned upon. "Will you and your lady be taking up residence in Alcott Park?"

Alcott Park was Alec's country estate in northern England. Kendra imagined that it was Lady Atwood's greatest wish to see Kendra hidden away in the countryside, so there'd be no faux pas committed by the newest member of their family.

Alec released Kendra's hand, shifting to look down the table at his cousin. "We'll travel to London tonight, then on to Alcott Park for a fortnight. Afterward, I shall be bringing Kendra to Venice to meet my relatives."

Kendra's stomach fluttered. As interested as she was in visiting Venice, to see the art and architecture and the wonder of its canals, she was uneasy about being introduced to the maternal side of Alec's family. His late mother, Alexandria, had been an Italian countess who'd fallen in love with Alec's father, Edward, on his Grand Tour. Kendra got enough disapproval from the English; she didn't need it from Venetian aristocrats too.

A footman leaned down, offering her a silver platter filled with meats. Grateful to focus on something else, she picked up the knife and fork. Bypassing the artfully arranged tongue, she selected two thick slices of ham.

"But will you settle at Alcott Park, Cousin?" Lady Mary persisted, her eyes on Alec as she took a sip of her champagne.

"No." Alec shook his head. "London is more agreeable for us to make our home."

"London society shall be greatly improved with your presence, Miss—ah, your ladyship," Muldoon spoke up, shooting Kendra an impudent grin. "Mayhap I shall see you around town."

Kendra noticed that his gaze slipped further down the table to where Lady Rebecca was seated. She suspected he was hoping that if they met, Kendra would be accompanied by Rebecca. In the last year, it had become clear to Kendra that the two harbored a mutual attraction, but neither one was prepared to act on it. Poor Irish reporters did *not* marry daughters of nobility.

Then again, Americans from the future didn't marry British aristocracy. Only the Duke and Alec knew that she was from the twenty-first century, but being a penniless American hadn't exactly made her a desirable match. The pained expression on Lady Atwood's face wasn't going to go away anytime soon.

"Not much chance of that," Sam growled at the reporter, as he sliced into the tongue on his plate. "She'll be traveling in circles high above you."

Muldoon wiggled his eyebrows. "I've learned to always expect the unexpected with M—with her ladyship. No offense, ma'am."

Kendra was more offended at being called ma'am, but decided that was probably a twenty-first-century pet peeve.

"You're my friends," she said simply, before turning her attention to eating her eggs, ham, and rolls. Except for the tongue—which was considered a delicacy—the champagne, and the iced fruitcake set in the middle of the table, the breakfast was like any other.

She was buttering a roll when she noticed a younger footman sidle into the dining room. He approached Harding and whispered in his ear. The shock that rippled across the butler's normally unflappable features sent a frisson of awareness through Kendra.

*Something happened.*

Harding carefully set the champagne bottle in an ice bucket before accompanying the footman out the door.

Kendra glanced at Alec, who was also regarding the door thoughtfully. "What do you think's going on?"

He said, "I have no idea."

Seconds ticked by, then Harding reappeared. He retrieved the champagne bottle and circled the table to the Duke. On the pretext of refilling his flute, the butler leaned down and murmured something in his ear. If Kendra hadn't already been on alert, the Duke's reaction would have been a red flag. His eyebrows flew up and he shot her a quick look. Nodding at Harding, he picked up his linen napkin, blotted his mouth, then carefully laid it on his plate.

"Forgive me, but I must attend to a matter," he announced, pushing himself to his feet. "Alec, would you and your lovely bride accompany me?"

Lady Atwood frowned. "Bertie, what—?"

"We shall only be a moment, Caro," he cut off his sister with a smile.

As soon as they exited the dining room, Kendra repeated her question: "What's going on?"

The Duke shook his head. "I'm not entirely certain. We have a visitor. A royal courier."

They followed the Duke to the Gold Salon, one of the castle's more ornate drawing rooms. Apparently, a royal messenger deserved the best. The courier waited in front of one of the Palladian windows, gazing at the gardens outside. He was a middle-aged gentleman wearing an exquisitely tailored green-and-navy frock coat buttoned tight around the torso before flaring into a full skirt that hit mid-calf. He'd kept his curly brimmed beaver hat on, but at their appearance, he swept it off to reveal a full head of curly brown hair and dipped into a graceful bow.

"Your Grace, my lord and my lady." His gaze traveled over them as he straightened. "I understand felicitations are in order. Forgive my intrusion during this happy time."

"Thank you," Alec replied. "But of course, that begs the question as to why you felt the need to intrude. What is this about?"

The courier looked taken aback at such directness. He hesitated, as though searching for the correct words. Finally, he said, "There's been an incident."

"An incident?" the Duke echoed.

"Yes. A tragic incident." The courier looked at Kendra. "We are aware of your ladyship's experience in investigating such things."

*We?* Kendra eyed the man in surprise, but before she could

question him, Alec said sharply, "My wife and I shall be leaving for our honeymoon shortly. Unless the King himself is asking for her ladyship's help with this . . . incident, I am going to bid you good day, sir."

"I understand your concern, my lord." The courier reached into his coat pocket and withdrew a letter. A royal wax seal held the flaps together. He handed the parchment to the Duke, but his eyes were fixed on Alec. "The King is indisposed. He is not asking for her ladyship's assistance in this matter."

Alec shook his head. "Then if the King isn't behind this request—"

"Not His Majesty, sir. *Her* Majesty. Will you postpone your honeymoon for the Queen?"

# THREE

A curious silence descended. Kendra wondered if everyone else was finding the moment as surreal as she was.

The Duke was the first to speak. "This incident," he said. "You are speaking of murder?"

It was a natural assumption. In the last year, Kendra had been involved in several such investigations. She knew her activities had been the cause of gossip among the Beau Monde, but uneasiness knotted her stomach at the idea that she'd drawn attention in royal circles as well.

"Possibly," the courier said cautiously. "Yesterday morning, Lady Westford was found dead in the Bowden Theater. 'Tis a theater in Covent Garden."

The Duke lifted his eyebrows in shock. "Lady Westford is dead?"

"Yes, I'm afraid so, Your Grace."

Kendra glanced at the Duke. "You knew her?"

"Yes, though I cannot claim we were close friends. Lady Westford has an interest in natural philosophy, and throughout the years, we've attended the same lectures at the Royal Society. It's rather unusual for ladies to go to such scientific forums. I found the countess to be intellectual and charming. This is a . . . a terrible shock."

Alec said, "I met Lady Westford when she launched her youngest daughter into society several years ago." He looked at the courier. "What happened?"

"It appears her ladyship fell from the upper balcony of the theater, my lord."

The Duke's eyes widened. "Good God, during a performance?"

"Ah . . . no." The man's gaze dropped to the hat that he was rotating in his hands. He was silent for a long moment. Again, Kendra had the impression that he was searching for the right words. At last, his hands stilled, and he lifted his gaze to the Duke's. "It's believed she fell on Sunday, when the theater was closed."

"I don't understand. Why was she at the theater when it was closed?"

"One of many questions, Your Grace."

"I have a question," Alec drawled, eyeing the courier. "Why is the Queen requiring my wife's involvement? Surely, the matter is being looked into by the proper authorities?"

"Bow Street's Chief Magistrate, Sir Nathaniel Conant, assigned an investigator—Mr. Parker—to look into the matter. London's chief coroner is currently in France, but Dr. Lucien Thornton, a respected physician, conducted the postmortem. He concluded that her ladyship accidently fell from the balcony to her death."

Kendra contemplated the man. "So her death has already been officially declared an accident?"

"Yes."

She frowned. "Then what's the problem?"

"There is speculation that she did not fall, that she . . . ah, that she jumped."

"My God." The Duke let out a shocked breath. "Suicide? I do not believe it!"

"Nor does Her Majesty," the courier said quietly. "Self-murder is such a vile, sinful act, and would cause great disgrace to the family, not to mention cast a shadow on Lady Westford's soul. Her Majesty is requesting that Lady Sutcliffe investigate the matter quietly, to remove all doubt."

"What is your name, sir?" Alec demanded, his green eyes narrowing on the courier. "You present yourself as a royal courier, but you clearly did not ride here on horseback, which is the fastest method used by messengers—even royal messengers. And you appear to be intimately familiar with the details of her ladyship's death."

A gleam of what might have been rueful admiration entered the other man's eyes. "Very astute of you, my lord. I am Mr. Boothe. I clerk for Mr. Disbrowe," he admitted. "I am acting on behalf of Her Majesty."

Kendra's uneasiness intensified. She didn't need the Duke or Alec to tell her that they were dealing with the inner circle of the Palace. The British royal family had become a constitutional monarchy centuries before, during Charles II's reign, but the Palace had more power today than in her own time. Maybe they couldn't toss her in the Tower of London—*could they?* —but they could probably make her life damned unpleasant if she fell afoul of them.

"Edward Disbrowe is Her Majesty's vice chamberlain," the Duke told Kendra.

"Why does the Queen want an investigation?" Alec asked. "Tongues will wag that Lady Westford committed self-murder regardless. No one can stop that from happening. I dare say not even Queen Charlotte."

Mr. Boothe nodded. "Unfortunately, rumors will always abound, given the suspicious nature of her death."

"You're not asking me to investigate an accident," Kendra said slowly, meeting the man's eyes. "You're here because of the third possibility. You think she was pushed."

A shadow crossed Mr. Boothe's face. "Her Majesty is concerned that foul means were employed. She wishes to know the truth."

*Unless the truth is uncomfortable, like a suicide.* Kendra pushed that thought aside, because it wouldn't deter her. She'd follow the investigation wherever it might lead and not let politics—or even a queen's discomfort—dissuade or distract her.

She kept her gaze on Mr. Boothe. "Why is the Queen taking such an interest in Lady Westford's death? Were they friends?"

The Duke cleared his throat. "I can answer that, my dear. Lady Westford is . . . *was* one of Her Majesty's ladies-in-waiting."

"She served Queen Charlotte for the last six years," Mr. Boothe added. "Her Majesty was quite rightly distraught when she received word of the tragedy yesterday afternoon."

"Where is the body now?" Kendra asked. "I'll need to see it, and the theater where she died."

"I'm not certain, but Dr. Thornton ought to be able to tell you. She was found at the Bowden Theater on Monday morning. Its doors are open."

*Open and doing business*, Kendra thought with a flash of irritation. *God.* It was incredibly frustrating that her nineteenth century counterparts didn't have any procedures in place to seal off crime scenes. Hell, they didn't even have an official police force, just a cobbled-together group of constables, watchmen, magistrates, and Bow Street Runners.

Mr. Boothe smoothed the brim of his hat before placing it firmly on his head. "Naturally, Her Majesty wishes to be kept informed of your investigation. You shall report your findings to me, and I will convey them to the Queen."

"And if I need to speak to the Queen?"

Mr. Boothe's reaction could only be described as shock laced with horror. "One does not *speak* to the Queen, my lady. A protocol must be followed. One first must request an audience and—"

"Her Majesty is asking for *my* help in this matter," Kendra reminded him.

Mr. Boothe waved his hand as if that detail was irrelevant. Probably because it was, Kendra mused. Queen Charlotte wasn't issuing a request; this was an order.

"The Queen has no information to share," he told her. "And even if she did, she cannot grant you an audience at this time. The King . . ." Mr. Boothe's mouth compressed into a thin, pained line, and he shook his head. "She is currently traveling to Windsor Castle to visit His Majesty."

His Majesty, King George III, who was currently incarcerated in the ancient fortress due to his madness. Kendra remembered that from the history books, although the King's illness was hardly a secret in this time. Five years ago, he'd been forced to hand over power to his profligate son, Prince George, making him the Prince Regent and ushering in the period known, fittingly, as the Regency.

"I have a royal coach at my disposal," Mr. Boothe informed them. "If we leave immediately, we ought to be in London by midafternoon."

Kendra said, "I'll be bringing my own team to help with the investigation."

Mr. Boothe blinked at her. "I beg your pardon?"

"I've worked with Dr. Munroe and Mr. Kelly on previous investigations. Dr. Munroe operates an anatomy school in London. I'd like him to examine the body. Mr. Kelly is a Bow Street Runner."

This was another thing that had changed, Kendra mused. In the twenty-first century, she'd been part of task forces and teams. But she'd always been a loner, the person who worked through holidays and happy hours. But here . . . here she was outside her jurisdiction. *Way* outside. She needed a team who could both help her navigate the labyrinth of rules and be openminded enough to accept her ideas and theories. Sam Kelly and Dr. Munroe had overcome whatever reservations they'd had about her, and treated her, for the most part, as an equal.

Ironically, she hadn't been so openminded herself, viewing both men as inferior because she had more than two centuries of knowledge on them. A common, modern-day mistake. By her standards, the era's technology was archaic and police procedure rudimentary at best, but she had soon realized that many of the people she met were still enormous assets.

"This is most unusual." Mr. Boothe frowned. "Bow Street was already involved, and Dr. Thornton—"

"Has determined that there was no crime," Kendra interjected.

"Lady Sutcliffe's request isn't as unusual as you asking a marchioness to investigate a possible crime, Mr. Boothe," the Duke put in with a faint smile. "I can vouch for both men, sir. And their discretion—which, I presume, is really your concern. Fortuitously, they are here at Aldridge Castle."

"I trust you to know what is best, Your Grace. I've left my card with your majordomo." His gaze moved to Kendra. "You will keep me informed, my lady." He gave a quick bow and swept out of the door.

The Duke exchanged looks with Kendra and Alec. "I shall have the carriage brought around immediately," he said, and also left the room.

Once they were alone, Kendra said to Alec, "I'm sorry. I know this is the last thing you wanted."

Alec huffed out a laugh. "I knew our life would be unconventional, madam-wife." He reached over to clasp her hand, lifting it to touch the simple gold ring that now adorned her finger. He smiled into her eyes. "I have what I want—you."

Kendra surprised him—and herself—by grabbing his coat lapels and yanking him in for a deep kiss. She gave a breathless laugh when she released him, smoothing out the creases she'd made on his coat. "I guess we both got what we wanted." She grinned. "Now, we'd better get moving. Even I know that when a queen wants answers, it's best not to keep her waiting."

# FOUR

A bride and groom leaving their own wedding breakfast early was simply not done. But the news that Lady Westford was dead sent shockwaves through half the wedding party. Kendra wasn't surprised when Lady Atwood still managed to glare at her, muttering darkly that all her fears were coming true. Thankfully, the lady was slightly mollified when the Duke revealed that Queen Charlotte herself had requested that Kendra look into Lady Westford's death.

She left them to speculate as she pulled Dr. Munroe, Sam, and Muldoon into the Gold Salon. Once there, Muldoon didn't waste time, asking bluntly, "How was she murdered?"

The reporter was tall and lanky, with reddish-gold hair, a prominent chin and cerulean blue eyes that surveyed the world with a sly, irreverent sense of humor. He was also a tenacious journalist—a skill she'd found useful in past investigations.

"I didn't say Lady Westford was murdered," she replied.

He gave her a cheeky grin. "You didn't say that she wasn't either. It's *you*, my lady. You've gained a bit of a reputation regarding your interest in unnatural deaths."

Kendra could hardly argue the point. It was, after all, the reason the Queen asked her to investigate, and why Lady Atwood continued to look at her as if she'd just drunk a glass of spoiled milk.

She said, "I've been asked to review Lady Westford's death, which was ruled an accident."

Muldoon's eyes sharpened. "Her Majesty disagrees, does she?"

"Let's just say she wants a second opinion."

"Who conducted the postmortem?" asked Munroe.

"Dr. Thornton." Kendra saw recognition flash in his eyes. "You know him."

It wasn't a question, but Munroe nodded. "Yes, Lucien and I are well-acquainted. I belong to the Metamorphosis Club that he founded."

The Duke frowned. "I'm not familiar with that organization."

"It's not a formal organization, Your Grace. It's more of an informal salon, allowing those in the medical community to discuss the latest advancements and theories in natural philosophy and medicine. Lucien—Dr. Thornton—is an excellent physician, with interests that go beyond merely writing prescriptions."

Kendra understood the implication. The medical establishment here was a bizarro world that adhered to a rigid hierarchy. At the top were physicians, who spent most of their time diagnosing their patients' maladies and prescribing treatments. Below them—or, rather, *beneath* them—were surgeons, who actually got blood on their hands in their attempts to save lives. Then came apothecaries, who acted like modern-day pharmacists, followed by barber-surgeons. This was a time when you could get your haircut and have minor surgery in the same visit.

An anatomist or medical examiner, like Munroe, was at the very bottom.

"I'd still like you to examine the body, doctor. Will that be a problem for you?"

He regarded her with steady gray eyes. "No. I'm certain Lucien won't be insulted either."

"Good." She looked at Sam. "Mr. Kelly—"

"I'd be honored ter assist you, lass."

She smiled. At barely five-six, with uptilted features and a mop of curly reddish-brown hair, Sam always reminded Kendra of an elf. Granted, an unkempt elf with a penchant for whisky. Today, though, he'd not only put on his Sunday best, but he'd combed his unruly hair and shaved. His eyes, as gold as Spanish doubloons, could gleam warmly with humor or appreciation when he held a glass of whisky or turn as flat and skeptical as any cop's she'd worked with in the twenty-first century.

"Before you accept, I should tell you that Sir Nathaniel Conant assigned a Runner to the case," Kendra added. "A Mr. Parker. Do you know him?"

"Aye, I do."

Kendra had to ask: "What's your opinion of him?"

"We're not mates."

"That doesn't surprise me," Muldoon interjected. "The man prefers giving pretty speeches and currying favor with his betters than actually applying himself to being a thief-taker. I suspect it's only a matter of time before he takes over for Sir Conant."

Sam's lips thinned, but he said nothing.

"I don't want to cause problems for you, Mr. Kelly. Those in charge don't like to have anyone second-guess their conclusions." Or question their authority. Territorial pissing contests wasn't confined to Kendra's era.

He shrugged. "I ain't worried."

"And where do I fit in, my lady?" asked Muldoon. "I'm not a Runner or an anatomist. I am but a humble scribbler."

Sam gave a snort. "You're a lot of things, Muldoon—humble ain't one of them."

"You're in a position to hear things, Mr. Muldoon." And in a time when she couldn't search databases for information, she'd Kendra had found his network of sources invaluable.

"I cover politics, not Palace intrigue."

"Sometimes the two overlap."

"Yes, but not with Her Majesty's household. The King made certain of that when he stipulated his bride never involve herself in politics before he agreed to wed her. Except for when the Queen quarreled with her son over him becoming the Prince Regent, she has always abided by the King's edict." His eyes gleamed. "Unless you think the Queen's lady-in-waiting could have been murdered by a political foe?"

"I wouldn't sound so excited if I were you, Mr. Muldoon," she remarked dryly. "It's too early to know what we're dealing with.

Right now, the official verdict is that her death was an accident. Our job is to find out if that's the truth."

⁓

There was no *fast* way to travel to London, but the Duke ordered six horses to pull the carriage instead of the typical four, which shaved some time off the four-hour journey. Horseback, which both Sam and Muldoon chose, was the fastest way to travel—roughly two hours to the city—and Sam promised to locate and arrange an interview with Dr. Thornton by the time they rolled into town around four.

Another carriage followed, filled with their trunks and a handful of servants—Kendra's maid, Alec and the Duke's valets, and Mrs. Danbury (the Duke's housekeeper) and Harding. The Beau Monde did not travel light.

"I can't imagine Dr. Thornton making a mistake in the cause of death," Munroe said, as the carriage rumbled down Aldridge Castle's long drive.

Alec shook his head. "I'm sorry, doctor, but I don't know how it could've been an accident. I've been to the Bowden Theater. Like most theaters, the balustrades are high. Too many young bucks attend performances while in their cups. If it was easy to fall off balconies, most of the Ton would already have brained themselves by now."

The Duke chuckled. "You have a cynical view of the Beau Monde, nephew."

"I have a pragmatic view of the Beau Monde, uncle. That leaves two possibilities. One, Lady Westford killed herself. But if so, it's a bizarre way to commit suicide, throwing oneself off a balcony in an empty theater. Why?"

"She was making a statement with her death," Kendra said.

"Pray tell, what sort of statement?" the Duke asked.

Kendra took a moment to consider the question. "I don't know. Maybe something happened at the Bowden Theater, something that made her feel that she couldn't live with herself anymore. Killing herself there might have been her way of drawing attention to the theater. A final, desperate act."

Horror flared in the Duke's eyes. "You don't think she was . . . she was assaulted at the theater?"

"It would explain the venue," she said, careful to keep her tone neutral. "We need to keep an open mind and investigate all possibilities, no matter how difficult."

The Duke nodded, his expression troubled as he turned to look out the window. Kendra suspected that he really wasn't seeing the patchwork of fields and hedgerows, or the metal-gray clouds pressing down in the horizon.

"The second possibility is murder," Alec said, returning to his earlier points. "I have the same problem with murder as I do with suicide. Why kill someone in such a peculiar manner in a public venue? Especially someone like Lady Westford, who is part of the royal circle?"

"Mayhap her killer asked her to meet him at the empty theater?" the Duke offered. "It could've been a clandestine meeting where they could speak freely, but something happened . . . an argument that turned violent."

"I'm not certain it's possible to be guaranteed privacy at a theater." Dr. Munroe's dark brows knitted over his gold spectacles. "Theaters—even small stages—are usually drafty places with a warren of rooms beyond the main auditorium. I don't think you can be assured privacy inside its walls, even if the theater is closed. Maids often are cleaning the rooms, and theater managers hire ratcatchers to contain the vermin."

"It's something to keep in mind," Kendra said, even as she thought: *rat catcher.*

Concern pinched the Duke's face as his gaze settled on her. "I agree with Alec's earlier point. Lady Westford is—*was*—no ordinary gentlewoman. She was part of the Queen's inner circle. Her death would not go unnoticed. If this was premediated murder, then we're dealing with a madman bold enough, ruthless enough, to kill someone at the very top of society.

"And," he added softly, "without Her Majesty's interference, clever enough to get away with it."

# FIVE

Coming from the bucolic peace of the country, returning to London was always a bit of a shock. With more than a million souls inhabiting what was once a Roman fortress, the city had a kinetic energy that was both appealing and appalling. Formerly affluent neighborhoods had fallen to ruin, becoming rookeries and slums that housed the working poor and the more criminally inclined. Poverty was grinding, with beggars and hollow-eyed men and women huddling in doorways and alleys, and raggedy children darting around the muddy streets.

While she'd seen the same—homeless encampments, hungry children, cities rocked by crime—in her own time, she didn't think she'd ever become used to the animals that shuffled through the streets of London. Cows, pigs, goats, sheep, stray dogs, and feral cats shared the thoroughfares and pavement with pedestrians, carriages, wagons, and horseback riders. The stench was like a punch in the face, the air thick with livestock's gamey odor, raw sewage, and rotting carcasses from nearby stockyards. Added to the stink was the smog from the city's numerous coal fires, which turned the already overcast sky a sickly yellow and brown.

"Good God," the Duke murmured, pulling out a handkerchief that his valet had wisely scented with Albany cologne. "I fear the smell is getting worse."

Kendra nearly smiled. He said that every time they came to London.

Munroe said, "'Tis a far cry from the fresh air you enjoy in

Aldridge Village, Your Grace. It will get better once we are beyond the slaughterhouses. Dr. Thornton ought to be at his residence on Curzon Street. I took the liberty of giving your coachman his address before we departed."

"Where would he keep Lady Westford's body?" Kendra wondered.

"Since her ladyship's death was declared an accident, the body was most likely released to her family. She will be at home until the funeral."

Kendra nodded as her gaze strayed again to the window. The stink of the stews slowly dissipated as they made their way toward the fashionable Mayfair District. An assortment of businesses, shops, and residences lined streets congested with service wagons carrying vegetables, kegs of ale, and bins of coal; a few horseback riders; and a steady stream of private carriages, hackneys, phaetons, and curricles. Children raced dangerously in and out of the traffic with brooms to sweep away the dung and dirt. London echoed with noise: people hailing acquaintances or arguing with shopkeepers, laughing with friends; ringing hammers as structures were repaired, rebuilt. or demolished; and the never-ending *clop-clop-clop* of horse hooves and the thrumming of wheels.

Coachman Benjamin skillfully steered the vehicle to Curzon Street, easing the carriage to a stop at the curb outside a pretty, three-story, white stucco townhouse. The carriage rocked as Benjamin and the stableboy, Dylan, leapt down. Dylan scurried to secure the horses while Benjamin came around to open the door and unfold the steps.

"Send word to Mr. Kelly at Bow Street that we've arrived," the Duke instructed the coachman as they descended.

"Aye, Yer Grace."

The group approached the house, and Alec used the simple brass knocker to rap the black-painted door. It took a few minutes, then the door creaked open, and a young uniformed maid peered inquiringly out at them.

"I am the Duke of Aldridge," the Duke said. "We are here to speak to Dr. Thornton."

The aristocrat didn't use what Kendra considered his "duke voice"—the upper-class accent so sharp it should've been registered as a deadly instrument—but the maid's eyes grew round regardless, and she immediately dropped into a curtsy.

"Oh, aye, Yer Grace. Dr. Thornton said ye'd be coming, and ter bring ye right up ter his study."

Munroe waved off the maid. "I know the way. Continue with your duties, Jenny."

The maid smiled, knees buckling in another curtsy. "Aye, Dr. Munroe," she said before scampering away.

Munroe glanced at them briefly as he led them to the staircase at the end of the hall. "Most members open their homes to host the Metamorphosis Club," he explained.

"I would enjoy attending one of your salons, if it's permitted, Dr. Munroe," the Duke said as they climbed the stairs. "Your discussions are, I'm certain, most fascinating."

"You would be welcome as my guest, Your Grace," Munroe said, and smiled. "During our last meeting, Mr. Dandridge introduced us to a new invention that you would find interesting. 'Tis an instrument that allows a physician to listen to the heart without having to press one's ear against the chest."

"A stethoscope," Kendra said automatically, even as she thought: *Holy shit, I live in a world where the stethoscope is a new invention.*

Munroe glanced at her in surprise when they reached the landing. "Yes, my lady. A stethoscope. Or, at least, that is what some physicians have begun calling it. René Théophile Hyacinthe Laënnec is the physician who designed the device, and he prefers the name *Le Cylindre*. Though Laënnec's invention is only a few months old, and has not yet been widely used outside of France."

*Damn, damn, and double damn.* It was the little details that always tripped up criminals—and, apparently, time travelers.

Thankfully, the Duke rescued her. "Her ladyship enjoys reading the medical journals I subscribe to," he said smoothly. "I believe there was a small article about *Le Cylindre* in one of them."

Munroe gave Kendra an admiring look. "If you have an interest in medical advancements, my lady, perhaps you would like to attend our meetings, as well."

An evening where she'd have to pretend surprise over tools and techniques that were outdated in her era? *Oh, joy.*

"Sounds interesting," she murmured politely, earning a knowing smile from Alec.

The anatomist led them down the hall to an open door. A quick inspection revealed a study clearly used by someone in the medical field. Shelves were crammed with books and scientific equipment, including microscopes, a couple of Leyden jars, and a black doctor's medical bag. No stethoscope that Kendra could see, but she also wasn't entirely sure what that would look like in this era. A desk sat in front of the window overlooking the street and a large oval table with at least a dozen chairs stood in the center of the room, below a chandelier. Both the desk and the table were strewn with newspapers, foolscap, and more books.

Kendra's eyes cut to a short, rotund man standing in front of the fireplace, sipping a glass of whisky. Early sixties, she estimated. He'd compensated for his balding pate by sporting bushy, gray mutton-chop side-whiskers. He was not contemplating the flames that were currently devouring the logs in the hearth. Rather, his gaze was fixed on a painting of a young blonde woman hanging above the carved mantle. His expression was one of intense sorrow.

Upon their entrance, he turned and summoned a smile that didn't quite dispel the sadness in his eyes. "Ethan! Good afternoon," he said. Kendra noticed the slight tremor in his hand as he set his glass on his desk. "Mr. Kelly gave me your message."

"Thank you for taking the time to receive us. This is the Duke of Aldridge, and Lord and Lady Sutcliffe. Your Grace, my lady, my lord, may I introduce Dr. Lucien Thornton."

"Your servant." Thornton bowed. "May I offer you refreshments? I shall summon Jenny to bring tea—"

"Thank you, no," the Duke said quickly. "We don't want to put you out any more than is necessary. We've come about Lady Westford."

"Yes, Ethan said as much in his message." Thornton licked his lips, his gaze darting between them. "I don't understand what you want with me. Were you acquainted with her, Your Grace?"

"A little. But I prefer country life over the city, so I didn't know her as well as I would have liked. Now, it's too late."

Kendra added, "You did the postmortem."

Something flickered in Dr. Thornton's eyes before they went carefully blank. "Yes."

Kendra kept her gaze on his. "You ruled the death an accident. I am going to ask you a question, and I would like you to think carefully before you answer: Was your ruling truthful?"

She saw the shock whip over his face as his eyes widened. "What are you suggesting? That . . . that I would *lie* about it? Why would I do such a thing?"

"Because you were being considerate of the family," Munroe said carefully. "If Lord Westford feared that his wife may have killed herself, he may have asked you to issue a different verdict."

"You must admit that it is very strange for her ladyship to have had such a mishap in an empty theater," the Duke added gently.

Thornton pursed his lips and dropped his gaze to the cluttered table. For a moment, no one spoke. Kendra was aware of the street noises, the crackle of fire in the hearth, the tick-tick-tick of the pendulum as it swung side-to-side in the large grandfather clock in the corner of the room. She was beginning to wonder if he would ever speak when he let out a heavy sigh and raised his eyes to meet the Duke's steady regard.

"I cannot speak to the lady's state of mind, Your Grace. But I know she visited that very theater the day before her mishap."

"She was at Bowden Theater on Saturday?" Kendra's tone was sharp enough to bring Thornton's eyes back to her. "How do you know?"

"Mr. Parker mentioned it. He said . . . ah, that witnesses described Lady Westford as being distressed."

"Distressed about what?"

"That I do not know. Mr. Parker didn't say."

"You haven't answered the question. Do you believe that Lady Westford's death was an accident?" Alec asked.

The doctor averted his gaze. "'Tis my official assessment."

*Another answer/nonanswer,* Kendra mused. "When is the inquest?"

"There is no inquest, as it was not a suspicious death."

Kendra stared at him. "*Not* a suspicious death, Doctor? The woman went into an empty theater, climbed to the top balcony, and fell to her death. If that's not suspicious, I don't know what is."

Thornton stiffened. "Given her ladyship's status, it was determined that it would be best for the incident to be resolved quickly."

"Who made that determination, Lucien?" Munroe demanded.

"Lord Westford's sensibilities—"

"Should never have been considered," Munroe snapped. "We take an oath to pursue the truth, Lucien. 'Tis what the Metamorphosis Club is about."

Thornton's jaw tightened. "I know what the club is about. I was one of its founders!" He drew in an uneven breath, and then raised a hand. "Forgive me, Ethan, but you tend to the dead. You have forgotten what it's like dealing with the living. The sensitivities that must be considered."

Munroe opened his mouth to respond, but closed it abruptly when Jenny materialized in the doorway.

"Beggin' yer pardon, sir." She flushed when everyone looked at her. "A message came for milady. Mr. Kelly'll meet ye at Lord Westford's residence. He said ter tell you: Her ladyship is at home."

# SIX

"I don't know what to think," Munroe admitted as the carriage barreled down the road. "I'm afraid Lucien must have acquiesced to Lord Westford's sensibilities and declared the death an accident, regardless of the truth. It's unacceptable."

Kendra met his troubled gaze. "Whatever he did—or didn't do—has nothing to do with you, Dr. Munroe. If mistakes were made, we'll put it right. It's interesting that Lady Westford was at the theater the day before she died there." And that bit of information meant they had to visit the theater sooner rather than later.

Now, though, her gaze was drawn to Westford's Georgian red-brick mansion in the exclusive St. James Square. Sam Kelly was waiting on the stoop with another man, both of whom walked down the pebbled path to wait for them to climb out of the carriage. When they had, Sam introduced his companion as Mr. Parker of Bow Street.

Kendra studied the other Bow Street Runner. Mid-thirties, and opposite Sam in every way: tall and lean, with honey-blond hair cropped in the fashionable Brutus style. His clothes were tailored and pressed, his cravat flawlessly tied, his Hessian boots polished—and dust-free. Unlike Sam, whose Sunday-best clothes were now wrinkled and grimy, his boots caked in mud, after his two-hour horseback ride to London. She recalled Muldoon's words that Parker was more politician than policeman. One look at him, and she decided the reporter was right.

Mr. Parker bowed. His blue eyes twinkled as they traveled over

Alec and Kendra before settling on the Duke. Like most politicians, Kendra reflected, he had an uncanny knack for zeroing in on the most prestigious person in the group.

"Mr. Kelly has explained that you have concerns over Lady Westford's death," he said with an ingratiating smile. "I can assure you, as far as Bow Street is concerned, it was an accident. The case is closed. You needn't have any fears on that score."

He didn't wink, but Kendra felt he might as well have. He was practically admitting there was a cover-up, and was damn proud of it.

"Excuse me, I need to see the body," Kendra said abruptly, brushing past him as she strode to the door. The customary funerary hatchment was hung above the knocker, and the curtains were drawn tight across the windows to indicate a death in the family.

Alec joined her, reaching past her to knock on the door.

"I say!" Parker exclaimed, flabbergasted, as he hurried to catch up. "I've just explained that her ladyship's death was an accident. There's no need to disturb his lordship."

Kendra shot him a frosty glance. "I heard you. Is it the truth?"

Parker's lips parted in surprise. "The truth . . ." He cast a quick glance around him, as if seeking support from the men against this madwoman. When none came, he pivoted back to Kendra, blue eyes narrowing. "The truth is something that Lord Westford may not want known, if you take my meaning, ma'am."

"I take your meaning, Mr. Parker," she said, and summoned a pleasant smile. "And I don't care what Lord Westford wants."

She caught Sam's quick grin and heard Parker's swift intake of breath as she turned and, bypassing the knocker, banged on the door.

"Can you not stop her?" Parker implored Alec and the Duke.

Alec just smiled, as the Duke remarked, "I'm afraid Lady Sutcliffe is not a stoppable sort of female."

Parker didn't seem to know what to make of that statement. "The family shouldn't be disturbed," he muttered. "They're in mourning."

The butler who opened the door a moment later reflected that sentiment. He was wearing black armbands and viewed Kendra and

Alec with a lofty expression. "The family has suffered a bereavement and is not at home to anyone," he intoned, and began shutting the door. Kendra wedged her foot across the threshold to prevent it from closing, and wasn't surprised when the butler's eyes bulged in astonishment.

She said, "I'm here for Lady Westford."

"You can't— It isn't— Lady Westford is—" the butler stuttered. He blew out an aggravated breath. "She is the reason the family is in mourning."

"We are aware of her ladyship's death," the Duke said, stepping forward. "I am the Duke of Aldridge, and this is my nephew, Lord Sutcliffe, his wife, Lady Sutcliffe, Dr. Munroe, and Mr. Kelly from Bow Street. I assume you are familiar with Mr. Parker."

Kendra had to suppress a smile. Now the Duke *was* using his "duke voice." It always got results, and today was no different. The butler was already standing rigidly, but his shoulders went back another half an inch and his chest puffed out. He schooled his features into the impassivity expected of a high-class butler. If he was confused by the Duke of Aldridge's desire to see a dead woman, he would never show it.

"Your Grace, madam, sirs." The butler swung open the door, allowing them into a spacious, black-and-white-marble-tiled entrance hall. The paneled walls were decorated with gilt-framed oil paintings and mirrors draped in yards of black crepe. An ornate staircase dominated one wall. At the top landing, a maid was sweeping. She paused briefly to peer down at the intruders, then hastily resumed her duties.

"Lady Westford is in the drawing room," the butler said. "Please, follow me."

They crossed the foyer to a pair of double doors beyond the staircase. Kendra eyed the black mourning hatchment positioned above the doorway like a vulture. God, it was depressing.

The butler wrapped his hands around the twin doorknobs and opened both doors with a swoosh. He stepped aside, letting them file past.

The drawing room's curtains were closed. The only light came from an oil lamp on a shelf, its meager glow barely reaching the open coffin positioned on a nearby table, and shadows pooled around the furniture. Even though Kendra knew it was customary to keep the dead at home until burial in this era, it was still weird to see the coffin in the drawing room. Flowers exploded out of vases positioned around the room. A nice touch, though Kendra had a feeling the blooms hadn't been sent by loved ones. More likely, servants had placed the floral arrangements around the coffin to combat the sickly scent of death that currently permeated the drawing room.

"I shall inform his lordship that you are paying your respects," the butler murmured, retreating.

Kendra glanced around. "Can we get more light?"

Alec walked to the fireplace. There was no fire in the hearth and the room was chilly. Kendra wondered if this was another way to keep the fumes from the decomposing body in check. Alec found tapers, lit one from the oil lamp, and then walked around the room lighting candles and more lamps.

She raised her eyebrows at him. "We can't just open the drapes?"

Alec shrugged. "It would be disrespectful."

It was one of those rules that made no sense. How was daylight disrespectful? Still, she wasn't going to argue. Instead, she moved over to the open coffin, studying the figure inside.

Lady Westford was tiny. Almost doll-like. Maybe a whisper over five feet, with dainty, birdlike bones. Someone had dressed her in a gauzy black dress with a black ruff encircling her throat. A few silvery strands in her thick, chestnut hair indicated her advanced years. Her heart-shaped face was relatively unlined, with delicate features that had been dusted with rice powder. Probably an attempt to conceal the greenish discoloration of decaying flesh.

All and all, Lady Westford looked perfectly normal.

*And that was completely wrong.*

Kendra had seen victims of suicide who'd plunged to their deaths. They did not look perfect or normal.

Leaning forward, Kendra tried not to grimace when she speared her fingers through the woman's thick hair. In the twenty-first century, it was standard procedure to don latex gloves when touching the dead. She was a bit of a germaphobe without the protective cover.

Not that it stopped her.

"Good God!" Behind her, Parker sucked in a shocked breath. "What the devil is she doing?"

Kendra ignored him. "I can feel deep lacerations of the occipital bone," she said, glancing at Munroe. He was studying the dead woman with an intensity that made her think that he shared her suspicion. "The back of her skull appears to be concave. We need to roll her over, doctor."

He jerked his gaze away from Lady Westford's face and helped Kendra flip the body.

"You can't do this!" Parker exclaimed. "Your Grace, she can't do this! 'Tis unseemly!"

"Her ladyship has her reasons," the Duke replied with remarkable calm, then focused on Kendra. "You *do* have your reasons?"

"I do." She began to unbutton the jet-black fasteners, peeling open the gown.

"God's teeth," Sam breathed as they crowded around the coffin.

"What . . . *what is this*?" Parker spluttered.

"Mostly livor mortis." Kendra let her gaze travel over the black-and-blue bruising that covered the dead woman's shoulders, spine, and buttocks. The other injuries, however, were not. Using her fingertips, she explored the nape of Lady Westford's neck, traveling down her spine and ribcage. The woman's bones were broken and shattered. She brought her fingers back to probe her skull. The trauma was concealed mostly by Lady Westford's hair, but it was impossible to ignore the misshapen shape of the occipital bone.

"What does that mean?" demanded Parker.

Kendra looked up at the Bow Street Runner. "It means, Mr. Parker, that Lady Westford didn't kill herself. She was murdered."

# SEVEN

Mr. Parker stared at her in speechless consternation. He began to shake his head, but before he could refute her proclamation, an angry shout drew everyone's attention to the door, where a man stormed into the drawing room.

"*What in God's name are you doing to my wife?!*"

Lord Westford was a large man, both in height and in width, with a sizeable paunch that strained the gold buttons of his green-and-brown-striped waistcoat. His fleshy features, framed by a lion's mane of white hair, were ruddy and quivering with his outrage.

Alec stepped in the path of the irate nobleman, forcing him to stop. "I'd advise you to calm down, my lord."

"Calm down? *Calm down?*" The earl pointed a thick finger at Kendra. "This female is mauling my wife!" He glanced into the coffin, and his eyes bulged. "My God," he sputtered. "You've *undressed* her? How *dare* you!"

Kendra met the man's incensed gaze. In truth, she couldn't blame him. If opening the drapes was considered disrespectful in this timeline, she only could imagine what it must look like for her to poke and prod at his deceased wife.

"I apologize, my lord," she said, taking her hands off the victim. "But this was necessary—"

"You are an abomination to your sex, madam!"

"Careful," Alec warned, his accent cold and clipped.

Lord Westford turned his blistering gaze on Alec. "I am aware that you married this . . . this American upstart." His lip curled. "Your wits must have fled. She is—"

"My ward," the Duke interjected. "And she is now my niece. You are understandably distressed, Westford." He softened his voice. "However, I must advise you not to say anything you may regret."

Lord Westford's chest swelled and his face turned an alarming puce. Most people were intimidated by the Duke of Aldridge, whose lineage could be traced back to William the Conqueror. Add to that, the Duke's incredible wealth. Those two factors normally earned deference. Kendra deduced that Lord Westford had an equally powerful pedigree and fortune—despite an earl being ranked below a duke—or he was simply too enraged to hold his tongue.

"I demand that you leave! I did not invite you here, Your Grace—"

"No, Her Majesty did," the Duke returned, never taking his eyes off Westford.

"W-what?" His jaw sagged.

"Queen Charlotte feared that the investigation into your wife's death was too hasty, and asked Lady Sutcliffe to review the matter."

Kendra had never seen a man's face change color so fast, going from deep crimson to ash gray. *The power of royalty.*

Westford shook his head. "My wife fell—"

"Your wife didn't kill herself," Kendra cut in, hoping that would alleviate Lord Westford's greatest fear, and he wouldn't cause difficulties in the investigation. *Unless he was the one who caused his wife to fall.*

"Lady Westford's neck is broken, the back of her skull crushed." She paused, searching his face to see if he understood the implication—or showed a flicker of guilt. But Westford's face remained carefully guarded, no longer even revealing his earlier anger. "Most of the discoloration that you see was caused by lividity—livor mortis. That means when the heart stops pumping, blood pools at the lowest points of the body."

He scowled. "I don't know what that has to do with my wife's mental state."

Kendra eyed him curiously. "You bring up a good point, my lord. What *was* her mental state? Was she depressed, or upset about anything in particular?"

"This line of inquiry is ridiculous!" In an instant, Westford reverted to his outrage. "Dr. Thornton declared Grace's death an accident, and I see no reason to contradict him."

"The physical evidence contradicts him," Kendra said. "Lady Westford's injuries are consistent with someone who fell backward. That's not the norm. People leap. They jump. They may even dive. But they don't do it *backward*. And they sure as hell don't twist around mid-flight so they land on their back."

Lord Westford blinked. Kendra wasn't sure if it was a reaction to the new narrative regarding his wife's death or the fact that she'd used the word *hell*. Ladies did not curse.

She went on, "Dr. Munroe is going to take the body for a more thorough examination."

"Absolutely not!" Westford huffed. "I shall not have my wife removed from this premises and dragged about like a . . . a sack of potatoes."

The Duke looked at the anatomist. "Would it be possible to conduct your examination here, Dr. Munroe?"

"It would have to be a visual examination, but yes."

Lord Westford's jaw tightened. "Dr. Thornton is an esteemed physician and has already shared his findings. Why should I consent to this?"

"Because it is the wish of Her Majesty," the Duke reminded him coolly. He drew out his pocket watch. "The hour grows late. I think the best course of action is for Dr. Munroe to stay and examine the body whilst we continue our inquiry at the theater. Do you have any objection to that, my lord?"

Kendra could see that the earl had plenty of objections, but once again Queen Charlotte's name was enough to silence him. He pressed his lips together in an angry line.

"Very well, Your Grace," he finally conceded. "But I want him to make quick work of it. I am expected elsewhere."

"I'll assist you," Sam offered, earning a slight smile from Munroe. "Thank you, Mr. Kelly."

Lord Westford's expression was stony. "Pentagross will show you out, Your Grace." With that, he turned on his heel and headed toward the door.

Kendra followed him. "I actually have a few questions for you, my lord."

"I don't have time for this nonsense."

"Are you familiar with the Bowden Theater?"

He stopped and turned to stare at her. She returned his regard and waited. After a moment, he blew out a breath. "I've attended a few performances there."

*I, not we.* "Your wife didn't go with you?"

"My wife and I did not share the same interests. She was, if you must know, a blue-stocking. She preferred attending lectures and seminars, when she wasn't with Her Majesty."

"We were at a few of the same lectures," the Duke said, approaching. "She was a delightful lady, and, as I didn't say this before, my condolences for your loss, my lord."

Lord Westford acknowledged the Duke's sympathy with a brusque nod.

Kendra asked, "Do you know why your wife went to the Bowden Theater on Saturday? Mr. Parker said that Lady Westford was distressed when she went there."

"I didn't tell you that—"

"No." She leveled a hard glance at the Bow Street Runner as he rushed over. "I heard it secondhand. Do you deny it?"

Parker frowned, taken aback. "Well, ah, no. Of course not. A few actresses told me that Lady Westford was distraught. That's why I thought she . . . may have . . ." He shot a sidelong look at Lord Westford and fell silent.

Lord Westford scowled. "I do not know why Grace was at the theater. Now, I—"

"Just a few more questions," Kendra interrupted. "When was the last time you saw your wife?"

The earl's eyes narrowed, but he replied, "Thursday morning. I was coming in from riding, and she was leaving."

"What time?"

"Eleven. Maybe a little later. I don't know. I didn't look at the clock."

"Where was she going?"

"I have no idea."

"You didn't ask?"

"No, I did not. She appeared to be in a hurry, as was I."

"Did you notice her mood—other than she seemed to be in a hurry?"

He was silent for a long moment, then shook his head. "She was preoccupied—which is normal for a lady-in-waiting. Being inside the Palace is . . . stressful, especially given the King's troubles. There are always worries when dealing with the royals."

"Did she tell you if anything was bothering her?"

"I just told you, no."

"And you never saw her on Friday, Saturday, or Sunday?"

"I dislike having to repeat myself, my lady. The last time I saw and spoke to Grace was Thursday morning."

Kendra contemplated him. "That's a long time to go without seeing your wife. Weren't you worried?"

"As a lady-in-waiting, Grace would spend days—and nights— with the Queen. Regardless, Grace and I have never lived in one another's pockets."

"Where were you on Sunday morning, my lord?" she asked.

Lord Westford's eyes lit up with fury. "Do you dare imply that I killed my wife?"

"I'm asking where you were on Sunday morning."

"Your Grace, this is—"

"A necessary line of questioning," the Duke said. "I've found the best way to deal with it is to answer Lady Sutcliffe's questions and be done with it."

The earl's broad face tightened. Kendra wondered if he'd resist answering out of sheer spite. Or perhaps arrogance. But he surprised her by saying, "I was with a friend."

"What's the name of your friend?"

Lord Westford's nostrils flared. "I will not have you disturbing my friends with senseless interrogation. And I find your implication that I killed my wife insulting, Lady Sutcliffe." He turned his hostile gaze on the Duke. "Your Grace, I have been more than generous with my time. I shall not answer another question. Good day."

The earl strode out the door without a backward glance. A few seconds later, the butler—Pentagross—materialized to escort them out. Parker frowned at Munroe and Sam, then followed Kendra, Alec, and the Duke outside.

"I must return to Bow Street," Parker announced, turning his collar up on his greatcoat as a gust of icy wind buffeted them. "I assume Mr. Kelly will be assisting you with your inquiries and my services are no longer required?"

"It is no disrespect, Mr. Parker. We are simply familiar with Mr. Kelly," the Duke said.

Parker waved that away. "I have plenty of other tasks that I must attend to. I wish you luck, and good day."

As the Bow Street Runner walked quickly down the street, Alec observed, "He seems remarkably sanguine for someone who has been replaced."

Kendra laughed. "If Mr. Parker has political ambitions, the last place he'll want to be is between Lord Westford and the Duke of Aldridge."

"And Her Majesty," Alec added, grinning.

The humor ebbed at they walked to the carriage.

"How did Dr. Thornton miss something so obvious?" Kendra asked, frowning. "I thought that he rushed the verdict to cover up a suicide, but he couldn't have thought Lady Westford killed herself."

"Maybe he truly believes it was an accident," the Duke said, holding onto his hat to prevent it from flying off in another blast of wind.

"Why didn't he insist on an inquest?" Kendra wondered aloud after they were settled in the carriage. "It's the proper procedure."

Personally, she considered inquests a waste of time. Their only purpose was to determine if the death was unnatural or natural causes, which they called a visitation by God. They didn't do a hell of a lot to identify the killer. But it still would've been more helpful than doing absolutely nothing.

She drummed her fingers on her knee, thinking. "We need to find out who Lord Westford's friend is, and if they were really together at the time his wife was falling to her death at the Bowden Theater," she said. "They had a strange relationship. He hadn't seen his wife in three days—four, really, since she was found Monday morning—and he wasn't alarmed."

"It's not that unusual in the Ton," Alec said.

Kendra met Alec's eyes. She couldn't imagine not being worried if she hadn't seen him in four days. "He didn't love his wife. He didn't express any regret that she was dead."

"Not everyone wears grief the same way," Alec pointed out. "And there are those who care more about society's sensibilities and their own reputation than justice."

"I agree with Kendra," the Duke interjected softly. "That man didn't love his wife."

Pain flickered across his face. Kendra knew he was remembering his own wife, Arabella, and daughter, Charlotte, both of whom he'd lost twenty years ago in a boating accident at sea. Arabella's body had washed ashore, but Charlotte was never found. More than twenty years later, and he still mourned. Meanwhile, the Earl of Westford had lost his wife two days ago, and couldn't be bothered to even look sad.

"He didn't love her," Kendra said. "The question is: Did he hate her enough to kill her?"

# EIGHT

The Bowden Theater was a four-story, buff-colored, neoclassical building within walking distance of Munroe's anatomy school. The Covent Garden area was an eclectic mix of bustling businesses and shops and street hawkers selling everything from fruit to flowers. Twilight lengthened the shadows, sending lamplighters up their wooden ladders to trim wicks and light the candles beneath the lamps' glass domes. Traffic was still heavy with wagons, hackneys, and horseback riders. Soon the commercial vehicles would fade, though, replaced by private carriages as the Ton began to emerge for their evening's entertainment. The colder-than-normal temperatures wouldn't stop the social whirl.

Coachman Benjamin deposited them at the front entrance of the Bowden Theater. They entered into a long, rectangular lobby decorated with a preponderance of gold. Enormous, gilt-framed mirrors were spaced between the windows to make the room appear even larger. Lining the walls were chairs and gold-painted Grecian sculptures. Kendra imagined the foyer would look spectacular in the evening, when the chandeliers and wall sconces were lit. But in the gray beams of late afternoon light, the lobby's décor appeared tawdry.

There were three sets of closed double doors positioned on the south wall. Muffled shouts, curses, laughing, singing, hammering, and sawing drifted through the wood panels. The cacophony rose several notches when they entered the auditorium.

Kendra had not yet set foot in a theater in this era. The design was similar to theaters in her own timeline, with seating facing the stage and orchestra pit below and divided into three sections. The biggest difference was a small horseshoe-shaped area in front of the stage that held half a dozen benches, and a spiked, wrought-iron fence separating the stage and orchestra from the audience. The vaulted ceiling soared to accommodate four balcony tiers flanking the stage. The balustrades on each level were baroque in style and painted gold (of course). Crimson velvet swag curtains with gold fringe carved out a space of privacy for each balcony box.

Kendra shifted her gaze to the stage, which was the source of the noise. She suspected that auditorium's acoustics amplified the sound, which was being generated by more than three dozen people scurrying across the floorboards. A handful of men and boys in rough garb were wheeling giant wooden scenery cutouts around actors that were rehearsing their lines, as well as clowns and harlequins that juggled and flipped and cartwheeled across the stage.

For just an instant, Kendra's head swam with a memory. More than a year ago, she'd snuck into Aldridge Castle—in her own era—by posing as an actor hired to be a servant for a Regency-themed fancy dress party. At the time, she'd considered the frenetic energy among the cast members to be controlled chaos. Two hundred years separated the productions, but the energy was very much the same.

A man's voice boomed above the din as he shouted at the men moving the scenery: "No, no, *no!* Blast you! I told you that the forest scene is in the opening act! I want trees! *Trees!* I don't want a goddamn castle! We've got less than two hours, so move your bloody arses!"

"'So are they all, all honorable men,'" another man's deep, beautiful baritone said, floating to the rafters. He swept his arm in a wide arc, reciting, "'Come, I speak to Caesar's funeral—'"

"Come I *to* speak *in* Caesar's funeral!" a striking woman, with red hair piled into a towering beehive, boldly painted red lips, heavy rouge, and kohl eye-liner, corrected him loudly. "Zounds, if you can't speak the Bard's words properly, you have no business on stage, you saddle-goose—"

"Strumpet!" the man thundered back. His insult brought guffaws from the scenery workers and a shriek from the actress.

"I wanted to bring you to the theater, but I didn't envision this," Alec said with a rueful smile.

Kendra gave them a quick sideways glance as they descended the auditorium steps. "Clowns? And harlequins?"

"They provide an amusing interlude between acts," the Duke told her.

"How many acts are there?"

"It depends, but an evening at the theater may last five hours or more," the Duke replied.

"Five *hours?* Seriously?"

"No one stays for the entire evening's performances. Patrons tend to come and go throughout the evening, and the Ton is always fashionably late," Alec assured her. "When we go, we'll arrive for the final performances—most of which are not on stage."

"Yes, after an evening at the theater, I've often wondered how we can claim to be the most intelligent species," the Duke commented dryly. "'Tis why I prefer my telescope, contemplating the stars. One has to hope there is more enlightened life than us in the universe."

They skirted the iron spikes. Kendra had to laugh when Alec explained the barrier was to keep the boisterous crowds away from the musicians, or from jumping on stage or pelting the actors with fruit if they didn't like the performance. *Intelligent life, indeed.*

"Who the devil are you?" demanded the man who'd been yelling at the stage crew. He strode toward them as they mounted the steps to the stage, gesturing wildly with his hands. "We're not open yet. You can't be here!"

Alec lifted a haughty eyebrow. "And you are . . . ?"

The man drew himself up to his full five-feet-ten-inch height. A shock of salt-and-pepper hair framed a wide, mobile face that changed from agitation to pride in an instant. "I am Mr. Antonio Myott. I am the director and manager of the Bowden Theater."

The deep, melodious voice coupled with his expressive face made Kendra almost certain that he'd been an actor himself at one time.

"I am Sutcliffe," Alec replied. "This is the Duke of Aldridge and my wife, Lady Sutcliffe."

Mr. Myott blinked. "We are honored by your patronage, of course, my lord, but we do not open for another two hours."

"We're not here for your performances," Alec replied.

"Then, pray, what business do you have here, sir?"

"Lady Westford," Kendra said simply.

The theater director's expression cleared. "Ah. I see. Well, unfortunately, you're too late, my lady. We are no longer selling tickets—she was removed yesterday."

Kendra stared at him. She knew that in this era, the general public was allowed to stroll through crime scenes, but selling tickets? "You *charged* people to view Lady Westford's body?"

Mr. Myott waved his hand. "It was Mr. Harvey's idea. He owns the theater. But the authorities were quick to remove her, so we hardly made any money. I suppose I can't complain, as it was distracting for my troupe to have folks traipsing through the auditorium during rehearsal."

"I see." Kendra had to swallow her outrage. "Can you tell me where she was found?"

A cagey look crossed Myott's face. "Mr. Harvey wouldn't want me to satisfy the public's curiosity without compensation."

Alec produced a coin, which disappeared quickly into Mr. Myott's pocket. Kendra doubted that Mr. Harvey would ever see it.

The theater director grinned and pointed to the row of seats on the edge of the pit. "That's where she was found. Bloody mess, it was. Looked like she broke her neck, the way her head was twisted."

Kendra eyed the seats Myott was pointing at. "There was blood?"

"Yes. We had a devil of a time getting it off the back of the seat."

Kendra asked, "Who found her?"

"Prudence and Edward." He gestured toward the two actors who had been arguing earlier, but who were now observing them, unashamedly eavesdropping. "They came in early to rehearse yesterday morning—"

"Gave me a terrible start, it did," Prudence interjected. She grabbed her companion's elbow, dragging him across the stage. "Thought it was a prop, or someone playing a trick on us. But then we went over to her, didn't we, Ed?"

"Aye." He nodded. "We realized instantly that the poor dear had shuffled off her mortal coil."

"Did you see anyone else around?" Kendra asked.

Edward shook his head. "Nay, no one was here save Prue and I. I ran out to fetch the constable and to send a message to Mr. Harvey and Mr. Myott."

Prudence said, "Edwina is usually somewhere about, but—"

"Do *not* mention that creature's name," Myott snapped. "I am surrounded by ungrateful wretches."

"'How sharper than a serpent's tooth it is to have a thankless child,'" Edward quoted with gusto.

Myott glared at the actor. "You need to remember the lines of the play you're currently in, you lout. Now, both of you, get back to work!"

Kendra held up a finger. "One moment. I have a few more questions."

"We don't have time for your questions, madam," Myott said.

"Maybe Prudence can escort us around," Kendra suggested. "That way, you can continue your business. We promise not to take much of her time."

"I'll do it," Prudence said before Myott could object. "I'm not working until the fourth performance, and *I* know my lines." That was said with a smug sideways glance at Edward.

Myott's jaw worked. "The doors open in less than two hours. That may seem like a lot of time, but—"

"We only need fifteen minutes. Twenty, tops," Kendra promised.

Myott didn't look happy, but he seemed to realize that he was wasting time by standing there arguing. He huffed out an exasperated breath and flapped an impatient hand at Prudence. "Fifteen minutes, no more! This ain't a bloody party. We've got a schedule to keep!"

Prudence grinned, her skirts belling out as she pivoted and moved to the stairs off the stage. "Don't mind Mr. Myott. It's been absolutely frantic around here since Clarice left," she confided as they joined her, clunking down the wooden steps. "Not even a by-your-leave, and she was supposed to play Portia too. Mr. Myott has been in a peevish mood ever since, even though we *do* have Sarah. The understudy," she identified, anticipating the question. "Personally, I think she's better than Clarice— There!" She paused in the aisle. "That's where we found the poor creature."

"Which seat exactly?" Kendra asked.

"That one, third seat off the aisle. It was really quite dreadful." Prudence's cheerful tone was at odds with her words. "She was just lying there, her neck twisted at a peculiar angle. And the blood . . ."

Kendra tuned out the actress as she studied the crime scene. She observed the balconies, mentally calculating the distance. The lowest was about ten feet off the floor. A fall from there might result in a sprained ankle or a few broken bones, but the chance of survival was high. The second- and third-tier balconies were iffier, depending how one landed.

"We need to go to the top balcony," she announced.

Prudence led the way down the aisle and through an arched door, to a wide, carpeted staircase.

"You mentioned someone named Edwina," Kendra said as they mounted the steps. "She didn't come in today?"

"I haven't seen her since Saturday evening. Mr. Myott thinks she took off because she was probably the first one to find the body. I reckon she finally returned to her family, the poor dear." Warming to the subject, Prudence explained, "She was burned something fierce in a fire at one of the theaters on Drury Lane. She'd come to London to be an actress, but afterwards . . . well, it ain't like folks would want to see *her* onstage. She helped Old Beatrice, our seamstress, with the costumes. Quite clever with a needle, she is."

Prudence flounced up the stairs. "It ain't uncommon for folks to leave, of course. We're a flighty lot." She glanced over her shoulder, shooting Alec a flirtatious grin. "But, I confess, I was surprised

Edwina didn't tell Old Beatrice she was leaving. It was a shabby thing to do, as Old Beatrice treated her well. And Mr. Harvey. Mr. Myott acts as though he's the one grievously injured, but it was Mr. Harvey who let her stay here at the theater. Felt sorry for her, I reckon. Still, probably gave her a fright if she found the body."

"Edwina lives here at the theater?"

"Yes."

"If she found the body, why wasn't she the one who contacted the constables?"

Prudence lifted one shoulder in a half shrug. "Plenty of folks get nervous around the law."

Kendra asked, "What's Edwina's last name?"

"Oh." Prudence's brow wrinkled. "I can't say that I know. We just called her Edwina."

Prudence paused on the third-floor landing to catch her breath, then continued up to the fourth level. When they reached the landing, she flung out a hand dramatically and announced, "Here you go!"

The entrance to each private box was framed by diaphanous gold silk curtains, which could be closed for the discretion of those inside. The space inside the boxes was small, with six Queen Anne chairs arranged in two rows facing the stage. Decorative sconces dotted each wall. A delicate side table was positioned next to the front row.

Kendra walked to the balustrade. Resting her hands on the rail, she estimated the height to be about three inches above her waist. Slowly, she leaned over the railing to peer down at the seats where Prudence had found Lady Westford's broken body. On the stage, the noise and activity continued. No one was paying them any attention.

Alec joined her. "What a horrid way to die," he murmured softly, his gaze on the seats below.

"Oh, I agree, sir. I can't imagine killing myself in such a way," Prudence piped up. "She must have been mad."

Kendra regarded the actress curiously. "Why do you think she killed herself?"

"Well, because everyone knows it." She shrugged. "She came here the day before she did it, you know. Right before our opening act. Lud, you should have heard Mr. Myott! He flew up into the boughs, told her that we had no time to answer her questions. You'd think Prinny himself was coming for the opening act." She rolled her eyes. "We don't even have a royal box."

"Were you here when Lady Westford came?"

"Well, of course. I'm the one who spoke to her first."

"What did she want?"

"To speak to Clarice."

"Clarice. The actress who left?"

Prudence's towering beehive bobbled as she gave an excited nod. "Yes. And when I told her that Clarice was gone, the lady looked like she was gonna cast up her accounts. Quite distressed, she was. Then she asked who Clarice was keeping company with, what she talked about."

Kendra frowned. "Did she get her answers?"

"Not really." The actress's painted lips curved into a sly smile. "Before she left, Clarice was boasting about having made an arrangement that could be lucrative for her."

"An arrangement . . . with Lady Westford's husband?" Alec guessed.

"Makes sense, don't it? The lady wouldn't have come the next day to pop herself off otherwise."

"You believe Lady Westford killed herself because her husband was having an affair with Clarice." Kendra thought of Lord Westford. What woman would kill herself over him?

"Well, it's obvious, ain't it? Her ladyship realized that her husband had betrayed her, and in an act of pure desolation, she returned on Sunday to fling herself off the balcony in the very theater where her husband's lover once trod the boards!" Prudence exclaimed, pressing her a hand against her bosom. "Lud! It's a tragedy worthy of the Bard himself."

"It's worthy of something, all right," Kendra muttered dryly.

"Your fifteen minutes are up!" Myott hollered from the stage below. "Prue, I want you down here *now!*"

Prudence darted over to railing, and bellowed, "Hang on!" In a softer voice, she added, "You bloody twit." Turning back, she grinned at them. "Anything else I can help you with?"

"When you spoke to Lady Westford, how did she seem?" Kendra asked. "Angry? Upset?"

Prudence looked confused. "I told you. She was upset when she found out that Clarice had taken off and we didn't know where she'd gone. Worried, I expect, that she couldn't confront the creature."

"Prue!" shouted the theater director.

"What exactly did she say when she asked you about Clarice? Her exact words? You're an actress; you have an excellent memory."

The compliment did the trick. Prudence beamed, then closed her eyes, frowning in concentration. "She asked to speak to Miss Clarice Chapman. Mr. Myott told her that Clarice had taken herself off like a thief in the night, and we didn't have time to talk about the bloody tart because we still had a performance to put on. She then wanted to know what Clarice had been up to, who she'd been seen with—"

"Prue! Get. Down. Here. *Now!*" Mr. Myott yelled again.

"Zounds! I'd better go before Mr. Myott has a fit." She pushed herself away from the balustrade, crossing the small space.

"If I need to talk to you again, how can I reach you?" Kendra asked before the actress left the private box.

Prudence paused. "I'm here from two 'til closing, every day except for Sunday. Might have to reconsider that, though," she added with a boisterous laugh. "Most of the action appears to be happening on Sundays."

～

While they'd been in the theater, a misty, purple-tinted twilight had fallen. The streetlamps now cast a demonic orange-red glow over the faces of the pedestrians and costermongers as they moved up and down the lane. The sweet, nutty scent of roasting chestnuts from a nearby street vendor made Kendra's stomach growl. She hadn't eaten anything since breakfast. *Her wedding breakfast.* Jesus, had it only been that morning she and Alec had exchanged vows?

She pushed aside that thought. *Focus.* "Alec was right earlier, about the balustrade being designed to prevent accidents from happening. Lady Westford was a petite woman, several inches shorter than me, and the railing was above my waist. The only way she could have gotten over it was to climb over."

"Maybe she did . . . in a moment of madness," the Duke said softly. "Maybe she climbed over, held on to the railing, and let herself fall backward. That would explain the position of the body."

"Why? Because she assumed her husband was having an affair with Clarice?" Kendra scoffed. As far as she was concerned, Lord Westford wouldn't inspire a woman to shave her legs, much less become so hysterical that she'd throw herself to her death.

"It's not unheard of." The Duke's gaze was troubled, as they returned to the carriage. "Lady Caroline Lamb slashed her wrists in the middle of a ball honoring the Duke of Wellington when Lord Byron spurned her."

Kendra shook her head. "The trajectory is still wrong for what you're suggesting, Your Grace. The seat she landed on wasn't under the balcony, but closer to the aisle. She'd need strength and momentum to achieve that kind of distance."

She noticed a boy standing next to Coachman Benjamin by the carriage.

"Lady Westford didn't kill herself," she added firmly. "Someone picked her up and threw her over the balcony."

"Dear God," the Duke said beneath his breath.

"At least we know the fiend is a man," Alec said. "A woman wouldn't have the strength to do it."

The Duke raised his eyebrows at his nephew. "Was a woman ever a consideration?"

Kendra smiled. "Don't ever underestimate women, Your Grace. But in this instance, I agree with Alec. We're looking for a man."

Coachman Benjamin stepped forward as they came up to the carriage. "Your Grace, this . . . person—"

"Oy! Ye're the Duke?" The boy, about ten years old, darted forward. His too-thin face was streaked with dirt and soot. Staring up at the Duke, he swiped his runny nose with the back of his hand. "If'n yer the nob, Oi gotta message fer ye."

The Duke's lips twitched. "I'm the nob. Let's see the message."

"Ain't on paper. Got it in me head. Thief-taker told me that Oi'd find ye at Bowden's and Oi'm ter tell ye . . ." His face scrunched in concentration. "The doc's done with his examination. You can find 'im at the doc's house." The boy's eyes shone with excitement. "The doc lives in the dead-house. Sawing and cutting up bodies for a livin', he does."

Kendra stifled a smile. *Bloodthirsty kid.* The Duke tossed the boy a coin, and then the urchin dashed away.

"The anatomy school isn't far." Alec eyed the traffic on the street. "We'll make faster time on foot."

As they started down the pavement, Kendra said, "I think we have an eyewitness to Lady Westford's murder."

"Edwina," Alec filled in.

Kendra nodded. "She lives at the theater, so, yes, I think that's likely. I also think it's likely that Lady Westford went to the theater on Sunday morning to meet Edwina. No one has heard from her since Saturday night." Uneasiness knotted her stomach as she looked at Alec and the Duke. "Lady Westford might not be our only murder victim."

# NINE

Dr. Munroe's anatomy school was an unassuming, three-story brick building in a shadowy pocket of Covent Garden. Deliberately unassuming, Kendra knew. Despite the messenger boy's ghoulish excitement, medical examiners in this time faced condemnation and superstition from the public.

The door was unlocked, so they let themselves into the darkly-paneled foyer. Oil lamps had been lit, guiding them down the hallway to Dr. Munroe's office. There, the door was open, light spilling into the hallway, and Kendra heard the murmur of masculine voices as they approached.

Munroe was sitting behind his desk, facing Sam, who was lounging in one of the wingback chairs. They held glasses of whisky.

Both men stood as they entered. "Your Grace, my lord and lady, you received my message," Munroe said, moving to the sideboard, which held several decanters. "Would you like a whisky? A sherry?"

The latter was meant for Kendra, as sherry was considered a ladylike beverage. Munroe may have accepted her presence in the autopsy room, Kendra reflected wryly, but he couldn't overcome his preconceived notions of what was a proper drink for women.

She didn't argue, though, accepting the glass and taking a sip of the fortified wine. Her gaze roamed the cluttered room. Shelves and tables were packed with a mishmash of scientific equipment and jars filled with cloudy liquid and weird bobbing shapes. A full-sized skeleton was wired together on a T-stand.

"What did you find out from your examination, doctor?" she asked, looking to Munroe.

He didn't answer immediately. "As you are aware, my examination was limited to a visual and tactile observation," he said slowly. "Without a proper autopsy, I cannot determine the exact nature of Lady Westford's injuries."

Sam gave a snort. "Seems obvious enough. You take a tumble from that height, you die."

"Not necessarily," Kendra said. "We're talking roughly forty-eight feet. Statistically, you have a fifty percent chance of survival. From that height, it's less about the fall, and more about how you land, what you land on, and what you're wearing. If Lady Westford had jumped, she would've been seriously injured, but she had a good chance of surviving."

"But she didn't jump," Alec murmured, his eyes on the amber liquid that he swirled in his glass. "She was thrown over."

Munroe nodded. "Yes, that's my conclusion. She struck her head against the back of a theater seat, along the occipital bone, fracturing her skull and causing the lacerations that you observed earlier, Lady Sutcliffe. The impact caused a severe cervical laceration—basically, she broke her neck. I cannot say if she died instantly, but the head trauma most likely caused her to lose consciousness, and she would have expired shortly after impact."

He hesitated, then added, "Naturally, she had considerable bruising, but there were contusions on her upper arms that I believe were at least a week old."

Kendra recalled Lord Westford's angry face as he strode toward her earlier. "Abuse?"

"I have no way of knowing that." Munroe pursed his lips and said carefully, "But the injuries are consistent with someone grabbing her upper arms hard, possibly shaking her."

"They were not sustained when the monster threw her off the balcony?" the Duke asked.

"There was bruising along her waist that was most likely caused when the fiend grabbed her and threw her over." Munroe took a sip of whisky. "She didn't struggle before she was thrown over."

The Duke lifted his eyebrows. "How can you be certain of that?"

"Lady Westford had no damage to her person, except for the injuries I just mentioned. No torn fingernails to indicate that she tried to claw her attacker, or self-defense wounds on her hands. I had her abigail bring me the clothes that she'd been wearing when she died, as well as everything that was found on her person. There was very little ruin, except for a tearing along the ruffle at the hem of her skirt. The cloak she'd been wearing was velvet, so made of sturdier material, and not as easily damaged, but it was scuffed along the hem as well. Hardly surprising for an outdoor garment, I suppose. The gown was made of a lighter muslin. If there'd been a prolonged struggle, the seams would have split open. Her shoes, stockings, and reticule had no dirt, smudges, or tears."

Again, Kendra was impressed with Dr. Munroe's thoroughness. It was why she wanted him on her team.

"The hem of her skirt could have been torn if she ran up the stairs to the balcony," she said. Regency gowns were not meant to be worn in marathons. She'd ruined a few dresses by doing just that— either trying to escape a killer or catch a killer.

"Or it was torn before she arrived at the theater," Alec countered.

"Not if she came directly from her home. Her maid would have noticed and wouldn't have let her leave the house with a torn skirt." Kendra could say that with considerable confidence, given that her own maid, Molly, was a stickler about such things.

Sam scratched the side of his nose as he regarded her. "Don't make much sense why she'd run up the stairs, lass. If a monster was after her, she'd do better ter flee outside the theater where she could get help."

"Unless she had no choice but to go up the stairs." Kendra took a long sip of her sherry as she imagined the scenario. "Her killer could have threatened her with a knife or gun to get her to go up to the balcony. Or he simply intimidated her with his size. Lady Westford was very petite. I don't think it would have taken much for her to feel threatened."

The Duke pressed his lips together. "What you're saying is the fiend deliberately stalked her like he would an animal, chasing her to the balcony because he intended to throw her to her death."

"And she reacted like an animal would, her only thought to get away from the danger," Kendra said quietly. "Fear has a way of making a person irrational. Once he got her to the stairs, she had no choice but to go up."

Alec frowned. "Yes, but she would have fought—like any trapped animal. There would've been defensive wounds."

Kendra shook her head. "Not necessarily. Some animals—and people—freeze in fear. Her assailant could have rushed her, grabbed her, and tossed her over the balcony before she had time to react. Lady Westford had to have been facing her killer. He saw her face— her terror—when he picked her up, when he threw her over . . . when she plunged to her death."

"God's teeth," Sam breathed. "The man is a monster."

Kendra could tell by the otherwise stunned silence that her words had painted the horror of Lady Westford's final moments. It took a moment, then Sam cleared his throat, the sound piercing the tension that wound around them.

"Why?" he asked. "If he was planning ter stop her claret, why chase her up the stairs? Seems like a lot of bother ter kill someone."

"I don't know," Kendra admitted.

The Bow Street Runner continued, "And why was she even at the theater? It was closed on Sunday."

"That I can tell you. We found out that Lady Westford was at the theater on Saturday, asking about one of their actresses, Clarice. Apparently, she's disappeared. I think Lady Westford arranged to meet with a girl named Edwina who works and lives at the theater. Unfortunately, Edwina is now missing."

Sam's eyebrows shot up. "You think she witnessed the murder and the fiend killed her too?"

"It's possible. Though I'm hoping she got away, since the only body we've seen so far is Lady Westford's."

"He could have caught her outside the theater," Alec pointed out.

Kendra glanced at her husband. "That's what I'm afraid of."

"I'll make inquiries," Sam said. He tapped his finger against his whisky glass, his expression thoughtful. "How did the villain know that Lady Westford was meeting this lass, Edwina, on Sunday mornin'?"

"It wouldn't be that difficult," Kendra replied. "Her husband would know her schedule. Even if she didn't tell him directly, he only had to ask the servants. I doubt they'd keep it a secret."

"You're thinking his lordship killed her?" Sam's voice was flat. There was no surprise in his gold eyes—they were all cop. Wary. Cynical. Seen-it-all.

"He has to be considered." As far as Kendra was concerned, the husband *always* had to be considered when a wife was murdered. "But the staff could have shared the information with a third party. Or been bribed to share it. Or the killer was watching her—or had someone watching her." She finished her sherry and set the glass down. "There are several scenarios."

No one said anything as they considered.

This time, Munroe broke the silence. "There's something I must tell you, my lady."

Kendra looked at him and the back of her neck prickled at the expression on his face. She couldn't quite decipher it. Caution? Fear?

He didn't go on right away. Kendra waited.

"I had a visitor on Friday morning," he finally said. "I believe that visitor was Lady Westford."

Whatever she'd imagined he'd say, this wasn't it. "I'm not sure I understand. How can you *not* know if your visitor was Lady Westford? Either she was or she wasn't."

"My visitor wore widow's weeds and was heavily veiled. Of course, I recognized that she was a gentlewoman from her speech and manners, but I've never been introduced to Lady Westford. I am aware we have attended many of the same events, but I don't know her voice. I certainly had no reason to suspect that she was my visitor." His black brows furrowed. "The only thing that stood out about my visitor was that she was extremely petite. The instant I laid eyes on Lady Westford earlier, I thought of the veiled lady."

Now Munroe's strange expression as he'd surveyed Lady Westford's body made sense. He hadn't been disturbed that Dr. Thornton had rushed to declare her death an accident—or, rather, that wasn't the only thing that had disturbed him. He'd recognized the victim.

Alec contemplated the anatomist. "Lady Westford isn't the only diminutive lady in society."

Munroe nodded. "Yes, I am aware of that, my lord, which is why I didn't mention it earlier. However, when I requested her maid bring me everything Lady Westford had worn on the day of her death, I also asked the girl if her ladyship had recently dressed in mourning. Understandably, she was reluctant to gossip about her mistress. Mr. Kelly convinced her to tell the truth." He glanced at the Bow Street Runner.

"She confessed that Lady Westford had dressed in a veil and widow's weeds on Friday," Sam told them. "She didn't know why."

The maid would never have asked, Kendra knew. No servant would question their betters.

"What did she want of you?" asked the Duke before he took a swallow of whisky.

"She wished to see a corpse that had been fished out of the Thames on Wednesday."

The Duke choked. Lowering his glass, he gaped at the anatomist. "I beg your pardon. Why the devil would she want to see a dead body?"

Kendra knew. Or had an idea. She asked, "Was the dead body a woman?"

Munroe's shadowed eyes met hers. "Yes."

"You think that corpse and Clarice the missing actress are one and the same," Alec guessed.

"It's a remarkable coincidence—and I don't like coincidences."

They went quiet for a moment, then Alec shook his head. "The timing isn't right. Lady Westford went to the theater to ask about Clarice *after* she viewed the body."

Frowning, Kendra shifted her gaze back to Munroe. "Did you show her the body?"

"When she arrived, she told me that she had read about it in one of the scandal sheets. I am aware there is a fascination for the grotesque, and tried to protect her from her own curiosity." His mouth curved in a faint smile. "Not everyone has your fortitude, my lady, when it comes to viewing the grislier aspects of our mortality."

Alec said, "Apparently, that didn't work."

"No. She was quite adamant, and . . ." His smile widened. "Well, your wife has disabused me of the notion that females are frail creatures. Of course, I was careful when I lifted the sheet, so only the woman's face was revealed."

Kendra eyed him curiously. "How did she react?"

"Because of the veil, I couldn't really see her face, but I thought she recoiled. In that moment, I feared that I'd made a grave error of judgement. But she rallied, and even stepped closer, leaning down to study the corpse. Naturally, I asked her if she knew the woman, hoping she'd be able to identify her. She said no. I then inquired whether she was looking for something in particular. She didn't respond. At the time, I thought she was too shocked to speak. Now . . . now I don't know what to think."

"And she didn't say anything else?" Kendra pressed.

Munroe shook his head. "She thanked me for my assistance and left. I escorted her to the front door and watched her get into a hired hackney. It was an odd encounter."

"Is the woman from the Thames still in the morgue?" Kendra asked.

"Yes. Normally, I would have already conducted the postmortem—one does not want to let these things go on for too long—and released the body to the authorities. However, she came to me late Wednesday and I already had several other cadavers on my schedule. I also was planning to travel to Aldridge Village for your nuptials, my lady." Munroe shot Kendra a fleeting smile, then set down his drink and stood. "I'd expected to see to her upon my return."

He snatched up a candelabra from his desk and walked to the door, where he paused and waited for the group to join him. Together, they walked down the long hall to the other end of the building.

Kendra had been to Munroe's morgue several times, but she still found it creepy when the anatomist opened the door and cold air wafted up from what seemed like a black abyss. The candle's flames flickered in a mad dance as the party descended the stone steps.

It was smart to use the basement for a morgue, as the naturally lowered temperature kept the rancid odor of death in check and slowed the decaying process of the cadavers. However, there were no chemicals invented yet to eliminate the stench entirely or to sterilize the subterranean chambers. Death had become embedded in the stone walls and floor and Kendra doubted that this building would ever be free of the odor. Would its future occupants ever wonder about the strange smell emanating from the basement?

She pushed the fanciful thought away as they moved into one of the chambers. The light from Munroe's candelabra illuminated shelves and counters that held the tools of the anatomist's trade—amputation saws, scalpels, dissecting forceps, scissors, knives and wooden buckets filled with pink-tinted water. A half-full whisky bottle was on the counter. Kendra almost smiled. This was her contribution, having convinced the anatomist to douse his hands with the spirits after he conducted his autopsies. Not exactly modern-day standards, but it worked as a rudimentary disinfectant.

Kendra's gaze traveled over the three narrow slabs. Only one was occupied, the cadaver's shape clear beneath the dirty linen sheet.

Munroe stared at the figure. "I don't understand . . ." he muttered, and hurriedly crossed the room. He yanked back the sheet to reveal the peaceful visage of an elderly gentleman. Munroe spun around so quickly that the flames of the candelabra he held flickered and threatened to go out.

Kendra's skin tingled, and in a flash of precognition, she knew what Munroe was going to say before he said it.

"She's gone." The anatomist gestured to the empty table behind him. "She was there. *And now she's gone.*"

# TEN

"*Gone*, sir? I-I don't understand."

Mr. Barts, Dr. Munroe's apprentice, stood next to the table that they occupied at the Green Lantern, a tavern with a low, timbered ceiling, a fire roaring in the rugged stone hearth, and a dark mahogany bar that ran the length of the far wall. Serving maids wove around the tables or worked behind the tap, handing out tankards sloshing with ale and plates piled high with meats and vegetables. The room was noisy with the clatter of cutlery and conversation, a homey congeniality that Kendra thought solidly middle-class, the customers mostly clerks, merchants, and shopkeepers.

Forty-five minutes ago, they'd retreated to the tavern to satisfy their hunger and wait for Mr. Barts. By the time the apprentice, a pale young man with wispy blond hair and a weak chin that disappeared into his cravat, came jogging through the tavern door, they were almost finished with their meal.

"The dead woman from the Thames is not in the morgue," Munroe said now.

Mr. Barts blinked. "But . . . *I* didn't move her. No one came to claim the body. It *must* be there."

"It's not. Please, sit down, Mr. Barts. Do you want any food? Something to drink?"

"Oh. Thank you, no, sir. I ate earlier." Barts had taken off his tricorn hat, but kept on his greatcoat as he pulled out a chair and sat. He frowned at Munroe. "This is most unusual, sir."

"Did anyone ask to see the body?" Kendra asked. She saw the

flash in Barts's pale eyes and knew he was thinking of the veiled lady, and clarified, "Not the woman on Friday."

"Oh." Barts's face fell. "No. No one."

"Did you notice anyone loitering outside the school?"

"No. Well, at least, I don't think so. I didn't notice anything out of the ordinary. Do you think—" Barts stopped abruptly, casting a quick look at Sam.

Munroe lifted his tankard. "Go on, Mr. Barts. If you have a suspicion, please, speak freely. You are amongst friends."

The young man's eyes darted uneasily around the table. With the exception of Munroe, she suspected that he didn't view them as friends. And maybe not even Munroe, who was his employer.

"I only . . . well, could a resurrectionist be involved, sir?" Barts said. "Stealing the body to sell to one of your competitors?"

Munroe's dark brows lifted in surprise. He was quiet for a moment as he considered the possibility. "I concede that this is a competitive business," he said slowly. "I have certainly vied with my fellow anatomists in purchasing bodies. However, we outbid each other—we don't steal from one another."

Kendra regarded him. "How difficult would it be to steal a body from the morgue?"

"It's never happened before, but I daresay it wouldn't be very difficult," Munroe admitted. "You're familiar with the building, my lady. If Mr. Barts and I were in our offices or in the operating theater, it would be fairly easy to go into the morgue without our knowledge. And the building has various entry points besides the front door. Someone could sneak in with no one the wiser."

"I locked up when I left in the evening, sir," Barts insisted. "I did it every evening when you were gone."

Munroe nodded. "I don't doubt you, Mr. Barts, as I had to unlock the door when Mr. Kelly and I arrived earlier. However, I never checked the other doors. I saw no reason to do such a thing. Someone could have broken in."

"I'll send me lads ter the flash houses, see if anyone's heard of a body being stolen." Sam angled his head as he considered the matter.

"'Tis a queer job for a housebreaker ter steal a body—queer enough that they'd most likely boast about it. And somebody would be paying them, 'cause they wouldn't be doing it on their own. These buggers would steal their own mum out of her bed and sell her for a guinea."

A barmaid, ample hips swinging like a pendulum, sashayed up to their table, her dark eyes on Barts. "W'ot can Oi get fer ye, love?"

"Oh." Barts seemed startled to be addressed. "Nothing. Thank you."

"Well, if ye change yer mind . . ." The barmaid gave him a wicked grin and wink that had Barts turning red and swallowing nervously.

Kendra addressed the apprentice when the maid swung to the next table. "You worked in the morgue when Dr. Munroe was gone?"

"No, I didn't conduct any postmortems. I taught a few classes for the students," he replied stiffly. "I also did paperwork and ordered supplies, as instructed by Dr. Munroe. Everything was normal. But I . . ." He looked to Munroe. "I didn't go down to the morgue, as there was no reason to do so until your return, sir."

"You did nothing wrong, Mr. Barts," Munroe reassured him.

They had no more questions for the apprentice, so Munroe dismissed him. Kendra watched Barts weave his way across the room to the door. After he'd disappeared, she turned back to Munroe. "Do you think Mr. Barts could be involved in the theft of the body?"

"Good God, no. Absolutely not."

Kendra didn't say anything, but she wondered if Munroe's faith was misplaced. Barts had been nervous. Sure, he *always* struck her as nervous. But Barts had access to the school and the missing body. Kendra didn't know how much assistants earned during this time, but she suspected that it wasn't much. Bribery was a long-standing practice. Barts could even rationalize it: Who would it hurt? The woman was already dead.

Frowning, Munroe picked up his tankard again. "Bodies are always valuable to those in the medical field. However, if the interest was dissection, I had two bodies in the morgue. Why only steal the woman? Women and children aren't worth as much as an adult male. Why—" He drew in a sharp breath, and something flickered in his intelligent gaze.

"You've thought of something," the Duke prompted.

"Yes. Possibly." He set down his tankard without taking a drink. "There was a peculiarity about the woman that I failed to mention. When the River Police brought her to me, she wasn't clothed. That's not the oddity," he added hastily. "I'm merely mentioning it to give you a full understanding."

Kendra nodded. "Go on."

He said nothing for a long moment. A strange expression had settled behind his eyes. Then he expelled a breath. "As I told you, I didn't have time to conduct a postmortem, so I cannot say the cause of death. But I can say, based on my visual examination, she was not shot, stabbed, or strangled. I believe—although I can't be certain— that she was in the Thames for only a day or two. In my experience, cold water can slow decomposition. The river is also dreadfully polluted, which hinders marine life. This allows the body to be more preserved than, say, if she'd been pulled from the ocean."

Kendra wasn't surprised. The stench coming off the river was like a living thing, and was also the main reason wealthier citizens abandoned their homes near the river to move west to the Mayfair District, which was conveniently upwind of the Thames.

"She had abrasions around her wrists and ankles," Munroe continued.

"Abrasions? Like she'd been restrained?" Kendra was careful to keep her voice neutral, even as her stomach did a quick roll.

"The marks would be consistent with some type of restraint—a sturdy material rather than metal, I'd say," he acknowledged cautiously. "She also had puncture wounds on the insides of her forearms."

The Duke looked to Kendra with apprehension. "Dear heavens. Is this the same kind of madman as before?"

When Kendra had first arrived in this period, they'd found the nude body of a young girl floating in the lake at Aldridge Castle.

Kendra had eventually killed the sadistic serial killer preying on prostitutes. Could they now be dealing with another likeminded madman? Was that why the body had been stolen? Was the killer afraid it would yield incriminating evidence upon closer scrutiny?

A chill prickled the back of her neck. "I don't know what we're dealing with—yet."

Munroe added quietly, "The restraints and puncture wounds weren't the most peculiar thing."

Kendra eyed him. "What else did you see, doctor?"

"It was what I didn't see. Livor mortis."

Everyone stared at him. The laughter and conversation around them seemed out of place for their talk.

"How is that possible?" the Duke asked.

"I know of only two possible causes. The woman was either severely anemic and had very little blood in her veins to produce lividity when she was killed, or she simply had no blood in her veins at all. The puncture wounds, the restraints . . ." Munroe shook his head, his gray eyes dark with worry. "I'm afraid that someone took this woman, restrained her, and then drained her dry."

The mood inside the carriage was somber as the horses trotted down the dark streets to Alec's residence at 25 Bedford Square. The amber glow from the interior brass lantern illuminated the lines on the Duke's face, making him appear older than his fifty-plus years.

He met Kendra's gaze. "This morning, we had one murder to investigate. Now it appears that we have two—if the woman from the Thames is connected."

*Three*, Kendra added silently. If Edwina had indeed witnessed Lady Westford's murder and had been caught by the killer.

But she didn't point that out. Instead, she said, "I don't see how they aren't connected."

She considered the timeline. On Wednesday, Jane Doe had been found in the Thames and delivered to Munroe's morgue. A scandal sheet had an article about the body on Thursday, and Friday morning, Lady Westford arrived to view the body. For some reason, the countess waited until Saturday night to go to Bowden Theater, inquiring about Clarice, the missing actress. The next day, Lady Westford was murdered. And now the body from the Thames—a body that may not have had any blood—had disappeared. *What the hell's going on?*

Kendra looked out the window when the carriage drew to a halt. They'd arrived at 25 Bedford Square. *My new home.* That was enough give her a jolt, momentarily pushing the murders out of her mind.

The Duke leaned forward to look at them as Alec assisted Kendra down the carriage steps. "This is not how I imagined we'd celebrate your wedding day."

The bells of a distant clocktower rang out. Kendra smiled up at the Duke. "The wedding was perfect."

He returned her smile. "It was. Good evening." He settled back in his seat as the coachman put up the steps and closed the door, then the carriage rolled down the street, quickly swallowed up by the ghostly fog that had drifted in an hour ago.

Alec drew Kendra's hand through the crook of his elbow and ushered her up the flagstone path to the distinguished brick mansion. The bells stopped—ten o'clock.

"Normally, the staff would line up to greet their new mistress," Alec told her as they approached the glossy black door, illuminated by two gas lamps on each side.

"That sounds tiring. I hope they don't do it every day."

Alec grinned. "They won't even do it tonight, as most of my staff is still at Alcott Park. We were supposed to stay here only one night before beginning our honeymoon there."

Kendra tilted her head to look up at Alec when they paused on the stoop. Keeping her gaze locked on his, she slid her hand down his arm in a slow caress until their fingers laced together.

"It doesn't matter to me," she whispered. "As long as I'm with you."

"I don't mind postponing our honeymoon—with one caveat."

The gleam in his eyes quickened her blood and made the breath evaporate from her lungs. She kept her eyes locked on his as he lowered his head. His warm breath feathered her lips, making them tingle, an instant before his mouth covered hers. Heat invaded her, melting her bones. Hands still linked, she pressed herself against him, gave herself up to him.

The hours of viewing death and speculating about the worst sort of humanity vanished like wisps of smoke. The night suddenly hummed with magic.

Kendra was breathless, her ears buzzing, by the time Alec broke off the kiss. He raised his head, his green eyes nearly black.

"The caveat," he whispered huskily.

Kendra barely heard him over the thrumming of her heart. "What is it?"

"Our honeymoon can wait." His mouth curled in a slow, sexy smile. "But I must insist on a honeymoon night."

Keeping her gaze locked on his, Kendra loosened his cravat, then raised herself on her toes to brush her lips against his ear. "I think that's a wonderful idea, my lord."

She didn't take her eyes off Alec as they entered the house, failing to notice the road to the park—and the shadowy figure watching them from the trees.

# ELEVEN

The next morning, Kendra sat in front of the vanity dresser while Molly styled her hair and cheerfully recounted household gossip. Telling the lady of the manor what was happening belowstairs was one of the duties of a lady's maid, and Molly took it seriously. Kendra learned that there were only four servants residing at 25 Bedford Square: Mr. Wakely, the butler; Mrs. Simmons, the cook; the head footman, Hugh (Molly said his name with a soft sigh); and the downstairs maid, Hannah, who was London-born and -bred. Until recently, Molly had lived her entire sixteen years within the confines of Aldridge Village.

"Mr. Wakely is a bit stiff-rumped, but likeable enough." Molly lowered her voice to a confidential whisper. "Oi think 'e's afraid of Mrs. Danbury, even though a butler outranks an 'ousekeeper."

Kendra couldn't blame the man. The Duke's housekeeper was formidable woman. Given their unexpected stay in London, the Duke had loaned Mrs. Danbury to assist in organizing Alec's household until the rest of the staff arrived. *God help them.*

"They're a bit afraid of ye too," Molly added as she tucked artificial flowers into Kendra's intricate braid.

"*Me?* Why are they afraid of me?"

Molly gave her a strange look. "'Cause they've never 'ad a mistress afore. If ye're displeased with them, ye can 'ave 'is lordship sack 'em."

"I'm not going to fire anyone."

"Aye, well, they don't know that, do they?" Molly grinned. "Oi reckon ye'll be a bit of a surprise for them—in more ways than one."

A soft knock at the door drew their attention. Molly finished pinning the last flower bud to Kendra's hair, then went to the door and opened it a crack. Kendra heard a murmured exchange.

The maid closed the door and returned to announce, "The Duke 'as arrived. 'E'll be in the mornin' room, 'aving breakfast."

Five minutes later, Kendra found the Duke standing in front of the long buffet, lifting one of the silver domes to inspect the scrambled eggs, stewed tomatoes, mushrooms, and slabs of ham. "Good morning, my dear," he said when he noticed her. His blue eyes twinkled. "Normally, I wouldn't presume to call on you so early, but given the circumstance, I didn't think you'd mind. Do you?"

"Not at all." She picked up a plate as Wakely came through the door with a silver pot of tea.

"Good morning, my lady. Would you care for tea or coffee?"

"Coffee, thank you." Maybe thanking servants wasn't the thing to do, but she wasn't going to worry about it. *You can take the girl out of the twenty-first century, but you can't take the twenty-first century out of the girl.*

"Where's Alec?" asked the Duke, sitting down at the table with his plate. "I thought he'd be at his bride's side."

"He's out riding."

The Duke reached for a toast point, then spread butter and jam on it. "I'm sure Alec would arrange riding lessons for you."

The mere thought of trying to control a thousand-pound animal made her mouth go dry. But she wasn't going to admit that. "I'm a little too busy right now," she said instead. "I've got to start a timeline to track Lady Westford's movements up until the day she died: where she went, who she met, what she was involved in."

"I took the liberty of having something delivered to you shortly that might help," he said.

She'd picked up a plate and spoon to ladle the eggs, but now glanced at the aristocrat over her shoulder. "What is it?"

He gave her a mysterious smile. "You'll find out soon enough."

"Okay. But just so you know, I've got a reputation for breaking the most hardened suspects in the interview room."

He laughed. "Duly noted."

Kendra brought her plate over to the table and sat down across from the Duke. "I realize that you didn't know Lady Westford well, but did you ever hear any rumors about her? Or Lord Westford?"

The humor faded from the Duke's face as he considered the questions. "Nothing that would result in her murder." He sighed and shook his head. "Caro would know, as she tends to keep up with town gossip."

"I can guess who she corresponds with—Lady St. James." Lady St. James was one of London's most notorious gossips. If there were any whispers swirling around Lady Westford, she would know. "I already decided to call on her today."

"She would know the on-dit. Of course, she'll also share whatever you discuss with her. I think Her Majesty was hoping for more discretion."

Kendra shrugged. "I don't have a lot of choice. I need information, and I need it fast." And it wasn't like she could tap into a slew of databases or the dark web. Here, all she had was Lady St. James.

The Duke lifted his teacup. "I have a few meetings at my club. I'm certain Lady Westford's death will be the main topic of conversation and there will be plenty of theories as to what happened." He sipped, then put down the porcelain cup. "I'll let you know if I hear anything interesting."

The door opened and Kendra looked over as Alec came through carrying a bouquet of dazzling yellow, orange-gold, and white daffodils, sprinkled liberally with soft blue forget-me-nots.

"Good morning, uncle," he said, but his eyes were on Kendra. Smiling, he brought the flowers to her. "For my lovely bride."

Surprised, Kendra stared at the bouquet. Then she pushed herself to her feet, her throat tightening unexpectedly as she accepted the gift. "They're beautiful."

"Wherever did you find daffodils at this time of year, Alec?" the Duke asked.

"Standish."

"Ah."

Kendra glanced at them in confusion. "Where's Standish?"

Alec smiled, lifting a finger to tease the stray curl lying against her cheek. "Not a where—a who. Barnaby Camden, the Earl of Standish. He has a prodigious fondness for horticulture, which he indulges with an impressive greenhouse at his London residence. I thought my wife deserved better than the posies hawked by street vendors. Standish gave me a tour of his collection, and a rather long-winded lecture on what every flower represents. Apparently, daffodils are hope for the future. I thought it was fitting for us and the future we will make together."

Kendra pressed her nose into the velvety petals, breathing in their delicate scent.

"I asked that he include the forget-me-nots because I never want you to forget where—*when*—you came from. I know that is who you are, sweetheart."

She let out a shaky breath, raising her eyes to her husband. "No one has ever given me flowers before."

There was a beat of silence. Then Alec shook his head. "How the devil did America win the war when it's populated by fools?"

Kendra gave a soft laugh. Romance had never factored into her life before. Her parents had choreographed her every waking minute until she'd enrolled in Princeton at the age of fourteen. Their attempt to exert their authority on her there had caused her to rebel, and they'd washed their hands of her. It had been a scary time, and survival had meant becoming laser-focused on her studies. Not that fourteen-year-old college students were invited to frat parties. Her classmates had viewed her as the child she was. She'd been alone, a social pariah. *A freak.*

As an adult, her life had revolved around her work. She could count the men she'd been involved with on one hand.

And not one of them had ever brought her flowers.

She had to swallow against the lump lodged in her throat. "Thank you," she said softly, looking into Alec's eyes.

He smiled. "My pleasure."

Wakely materialized at the door. "A delivery has come for you, ma'am."

Kendra raised her eyebrows at Alec, but he shook his head. "I brought my delivery to you personally."

"Ah," said the Duke, wiping his mouth with a napkin and rising from the table. "This one's from me."

Kendra smiled as soon as they entered the foyer and she saw two footmen struggling with a large, heavy object wrapped in canvas. She didn't have to see under the covering to know what it was—a slate board.

"It's perfect, Your Grace." She had to blink when her eyes suddenly blurred. "It's all absolutely perfect."

# TWELVE

After installing the slate board, Kendra and Alec traveled to Lady St. James's townhouse via carriage through streets shadowed by low-bellied clouds that obscured the sun, threatening rain or sleet. Kendra knew that the colder-than-normal temperatures and seemingly never-ending sunless days were not only making farmers nervous, but also the general population. In the future, this period would become known as the "Year Without a Summer," thanks to the previous year's volcanic eruption of Mount Tambora in Indonesia. Kendra had read about the event in history books, but they didn't convey the bleakness of the crop failures and food shortages, as well as the underlying fear that the new weather pattern meant the world was ending.

The carriage stopped outside Lady St. James's home. Eleven o'clock in the morning was not only an unfashionable hour to call upon a member of the Ton, but it was also considered shockingly rude. Lady St. James' butler certainly looked appalled when he opened the door to find Alec and Kendra on the stoop. He quickly composed himself when he realized who was calling, and hurried off to deliver Alec's card to Lady St. James's lady's maid, who would then give it to her mistress. Still, the fact that he left the Marquis and Marchioness of Sutcliffe standing in the entryway rather than escorting them into the drawing room revealed how they'd discombobulated the man.

When the butler returned, his face flushed red at the faux pas as he told them that Lady St. James was at home, but would be a few minutes before she joined them. He ushered them into Lady St. James's fussy parlor—an eye-popping mishmash of ancient world, Asian, and baroque decorating elements—and had a maid bring in a tea tray and dishes of fruit and bite-sized cakes.

Kendra was standing in front of one of the cluttered tables, studying the laughing head of a deity in gray stone, either from the Ming Dynasty or a clever forgery, when Lady St. James scurried into the room in a flutter of ribbons and ruffles.

"My Lord Sutcliffe, Lady Sutcliffe," she greeted somewhat breathlessly.

Kendra turned to look at the countess, who favored styles more suited to a young debutante rather than a woman approaching her mid-fifties. Today, she'd dressed in a pink-and-white floral glazed chintz with a deep pink sash tied into an extravagant bow beneath her ample bosom. A lace cap covered brown hair streaked with gray. She'd draped a gold-fringed paisley shawl over her shoulders and clutched a pink feathered fan, which she now unfurled and waved in front of her face, even though the room was cool.

"This is an unexpected pleasure," she continued, deliberately slowing her pace, a wide smile creasing her plump face as Alec pushed himself to his feet and gave an elegant bow.

He said, "Forgive us for calling on you at this ungodly hour. I know it's unorthodox."

She tittered. "One might say that it is more unorthodox that you are calling upon me this morning instead of embarking on your bridal tour, my lord." Her brown eyes gleamed with sly amusement. "My dear friend Lady Atwood informed me that after the wedding you would be traveling to Venice to introduce your bride to your relatives. You were wed yesterday, were you not?"

"We were indeed." Alec waited politely until Lady St. James and Kendra sat down before he took his seat again. He gazed at the matron. "Unfortunately, we were forced to postpone our honeymoon."

Lady St. James snapped her fan shut. "Does this have anything to do with the tragic death of Grace Taylor-Clarke, the Countess of Westford?" She smiled at their surprise. Reaching for a small pitcher, she splashed milk into her porcelain cup before pouring tea. "Everyone in town is talking about the poor creature."

"What are they saying?" Kendra asked.

"Well . . ." The countess picked up her teacup and studied Kendra over the rim. "Word is that it was a bizarre accident, falling off the balcony in the Bowden Theater. Of course, no one believes it."

"What *do* they believe?"

"Why, that Grace threw herself off the balcony, of course. Though now I'm thinking that she was murdered."

Kendra raised her eyebrows. "Why do you think that?"

Lady St. James's laughed lightly. "Why? Because you are here, my dear."

Kendra acknowledged that with a smile. "What can you tell us about Lady Westford?"

"What precisely do you want to know?"

"What kind of person was she?"

The countess took a slow slip of her tea as she considered. "She was, as I'm certain you know, one of the Queen's ladies-in-waiting," she said finally, setting down her teacup. "I found her to be a serious sort. Always reading—and not *interesting* books, either. They were about natural philosophy or medicinal plants. Can you imagine? And she attended lectures at the Royal Society. Quite unusual for a lady." She leaned forward slightly. "Then there is—*was*—her association with Mr. Goldsten."

Kendra regarded her. "Mr. Goldsten?"

"He's a surgeon." She hesitated, then lowered her voice to add, "And a Jew."

"What exactly was her association with him?"

The matron offered Kendra a teasing smile. "I suppose I can discuss this with you, since you are now a married lady. You could say that Grace had a particular *fondness* for Mr. Goldsten."

"They were having an affair?"

Lady St. James gave a surprised laugh. "You are very blunt, my dear. Yes, that's the on-dit. However, I will concede that they conducted themselves with great discretion. Most likely because the Queen is a stickler when it comes to propriety. A bit hypocritical, if you ask me, since her own son, the Prince Regent, can hardly claim to be a paragon. Or her other sons and daughters, for that matter." She sniffed. "Though I will allow that Queen Charlotte has always been straitlaced, with nary a word spoken against her when it came to her marriage vows."

Kendra wasn't interested in royal gossip. "Did Lady Westford's husband know?"

"Certainly." Lady St. James flicked her hand in a gesture of casual dismissal before reaching for a cake. "They've led separate lives for ages. It's common knowledge that Westford has had a left-handed wife for nearly thirty years."

"A what?"

Alec was the one who answered. "A mistress," he told Kendra, then asked Lady St. James, "Who is she?"

"Hetty O'Leary. Or is it Heather? No matter." Lady St. James bit into the cake, chewed and swallowed. "She was an actress when she met Westford. By all accounts, they fell madly in love and his lordship set her up in a villa. In St. John's Wood, of course."

Seeing Kendra's confusion, the countess explained, "St. John's Wood is famous—or is it infamous? —for housing the mistresses of gentlemen. 'Tis where Prinny set up his morganatic wife, Mrs. Fitzherbert. Though she may have moved there after their relationship ended. 'Tis difficult to keep up with his many loves. Mrs. O'Leary has been giving Westford a score of by-blows ever since. It's all very . . . domestic."

Kendra didn't know why she was startled by this information. She'd been here long enough to know that for all its rules and regulations that restricted behavior (mostly the behavior of women), the Beau Monde had a hedonistic streak as wide as the Atlantic Ocean. No one batted an eyelash when gentlemen kept mistresses— or, apparently, an entire second family—on the side. But it was hard to reconcile the haughty man she'd met yesterday with this story of a double life.

"How many children do they have?" asked Alec, taking a sip of his tea.

"Oh, good heavens, I'm not certain. It's not like *that* family is part of proper society. The eldest son, though, was trained as a barrister, and is currently working in the House of Commons as a clerk." The countess finished her cake. "I believe Mr. O'Leary has ambitions to hold office in Parliament—a desire no doubt fostered by his lordship."

"And Lady Westford? How did she feel about her husband's second family?" Kendra asked.

Lady St. James's lips curled in an indulgent smile. "You and Sutcliffe have clearly formed a love match. Of course, *I* knew that the instant I saw this rapscallion cast his eyes at you." She picked up the feathered fan to give Alec's arm a playful rap. "Not everyone is so fortunate, though. Lady Westford had her first season the year after I was presented, you know. She was Miss Grace Morton then. Such a dainty thing. I was positively green with envy over her figure—which she maintained throughout the years, despite having three children. Not an easy thing to do. Children wreak havoc on one's form," she said, sweeping her hand to indicate her own plump figure. Then, without a hint of self-awareness, she picked up another cake to nibble. "I'm certain she could have had her pick of beaux, but her father had already arranged a match with Westford's father. Henry was Viscount Dorsten at the time; a good catch, but the estates were impoverished."

"And Miss Morton supplied the fortune," Alec murmured.

"Yes. It's been said that the union was satisfactory for both parties."

Alec said, "I was presented to their daughter during her first season several years ago."

"That must have been the youngest. Lady Matilda Taylor-Clarke—now Lady Ross. Married an Irish lord, of all things. Although a step up from the match made by their eldest daughter, Lady Hannah, who married beneath her with Mr. Charles Nettlemyer. His family is in the banking trade. Excessively wealthy, which, I suppose, helps one overlook their lack of pedigree."

"It does indeed," Alec agreed easily.

"Their youngest is a son, thank goodness. The estates are secure, although the viscount is a bit of a scapegrace. Then again, young bucks ought to sow their wild oats before doing their duty."

"How old is he?" Kendra asked.

"Five and twenty, I think."

"And Mr. O'Leary? Is he younger or older?"

"Older. Why does that matter?"

Kendra had some thoughts on that, but pivoted. "Mrs. O'Leary was married before?"

"I don't believe so. Why do you . . . oh, because she styles herself as *Mrs.* O'Leary?" Lady St. James shook her head. "Sometimes mistresses, like unmarried housekeepers, adopt the title of Mrs. It's a mere formality, nothing more."

"Do you know if Lady Westford was having any difficulties with Mr. Goldsten?"

"I haven't the faintest idea. Mr. Goldsten is hardly in my social circle."

"No, but Lady Westford was."

"True, but as I said, they have been most discreet in their relationship."

"What about if she was having trouble at . . . work?" Was being a lady-in-waiting, *work*? What did a lady-in-waiting actually *do*? Kendra realized she had no idea.

Lady St. James laughed delicately. "Oh, there's always troubles. Royal court is rife with politics and petty jealousies, and squabbles between the Mistress of Robes and Lady of the Bedchambers, vying for Her Majesty's attention. I honestly don't know how our poor Queen can abide their cattiness in addition to the King's indisposition. Especially when he is in one of his spells and imagines he's in love with one of the Queen's ladies. Her Majesty was quite distraught when the king pursued her Lady of the Bedchamber, Lady Pembroke."

"I suspect they are careful not to expose their rivalries in front of Her Majesty," Alec commented, adroitly sidestepping the reference to the King's madness.

"Very true," conceded Lady St. James, pausing to refill her cup with milk and tea. "Grace was the Queen's lady-in-waiting for six years. While one must always tread cautiously in court, she may have confided in one of the other ladies. I would imagine she formed friendships there."

She took a dainty sip of tea before setting the cup down carefully. "I heard that Lady Melville, Lady Macclesfield, and Lady Bath have accompanied Her Majesty to Windsor Castle this week, but Lady Harrington is having a ball tonight. She is one of the Ladies-of-the-Bedchamber. If Grace confided in anyone about what was happening in her life, it would be the Saint—Lady Jane Harrington. I would be delighted to introduce her to you if you are attending this evening, my lady?"

Kendra managed to bite back a sigh, glancing at Alec. "I guess we're going to a ball."

# THIRTEEN

A cold gust of wind forced Sam Kelly to grasp the brim of his tricorn hat to prevent it from lifting off his head and sailing down the street as he stepped out of the butcher shop. His feet were already aching from having spent the morning quizzing every street vendor and shopkeeper in the vicinity of Bowden Theater. No one knew anything about the missing girl, Edwina. The closest Sam came was a nearby baker, who told him that Edwina had purchased a loaf of bread on Sunday morning. He hadn't seen hide nor hair of her since, which, now that he had a chance to reflect on it, was apparently most peculiar, as it was her habit to buy bread or pasties from him every other day.

This did not bode well for Edwina.

Sam scanned the area, studying a young girl in a tattered dress and wool shawl setting up a crate of oranges on the corner. He waited until the cart hauling bags of grain lumbered past, then sprinted across the street, careful to avoid the fresh dung.

The girl was no more than ten, but her voice rang out strong and true: "Two a penny! Come an' get 'em afore they're gone!" She looked at Sam at his approach. "Ye wan' an orange, sir? Priced right, they are!"

"I'd prefer information." He dug out a penny.

She focused on the coin, but it didn't stop suspicion from tightening her thin face. "About what?"

"Edwina. She works at Bowden Theater."

She narrowed her eyes at him. "Are ye a Beak? Edwina don't like Beaks."

"Why don't she like . . . er, officers of the law? Has she committed a crime?"

"Folks don't need ter commit crimes ter not like Beaks," the child scoffed, pulling her shawl tighter around her scrawny shoulders.

Sam acknowledged the sentiment with a slight nod. "What was Edwina's reason?"

"Same as most folks." The little girl's chin jutted up in a gesture that was both defiant and oddly vulnerable. "They ain't ter be trusted. She was hurt somethin' terrible when she worked at Finnigan's Theater. When she complained ter the watchmen and constable, they laughed. Said they'd look into it if she was a bit more friendly ter them.

"And it ain't just Edwina," she added, her lip curling. "Beaks don't care about workin' folk. Me ma was sent off ter Botany Bay 'cause a nob accused her of filching his handkerchief. Ma said she didn't take it, but they didn't believe her, neither."

Sam's lips tightened. The story was common enough. "I'm sorry about your ma."

"Oi suppose being deported ter Australia is better'n hanging," the child said with a contemptuous sniff.

"What's your name?"

"Why should Oi tell ye?"

"I reckon this is a normal spot for you, if you know Edwina. It wouldn't be difficult ter find out," he pointed out mildly.

She scowled at him. "Bridget."

"Edwina seems ter have confided a considerable amount in you, Bridget."

"Folks don't like lookin' at her, 'cause her face is burned. But Oi'd talk ter her when she'd buy me oranges. She told me Oi reminded her of her little sister."

"Did you hear what happened at Bowden Theater?" he asked, and watched fear darken the little girl's eyes before she averted her gaze to the oranges in the crate at her feet.

"Aye," she whispered. "A gentry mort cocked up her toes. Edwina didn't have nothin' ter do with it."

He contemplated her tense face. "You seem awfully sure of that."

She lifted her eyes to meet his. "Oi am."

The child could simply be speaking out of loyalty to her friend, but Sam's gut told him that there was something more. "Were you here on Sunday, selling your oranges?"

She shifted her gaze, focusing on two horseback riders trotting by.

"Bridget. This is important. Edwina might be in danger."

"Oi know," she said softly. "Oi saw her. She was running and a man was chasin' her. He weren't no watchman, neither." She shivered, but it wasn't from the cold. She pinned Sam with her accusing eyes. "The last time Oi saw anyone that scared was when me ma told me that she was gonna be transported ter Botany Bay."

"Did you hail a watchman for help?"

Bridget said nothing, simply stared at him with her bruised, reproachful eyes.

"God's teeth, how can the law help if no one reports crimes?"

"The law don't help when we *do* report crimes," she shot back. "And since the man was dressed like a swell, the *law* would be thinkin' that he was chasing Edwina 'cause she stole somethin' from him."

The girl was probably right. Sam blew out a breath. "What time was this?"

"The bells rang—little after ten o'clock."

"Can you describe the man?"

"Nay."

"Young or old? Short or tall?"

The girl shrugged. "He had on a hat, and his collar was turned up." She bit her lip, thinking. "Young enough, Oi reckon. He wasn't bacon-fed neither. Fit enough ter run fast." She gave Sam a once-over. "He was taller than ye."

The defiance suddenly drained out of her, leaving her small face ashen and pinched. "Oi haven't seen Edwina since," she said. "Oi reckon the man caught her and Oi won't be seein' her again."

Fifteen minutes later, Sam clumped up the stairs at 25 Bedford Square behind the Marquis of Sutcliffe's stiff-necked butler. In the library, his gaze immediately went to Kendra, writing on the slate board.

"Did you learn anything?" she asked when he joined her.

"Aye, a bit. I see you've acquired a slate board." It was, he'd always thought, a clever way to organize the various bits and pieces of an investigation. He'd even suggested setting one up in Bow Street, but they'd been less than receptive.

"The Duke had it brought over," Kendra told him.

Sam studied the timeline she'd written on the slate board, beginning with Wednesday, when the body was found in the Thames and delivered to Munroe's morgue, then Friday, with Lady Westford viewing the body, to Sunday, when she was murdered.

"A girl selling oranges on the street saw Edwina on Sunday morning fleeing from a man," he said. "A little after ten o'clock."

She gave him a sharp look. "Why are we just hearing about this now?"

"The girl—Bridget—didn't report it. Said Edwina doesn't trust the law, and she doesn't either. Her ma was deported." Sam lifted a shoulder in a half shrug. "A lot of folks are like that. Or they just want ter mind their own business rather than get involved."

Kendra blew out an annoyed breath. "How can cops help when no one speaks up?"

Sam scratched the side of his nose to hide his confusion. What, he wondered, was a cop? American slang for Bow Street Runner? Still, he got the spirit of what she was saying. Apparently, folks in America had the same mistrust of the law as they did in London Town.

"Was she able to describe the man?" she asked.

"She said he wasn't fat, not elderly because he was fast, taller than me, and dressed like a gentleman." He watched her write it on the slate board. "A description I reckon fits most of London."

"Not everyone. Lord Westford is too big and old to have been chasing Edwina," Kendra pointed out. "Of course, that doesn't mean he didn't hire someone to do it."

Sam shook his head. "Most assailants hired ter commit murder come from the stews. They wouldn't be dressed like a gentleman."

Kendra looked thoughtful. "That's not enough to eliminate the possibility. I found out that Lord Westford has another family."

Sam kept his expression neutral as Kendra explained. He wasn't surprised. Such arrangements were common enough, especially in the Polite World, where marriage was more often about business than love.

"Mr. O'Leary—Westford's illegitimate son—is young and most likely dresses like a gentleman," Kendra pointed out when she was done.

Sam couldn't mistake the implication, but had to argue, "Why would Mr. O'Leary wish ter harm her ladyship? They've no connection other than she was married ter his father."

"Mr. O'Leary is older than Lord Westford's biological son, but because of the circumstance of his birth, he won't inherit the title or money. That could make a person bitter."

Sam shook his head. "Mr. O'Leary's half-brother will naturally inherit the title and entailed estates, but that doesn't mean Mr. O'Leary or any of Lord Westford's illegitimate offspring will be left penniless. In fact, Lord Westford appears ter have taken an interest in their welfare, if the oldest was trained as a barrister and now works in Parliament. Not every nobleman cares what happens ter his by-blows."

He paused, then added, "Mr. O'Leary may resent the circumstance of his birth, but he had no reason ter murder his father's wife. Her death changes nothing about his circumstances."

"I know how difficult divorce is in this ti—" She broke off abruptly, a strange expression crossing her face, and said firmly, "In England."

"I reckon in America it's easier ter get a divorce," he said carefully, even as he wondered at her reaction. It wasn't the first time that the lass had stopped herself, as if she was about to speak out of turn. Sam had known Kendra Donovan—Lady Sutcliffe now, he corrected himself—for more than a year. For all her spunk and cleverness, she was . . . peculiar. She had a broad understanding of the criminal element that Sam had never seen in his fellow men, much less in a woman.

The Duke had once hired him to investigate her background, how she'd come to England. And he'd found . . . nothing. *Absolutely nothing.* That was an oddity he couldn't explain. Everyone left some kind of trail: a name on a ship manifest, or a captain or crew member who recognized her. She was too pretty and, yes, too peculiar, with her American accent and strange ways, to *not* be remembered.

She was a puzzle, to be sure, but he realized that it didn't matter. He'd follow the lass to the ends of the earth if she asked it of him.

"Will Lord Westford be able to marry Mrs. O'Leary now?" Kendra asked, bringing his attention back to the topic at hand.

"It's possible, but it would certainly cause a scandal," said a new voice. The Marquis of Sutcliff sauntered into the library. "Even if he did marry her, it would change nothing. Mrs. O'Leary's children would still have been born out of wedlock."

"Mr. Kelly said the same thing," Kendra admitted. She tapped her chin with the piece of slate. "Maybe it has less to do with the children and more to do with Lord Westford marrying the woman he loves. He wouldn't be the first husband to hire someone to kill his wife in order to marry his mistress."

Alec moved to the sideboard and pulled a stopper out of crystal decanter. "Lord and Lady Westford were married comfortably for thirty years. Why murder her now?"

"How do you know their marriage was comfortable?" she challenged.

Alec gave a quick laugh. "Touché. However, Lady St. James is a reliable source for this type of information, I believe. Mr. Kelly, a glass of whisky?"

"Aye, thank you, sir." Sam eyed the glass appreciatively as Alec brought it over to him.

Kendra said, "One never knows what goes on behind closed

doors—not even Lady St. James. I think you should ask Lord Westford if he's planning to marry Mrs. O'Leary."

Sam stared at her with the same shock as her husband.

"You want me to interrogate his lordship about whether he's going to marry his mistress?" Alec said. "And I suppose I ought to ask if his wife was in the way?"

"Interrogate is a strong word. Consider it collecting information."

"Oh, I'll be sure to tell him that when he gets insulted by the implication that he had his wife murdered," Alec muttered, taking a swallow of his whisky.

"I don't care about his feelings. He rushed to have his wife's death declared an accident, to shut down any investigation. I don't like it."

"Very well."

"Ask him if he was aware of his wife's affair with Mr. Goldsten," Kendra added.

Alec smirked. "To confirm, you want me to quiz him about murdering his wife, whether he's going to marry his mistress, and if he knew about his wife's *amoretti*."

Kendra returned his smile. "You don't have to do it in that order."

Sam took a moment to enjoy his sip of whisky before asking, "You really don't think Lord Westford killed his wife, do you, lass?"

Instead of answering, she regarded him. "You don't?"

"Nay." He paused to formulate his thoughts. "People kill for all sorts of reasons. But this. . . it was too public. Seems ter me, there are any number of ways ter rid yourself of an unwanted wife without drawing this kind of attention."

Kendra surprised him by nodding. "I agree, Mr. Kelly. I can think of a dozen ways to kill someone that is more efficient and private, and where you wouldn't have to worry about possible witnesses like Edwina."

God's teeth, *Sam* didn't even know that many ways to kill.

"But he's still a suspect until he can be eliminated," Kendra continued, and began to pace. "I'm more interested in Lady Westford's connection to the first murder victim, Clarice."

"We don't know the body found in the Thames was Clarice," Alec said.

"You're right, but the timing works. And Lady Westford was asking about Clarice. That's not a coincidence."

"Aye, but Lady Westford saw the body in the morgue," Sam said. "If it was Clarice, why would she be asking about her the next day?"

"There might not be a lot of marine life in the Thames, but being in the water for a couple of days has a way of changing a person's appearance," Kendra pointed out. "Maybe Lady Westford wasn't entirely sure the body she saw *was* Clarice, and wanted confirmation."

"It's queer thing, with the woman's blood drained and then the body stolen." Sam wasn't a superstitious or devotedly religious man, but he tightened his hand on his glass to stop himself from making the sign of the cross.

Kendra said, "We need to find the connection between the woman from the Thames—Clarice or not—and Lady Westford. I've sent Muldoon a message to see if he can locate the article that caught Lady Westford's eye."

"I'm gonna speak ter Lady Westford's household and stable staff," Sam said. Servants of the nobility could be uppity, but he had more authority with them as a Bow Street Runner than with his betters. "Maybe they knew what her ladyship was involved in."

"Dr. Munroe mentioned that Lady Westford arrived by hackney on Friday." Kendra turned to study the timeline. "It's likely that she did the same on Sunday. That tells us something."

"Aye. She wanted secrecy." Sam tipped back his glass to finish his whisky as the door opened and the butler entered, carrying a silver salver with a single folded piece of foolscap.

"A message has come for you, my lady."

Kendra opened the paper, explaining, "I sent a message earlier to Dr. Munroe to ask if he knows Mr. Goldsten."

"Mr. Goldsten?" Sam asked.

"Lord Westford wasn't the only one unfaithful in the marriage."

"Ah."

Kendra smiled. "Dr. Munroe knows Mr. Goldsten, and has agreed to introduce me."

# FOURTEEN

Mr. Goldsten was not a physician; he was a surgeon—or, in this century's vernacular, a sawbones—who'd set up his surgery in Blackfriars, a section of London that had taken its name from the black-robed friars who had once lived in the priory on the banks of the River Thames. The priory was long gone, first gutted by King Henry VIII, with his dissolution of monasteries, and converted into factories and residences, then destroyed by the Great Fire that had burned most of London to the ground in 1666.

Only a few crumbling stone walls of the old monastery remained amidst a warren of timbered taverns, warehouses, shops, and shabby dwellings. It was, Kendra mused, a far cry from the Blackfriars of the future, with its sleek, soaring glass-and-steel skyscrapers.

Kendra was also amazed to see the River Fleet, which gurgled and gushed through the neighborhood to the Thames. The waterway would eventually vanish beneath concrete and asphalt, becoming one of London's lost rivers. Even now, construction was taking place, changing the cityscape into what it would someday be. *And I am witnessing it firsthand.*

"I've known Mr. Goldsten for more than three years," Munroe said.

Kendra dragged her gaze away from the window to look at the anatomist, who was sitting across the carriage from her. When she'd picked him up ten minutes ago, she'd given him a brief rundown of what she'd discovered, including Lady Westford's supposed relationship with Goldsten.

"We became acquainted mostly through the Metamorphosis Club," he continued. "But we were not close, and I had no idea that he'd formed an . . . attachment to Lady Westford."

"He never spoke about her?" Kendra asked as the carriage came to a halt. John, the head groom who ran Alec's stables but performed the duties of coachman when needed, jumped off his perch and opened the door.

Munroe shook his head. "No. But our conversations centered around medical advancements and natural philosophy."

Kendra descended from the carriage and paused to scan the street. The general seediness of the area extended to the people, mostly tradesmen, laborers, shopkeepers—men, women and children—and, because the Thames was so close, dockworkers and sailors. Mixed races, she noted. Those hurrying about their business gave them—or, rather, her—sidelong glances. The men loitering in the alleyways, however, watched them with eyes crafty enough to make her dip her hand inside her reticule and close her finger over the muff pistol.

Out of the corner of her eye, Kendra saw John shift his stance as well, bringing up his blunderbuss to hold crosswise against his chest. The message was clear: *Don't mess with us.*

The anatomist guided her toward a narrow red-brick building with sash windows. It had clearly once been pretty but was now derelict, the bricks chipped and smudged with soot. The white paint on the door and window trims had gone gray with grime and age, some of it peeling away to reveal rotting wood.

The inside wasn't any better. The lobby—which Kendra suspected had once been an entrance hall—was dingy and spare. Men occupied the rows of chairs. Most appeared to be suffering from gunshot or knife wounds or looked as if they'd been in an accident or brawl, their flesh bruised, bones broken, eyes swelled shut. A handful of men looked ill, their skin pale and sweaty, their eyes dull and sunken into dark hollows. One man's face was deformed with oozing ulcers.

Bad, but the stench was worse. Kendra was struck forcibly by body odor, blood, decay, infirmity. She breathed shallowly and was relieved when Munroe strode quickly through the room, nudging open a door on the far wall.

Unfortunately, the putrid odor followed them. Or maybe it awaited them in the next chamber—the smell of disease, maybe death. There were about a dozen occupied cots here. Some patients were sleeping, their chests rattling with every labored breath. Others were staring at the ceiling with a vacant look in their eyes. Maybe opium. Or maybe just imagining themselves in another place.

Kendra focused on activity on the other side of the room. About five men, all of whom were barely old enough to shave, were clustered around a man lying on a cot, and watched an older man on a stool carefully peel a bandage from the man's bicep. Instead of wearing white lab coats, everyone but the patient was wearing blood-spattered aprons over their regular clothes.

"There doesn't appear to be any infection, which I attribute to the marigold and honey ointment that was applied after the wound was cleaned and stitched," said the man that Kendra assumed was Mr. Goldsten. Leaning forward, he eyeballed the injury, then gave a satisfied sigh as he straightened. "Let's see your range of motion, Mr. Eastman."

The patient stared at him without comprehension. "Me w'ot?"

"Lift your arm . . . yes, like that. Now please move it in a circular motion. How does that feel, Mr. Eastman?"

"Better than when Oi 'ad a cheese-toaster stickin' in there."

"Indeed." Goldsten hoisted himself to his feet. "Mr. Beane, please reapply the salve and dress the wound with new wrappings." He handed a jar and strips of linen to an earnest-looking young man with curly brown hair. "Afterward, you may return to your duties, Mr. Eastman. But no more squabbles with midshipmen who fight with a dirk rather than their fists."

The surgeon turned, eyes widening in surprise when he realized he had a new audience. "Dr. Munroe! I didn't realize you were here." His gaze slid to Kendra and he waited for introductions.

Munroe obliged. "Mr. Goldsten, may I introduce Lady Sutcliffe. My lady, this is Mr. Goldsten."

"Lady Sutcliffe. This is a pleasure."

He bowed, but he didn't smile. There was an intensity to his expression that made Kendra think he rarely smiled. She estimated him to be around Lady Westford's age, somewhere in his mid-fifties. He was attractive, with a full head of hair, once black, but now pewter gray. His face was thin, worn down by worry, age, and exhaustion. Like Munroe, he had spectacles pinched on the bridge of his narrow nose. The hazel eyes behind the lenses were serious, guarded. His clothes, beneath his stained apron, were rumpled, his cravat hastily tied. Clearly, being fashionable was not a priority.

Goldsten was, Kendra decided, the opposite of Lord Westford almost in every way. *And that's interesting.*

"Do you hope to become a patroness for surgeries serving the destitute, my lady?" he asked, his eyes steady on hers.

"Was Lady Westford a patroness for your clinic?" Kendra asked.

He sucked in a quick breath. After a moment, he said, his tone careful, "Lady Westford was a generous woman. She wanted to help those less fortunate than herself. Were you friends?"

"No." Kendra glanced around, noting that there were several eyes on them. "Maybe we should go somewhere more private to talk?"

"Yes, that would be wise. Let's go into my laboratory." He paused, then shook his head. "On second thought, there's a coffee shop down the street. My laboratory is not set up to accommodate a lady's sensibilities."

"I'm fine with your laboratory," she assured him.

Munroe said, "Lady Sutcliffe has attended my autopsies on occasion. Smelling salts will not be required, Mr. Goldsten."

"Very well," Goldsten replied, peering at her curiously. "One moment." He turned to address his apprentices. "Mr. Beane, escort Mr. Eastman out when you are finished. Mr. Dawes, please take over the care of our next patient. You've assisted me enough times in setting broken bones."

"Yes, sir," said Dawes, a handsome youth with curly, ginger hair. He'd been one of the apprentices staring at Kendra with open curiosity, but he now tore his gaze away to follow Goldsten's instructions.

"You may have to expand your facility soon, Mr. Goldsten," Munroe commented as they followed the man to an archway that led to a short hallway. "You have no shortage of patients."

"'Tis one of the benefits of being located so near the docks." Goldsten shot them a wry smile that temporarily lifted the weariness from his face. "Sailors enjoy celebrating their return to London by imbibing too much, and that inevitably leads to arguments that are settled with weapons and fists. Dreadful, of course, but it gives me ample specimens to experiment with new wound treatments without being on the battlefield. You're right about the space, though, Dr. Munroe. I've spoken to Mr. Dawes' stepfather about renting a larger building in the area. Mr. Stevens is the largest landlord in Blackfriar."

"Convenient to have Mr. Dawes as an apprentice then," murmured Munroe, and earned another fleeting smile from the surgeon.

"It is."

"Tell me, do you still work at St. George's?" Munroe asked.

"Oh, yes. Although for how long, I don't know. I may be in desperate need of space here, but St. George's is in desperate need of renovations. The building is falling down."

Mr. Goldsten pushed open the door that led to his laboratory. Several windows on one wall allowed daylight to stream across counters and tables that displayed a smorgasbord of horrors. Pickled organs floating inside jars. A jumble of bones and skulls—human and animal. On one table, there was a full-length mummified body. On another was—*holy crap*—a human arm, its pale, waxy flesh sliced open to reveal muscles, tendons, and veins.

Aware that Goldsten was watching her—probably waiting for her to faint—Kendra schooled her features into impassive lines.

"Please, have a seat." Goldsten indicated the chairs in front of his desk. He waited until they'd settled before he dropped into his own seat. "What is your visit really about, my lady?"

Kendra had to appreciate his directness. "Lady Westford's murder."

He gave a surprised jerk, then went utterly still. "What are you talking about? It was a tragic accident."

"You don't really believe that, do you? You think that Lady Westford went into an empty theater, climbed to the top balcony, and *accidentally* fell over the railing?"

She was watching him closely, and saw the quick flinch before his expression went carefully blank.

"I cannot presume to know what happened," he said stiffly.

"There can be no doubt that her ladyship was murdered," Munroe said gently. "I examined the body myself."

Goldsten frowned at Munroe. "Dr. Thornton conducted the postmortem. He ruled it an accident."

The anatomist blew out an uneasy breath. "I can only surmise that Lucien issued that verdict because Lord Westford pressured him to do so."

"Do you know anybody who would wish to harm Lady Westford?" Kendra asked Goldsten.

"Why would I know such a thing?"

Kendra contemplated him for a long moment. "We know that you and Lady Westford were involved."

His throat worked as he swallowed. "We were friends. Suggesting anything else is unseemly and would besmirch the lady's reputation."

"The lady is dead, Mr. Goldsten, and past caring about her reputation."

His gaze fell to the papers and books strewn across his desk. "Reputations aren't only about the present, my lady. They're about the future," he said softly. "Our reputation today becomes our legacy of tomorrow. Sometimes it's only our legacy that we pass on in the world."

"I'm not interested in exposing Lady Westford's romantic life,"

Kendra said, impatient with proprieties. "The woman was *murdered*. If you and Lady Westford were friends, as you say you were, she may have confided in you. Did she ever talk to you about her husband, her marriage?"

Goldsten looked up. "No, not really. Grace—Lady Westford and I shared the same interests in medicine and natural philosophy. She was passionate about it, and even kept up a correspondence with Mr. Edward Jenner. She greatly admired his attempts to eradicate smallpox."

Kendra had to control her shock. Edward Jenner was responsible for creating the first vaccine. Hell, he had *coined* the word "vaccine." Would she ever get used to living in the same era as people she'd once read about in history books?

"An unusual lady," Munroe murmured. "I regret not becoming better acquainted with her."

"Lady Westford's interest in medicine was inspired by her sister, who perished from typhus when she was quite young," Goldsten said.

Kendra circled back to why she was there. "I've been told Lady Westford was estranged from her husband. That he has a mistress, another family."

Goldsten's brow creased in puzzlement. "Yes. What of it?"

"Maybe Lord Westford wasn't happy with the arrangement."

"Lady Westford rarely spoke of her husband other than to say that they married young and for reasons that had nothing to do with the finer emotions." His tone was stiff. "It isn't unusual in certain circles, my lady."

"She never mentioned any arguments she and her husband had? Or that she was afraid of him?"

"No. She wasn't afraid of her husband."

"She told you that she wasn't afraid of him?"

"Well, no—"

"She just never talked about him. So you don't know for sure."

Goldsten lifted his hands, palms up. Kendra noticed blood in the creases—not his, but belonging to the countless patients he'd worked on today.

"I can't help you with that kind of gossip, Lady Sutcliffe," he said.

"Did she mention having difficulties with anyone else?"

Frowning, he dropped both his hands and his gaze to the desk. "No."

Kendra watched him fiddle with pieces of foolscap, tidying them into a pile. "No one that she was afraid of or troubled by?" she pressed.

His restless fingers stilled. He looked to the window and the gray clouds framed between the neighboring buildings. Kendra thought she saw sadness in his eyes as he said, "No, no. Lady Westford wasn't a person that you could dislike, much less hate."

"When was the last time you saw her?"

He slowly brought his gaze back to hers. "I'm not certain. I think it was when we attended a lecture on typhus given by Monsieur Chevalier. He's a French physician who was in Napoleon's army when they retreated from Moscow. He witnessed the devastating death toll from the disease."

"When was the lecture?"

He sifted through his periodicals, papers, and books until he found a tattered leatherbound journal. He spent a minute flipping through the pages until he found the one he wanted. "Thursday, August 28."

"And that was the last time you saw her?"

"Yes." But his gaze skittered away.

Kendra eyed him, then asked, "What was her mood like on that day?"

"She was . . . she was troubled by the King's illness," he replied. "She'd recently traveled with Her Majesty to Windsor, and witnessed firsthand the treatments being used on the King. It disturbed her."

An icy chill raced down Kendra's arms. More than a month ago, she'd spent time in a madhouse. She was all too aware of the treatments prescribed in this century.

"Do you know why she would be at Bowden Theater on Sunday morning?" Kendra asked.

The sudden change in topic seemed to confuse Goldsten. He frowned. "What? No."

"She never talked about the Bowden Theater?"

Goldsten shook his head. "No."

"What about an actress named Clarice?"

"What? Who? No, I don't recall her mentioning that name."

He was, Kendra decided, a very bad liar. The room was cold, but she detected a gleam of sweat on his brow. She said nothing, letting the silence spin out until he finally met her gaze.

"Mr. Goldsten, I am trying to find out who killed your friend," she said at last. "You need to be honest with me."

An emotion she couldn't decipher flared behind his eyes, and then he pushed himself to his feet in a jerky movement. "I've told you everything that I know. I'm afraid I must return to my patients."

"One more question." She kept her gaze on his as she stood. Goldsten's reluctance to continue the inquiry was palpable. "Where were you on Sunday morning?"

He inhaled sharply; he knew exactly what she was asking. If he was insulted or outraged by the question, he didn't show it. His voice was oddly flat when he said, "I was at St. George's in the morning. By afternoon, I was here. Sunday is not a day of rest for the sick, diseased, and dying, Lady Sutcliffe. Now, I really must beg your leave."

Kendra and Munroe followed the surgeon back to the patients' ward. Mr. Dawes paused his administrations and began, "Mr. Goldsten—" but Goldsten shook his head.

"Hold your inquiry, Mr. Dawes, until I return from escorting our guests out." He strode across the room, opening the door to the waiting room.

Munroe stepped across the threshold, then stopped, turning to face the surgeon. "We both joined the Metamorphosis Club because we share the belief that scientific knowledge can only be advanced through research. Our quest for truth makes society uncomfortable, just as Lady Sutcliffe's makes people uncomfortable."

Goldsten nodded. "I understand, but I have no more answers for you. Good day, Dr. Munroe, Lady Sutcliffe."

Kendra crossed the lobby, aware of dozens of eyes on her. But only one pair of eyes made the space between her shoulder blades itch. As Munroe pulled open the front door for her, she glanced back to see that for all his talk about getting back to his patients, Goldsten hadn't moved from his spot. And even from this considerable distance, Kendra recognized the naked fear in his eyes.

# FIFTEEN

"When you care about a person who is murdered, you don't forget the last time you spoke to them," Kendra said quietly as they walked down the pavement to the carriage. The phenomena, she knew, was called trauma anniversaries. "He's either lying outright or not telling us everything."

Munroe let out a pensive sigh. "I don't know what to say other than that Mr. Goldsten's evasiveness is troubling."

"Miss Don—Lady Sutcliffe!"

The shout had Kendra pivoting around. Phineas Muldoon was jogging toward them.

"Dr. Munroe," the Irishman added, doffing his hat as he came to a stop in front of them.

Kendra surveyed his face, flushed from the cold wind. "How'd you know I was here?"

He gave her an impudent look, tapping the side of his nose. "I have my ways." When she merely lifted her eyebrows, he grinned. "And I happened to encounter Mr. Kelly at Whitehall. He was searching for Mr. O'Leary at the time, and mentioned that you were making inquiries of Mr. Goldsten. He was involved with Lady Westford, was he?"

"That's what we've been told. He confirmed they were friends."

"Probably that's all he'll confirm. He'd never admit to having an intimate relationship with a lady, married or not. He'd want to protect her reputation." A shadow crossed the Irishman's face, leaving it brooding. "Common folk know their place, Lady Sutcliffe, and it isn't to marry above their station."

Kendra had a feeling he wasn't referring to Goldsten and Lady Westford's relationship anymore. Maybe that's what compelled her to say, "I'm a commoner. You could say I married above my station." *And out of my own time.*

Muldoon's morose expression lifted and his blue eyes twinkled. "If I may be so bold, there is nothing common about you, my lady." He glanced at the carriage. "Are you returning to the morgue, or home?"

"Neither. St. George's hospital. Mr. Goldsten said he was working there on Sunday."

"Ah. And you'll be wanting to confirm his alibi. May I join you? I have something of interest to share with you."

"Of course." She waited until they'd joined her in the carriage and it was underway before she asked, "Did you get my earlier message, Mr. Muldoon?"

His wide mouth curved into one of his sly smiles. "Mr. Kelly told me that Lord Westford spends most of his time with his mistress— Mr. O'Leary being a product of that union. Are you thinking that the earl murdered his wife to be free to marry his lady love?"

"A husband always needs to be looked at when his wife is killed, but I'm also looking elsewhere."

"Mr. Goldsten."

Kendra lifted her eyebrows. "Mr. Muldoon, I'm starting to think you wanted a ride to fish for information rather than share anything you found out."

He grinned, unabashed. "Can't fault me for being curious. Personally, I think it's more likely that the English nobility will kill for money and power rather than for love, but what do I know? I'm just a poor Irish scribbler."

"Mr. Muldoon—"

"Yes, I got your earlier note, my lady. I spent my entire morning hunting for the article, and even had to venture into my competitor's territory, call in a few favors—"

"Mr. Muldoon, I'll hire a marching band and give you a parade later for all the work you've done. Right now, I'd like you to tell me what it said."

He laughed. "I have something even better, my lady."

He reached into the pocket of his greatcoat and pulled out a battered and stained copy of *The Morning Post*, which smelled a little like fish. Handing it to her, he said, "The article you seek is at the bottom of the page."

"'Beauteous Mermaid Found In River'?" Kendra read aloud, then raised her eyebrows at Muldoon.

He chuckled. "*The Morning Post* scribblers are a creative lot."

Kendra could only shake her head. Then again, she could hardly pass judgement. She'd scanned enough tabloid headlines announcing secret alien autopsies or Bigfoot sightings, let alone the outlandish clickbait that ran rampant on the Internet.

Lowering her eyes, she quickly read the article. The more scandalous broadsheets were just beginning to incorporate illustrations—the more outrageous the better—but *The Morning Post* was still dense in print.

**In the wee hours of the morning, the Thames Police discovered the body of a beautiful young woman, clad only in seaweed, floating on the waves. Mr. Tibbs, a local fisherman, described the creature as having an uncommon loveliness, with pitch-black hair and a heart-shaped mole on the left side of her face. Tales of enchanting sirens and mermaids have long been part of sea lore, and Mr. Tibbs admitted that if the lady in question had sported a fishtail as opposed to being whole of limb, he would have given credence to her being a magical creature. Mr. Cranston of the Thames Police said that, as there were no obvious wounds, they believe the beauty was bathing when she fell into the Thames and drowned. The cadaver was transported to the morgue of Dr. Ethan Munroe, who runs a notorious anatomy school in Covent Garden, where he instructs his pupils in the ghoulish art of dissection.**

Kendra handed the newspaper to Munroe to read for himself.

"We need to find out if Clarice had a beauty mark. It could be the thing that caught Lady Westford's attention, if she was already familiar with Clarice. Mr. Muldoon, take this article to Bowden Theater and ask for Prudence. See if she can confirm that this description matches Clarice. And find out anything else you can about the actress. When we were at the theater yesterday, we were more focused on Lady Westford's murder than Clarice's disappearance."

Muldoon gave Kendra a jaunty salute. "Aye, aye, captain."

"This is . . . rubbish!" Munroe exclaimed, rattling the newspaper irritably. "'Notorious anatomy school,' indeed! And 'instructs his pupils in the ghoulish art of dissection'—*ghoulish?*"

He crumpled the paper in disgust before Muldoon snatched it back from him and smoothed it out on his knee.

"There is nothing notorious nor ghoulish about my school!" Munroe went on. "It is this kind of fearmongering that keeps England's medical community behind the rest of Europe. How can they expect surgeons to successfully operate on the wounded if we don't know basic anatomy? My God, even France realized that! Their government *supplies* their surgeons with unlimited cadavers to dissect, even if those are only sent to one teaching school. I—" He caught Kendra's eye and broke off, blowing out a frustrated breath. "Forgive me for my diatribe, my lady. This has been a sore point for me and my colleagues for years."

"The rules are archaic," she agreed sympathetically. She turned to her other companion. "Mr. Muldoon, when you're at the theater, also ask if anyone knows whether Clarice suffered from severe anemia."

"Now that's a peculiar request. May I ask why?"

Kendra glanced at Munroe. "Do you want to explain, doctor?"

"I didn't have a chance to conduct an autopsy, Mr. Muldoon, but my visual examination noted that the body showed no signs of lividity. She was either severely anemic or she had no blood coursing through her veins at the time of her death."

Muldoon's eyes widened. "Maybe she *was* a mermaid. Or, in Ireland, there are tales of a *Dearg-due*. A beautiful woman who transfixes her victims, then drinks their blood."

"Maybe you should consider writing for *The Morning Post* yourself, Muldoon," Kendra said.

The reporter laughed. "I didn't say a *Dearg-due* killed the poor creature. I was simply reminded of the old folktales." He then turned his attention to Munroe. "What stopped you from conducting the postmortem? Did someone claim the body?"

"What exactly did Mr. Kelly tell you?" Kendra asked.

"We spoke of Lord and Lady Westford's marriage—which I already knew about from *my* inquiries. He said that Lady Westford had been interested in a body pulled from the Thames and transported to Dr. Munroe's morgue. Again, I was aware of this because of your note inquiring after the article. He did mention that the drowned woman in the article might be an actress named Clarice, who worked at the Bowden Theater, the very same theater where Lady Westford died. Interesting coincidence. He did *not* mention a mermaid drained of her blood." He crossed his arms in front of his chest. "Or whatever else you two are hiding. Must I remind you of our deal to share information?"

"Fair enough. You know everything—except that the body was stolen from the morgue."

Muldoon stared at her. "The body was *stolen*?" He cut his gaze to Munroe, then began to laugh. "God knows there's plenty of body snatching going on. 'Tis why families hire watchmen to patrol graveyards at night. But anatomists like you, Dr. Munroe, tend to be the recipient of those bodies. I've never heard of a resurrectionist stealing a corpse from an anatomist before."

"It's not amusing, Mr. Muldoon." Munroe scowled at him. "We do not know who stole the body or why. Unfortunately, I was also only able to do a visual examination when I had it on my table, which is why I cannot say with one hundred percent certainty that the creature had no blood circulating in her veins, even though the lack of lividity suggests it. She did have bruising around the wrists and ankles, and puncture wounds on the inside of her arms."

"*Puncture* wounds?" Muldoon's eyebrows flew up. "Like she'd been bitten?"

Munroe's look was derisive. "Surely you don't believe in your Irish folktales of vampires or *Dearg-dues* sucking the blood out of their human victims?"

Kendra expected Muldoon to laugh off such a suggestion. He smiled, but it didn't quite reach his eyes.

"Mayhap I'm just Irish enough not to dismiss the mystical world, Dr. Munroe. As your own Shakespeare wrote, 'There are more things in heaven and earth, Horatio, than are dreamt of in your philosophy.'"

Kendra couldn't argue with that. Hell, she was a time traveler. But she drew the line at vampires. "I think we can scratch Count Dracula off our list of suspects, Mr. Muldoon," she remarked dryly.

"Vlad Drăculea wasn't a count—he was a prince. In Walachia, Romania, I believe." Muldoon lifted his eyebrows when they stared at him in surprise. "What boy doesn't love a good story about a brutal, bloodthirsty, fifteenth-century prince terrorizing Europe by impaling his enemies? Do you know that it was said that Vlad insisted upon dining amongst his victims, soaking his bread in their blood?"

"Good God." Munroe was horrified.

Kendra had been thinking about the Dracula created by Bram Stoker. But the author of that book wouldn't even be born for another thirty years.

For a long moment, no one said anything as the carriage moved forward. The noises of the street—the clopping of hooves, the thrumming of wheels on cobblestone and gravel, the cries from the costermongers as they touted their wares—seemed too normal a backdrop for their discussion.

Muldoon broke the silence. "Mr. Kelly told me that you have a witness, and he's got his lads searching for her. She's most likely dead."

Kendra frowned. "Why do you say that?"

"It's been three days since anyone's seen her. Mayhap she'll be the next mermaid the River Police fish out of the Thames."

Kendra already considered his grim prediction a likely scenario. London might not have CCTV cameras on every corner in this time, but it had a million-plus eyeballs. Edwina, with her scarred face, would be noticed.

She looked out the window as seedy gave way to stylish, Hyde Park's velvety lawns of deep green dotted with sheep. Not the fluffy white sheep that she was used to seeing in the countryside. Here, the sheep's fleece had turned a dingy brown from living in London's smog. St. George's Hospital rose up on the other side of the thoroughfare.

"I shall make my way to the Bowden," Muldoon said once the carriage stopped and he had leapt down. "I'll let you know if I discover anything, my lady."

"Come to Bedford Square tomorrow morning, nine a.m. We'll have a briefing."

Muldoon cocked his head. "Very well. But why not this evening? I ought to know something by then."

Kendra let out a heavy sigh. "I can't tonight. I have to go to a ball."

Muldoon grinned. "You make attending a grand society soiree sound like you're walking to the gallows, my lady."

"I don't see much of a difference, Mr. Muldoon."

# SIXTEEN

St. George's Hospital resembled Mr. Goldsten's surgery, Kendra supposed, except on a much grander scale. As they walked up the steps of the neoclassical mansion, Munroe explained that the hospital had once been the London residence of Viscount Lanesborough, back when Hyde Park was nothing more than open fields. Like many wealthy families, the Lanesboroughs moved to more fashionable neighborhoods on the West End of London when the area urbanized. At the time, Lanesborough House had been taken over by medical staff who were unhappy with their facilities in the Westminster Infirmary, and they had rechristened it St. George's Hospital.

"I studied here for a time under John Hunter—one of the most brilliant anatomists I've ever known," Munroe said, opening the door for Kendra. "In fact, he was the reason I decided to become an anatomist and open a school rather than continue as a physician."

Munroe let out a soft sigh as they entered the waiting room, his gaze regarding the cracks in the walls, the crumbling crown molding, the peeling paint and scuff marks on the floor. "I confess, it's difficult for me to see St. George in such poor shape these days. The faculty is hoping to tear it down and build another in its place."

The interior did have the sad aura of an aging beauty unable to stop the ravages of time, Kendra thought. Unlike Mr. Goldsten's clinic, all kinds of patients occupied the waiting room chairs. Poor and working class, judging by their clothes. The upper classes—nobility or the nouveau riche—consulted physicians who made house calls. In a world of haves and have-nots, it was always nice to be the former. *Will that ever change?*

The stench was a little less oppressive here than in Goldsten's surgery, but not by much. Kendra didn't have to breathe shallowly or only through her mouth, but sickness had its own smell. As they crossed the room to the staircase, she was conscious of eyes, dulled by disease or drink or glittering with pain, tracking their progress. The sick muttered and moaned, hacked into dirty rags, or sat in quiet stupors.

"St. George has more than two hundred-fifty patients in fifteen wards," Munroe told her as they climbed. He paused on the next landing, where the long, wide hallway was a beehive of activity. Women wearing blue aprons over stiff, black bombazine dresses and carrying chamber pots and wooden buckets hurried in and out of rooms. A few men, also wearing aprons, theirs smeared with blood or bodily fluids, were making their rounds. Kendra could hear the dull murmur of conversation punctuated by sobs and shrieks coming from behind closed doors.

Kendra and Munroe received a few curious glances, but no one stopped to inquire about their presence. Munroe held out a hand to catch the attention of two women—one tall and thin; the other short and round—scurrying past with armloads of fresh, folded linens.

"Is Mr. Dandridge or Sir Preston working today?" he asked, earning an impatient look from the tall woman.

"Sir Preston is with a patient. Mr. Dandridge is currently in surgery." She shifted the bundle in her arms, pointing to a nearby door.

Munroe nodded. "Carry on, Sisters."

The women darted off, skirts flapping around their heels. Munroe opened the door, and Kendra stepped into a long, narrow room. Daylight streamed in a bank of windows, but oil lamps had also been lit, as well as a massive fireplace on one wall. There were fifty occupied cots, and Kendra identified at least a dozen medical staff—doctors and nurses—moving between patients. They seemed inured to the screaming, weeping, muttering, and cursing around them. Or the sound of urine hitting porcelain as a man with angry red, pus-filled boils covering his face stood pissing into a chamber pot. Another patient was vomiting loudly into a bucket.

Privacy was a luxury the poor could not afford.

Kendra had spent six years as an FBI profiler, viewing the ghastliest of crime scenes. In that time, she'd become hardened to dealing with the dead. It was ironic, she mused, that her stomach now roiled as her gaze traveled over the living. *If you can call this living…*

Munroe looked at her. "It can be overwhelming. We can wait for Mr. Dandridge elsewhere."

Kendra swallowed. "No, I'm fine. Which one is Mr. Dandridge?"

"Over there." Munroe walked toward a man sitting on a three-legged wooden stool at the end of a cot. The patient, restrained by leather straps, screamed and thrashed. Even with the restraints, two men tried to control the man's movements by pressing down on his shoulders and knees. Three young men were standing to the side, observing the procedure.

Kendra caught the flash of steel as Mr. Dandridge leaned over his patient. She gave him a brief look: mid-thirties; lean face, with black, curly hair; olive complexion. Fine lines fanned out from the outer corners of his eyes, likely the result of habitually narrowing them in concentration.

She turned her attention to the scalpel he held. His motion was quick, efficient. A slice, then he tossed something into a copper bowl held by a stern-looking nurse. It made a faint *thunk*. He repeated the slice, the toss. *Plink*. Kendra inched closer to see inside the bowl. It took her a moment to identify the three bloody lumps of flesh: *toes*.

Finished with the amputations, Mr. Dandridge set aside the scalpel and picked up a needle and thread from a small silver tray. "This young fellow is fortunate," he said, addressing those who were observing.

*Fortunate?* Kendra thought. She glanced at the patient's face, twisted in agony. His hair was matted with sweat. He'd quit screaming and was now emitting ragged moans each time the needle pierced his cut flesh as Mr. Dandridge skillfully sewed the skin together. The seam was tight, but blood oozed out, smearing the surgeon's fingers.

"The injury had become gangrenous," Mr. Dandridge continued, without looking up from the task at hand. The needle went in and out in a steady rhythm. "If he had waited longer to seek medical attention, the entire leg would have become infected and I— or another surgeon—would've been forced to remove it."

Mr. Dandridge snipped off the thread with a small pair of scissors from the tray. He tied a knot, then dumped the scissors and needle. Rising, he wiped his bloody hands on his apron. His next patient would be treated with those same hands.

"William," said Munroe, drawing the surgeon's attention.

"Ethan." Dandridge smiled, came over. "What brings you to St. George's?"

"Business. May I introduce Lady Sutcliffe? My lady, this is Mr. Dandridge—our most skillful surgeon."

"I saw your skill, Mr. Dandridge." Still, she had to ask, "Was there nothing you could have given the patient to reduce his pain? Opium?"

"Gin is less expensive. And we gave him almost half a bottle. Unfortunately, he must have developed a tolerance for it, as it did not have the effect it ought to have had."

Someone groaned and began retching into a bucket. Dandridge's eyes twinkled with amusement. "Shall we adjourn to a more pleasing environment? Ladies rarely tour our facilities, although when they do, they tend to confine themselves to the women's wards."

They fell into step with the surgeon as he walked toward the door. Dandridge gave Kendra a sidelong look. "Are you here because you are interested in becoming a patroness to the hospital, my lady?"

Apparently, Kendra mused, the only reason ladies toured hospitals and clinics was to become patronesses.

"I'm here because I'm looking into the murder of Lady Westford."

Dandridge was reaching for the doorknob. Kendra noticed how

those skillful fingers, so steady only moments ago as he sliced off three toes, spasmed. He stopped to stare at her. "*Murder?*"

Kendra studied him closely. "You sound surprised."

"I am." A troubled frown creased his brow. He pushed open the door. "I'd heard about Lady Westford's death, of course. But I was told it was an accident."

They walked down the hall, passing a few doctors, more nurses. Dandridge opened a door, then stepped back to allow them to enter. He'd brought them to what appeared to be a doctors' lounge. Bookshelves lined two walls, crowded with heavy tomes and medical instruments. A long buffet, located in front of a large window, gleamed with silver coffee- and teapots, a porcelain pitcher of ale, and crystal decanters. A fireplace took up another wall. Seven tables were scattered around the room. Three young gentlemen, still wearing their stained aprons, crowded around one table, whispering as they passed around an object. An old man with thick spectacles perched on a bulbous nose was reading a newspaper at the next table.

"Mr. Dandridge!" said one of the young men, as he glanced up and saw the surgeon. "We've been examining your *Le Cylindre*. Marvelous bit of engineering—simple, yet effective. My uncle is a physician in Manchester and would be interested in this for his practice. It ought not be too difficult to manufacture the device himself."

Kendra eyed the object with some interest. No one in the modern era would have looked at this simple wooden cylinder, about six inches in length and an inch and a half in diameter, and identified it as a stethoscope.

The old man at the other table snorted. "I've been using the ears that God gave me to listen to my patients' heartbeats for sixty years. I don't need anything designed by a Frenchie to practice medicine."

"Probably *wants* his ear against a lady's chest," whispered a pimply-faced youth, and the table erupted in laughter.

"Eh? What did you say, young Paulson?" The old man squinted at him.

"Maybe Mr. Dandridge would allow you to borrow *Le Cylindre* as a hearing aid, if you wish to eavesdrop on our conversation, Dr. Carter." Laughing, Paulson set the stethoscope on the table and jumped to his feet. His friends followed, and the trio rushed out of the room.

"Bloody young pups," muttered the old doctor, his wiry eyebrows twitching irritably as he rattled his newspaper and returned to his reading.

"Would you care for a drink?" Dandridge asked, crossing the room to the buffet.

"Thank you. Coffee," Kendra said.

He lifted the pot, poured her a cup. "Milk? Sugar?"

"Two sugars, no milk."

"I shall pour myself a cup," Munroe said.

They carried their drinks to the table that the young men had vacated. Kendra picked up the primitive stethoscope, inspecting it more closely.

Dandridge said, "I was intrigued when Monsieur Laënnec wrote about his invention. I am fortunate to have a cousin living in France, who managed to get his hands on one and send it to me. 'Tis a modest design, but I envision that it can be improved in the future."

"I can envision that too," Kendra said with a slight smile, setting down the old-fashioned instrument.

"Now, what's this about Lady Westford?" Dandridge prompted. "I heard she fell off a balcony in a Covent Garden theater. A tragedy, but an accident nevertheless."

"How well did you know Lady Westford?" she asked, picking up her cup. She tried not to make a face when she took a sip of the weak brew.

"She was a patroness at St. George's, and is one of the ladies I spoke of visiting on occasion. She also attended lectures at the Royal Society, where we had many interesting conversations. I was shocked and saddened when I heard of her accident."

"Except it wasn't an accident."

"So you say." He fixed his gaze on her. "Who told you that it was murder?"

"The evidence."

His eyes narrowed. "What evidence?"

"Let's just say it would require considerable effort for Lady Westford to accidentally fall over the railing."

Kendra recognized the flash of uneasiness in Dandridge's eyes, and knew what he was thinking.

"She didn't commit suicide either," she added quietly.

He sucked in a breath. "You are very blunt, my lady."

"When it comes to murder, I find it's best to be blunt." Kendra's gaze strayed to the elderly gentleman at the next table. He was pretending to be absorbed in reading his newspaper.

Dandridge shook his head. "No. I cannot believe that. Who would wish to harm her?"

"That's what I intend to find out." The comment prompted the elderly doctor to glance at her once quickly.

The lounge door opened and two gentlemen walked in, talking in low voices. One was small and wizened, with wispy gray strands combed over his bald pate and silver spectacles that matched the curved silver handle of his cane. The other man was tall and barrel-chested with a shock of white hair framing a broad, ruddy face. Kendra clocked the old man to be eighty—or nearly so—while his colleague could've been anywhere from his early forties to early sixties. He'd moderated his stride to match the old man's, but Kendra sensed a leashed energy in him.

They broke off their conversation when they spotted the trio at the table. The old man tapped his way to their table as the other man made a beeline for the sideboard. Kendra noticed how the younger man's ice-blue eyes scanned the room, taking in everything. Bypassing the coffee and teapots, he reached for one of the decanters, splashing whisky into a glass.

*The nineteenth-century's mantra: it's always five o'clock somewhere.*

"Ethan," the old man said, smiling, and his eyes, the color of washed-out denim, pinned Kendra with an inquiring look. "You brought us a guest."

"Sir Preston, may I introduce Lady Sutcliffe," Munroe said.

"My lady, this is Sir Preston. He is a chairman at St. George's and one of the founders of the Metamorphosis Club."

The old man gave a little bow. "'Tis a pleasure, my lady."

"And this is Mr. Burnell, one of our St. George's surgeons," Munroe continued when the other man walked over.

"Munroe is giving you a tour of St. George's, I see," Burnell said. "If you're considering donating to the hospital, I would be remiss not to urge you to save your money for a new hospital, rather than trying to save an old one."

Sir Preston frowned. "Let's not be so hasty in tearing down what could be repaired."

"Lady Sutcliffe is not here for the hospital. She's here because she believes Lady Westford was murdered," Dandridge told them, tossing Kendra an inscrutable look.

Both men looked startled by the blunt statement. But Burnell's surprise faded quickly into amusement. "Indeed? And what gossipmonger has spread this tale? No doubt old biddies who relieve their boredom by inventing far-fetched fantasies."

His lip curled with contempt, and Kendra's fingers tightened on her coffee mug. *Oh, I know that look.* For the first fourteen years of her life, she'd seen that look on her parents' faces. They were brilliant scientists, but they each had the emotional IQ of a crocodile.

"This isn't about gossip, Mr. Burnell," she said. Maybe she didn't have Alec and the Duke's cutting upper-class accent, but her tone was frosty. "It's about the evidence. Lady Westford didn't accidentally fall—or kill herself."

The smile remained cemented on his face. "And how, pray tell, did you come across this so-called evidence, madam?"

Munroe spoke up. "I examined the body myself. I concur with Lady Sutcliffe. This was no accident or suicide."

The smile vanished. "I thought Thornton ruled it an accident?"

"He was wrong," Kendra stated. "How well did you know Lady Westford?" She let her gaze drift between the men.

"This is extraordinary," Sir Preston murmured, frowning. "Are you absolutely certain, Ethan?"

"Yes."

"My goodness," Sir Preston muttered. "My wife and I were well-acquainted with Lady Westford. The countess was interested in our work here at St. George's, and we attended many of the same social events. We were distressed to learn of her death. And now this . . ."

"I knew her well enough," Mr. Burnell replied, studying the amber liquid in his glass. "We had many conversations about raising funds for a new hospital. This building has been here for almost a hundred years. Personally, I doubt that we'll get another twenty out of it."

"When was the last time you saw her?" Kendra asked all three men.

Dandridge answered first. "A few weeks ago, at the Royal Society. They had a fascinating discussion on using electricity to reanimate dead tissue." His voice warmed with excitement. "It brings up a host of possibilities. I just amputated three toes of a local wherryman. But what if we could harness the forces of electricity to stimulate dying flesh, bringing it back to life? What if we could offer treatment rather than amputation?"

"Balderdash!" The old man at the next table gave up all pretense of reading his newspaper. "What you say is sacrilege, Mr. Dandridge. Only God can bring back the dead!"

"We are men of science, Dr. Carter—not clergymen." Burnell matched the physician's glower. "You may waste your time praying for cures to society's ills, but the future will be shaped by natural philosophy and medicine. We must challenge ourselves and push past absurd barriers that are little more than superstition."

"By tampering with nature? By playing God?" Dr. Carter threw aside the newspaper in disgust and hoisted himself to his feet, practically vibrating with outrage.

Dandridge shook his head. "We play God every time we save a patient's life, Dr. Carter. If I hadn't operated on the wherryman, gangrene would have spread and eventually killed him."

"Mr. Dandridge makes a strong point," Sir Preston interjected, earning a furious look from Dr. Carter.

"Bah! I am aware of that *club* that you formed, sir! Mark my words, you shall regret toying with matters of which you know nothing. And you"—he scowled at Munroe—"with your dissections and experimentation. 'Tis blasphemy, and I will not listen to any more of this drivel." He stomped to the door and slammed it after him.

Burnell's lip curled. "That old relic still believes that disease is caused by an imbalance of bodily humors."

"Some individuals have a difficult time letting go of their former views," Munroe said quietly.

"You've always been too sentimental, Ethan. The man is archaic and should be drummed out of the medical profession." Burnell blew out a breath, glancing at Kendra. "I was also at that lecture, my lady. Like my colleague here, I believe electricity will prove useful in medicine, although I sincerely doubt that it will bring the dead back to life."

"My point is that we don't know what it may do until we *try*," Dandridge said stiffly.

No wonder Mary Shelly had been inspired to write *Frankenstein*. In fact, at this very moment, Kendra realized, the author was writing a masterpiece that would launch a new genre of fiction—and a million Halloween masks.

Kendra pushed away the distracting thought to ask, "Did you speak to Lady Westford at the lecture?"

"We tend to gather afterward to discuss what was presented," Burnell said. "And, yes, Lady Westford was in that group."

"How was her mood? Did she seem to be worried about anything or anyone?"

Burnell pursed his lips, frowning into his glass. "I don't recall anything unusual. We spoke about the lecture, of course, and certain advancements that have been reported in the medical journals. She didn't appear melancholy or fretful."

"That was the last time you saw her?"

"No, she came to St. George's last week. I saw her, but I didn't speak to her."

Kendra glanced at Dandridge. "Did you see her? Speak to her?"

"No. I mean, yes, I saw her, as well, but I didn't speak to her. She was with Mr. Goldsten."

*So, not two weeks ago.* Kendra wasn't surprised that Goldsten had lied. She was surprised that he'd lied about something so easily checked.

"What was she doing with Mr. Goldsten?" she asked innocently.

Dandridge started to speak, but Sir Preston cut in: "Lady Westford visits periodically. She invested time and money in the hospital, and she felt it was her duty to keep an eye on things. She had expressed concern over the mortality rate of mothers and their babes."

"Lady Westford and Mr. Goldsten were having an intense conversation when I saw them," Burnell said.

"Intense?"

"A bit of a row, if you must know. It's why I didn't approach. One doesn't want to become embroiled in someone else's quarrel."

"Did you hear what the quarrel was about?"

Burnell shook his head.

"Were you working at St. George's on Sunday morning?" Kendra asked the group.

Dandridge frowned. "Why do you ask?"

"Isn't it obvious, Dandridge?" Burnell said, his eyes on Kendra. "That's when Lady Westford died—or was killed, supposedly."

"Good heavens!" Sir Preston exclaimed. "Young lady, surely you cannot believe we—anyone here—would have harmed Lady Westford?"

Kendra glanced at the old man and thought, *Not you.* Physically, Sir Preston would never have been able to throw Lady Westford off the balcony, much less chase her up the stairs or Edwina down the street.

"It's a simple question." Kendra turned back to Burnell. "Why not answer?"

He smiled. "I have a suspicion that there are no simple questions with you, my lady. However, I shall answer. I didn't work on

Sunday. And since the direction of your inquiry is rather obvious, I shall state now that I did not murder Lady Westford. She was a patroness here, and I was quite optimistic that she would be spearheading the campaign to fund a new hospital."

She'd come here just to verify Goldsten's alibi, but something— just a whisper—made her Spidey sense tingle.

"I *was* here on Sunday," Dandridge said. "And I shall repeat what Mr. Burnell said: I did not kill Lady Westford. The very idea is ridiculous."

Sir Preston exhaled, clearly irritated. "On Sunday morning, I was at church. You can verify that with my wife."

Kendra nodded. "Since you were here on Sunday, did you see Mr. Goldsten?" she asked Dandridge.

He frowned. "Yes, briefly. He was working the women's ward."

"He worked the entire morning?" she pressed.

"Well, I don't know. We did not work together."

Kendra figured she'd better keep asking questions while she had a captive audience. "Did Lady Westford ever mention a woman named Clarice?"

They looked confused. Burnell spoke first. "Not to my recollection. Who is she?"

"Another woman who might have been murdered."

Burnell lifted a brow. "Might have been? You don't know?"

Munroe said, "The Thames River Police brought a woman's body to my school. I didn't have a chance to conduct a postmortem, but I believe she was exsanguinated or lost a considerable amount of blood before her death."

Burnell was clearly intrigued. "Self-inflicted?"

"I don't believe so. There was bruising that indicated restraints, and two puncture marks on the inside of both arms."

"My God. What is this about?" Sir Preston demanded, but Burnell ignored him.

"Fascinating. I would, of course, be interested in observing the postmortem when you do conduct it, Munroe."

Munroe hesitated only slightly, then shook his head. "Unfortunately, that won't be possible. The body was stolen."

"*Stolen?*" Burnell stared at Munroe, stunned. "Are you certain?"

Munroe smiled wryly. "They don't just get up and leave, you know."

Burnell shook his head. "Who would steal from *you?*"

"I heard Mr. Percy paid an ungodly sum to obtain only an arm from a man who had leprosy," Dandridge said, looking shaken.

The image of the leg in Goldsten's laboratory flashed through Kendra's mind. She'd assumed it had come from one of his patients, like the toes Dandridge had collected, but now she wondered if he'd purchased it on the black market.

Kendra circled back to the victim. "When you last saw Lady Westford, how did she seem?"

Burnell studied Kendra like she was a new species he'd discovered. After an uncomfortable beat, his mouth curved into another smile. "Forgive me, Lady Sutcliffe, but it is rather unusual for a gently-bred woman—or any woman, really—to be making these types of inquiries. Do you fancy yourself a Bow Street Runner?"

His amused condescension scraped her nerves more than his probing gaze, but she managed to summon a cool smile of her own. "Given your association with Lady Westford, I would think you'd be used to women having unusual interests, Mr. Burnell."

"Yes, she was indeed an enlightened female," Sir Preston said. "Which is why it's preposterous to think any one of us would wish to harm her. She supported our causes. Now . . ." He pulled out his pocket watch and checked the time. "I'm afraid I must go." The old man picked up his cane and leaned on it briefly as he eyed Kendra. "If I can be of any further assistance, let me know, madam. Good day."

Dandridge set down his coffee cup and pushed himself to his feet. "I'll accompany you, Sir Preston."

The surgeon picked up his stethoscope and slipped it into his pocket before leaving with Sir Preston. Burnell, Kendra noticed, seemed to find his colleagues hasty departures amusing.

"You didn't say where you were on Sunday morning, Mr. Burnell," she noted.

"No, I didn't." He smiled. "Even God had a day of rest, my lady. I was at home. Enjoying my day of solitude."

"I take it that means you don't have a wife?"

"My wife died several years ago."

"I'm sorry. Can anyone else verify you were at home?"

His smile thinned. "Solitude is derived from the Latin *solus*. By oneself."

"Your housekeeper?" Munroe put in.

"I do not have live-in servants. Given my schedule, I find that would be a frivolous expense. I do have a maid who cleans once a week, but I am not such a pagan to require her to work on the Lord's day." He finished his whisky and set down the glass. "This has been . . . interesting, my lady. Munroe." He nodded and sauntered across the room.

Kendra waited until the surgeon was gone before turning to Munroe. "Does he have a big house?"

He raised his dark brows at the question. "I'd say it's a modest dwelling. Why do you ask?"

"I'm just wondering how he's able to fit his giant ego into such a small space."

Munroe chuckled. "I know Burnell can come across as insufferable, but he's a highly skilled surgeon. And probably one of the most vocal proponents for medical advancements in the Metamorphosis Club, aside from Sir Preston."

"I'm sorry if my questions will cause problems for you with your colleagues."

"They'll understand, once they've had a chance to think about it."

They stepped back into the hallway, which seemed even more chaotic after the calm of the lounge area.

"Mr. Goldsten was telling the truth—he *was* here on Sunday morning," the anatomist pointed out as they descended the stairs.

"Yes, but this is a big place. Lots of entry and exit points. He could have slipped out for a couple of hours, with no one the wiser." She glanced at Munroe. "More importantly, Goldsten lied about the last time he saw Lady Westford."

Munroe said nothing.

The wind slapped them in the face as soon as they stepped outside. Kendra lifted her gaze to the dark clouds blowing in from the north. Rain, definitely. Maybe even snow, which would send even more people into a tizzy that the sun was dying and they were facing the end of days.

Yet it wouldn't stop the evening's various parties and balls. Unfortunately.

"I cannot believe Mr. Goldsten had anything to do with Lady Westford's death," Munroe said at last.

Kendra didn't respond as they strode quickly to the carriage. But she heard the underlying note in Munroe's voice. Dread. Maybe even fear.

*He doesn't want to believe it. But he's beginning to have his doubts.*

# SEVENTEEN

Kendra instructed Coachman John to drop Munroe off at his anatomy school before traveling on to Curzon Street. She'd briefly considered asking the anatomist to accompany her, but discarded the idea even before it was wholly formed. She needed answers from Dr. Thornton, and she didn't give a rat's ass about this era's sensibilities. She'd already caused enough tension between Munroe and his colleagues; she didn't want to be responsible for an even greater rift.

Fifteen minutes later, she knocked at Dr. Thornton's door. The same maid as the day before—Jenny—answered.

"Hello. Is Dr. Thornton at home?" Kendra asked.

The girl's brow furrowed in confusion. Maybe it was the use of "hello," which wouldn't become a common greeting until the advent of the telephone. Or maybe it was because Kendra was alone. Married women of the ton might not need chaperones to accompany them everywhere, but it was still outside the norm for them to visit a gentleman alone.

Jenny swallowed and made a visible effort to compose herself. "Aye. Is he expecting ye, ma'am?"

"He'll see me."

"Oh." She opened the door wider, stepping back to allow Kendra into the hallway. "If ye'll wait here—"

"Is he in his study?"

"Nay. He's in the drawing room."

"Take me to him." Kendra didn't wait; she began striding toward the stairs. Guilt pinched her for putting the maid in an awkward position, but she didn't want to give Dr. Thornton any chance to prepare for her. Not that he'd be able to prepare for the questions that she planned to ask.

Jenny scrambled past her and up the staircase. On the landing, she turned in the opposite direction of the study. Another open door revealed a small drawing room decorated in seafoam greens, fragile blues, and buttery yellows. Tasteful and feminine. Kendra's eyes flicked to the oval portrait above the marble fireplace, both a focal point and a position of honor. In the twenty-first century that position would be held by enormous flat-screen TVs. What that said about her time, she didn't know.

The portrait was of the same blonde woman in the painting in the study. Kendra had a feeling that she was the one responsible for the drawing room's décor.

Kendra had only a brief moment to observe Dr. Thornton before Jenny announced her presence. He was sitting at a small table in front of the window, engrossed in a book, with a teacup on the table.

"Dr. Thornton, sir, her ladyship is . . . she wants ter speak with ye."

The doctor glanced up, surprise widening his eyes when he saw Kendra in the doorway. "My lady." He started to rise.

"No, please, don't get up."

He ignored her, putting aside his book and bowing briefly. "Lady Sutcliffe. What can I do for you? Jenny, take her ladyship's cloak, bonnet, and gloves, and bring another cup of tea."

"Thank you, but I won't be staying long."

Thornton hesitated, then said, "Very well. Jenny, you may go. Please, have a seat, my lady."

"This is a lovely room," Kendra said as she sat down. Her original intention had been to go after the doctor hard, but instinct now had her choosing a different tactic. "Your wife?" she asked, her gaze shifting again to the portrait as she tugged off her gloves.

"Yes." The word was laced with sadness. "Mrs. Thornton was a lady of remarkable refinement."

Kendra had noticed the old-fashioned clothes the woman wore, with a full, swagged skirt, fitted bodice, and lace-trimmed square neckline.

"We were married for only a short time when Elizabeth developed diabetes mellitus," he continued, his face sagging as he, too, gazed at the painting.

"My condolences," Kendra said quietly. Diabetes mellitus would eventually become known as type 1 diabetes. There was no known cure, not even in her timeline, but at least there were treatments that prolonged life in the future. Here, Thornton's marriage had been doomed by his wife's diagnosis.

"I was a young physician at the time, but I recognized the signs. She followed the diet suggested by the physician Thomas Willis and the Scottish surgeon John Rollo, limiting carbohydrates and focusing on meats. Then, of course, there were the endless herbal treatments—sodium bicarbonate, potassium salts, chalk—even opium, and bloodletting . . ." He sighed heavily. "I knew, of course. I'd studied the disease in medical school, and I knew there was no cure. 'Tis in the blood, you see. I could only watch her . . . disappear."

"How old was she?"

"Four-and-twenty. We grew up together, and married as soon as I finished my medical training when I was twenty. We moved here, and Lizzie decorated each room. After . . . after she was gone, I couldn't bear to change anything. Now, it comforts me to be surrounded by the things that she personally selected."

"The Duke of Aldridge lost his wife and daughter when they were young. He says that not a day goes by when he doesn't think of them."

Thornton's smile was one of understanding, a shared sorrow. "Then he knows that once you have found the love of your life, there is no replacement. But you didn't come to quiz me about my late wife, did you, Lady Sutcliffe?"

"No." She kept her tone quiet, neutral. "Why did you rule Lady Westford's death an accident? You must know that it was not."

He drew in a swift breath. "There is no way we can be certain—"

"Yes, there is. I saw the railing on the upper balcony, and she was a small woman. She couldn't have accidentally fallen over it."

"Yes." He surprised her with his quick agreement. "But there is another option."

"She didn't commit suicide. For her to do that, she would have had to climb over the railing—"

"Which she could have done."

"And she would have had to shove herself away from the railing with enough force to land on seats several feet away. I don't know if she had that kind of upper body strength, doctor, but why bother? If she wanted to commit suicide, why not just jump?"

"My examination concluded that Lady Westford's skull was fractured, many other bones shattered. And she broke her neck. All consistent with falling off a balcony from that height."

"Also consistent with being *thrown* off a balcony."

She contemplated Thornton. Sweat was beginning to glisten on his upper lip.

"Your decision shut down the investigation, doctor," she went on. "Who told you to rule it an accident? Lord Westford? Or someone else?"

"You cannot be certain—"

"I can. The evidence points to murder, not suicide, which you would have known if you'd bothered to properly investigate," she snapped.

He went rigid. "I'm a physician, not a Bow Street Runner. I was asked to determine how she died, which I did!"

"You could have left it indeterminate, and an inquest would have been called. In fact an inquest *should* have been called, regardless. It's highly irregular that it was not."

"Do you know what an inquest entails, Lady Sutcliffe?" He thrust up his chin, his eyes catching fire. "If the victim cannot be seen *in situ*, then it is laid out for everyone to view. Often naked. Usually in a tavern. No husband would ever wish to see their wife displayed in such a manner for the jurors to gawk at and to satisfy the public's salacious curiosity. 'Tis unthinkable!"

"Are you saying it was Lord Westford who asked you to rule it an accident, to avoid an inquest?"

"I didn't say that!" Suddenly, he shoved himself away from the table, sending what was left in his teacup sloshing onto the tablecloth. The lines on his face deepened as he turned to stare out the window. "Lady Westford was a lady-in-waiting to the Queen. Can you imagine the embarrassment? I truly thought the lady committed suicide and wished to preserve Lady Westford's dignity."

Kendra got to her feet as well. "All you did was preserve a murderer's anonymity, doctor."

Thornton drew in a harsh breath. "I don't know how you can be so certain—"

"There was a witness," she said.

"Someone witnessed Lady Westford being murdered? What did she—or he—say? Can that person identify the monster?"

Kendra eyed the doctor. Natural questions. Except, in her experience, people tended to place the masculine pronoun before the feminine. "What did *he*—or she—say?" Was it a quirk, or was it a subconscious slip of the tongue by someone who knew the witness was female?

Thornton wasn't the killer, she knew. He was too old and not fit enough to be the one running after Edwina, and she was almost certain those people were one in the same.

But he knew something.

"The witness has disappeared." *Do you already know that, doctor?* "Not for long, though. We're following several leads and are close to finding her," she lied. "When we do, we'll have Lady Westford's killer."

"Good. That's good."

"It is." She kept her eyes on him as she tugged on her gloves. "Do you know a woman named Clarice? She's an actress."

"No. No, I don't." He licked his lips. "What does she have to do with Lady Westford's death?"

"That's what I'm going to find out." She gave him a hard look.

"If you remember anything, or have something to tell me, doctor, send word to 25 Bedford Square." She waited a beat. When he didn't reply, she added, "Thank you for your time, Dr. Thornton."

"I'll have Jenny show you out." He moved to the bell-pull.

"Don't bother. I can find my way to the front door."

He could have handled that better. But, by God, she'd taken him by surprise, just appearing like that and asking those damnable questions. Lady Sutcliffe was an odd creature, to be sure, but there was no denying her intelligence. Those rapier-sharp eyes of hers, that seemed to bore right into his brain. See into his very soul.

She *knew*. Maybe not the who or why. But she knew that he'd been asked to rule the death an accident.

No, not asked. *Told.* It had been an order, one that he dared not disobey.

Listening to Lady Sutcliffe's footsteps fade as she descended the stairs, Lucien Thornton searched his pockets and found his linen handkerchief. His fingers trembled as he mopped the sweat off his face. He'd begun perspiring the minute Lady Sutcliffe pinned him with her perceptive gaze. *It wasn't supposed to be like this.*

Slowly, shuffling like the old man he was now, Thornton crossed to the window. The position gave him a good view of the street below, the carriage waiting at the curb. Lady Sutcliffe appeared a moment later. Her stride was not dainty or ladylike. Nothing like his Elizabeth.

She did not look back or up at the window. The coachman rushed to assist her into the carriage, before climbing back onto his perch. A second later, the carriage pulled away from the curb, joining the traffic rolling down the street.

Lucien released the breath he'd been holding, but that didn't ease the heaviness in his chest. Long ago, he'd read how peine forte et dure had been used as a punishment for those who refused to plead guilty in court. Prisoners were forced to lie with a board on top of them and stones were slowly added, until the prisoner issued a plea or was crushed to death. Lucien had no board or stones on him, but the sensation of his chest being squeezed felt real.

*This should have been a simple matter*, he thought. Declare Lady Westford's death an accident, avoid an inquest, and bury her—and any possible investigation.

*What to do, what to do . . . ?*

He turned away from the window and went to his desk. He found a scrap of foolscap in one of the drawers. Uncapping the vial of ink on the writing stand, he picked up a quill and dipped the nib into the ink pot. He had to think for a long moment about what to write. Better to keep it brief and innocuous, he decided. This discussion required a private, face-to-face meeting.

Once he got the words down, he sanded the paper and carefully folded it. Hoisting himself to his feet, he moved to the sideboard, where he poured a generous four fingers of whisky into a glass. Whisky was meant to be sipped, savored, but he tossed it back like a shipman at the local tavern. He gasped as the spirit hit the back of his throat, burning its way to his belly. Unfortunately, it did nothing to dispel the cold fear that had begun pumping through his veins.

*Or is it guilt?*

He refilled his glass and walked to the fireplace, lifting his gaze to view the ageless features of his wife.

"What have I done, Lizzie?" he whispered.

He'd been so sure, the vision so clear, but now . . . now he was questioning everything. Lady Westford's death changed things. Tainted what was supposed to be pure.

His stomach churned with whisky and horror. "Oh, my God, what have I done?"

# EIGHTEEN

By the time Kendra made it back to Bedford Square, the rain she'd predicted earlier had begun to fall. She sprinted up the steps and into the foyer without getting too damp. Wakely materialized to take her coat, bonnet, and gloves, and to deliver the news that Alec was still out and the Duke had come and gone, promising that he'd speak to her at Lady Harrington's ball later that evening.

As she made her way to the library, Kendra wondered if the Duke had discovered something that he would impart at the ball or if she was reading too much into it.

Wakely sent a footman to light candles and start a fire in the library's hearth. Kendra was grateful for the assistance, since it took her three times longer than her nineteenth-century counterparts to get a flame from the tinderbox. After the footman finished, the library glowed with a warm, buttery light. Kendra was grateful to be indoors as the windowpanes rattled with each gust of wind and the rat-tat-tat of rain hitting the glass.

She picked up the piece of slate, but merely stood there and stared at the names she'd written on the board. Lord Westford, Mr. Goldsten, Dr. Thornton.

Lord Westford was the husband, and therefore a suspect. He'd pressured Dr. Thornton into declaring his wife's death an accident, tying it up nice and tidy. Thornton had said it was the action of a husband wanting to save his family the embarrassment of an inquest. That was possible. But it was also possible that the earl had hired someone to get rid of his wife. Why now, though? They'd been married for more than thirty years. What could possibly be the motivation after all this time?

Then there was Goldsten. The man had lied about the last time he'd seen Lady Westford. Was he afraid he'd come under suspicion if his argument with Lady Westford became public knowledge? It happened. People sometimes panicked when questioned, said something rash or irrational. But Kendra couldn't shake the feeling that Goldsten was hiding something.

Her gaze slid to another name on the slate board: Clarice. What was her connection to Lady Westford? And was that association responsible for Lady Westford's murder?

*How could it not be?*

Movement in the doorway caught her eye, and she found her husband leaning against the doorjamb, watching her. He'd discarded his greatcoat, hat, and gloves, but was still wearing his form-fitting dark green coat and buckskin breeches, wet from the inclement weather. His riding boots had been polished that morning, but were now caked in mud. His dark hair glistened with drops of rain.

Her fingers twitched with the desire to run her fingers through his locks. "How long have you been standing there?"

Alec smiled as he straightened and came toward her. "Long enough to admire my wife's many attributes," he said, lowering his mouth to hers for a kiss that sent her pulse hammering. He carried the scent of the rain and cold, and something uniquely him.

"Good afternoon, wife," he murmured, lifting his head.

"Good afternoon, husband." She smiled up into his eyes, and gave into her impulse, stroking his hair. "You were caught in the rain. You need to get out of your wet clothes."

"Maybe we both need to get out of our clothes."

She laughed when he nuzzled her neck. "Tempting. Very tempting." She angled her head to give him better access. "Did you learn anything interesting from Lord Westford?"

He sighed, then released her. "Not a damn thing." He walked to the sideboard and pulled the stopper on the brandy decanter. "I spent the day riding around London, trying to locate the bloody man. He was not at his residence, and he left no hint of his whereabouts." He poured himself a glass of brandy. "I went to all his haunts, but no one had seen him. It finally occurred to me that he might be at his villa in St. John's Wood."

"He was with his other family."

"Yes, but he'd taken Mrs. O'Leary and the children to the country. Miserable day for a jaunt into the countryside, if you ask me. It started raining on my return to the city."

"He isn't exactly in mourning, is he?"

"No." He took a long sip of his brandy. "What about you? Did you find out anything from Mr. Goldsten?"

"Yes. He didn't admit to having an affair with Lady Westford—"

"He wouldn't."

"Yeah, I know. A dead woman's reputation is more important than getting justice for her murder." She couldn't stop herself from rolling her eyes. "Lady Westford doesn't care about her reputation anymore. Why should everyone else?"

Alec looked thoughtful. "Is that true, though? We spend our lives creating and cultivating our standing in the world. Like land and estates, it's one of the few things that survive us. It's how we're remembered."

"Mr. Goldsten said the same thing."

His mouth curved as he regarded her. "But you don't agree."

She expelled a heavy breath. "I understand the principal, but I don't agree if it impedes a murder investigation. Mr. Goldsten also lied about the last time he saw Lady Westford."

"Well, then. That is suspicious."

"Maybe. Or he wants to distance himself from the investigation." She paused. "We confirmed his alibi, that he was working at St. George's on Sunday morning. But it's a big, busy place."

"You think he managed to sneak out?"

"It's possible. He's hiding something. So is Dr. Thornton. I went to see him about covering up the murder. He was nervous."

Alec's mouth curved. "I can imagine. But he's not young enough to have been the one chasing the girl afterward, surely?"

"No. But I told him that there was a witness, and he asked if she—or he—could identify the killer. In that order."

"You think it odd that he guessed the witness was a female?"

"You don't?"

"Not necessarily. On Sunday morning, there'd be plenty of women on the streets. Milkmaids and laundresses. Female costermongers like Bridget. Maids hired to scrub floors. It might be natural to assume the witness would be a woman."

"Plenty of young boys sweeping the streets too." Kendra turned back to survey the slate board. "Lady Westford wasn't the only one murdered. Clarice—assuming it *is* Clarice—was the first victim. She was restrained and possibly exsanguinated."

"Bizarre."

"It could be ritualistic. Muldoon told me about an Irish vampire demon called *Dearg-due*, who drains people of their blood."

"He can't believe—?"

She laughed. "Hardly. He's just a writer with an active imagination. Still, there are such things as death cults," she said, her humor fading. "Satanic or vampiric—or whatever demon or monster is currently in vogue. I've dealt with them in my time. I doubt if it's any different now."

"One hears rumors about people practicing paganism, of course. And no one knows more than you and I that there are still those who partake in hedonistic gatherings, like the Hellfire Club."

Kendra saw shadows enter Alec's eyes, and knew he was thinking of his late brother, Gabriel, who'd been involved with such a club. Gabriel hadn't realized the danger until it was too late.

She walked over to him to lay a comforting hand on his wrist. Beneath her fingertips, she felt the warm flow of his blood, the steady pulse of his heart. The earlier whisper she'd had at the hospital stirred again. *Blood.*

"Maybe . . . we're dealing with something less exotic," she said slowly. "Bloodletting is a common treatment for disease and illnesses."

Alec eyed her. "What kind of surgeon or barber would be so green as to take *all* her blood?"

Frowning, Kendra returned to the slate board. "I saw a lot of young men—apprentices—at Mr. Goldsten's clinic and St. George's Hospital. What if Clarice was ill and an apprentice tried to help? They didn't realize that they'd taken too much, accidentally killed her, panicked, and dumped the body in the Thames?"

"I still can't imagine even an apprentice being that inexperienced—or foolish—to remove all her blood."

"Maybe it wasn't all her blood. Maybe it was just enough to make her severely anemic. We don't know how she died."

Alec didn't look convinced. "Putting that aside, what is her connection to Lady Westford?"

"We know that Lady Westford was interested in medicine. She attended scientific lectures and was a patroness at St. George's. She was involved with a surgeon." Kendra began to pace as she considered the possibilities. "St. George's caters to both men and women. If Clarice was ever a patient, they could have met there."

She paused, then turned slowly to look at Alec. "Our suspect list is going to get longer."

"If you're talking about every physician, surgeon and apprentice at St. George's, I'm going to have to buy you another slate board."

Kendra laughed. "Hopefully, Lady Westford confided in Lady Harrington, and we can narrow that list down."

# NINETEEN

As far as Kendra was concerned, balls were like walking through a minefield. One misstep and you could commit a social gaffe that would be gossiped about for weeks. Or, for Kendra, say something that would only be understood by the attendees' descendants. It was stressful enough to be ogled by a hundred catty society matrons without having to worry that you could screw up the space-time continuum.

Still, as bad as it was to attend a ball, it was worse preparing for one. Kendra didn't have a fairy godmother waving a magic wand and zapping her into party-readiness. She had Molly.

The former tweeny took on the task with gusto, marching around with a militant gleam in her eye as she ordered footmen and maids to haul up buckets of hot water and honeysuckle salts for Kendra's bath, and insisted on washing Kendra's hair herself.

"Mrs. Danbury said ye'll 'ave ter mind yer manners with Lady 'Arrington," Molly said, scrubbing Kendra's head with a concoction that had all the ingredients of a salad dressing. "She's a lady-in-waitin' ter the Queen."

"I know."

"Mrs. Danbury says she's a lady of great virtue, like the Queen 'erself. Close yer eyes." Molly poured a pitcher of lukewarm water over Kendra's head. "A right miracle that is, Mrs. Danbury says, given 'oo Lady 'Arrington's sister is." The maid brought a towel over to rub the excess water out of Kendra's hair.

"Who's her sister?" Kendra asked from beneath the towel.

"She *was* Lady Worsley, but she took back 'er maiden name of Flemming when Lord Worsley cocked up 'is toes. 'Ere." Molly whisked the towel off Kendra's head, handing her another with which to dry herself as she stepped out of the tub.

"Their marriage was right wicked," Molly continued, waiting for Kendra to put on a robe before ushering her to a small footstool in front of the fireplace. "Lady Worsley admitted ter 'aving scores of lovers, and even ran off with one, 'oo is said ter 'ave fathered 'er babe." She picked up a bellows, pumping its handles to give the crackling fire an extra boost. "Lean forward."

Kendra knew the drill. She stuck her head as close to the flames as she dared. She had never thought she'd miss a hairdryer.

"Lord Worsley sued 'er and 'er lover," Molly continued cheerfully. "But *she* said that it was 'er 'usband 'oo gave 'er lover permission ter see 'er naked in the bath! It was a right scandal, it was."

"I can imagine." But why was Kendra shocked? Human nature didn't change. Sex scandals didn't start in Hollywood. Or even ancient Rome. They'd been around forever.

Kendra's thoughts drifted to Lord and Lady Westford's open marriage. He had his left-handed wife and family on the side, plus who knows how many other mistresses. It looked like Lady Westford had also taken lovers, the last being Mr. Goldsten. Supposedly, both were satisfied with the arrangement. But if that wasn't true, did it have anything to do with her murder?

The earl had to stay on the list, but Kendra was beginning to think that Lady Westford's murder was connected to something bigger. Something more sinister.

"Then Lady Worsley accused another nobleman of giving 'er the clap," Molly went on, happily scandalized. "After 'er 'usband died, she became a demi— a demino— demi—"

"Demimondaine," Kendra supplied. This era's version of a high-class call girl.

"Aye. That's the word."

"Mrs. Danbury told you all this?" Kendra couldn't imagine the formidable housekeeper gossiping with Molly in such a way.

"Ooh, well . . . nay," the maid confessed with a sheepish look. "'Annah told me about 'er when Oi said ye'd be goin' ter a ball given by Lady 'Arrington."

"Hannah?"

"Oi told ye, she's 'is lordship's scullery maid." The maid retrieved a hairbrush from the vanity. "Scoot forward. Oi got some work ter do untangling these knots."

Kendra always found it vaguely embarrassing to spend so much time on primping, but an hour and a half later, she couldn't argue with the results. Molly might not be a fairy godmother, but she could create magic. The maid had styled Kendra's hair high on her head, with a few loose tendrils she had painstakingly curled with heating tongs. Diamond hair ornaments twinkled like stars in Kendra's raven locks.

Kendra thought the hairstyle made her neck look impossibly long. Or maybe that was the low-cut bodice of the silver gown Molly had selected. The thin silk shimmered like moonlight with every twist and turn of her body.

"Ooh, me lady, ye look ever so beautiful," Molly breathed, taking a step back to admire her own handiwork. "Ye'll be needing these," she added, dashing to the wardrobe. She returned with a black velvet hooded cloak with a silver satin lining, and long white satin gloves. "'Tis a soft rain now and Oi don't want ye ter get yer hair wet."

Kendra was tugging on the gloves when Alec came through their connecting doors. Unlike the hours she'd spent getting ready, Alec had probably spent twenty minutes, but he looked damn good in what could probably pass for a tuxedo in her era. The exception was the snowy white cravat, instead of the modern bowtie.

"Perhaps we ought to stay home tonight," he said, his mouth curving as he walked toward her. "I shall be fighting every man who ogles my wife." He took her gloved hand, lifting it to press a kiss on her knuckles. "You are a sight to behold, my love."

She smiled into his eyes. "You're not so bad yourself, my lord."

Surprise flashed across his face, then he let out a laugh. "A high compliment, indeed." He glanced at Molly. "You did splendidly,

Molly. I daresay, a French or Swiss lady's maid could not have done better."

"Ooh! Thank ye ever so much, me lord!" Blushing, Molly pressed a hand to her chest as she stared at Alec with starry-eyed devotion.

Kendra captured Alec's arm, steering him to the door. "Come on, darling. My maid is about to swoon, and I don't have the time to find the smelling salts."

Carriages clogged the rain-slicked streets as the Beau Monde ventured out in search of entertainment. Kendra suspected that the Harrington Ball would be just one stop of many parties to keep them occupied until the wee hours of the morning.

"I've been told that Lady Harrington won't be shocked by Lord and Lady Westford's open marriage," Kendra mused.

"Are you referring to the countess' mother-in-law?"

She lifted her eyebrows. "I was actually talking about her sister. Her mother-in-law?"

"Who told you about the Sinner?"

"The Sinner?"

"Seymour Fleming, the former Lady Worsley—Lady Harrington's sister. Her escapades landed her with the moniker the Sinner."

"Molly said Lady Harrington is considered a paragon, while her sister seems to enjoy shocking society. She didn't tell me about the nickname or her mother-in-law."

"Molly is too young to remember Lady Caroline—the countess' mother-in-law. She died several years ago, but her scandalous reputation lives on in the Ton. She had so many affairs—with women as well as men—that she was actually thrown out of the Female Coterie."

"And that is?"

"A club whose members are high-ranking ladies in society. Lady Caroline reacted to the insult by forming her own club—the *New Female Coterie*."

"Not the most original name."

"No, but its members were quite original. She invited demi-reps, courtesans, and ladies of Quality who were considered 'fallen women' like herself into the club."

"And your aunt looks at *me* like I've crawled out from the sewer," she muttered, shaking her head. "How did her husband take it?"

"Lord Worsley was as promiscuous as his wife. Caroline bore him seven children—whether they were all his children is debatable, but he did claim them all—and he seemed happy enough in the marriage. He was a frequent visitor to the brothel at King's Place in St. James, which, ironically, was where his wife's club met. Are you shocked, darling?"

"I'm . . . I don't know what I am," she admitted. "I guess Lord and Lady Westford's open marriage is more common than I realized."

"It's common enough. Though there are plenty of husbands and wives who are devoted to each other. The King and Queen, despite their recent trials, have never strayed from their union, even though the King, in his madness, became lovestruck with a few ladies. My own mother and father were unified in their love. And our own Duke . . ."

He didn't need to remind her how devoted the Duke had been to his wife, Arabella. And there was Dr. Thornton. Kendra could clearly see how much he'd loved his wife.

Alec asked, "What about your parents?"

Kendra blinked, surprised. "My parents?"

"Yes. You've told me the reasons they married, as an experiment—"

"*I* was the experiment, to prove their theory that positive eugenics could create a better world. I failed, and so did their marriage."

"You didn't fail, my sweet. Your parents failed, by not seeing what a precious gift they were given. But I digress. Did your mother or father have any dalliances outside of their marriage?"

"*Ew.* I can't imagine them having a dalliance *inside* their marriage!"

Alec laughed. "They must have, for you to be born."

"In my time, there are ways . . ." She shook her head. She really didn't want to imagine *anything* with her parents. "My parents didn't have a traditional marriage, but I can't imagine them having affairs. They were too focused on their experiment. And, like I said, once I failed, their marriage was pointless. My parents never did anything that was pointless."

She paused, thinking back. "They never argued. I'm sure it was all very civilized when they dissolved the marriage and moved on with their lives. Last I heard, my mother was working for CERN in Switzerland, and my father had remarried. He has two more children—new experiments. God help them."

Alec eyed her. "So, your parents had a business arrangement, like many of the marriages formed in the ton. I told you, sweet, we have much more in common than you realize."

"I keep realizing that human beings don't really change."

"In the broader sense, perhaps. But individuals can change. I knew I would have to marry one day and hoped to form an amicable arrangement. Once the line was secure, we could go our separate ways."

Kendra stared at her husband. "You actually considered an open marriage?"

"I never thought of it as an open marriage, but definitely a business alliance. Then a beautiful, mysterious American came into my life, and I was changed forever."

"So, no open marriage in our future?"

"I shall call out any man who dares lure you away."

"I'll do the same with any woman. And I'm an excellent shot." She grinned. "You're right. We do have a lot in common. I think we make an excellent team."

He patted his lap. "Why don't you come over here and prove it."

She faked a glare. "And have you mess up my hair? Not on your life!"

"I knew it would happen eventually." He let out an exaggerated sigh. "You're beginning to sound just like a wife."

# TWENTY

Kendra had been in elevators filled to capacity with more breathing room than Lady Harrington's ball. In the slang of the day, the party was a crush, which was to say it was a smashing success. Good for Lady Harrington, but bad for her and Alec, as they were forced to fight their way through the warm bodies crowding the grand foyer to the elaborate staircase that curved to the upper level. It didn't help that they were stopped every other minute by well-wishers congratulating Alec on his marriage and wondering when he planned to whisk his bride off on their honeymoon. Kendra had to admire the ease with which Alec dealt with the curiosity and gentle teasing. She kept mostly silent, which was for the best, since her inclination was to tell them to mind their own damn business.

Kendra breathed a sigh of relief when they were finally disgorged into the ballroom. It had been designed by John Nash himself, with a wraparound balcony and short flight of stairs down to the dance floor. Alec snagged two champagne flutes from a passing footman, handing one to Kendra as she watched the quadrille below, the orchestra playing in the corner.

Kendra let her gaze roam over the elegant throng, noting the glitter of diamonds, the blaze of sapphires, rubies and emeralds. "What kind of security does Lord and Lady Harrington have? There's got to be at least a million dollars of jewels in this room."

Alec chuckled. "That's what you think of when you look around?"

"That was my first thought, but now I'm wondering what

everyone is hiding." She watched the dancers spin in graceful patterns around their partners. The scene looked like something out of a fairytale, but that was deceptive.

Or maybe not. Every fairytale had something evil at its core. How many of these couples were in dysfunctional marriages, abusive relationships? How many envied the other's social position or luck at the gambling tables?

Pride, greed, lust, anger, sloth, gluttony, and envy—the seven deadly sins were alive and well, and slithering around the ballroom like the serpent in the Garden of Eden, Kendra thought. Which of the deadly sins was she dealing with in Lady Westford's and Clarice's murders?

She sipped her champagne. "Keep an eye out for ruffles."

Alec laughed. "I don't have to. Lady St. James is standing over there, near the orchestra, talking to Lady Colburn."

Kendra found the countess, who was resplendent in green taffeta with, yes, several tiers of lace-edged ruffles. Diamonds and emeralds circled her throat and gloved wrists, and twinkled in the tiara atop her head.

"Kendra! Sutcliffe!"

Kendra glanced around to find Rebecca pushing through the knots of partygoers, followed by her parents and the Duke.

"Becca," Alec said, smiling as he looked her over. "You look lovely."

Rebecca's maid had fashioned her auburn hair into complex braids and curls, embellished with seed pears and tiny blue flowers. The elaborate style contrasted with her modest silk gown, a lighter shade than her cornflower blue eyes.

"I pale in comparison to your wife, Sutcliffe," Rebecca said. "Oh, my, Kendra, you are simply ravishing."

"Marriage agrees with you, my dear," Lord Blackburn said, beaming at Kendra.

"When did you arrive in London?" Alec asked.

"This afternoon," Rebecca replied, and shot a grin at her

parents. "Papa decided that there was less danger coming to London than having me run away to town by myself."

"My daughter is quite headstrong." Lady Blackburn laid a hand on Rebecca's shoulder as she smiled at Kendra. "You really do look marvelous, my lady."

"My maid worked for hours and hours on me," Kendra commented, earning a laugh from Lady Blackburn.

"I'd say that she had good material to work with." Lady Blackburn searched Kendra's face with intelligent eyes. "Bertie told us that you've determined that Lady Westford was murdered. Have you learned anything of interest?"

"Several things, but I'm not sure where they fit at the moment. Did you know that Lord Westford had another family?"

Rebecca gasped and glanced at her mother, and her eyes widened when she saw the truth on her face. "Mama? You knew?"

"I was aware," Lady Blackburn said quietly. "This is not a new arrangement. Nor is it a secret."

"So I've been told," Kendra said. "Do you also know about Mr. Goldsten?"

"I know about her *friendship* with Mr. Goldsten," Lady Blackburn said slowly.

Kendra eyed the matron. "At Aldridge Castle, I thought you said that you were acquainted with but not close to Lady Westford."

"That's true. But gossip travels—even to the countryside." Lady Blackburn's lips quirked. "And I've attended a few of the same salons as Lady Westford."

"I'm curious, my lady, are you a patroness for St. George's Hospital?"

"Not a patroness, no. But I am involved in helping hospitals that serve the community—St. George's is one. Unfortunately, the hospital is in a sad state these days. I'm of the mind that it can be repaired, but Lady Westford believed we should be raising funds to tear it down and build anew." She hesitated. "I believe St. George's was where Lady Westford met Mr. Goldsten."

"What do you know of Mr. Goldsten?"

"I'm acquainted with most of the medical staff at St. George's. Mr. Goldsten always struck me as someone dedicated to the art of healing. A very serious-minded individual. Ambitious."

Kendra picked up on the last word. "Ambitious?"

"He not only works at St. George's, but he opened his own surgery in Blackfriars." She tilted her head, leveling a shrewd look at Kendra. "Surely you can't think he had anything to do with what happened to Lady Westford?"

"I don't think anything at this point." Nothing that she felt comfortable sharing, anyway. Kendra caught the Duke's eye. "Would you walk with me, Your Grace?"

He smiled, offering her his elbow. "It would be my pleasure, my dear."

Alec stretched a hand to Rebecca. "Becca, would you care to dance?"

Lord and Lady Blackburn followed Alec and their daughter to the dance floor, although Kendra was aware of the thoughtful glance Lady Blackburn tossed at her over her shoulder.

"I assume you want to quiz me about my day," the Duke said as they began their stroll along the perimeter. Casually, he took Kendra's empty champagne flute, exchanged it for two full ones, then maneuvered her into an alcove so they wouldn't have to fight their fellow attendees milling around them.

"Did you learn anything interesting?

"A lot of gossip, mostly benign. There was one tidbit, though." He took a swallow of champagne. "Apparently Lord Westford was enraged when he learned about his wife's latest paramour."

"I thought their open marriage was acceptable to both of them."

"It was . . . until Lady Westford became involved with Mr. Goldsten."

"Ah." She wasn't surprised by the antisemitism in this age. God knew, she'd seen enough of it in her own timeline. Would it ever end?

"He was in his cups and complaining that she was making a mockery of their bloodline by taking up with a Jew." The Duke paused to draw in a deep breath, his gaze meeting hers. "He was furious. He said that he could kill her."

"Those were his exact words—he could kill her?"

"Yes. It's not particularly pleasant, but it *is* a figure of speech."

"And yet his wife is dead," Kendra murmured, her gaze straying to the dance floor. She could see Rebecca beaming at Alec as she drew herself up into a graceful plié before swaying sideways to the music.

"The incident happened several months ago, when the affair came to light," the Duke went on. "He was foxed and spoke in anger. If he was serious, surely he wouldn't have waited so long to do something about it."

Kendra shrugged. "We know that he didn't commit the actual murder. Maybe it took him that long to find someone to do it."

"My acquaintance with Lord Westford is limited, but I still cannot believe it of him."

Kendra scanned the ballroom again. "Is he here tonight?" Every rich person in London seemed to be crammed into the mansion.

"Lord Westford? No, he's in mourning."

"Yeah, well, he's not grieving at home. Alec said he couldn't locate him today. He took his family—his *other* family—to the country."

The Duke frowned, but said nothing.

She flicked him a look. "By the way, I've sent messages for a briefing tomorrow morning. I've come up with another theory that I want to run by everyone. It'll expand our suspect list."

"Interesting. I shall be there."

"Now . . ." She tipped her flute and finished her champagne. "I need to find Lady St. James so she can introduce me to Lady Harrington."

"You don't need Lady St. James for that, my dear. Jane and I have a long friendship. I shall introduce you."

⁓

At sixty-one, Lady Jane Harrington was still attractive, with a fine-boned face that sagged a bit here and there but was remarkably free of wrinkles. In a time before laser and skin peels, injections and fillers, Kendra knew this was primarily due to studious avoidance of the sun. The matron's hair, more silver than brown, was swept into an elaborate updo and was decorated with diamonds and pearls that matched her drop earrings and a glittering necklace that looked like it could bankroll a small country.

Lady Harrington stood on the sidelines with several other matrons, including Lady St. James, whose eyes lit up at their approach. "Your Grace, Lady Sutcliffe, good evening." She snapped her feathered fan shut. "May I introduce you to our hostess, Lady Harrington? And this is—"

"Bertie, how are you?" Lady Harrington interrupted, stepping forward with a hand outstretched to the Duke. "It's been ages since I last saw you. Still prefer the fresh air of the country over the frivolities of town?"

He bent to plant a chivalrous kiss on the back of her gloved hand. "The skies in London confound me. I can never make out the stars through the smoke. Although the ceaseless clouds and rain have made it difficult for me to use my telescope at Aldridge Castle as well." He returned her smile. "You look charming as usual, Jane."

"You may need to purchase a pair of spectacles, Bertie, but thank you for your kind words. And this must be your ward, Miss Donovan. Except"—she tapped the lace-trimmed fan against her chin as she surveyed Kendra—"she's no longer a miss, is she? She married that devilishly handsome nephew of yours."

"She did," said the Duke. "Jane, this is Kendra, Marchioness of Sutcliffe. Kendra, may I introduce Jane Stanhope, Countess of Harrington."

"I can see why Sutcliffe took himself out of the marriage mart when he met you, Lady Sutcliffe. You are quite lovely, my dear. Would you care to walk with me for a moment?"

Kendra had been wondering how she could extract the countess from her group of friends, and was a little surprised when Lady Harrington was the one to arrange it. Lady St. James's smile drooped a little, undoubtedly disappointed that she wouldn't be able to eavesdrop on their conversation.

Kendra fell into step beside the matron. For a moment, they didn't speak, instead listening to the music and the underlying sounds: the murmur of conversation, laughter, the whisper of silk, satin, and velvet skirts.

"I actually came here tonight because I wanted to speak with you, my lady," Kendra said in a low voice, glancing at the aristocrat's regal profile.

"I know."

She lifted her eyebrows. "You do?"

"Of course." Lady Harrington kept her gaze fixed on the crowd, smiling and nodding as they swept by. "I am one of Her Majesty's Ladies of the Bedchamber. I not only serve the Queen, but I care about her a great deal. I saw how disturbed she was when we learned about Grace's death." She shot Kendra a quick look out of the corner of her eye. "We are aware that it was ruled an accident, but that won't stop rumors from suggesting something else."

"Suicide."

"Yes. The idea was extremely vexing to Her Majesty. Grace would never do such a vile thing. I have heard about you . . . and your investigations." That was said with another glance, her eyes glinting with amusement. "Amelia quite enjoys sharing every tidbit of information she comes across."

"Amelia?"

"Lady St. James."

"Oh. Yes, she does."

"Amelia can be an entertaining companion, but I have little time or use for gossip. When you or your family are the ones whispered about, it can be quite tedious. You've no doubt heard about my notorious mother-in-law and sister." She pinned Kendra with a shrewd look. "No need to answer that, my dear. I can see that you have. Well, that is neither here nor there. The stories I've heard about *you* are much more interesting."

"You were the one who told the Queen about me," Kendra said.

"Her Majesty had heard rumors before, but yes, I am the one who suggested that your unusual expertise could be utilized to find out the truth about Grace's death." She gave a small smile. "I do apologize for ruining your honeymoon."

"Why didn't you come to me directly and ask me to look into the matter?"

"I am used to the politics of the royal court—very little is done directly, my dear. Besides, I'm familiar with your husband." She smiled at Kendra as they turned a corner. "Only a royal decree would have stopped him from whisking his bride off on a honeymoon. A royal request is just as good."

Kendra said nothing. She didn't like being manipulated, but at the same time, she had to admire the woman's strategic skills.

"The evidence indicates Lady Westford was murdered," she said at last.

Lady Harrington didn't express shock or horror. Instead, she maintained her pleasant expression, nodding. "I feared it would be so. An accident is simply too bizarre. Have you any thoughts on who could have done such a despicable thing?"

"It's early days. When was the last time you saw Lady Westford?"

"Friday. We were together with Her Majesty at Buckingham House."

*Buckingham House—before it became Buckingham Palace.*

"What time was this?"

"The Queen required our presence at three. We stayed until two the following afternoon."

That explained the gap in time from when Lady Westford viewed the body at the morgue and when she showed up at Bowden Theater. "How did she seem to you?"

Lady Harrington was quiet, then said, "Grace was a bit of bluestocking. Did you know?"

Kendra frowned at the non sequitur. "I've been told that she had an interest in science. Medicine."

In another era, Lady Westford could have been a doctor or scientist herself, not reduced to the sidelines, she reflected.

"Yes. She was fascinated by both old and new techniques," Lady Harrington murmured, her gaze moving over the dancers gliding across the floor. "She was also an avid gardener. I am not speaking of pretty flowers. She was interested in herbs for medicinal purposes. Did you know that her sister died of typhus?"

"Yes."

She glanced at Kendra, seemingly pleased. "You have found out a great deal in a short amount of time, Lady Sutcliffe. The tragedy influenced her. She advocated for more aggressive methods to finding cures for diseases. I am telling you this because I want you to understand that Grace was not someone with windmills in her head. She was very intelligent and thoughtful." Another flickering smile. "She was not like Amelia. She didn't gossip."

The matron unfurled her fan, using it to combat the stifling heat from the press of bodies around them. "The ball is a success, but it is quite warm in here. Let us step outside, shall we?"

Kendra followed Lady Harrington through the French doors to the veranda. She welcomed the rush of cold air as they stepped outside. Several torches had been lit to drive the shadows into corners and crevices. The evenings' drizzle had stopped—or paused—but the veranda's tiles were wet enough to dampen the hem of their skirts. A handful of couples was already outside, using the terrace as a respite from the overheated ballroom. And, given the young ladies who were accompanied by gentlemen, a reprieve from the watchful eyes of chaperones.

Lady Harrington stopped near a green topiary, snipped and shaped into a geometric spire, away from the listening ears of the other terrace occupants. "Grace tended to be serious of mind," she said. "But she'd become more somber than usual."

"You noticed this on Friday?"

She shook her head. "Her mood changed before that. A month, at least. Maybe more. She was blue-devilled. I approached her about what might be ailing her, but . . ." She lifted one shoulder in a dainty half-shrug. "Grace was one to keep her own counsel. I discovered her alone in one of the palace's antechambers, weeping."

"When was this?"

"A few weeks ago. I can't give you an exact date."

"Did you ask her why she was upset?"

"Of course. She dismissed my concern initially. I pressed, and she finally confessed that she was having difficulties with the men in her life."

"Men, plural? Not man?"

"Definitely men. I assume she meant her husband and Mr. Goldsten." Lady Harrington's eyes glinted with humor. "I may be called 'The Saint,' but that doesn't make me deaf and blind to reality, my dear. I am fortunate to be blessed in my marriage. However, I know, more than most, that not everyone is."

"Did she tell you what kind of trouble she was having with these men?"

"Not in so many words, but I know Henry—Lord Westford. He would not have been pleased that his wife had a friendship with a Jew. He's a pompous prig. Like many, he forgets that the Jewish people are as English as any of us."

"I heard that he wasn't happy about their relationship," Kendra acknowledge. "Do you think he could have had her killed because of it?"

Lady Harrington narrowed her eyes. "Very clever of you to suggest that Henry wouldn't have done the deed himself. As I said, he's a pompous prig, and pompous prigs excel at being quarrelsome, but shy away from physical confrontations. Henry wouldn't have laid his hands on Grace in a violent manner."

Kendra wondered if that was true, recalling the old bruises on Lady Westford's arms. Someone had laid their hands on her before her death. If not Lord Westford, was it Goldsten? Or someone else?

"My instinct is to say no, Henry would never have arranged for Grace's murder," Lady Harrington continued. "I trust my instincts, but I have to ask myself if I truly believe it, or if I believe it because I can't imagine a person that I know could be capable of such evil?"

Lady Harrington shook her head and sighed heavily. "I have spent many years behind palace walls, Lady Sutcliffe. In that time,

I've learned that most people wear many faces. They cloak their true nature to further their cause. Society may criticize and condemn my mother-in-law and sister, but neither one of them pretended to be something they were not.

"So . . . I don't know," she added, her gaze somber. "I don't know if Henry hired someone to kill Grace."

Kendra nodded. "What about Mr. Goldsten?"

Lady Harrington moved to the stone balustrade. Bracing her hands on the railing, she stared out into the gardens. The clouds had thinned into gossamer strands, allowing moonlight to wash the trees and shrubbery, still dripping from rain, in quicksilver. Hauntingly beautiful, but Kendra doubted Lady Harrington was seeing it at all.

"I remember when Grace first met Mr. Goldsten," the matron said softly. "It's been many moons since we were fresh-faced innocents, but I could see something in her then. A lightness of spirit that I hadn't seen before. She was happy. Until . . . she was no longer." Lady Harrington tilted her head to meet Kendra's eyes. "There is nothing so disheartening as a love affair turned to dust."

"Their affair was over?"

"Yes."

"Why? Did she say?"

"Not when I found her weeping. But several days later, I quizzed her again, and she admitted there was another woman. Younger, prettier—of course."

Kendra straightened up. "What was her name?"

"I don't know. I'm not certain Grace knew."

"How'd she know that the other woman was younger and prettier?"

"She saw them together. Grace called upon Mr. Goldsten at his clinic and saw him leaving with the creature."

"That seems pretty innocuous. Why did she assume he was being unfaithful?"

"I asked her that as well. But from what she said, it wasn't one thing, but many. He'd grown distant, preoccupied. Then, when she asked him about the woman, he acted oddly and lied. He said she was the wife of one of his apprentices, that he was walking with her because the streets around his surgery are unsafe. Mr. Goldsten's apprentices are all young men; Grace was quite certain none had a wife. She told me Mr. Goldsten became quite upset when she pressed him for answers. He said that if she trusted him, she would never mention the subject again.

"Suspicious," Kendra agreed. "Did Lady Westford ever mention a woman named Clarice?"

Lady Harrington gave her a sharp look. "No. Do you think she may be the other woman?"

"I'm not sure. What was Lady Westford's mood like when you saw her on Friday?"

A sudden gust of wind stirred the trees and shrubbery, scattering rain drops to the ground. The flames from the surrounding torches flickered madly, plunging Lady Harrington into shadow, making it impossible for Kendra to read her expression.

"She was late in arriving at Buckingham House," the matron replied. "Grace was well-named: her manners pretty, her comportment always graceful. But on Friday, she seemed to have butter on her fingers. She dropped the sewing kit twice, and accidently knocked over her teacup while serving tea.

"She was in a brown study. Her Majesty spoke to her several times, but it was as though she never heard her. I knew something dreadful must have happened. I managed to get her alone, but she dismissed my concerns. Except . . . she said the strangest thing."

Kendra waited.

Lady Harrington took a breath. "*Exitus acta probat.*"

"The outcome justifies the means," Kendra translated.

Lady Harrington lifted her eyebrows. "You know Latin?"

"A bit. Did you ask her what she meant by that?"

"I was about to, not only because it was so peculiar, but because of how she looked when she said it."

"How was that?"

"She looked afraid, Lady Sutcliffe. I was summoned by the

Queen and never had the chance to ask her about that comment, or the fear that I saw in her eyes," she said in a voice aching with sadness. "Now, I never will."

153

# TWENTY-ONE

"*Exitus acta probat.*" Rebecca paused in spooning up lemon cream from the delicate blue Wedgwood bowl she was cradling in her palm. "Whatever does that mean?"

"The outcome justifies the means," the Duke answered, ladling lemonade from a crystal punchbowl into his glass. "If I'm not mistaken, 'tis a quote from Ovid's *Heroides.*"

Kendra sipped her weak lemonade. She'd shared what Lady Harrington had said with Alec, Rebecca, and the Duke when they'd come into the refreshment room. Candlelight cast a mellow glow over the people gathered around linen-clothed tables that practically groaned beneath the weight of cakes and custards, fruits and ices. The French doors had been thrown open to the veranda, the fresh night air leaving the room much cooler than the ballroom.

"The timing is interesting," Kendra said. "We know that Friday morning, Lady Westford viewed the body in the morgue. When she arrived at Buckingham P—House, she was out of sorts, and then, later, afraid."

"That seems the obvious connection, but you said that Jane thought Grace has been disturbed for a while," Alec said. "A month, at least. If that's true, it wasn't because of the woman in the morgue."

"Disturbed because she'd seen Mr. Goldsten with a woman. When she confronted him, he lied and became defensive. Prior to that, Lady Westford confided that Mr. Goldsten was growing distant. She worried that she was losing him to another woman."

Kendra didn't believe Lady Westford's murder had anything to do with a soured love affair. The earlier inkling that she'd had was growing stronger, but she needed to follow the threads.

"Nothing can be solved this evening." Alec drew Kendra's hand through the crook of his elbow. "I shall bid everyone adieu, and take my bride home."

"Good heavens, Sutcliffe, it's not even midnight," Rebecca teased. "You never used to be a humdrum fellow."

"My nephew has never been a married man," the Duke said, smiling. "Good night, nephew."

"Good night, uncle, Becca."

"I'm having a briefing tomorrow morning at nine," Kendra said to Rebecca. "You're invited, if you're interested."

The other woman's face lit up. "I shall be there."

The street was relatively quiet except for the snort and shuffle of horses and the rattle of wheels as carriages arrived and departed. Coachman John had the steps down and the door open for them. After climbing inside, Kendra gave a surprised gasp when Alec scooped her up and set her on his lap.

She laughed as Coachman John hastily slammed the door shut. "I think you just shocked your coachman," she said.

"He'll get over it," Alec murmured, kissing her. "We never danced. I suggest we remedy that when we get home. A waltz with my wife in the moonlight."

"There's very little moonlight." Awareness danced across her skin when Alec found a particularly sensitive spot below her ear with his lips.

"Don't be quarrelsome, wife."

Kendra framed Alec's face with her palms, looking into his eyes. "A waltz sounds like an excellent plan."

---

"This is a blasted plan! Who's the beetle-headed fool that came up with it?" Elias Palmer demanded as he scrambled off the muddy ground. His ankle felt like someone was jabbing it with a pickax. "Bugger it!" he cursed, limping forward to wrestle the shovel that had fallen out of the muck.

"Ye might want ter keep yer voice down, Elias," warned his partner, Daniel Johnson. Even as he spoke, he shot a nervous glance around the graveyard. The moon was worrisome. When they'd started earlier, the clouds had been ideal for their purpose. The light rain hadn't been quite so ideal, of course, especially when it came to digging the newly covered grave.

"The Charlies ain't gonna be making their rounds ternight," Elias snapped, although Daniel noticed that he did lower his voice. "Colder than a witch's tit, it is."

He was right about that. Daniel could see icy plumes with every puff of his breath. If the watchmen patrolled the graveyards at all, they'd make quick work of it so they could hurry back to their pubs, all toasty warm, and plant their fat arses in the chairs, enjoying their pints.

Still, the moon—now unfettered by clouds—was worrisome. In its silvery rays, Daniel could see every pit and pore on Elias's ugly face, as well as the glimmer of fear in the eyes of the two street brats they'd hired to help this evening.

"C'mon, Danny," Elias growled. "Get a move on! We gotta dig another couple of feet ter get ter our prize."

For the next ten minutes, the only noise in the graveyard was the wind as it shimmied through the trees and tombstones, the whisper of spades sinking into the ground, the spray of mud, and the muted grunts and huffs as they put their backs into their work. Despite the cold evening, Daniel could feel sweat bathing his face, sliding down his spine.

"Oi'm getting' ter old fer this," Elias muttered. "Me bones are—" He broke off his complaint when their spades simultaneously hit wood, the dull *thunk* loud enough for Daniel to flinch and cast a wary glance around.

No Charlies came running out of the darkness.

He swung his eyes to his partner, saw the mutual elation lighting Elias' face. Invigorated, they dug faster, clearing the dirt away. Within minutes they were able to toss their spades aside. Jumping into the pit, they braced their feet on each side of the coffin.

"Oye, ye two!" Elias thrust a finger at the boys. "Get me the rope and those fokking crowbars. Move!"

The boys scrambled to retrieve the tools of the trade, lowering them to Elias and Daniel.

"Are we gonna see the dead bloke?" asked the younger boy. His Adam's apple bobbed up and down. Daniel couldn't tell whether it was from excitement or fear.

"Nay. 'E'll be buried in a shroud, ye daft whelp. Don't ye know anythin'?" Elias snapped.

Daniel and Elias used the crowbars to pry off the coffin's lid. With a grunt, Daniel hauled himself out of the grave, then waited while Elias lifted the coffin's lid up to him.

He nearly had a heart attack when the boys shrieked, their faces ghostly white in the moonlight.

"Shut yer blasted mouths!" Daniel whispered. "Do ye want ter be sent ter Newgate?"

"That ain't no bloke!" gasped the older boy.

"W'ot?" Elias glanced down, and nearly jumped. "Bloody 'ell!"

Daniel had thought graverobbing had cured him of any superstition, but now horror rose up inside him as he stared into the open coffin. The man who'd died and had been buried only yesterday was there, his big body sewn into a shroud. But he wasn't alone. Lying on top of him was a woman, naked as the day she was born. And her eyes . . .

God in heaven, *she had no eyes.*

Daniel fought the urge to turn tail and run. "What the bleeding hell is this?"

Elias said nothing for a moment, then glanced up at Daniel. The gleam in his partner's eyes wasn't fear. Elias's mouth curved in a wide smile, revealing his broken, tobacco-stained teeth.

"I'll tell ye what this is, Danny-boy. It's a two-fer: two bodies fer only one hole dug!"

# TWENTY-TWO

By the time Kendra stood in front of the slate board the next morning, the sky was a dazzling blue, clear of both clouds and smog —a rarity in London. Sunshine streamed through the library's windows, reflecting off the many silver domed trays hat had been brought in by the servants, supervised by a stoic Wakely.

"Will that be all, madam?" the butler asked.

Kendra noticed how his gaze strayed to the slate board. Except for the small flicker in his eyes, she couldn't guess what he was thinking. Probably wondering who the hell his master had married.

"Yes, thank you."

She waited for Wakely and the staff to file out of the room before she poured herself a cup of coffee, then walked back to the slate board to review her notes. She was savoring her first sip when she heard the clump of boots and swish of skirts. A moment later, Rebecca and the Duke came through, and with them the scent of fresh, cold air and horses—the latter explained by the riding habits that they wore.

"Good morning," Rebecca greeted cheerfully. She walked to the side table and helped herself to a cup of tea. "Duke and I met Sutcliffe in the park on our way over, and we had a lovely gallop. You must learn to ride, Kendra. You don't know what you're missing."

*Broken bones, probably.* But Kendra kept that opinion to herself.

Rebecca and the Duke spoke of the previous night's ball as they piled their plates with the classic English breakfast. They had just sat down at the table when Alec arrived with Sam and Muldoon. More greetings were exchanged, more plates filled. Kendra had to admit that having a briefing during breakfast was vastly better in the nineteenth century than in her own time.

"Dr. Munroe is not coming?" the Duke asked, glancing at the empty chair at the table.

"I invited him," Kendra said. "We can catch him up when he gets here." Her gaze roamed around the table and settled on Muldoon, who was slathering freshly churned butter on his bun. "Let's start. Muldoon, did anyone at Bowden Theater think the description of the woman from the Thames matched Clarice?"

"I got something even better." The reporter grinned as he set down his knife and bun. He yanked from his pocket a neatly folded piece of paper. He unfolded it several times, then flipped it around to reveal a poster for *The Merchant of Venice*. Below the title and performance dates was a black-and-white illustration of a beautiful, dark-haired woman. The artist had drawn her looking over her shoulder, head tilted, a coquettish half-smile curving her lips.

And a mole in the shape of a heart on her left cheek.

"Prudence said they printed these up two weeks ago," Muldoon explained. "They were supposed to go out this week. 'Tis one of the reasons Mr. Myott is so vexed that Clarice took herself off."

"This woman certainly matches the description in the newspaper," Kendra said.

"I found out something else." Muldoon paused—purposefully dramatic, Kendra thought.

Sam must have thought the same, because he narrowed his eyes and snapped, "Out with it, then!"

"Clarice isn't the only actress to have gone missing from Bowden Theater." Muldoon smiled at their surprise. "Prudence told me that an understudy by the name of Isabella Russo disappeared a couple of months ago. No one thought anything of it; actors come and go in theater companies all the time, you understand. Especially understudies, who grow weary of waiting for their turn on stage. But Prudence said that Isabella left without telling anyone. And no one has heard from her—or about her—since." His smile fell away, leaving his expression grim. "Rather ominous, don't you think?"

"Two women missing from the same theater . . ." The Duke looked at Kendra. "You say that we are not dealing with a madman who preys on women, but I'm not so certain."

"We don't know what we're dealing with yet," she said quietly. But she was beginning to suspect. "We need to add Isabella Russo to our list on inquiries."

She turned to Sam. "Mr. Kelly, can you send some of your men around to other theaters? Find out if they've had actresses who left without telling anyone."

The Duke drew in a quick breath. "Then you *do* think we're dealing with the same kind of monster as before!"

"I actually don't. Not like before, anyway," she said slowly. "I can't explain it, but this is different. No less evil, but different."

Rebecca took a sip of tea, then set down her cup. "You think Clarice is the woman you mentioned last night, the one that Lady Westford saw keeping company with Mr. Goldsten."

Kendra's gaze fell on the poster. Younger and prettier. "Yes, I think so."

"But how does this Isabella connect?" Rebecca wondered. "Unless it's just a coincidence that she, too, disappeared."

"I don't like coincidences. And if we find more missing women, then it's definitely *not* a coincidence." Kendra hesitated, searching for the right words. "Lady Westford was known for having a strong interest in science and medicine. It's possible Clarice had a bloodletting treatment. It would explain her being exsanguinated."

Rebecca, who hadn't been privy to that information, gasped. "Dear heaven. What are you talking about?"

"The poor woman had been bled dry," Muldoon replied, his eyes on Kendra. "God save me from the barber so inept that they took every drop of blood."

"We don't know if all of her blood was taken," Kendra reminded him, and narrowed her eyes in warning when he opened his mouth. "Do not start talking about vampires again. We are *not* dealing with the supernatural."

Muldoon grinned at her. "Ah, but none of this seems *natural,* my lady."

Snagging two bacon strips, Kendra stood up and circled to the slate board.

"Let's focus on what we know," she said. "Two women are dead. Lady Westford read the newspaper article and recognized Clarice. She went to Munroe's to confirm her suspicion." Kendra took a bite of bacon, chewed, and swallowed before continuing. "Lady Harrington told me that the Queen wanted them on Friday. They were with her until Saturday afternoon."

"That explains why she didn't go immediately to the theater to inquire after Clarice," Alec said.

Sam paused in shoveling his scrambled eggs into his mouth. "Aye, but it don't explain why she didn't identify the body ter Dr. Munroe."

Muldoon tapped his finger against his tankard of ale. "More to the point, why'd she go to the theater on Saturday at all? She verified that Clarice was dead. Why inquire about her afterwards? Unless . . ." He flashed Kendra a cocky grin. "Maybe she believed the creature had risen from the grave."

Kendra rolled her eyes. "I think we're dealing with a more mundane explanation, Mr. Muldoon."

"Such as?"

"Lady Westford was conducting her own investigation," she said, laying out her theory. "She didn't go to the theater to see if Clarice was there. She wanted to know if Clarice had been seen with anyone, talked about anyone. Unfortunately for her, it was Saturday night. The troupe was busy. No one had time for her."

She pointed at Edwina's name on the slate board. "Edwina lives and works at the theater. It makes sense that she observed this and approached Lady Westford, arranging to meet her the next day at the theater."

Muldoon leaned back in his chair, surveying the slate board. "A reasonable assumption, I suppose. Although I can't imagine Lady Westford conducting her own investigation."

"Why, pray tell?" Rebecca asked. "Because she's a woman?"

"Well, ladies of the Beau Monde typically don't concern themselves with the murder of a lowly actress, much less investigate the murder themselves," he replied, his tone light.

Kendra could tell that Rebecca was not amused by his observation. "That is a rather narrow-minded point of view, Mr. Muldoon," she said. "As a lady of the Beau Monde, I can tell you that we aren't all feeble, featherbrained females only interested in the cut of our gowns, sir."

The reporter's eyes widened, and it seemed to occur to him that might have put his foot in his mouth. "I never said—"

"I understand *exactly* what you are saying, Mr. Muldoon. You've made your position abundantly clear."

If Rebecca lifted her nose any higher, she'd be staring at the ceiling,

Muldoon cast a glance around the table, obviously looking for help. Sam muttered something under his breath that sounded suspiciously like "chucklehead," while Alec and the Duke focused on eating their breakfast.

Kendra deliberately put the focus on Sam. "Mr. Kelly, any leads on Edwina's whereabouts?"

"Not exactly. I've had me lads talking ter stagecoach whips and wherrymen. No one had a passenger meetin' the girl's description. However, one of the keel bullies said they might've seen a scarred-face chit in the area."

"Keel bullies?"

"Dockworkers who unloads or loads coal vessels," Alec explained, and looked at Sam. "Why couldn't he be certain it was her?"

"He said it was dark and he'd been drinking. And the chit's face was half covered with a scarf. He didn't think she was a bunter, which is the usual strumpet plying their wares about the docks."

"This is good news," the Duke said, glancing around the table. "If the dockworker really did see Edwina, then she's alive."

"For now." Kendra realized how pessimistic she sounded when everyone stared at her. "We're not the only ones looking for her. She can identify the killer."

Rebecca shivered. "The poor girl."

"If she was seen at the docks, maybe she was trying to book passage out of England," Kendra said.

"Aye, we looked into that," Sam replied. "No one admitted ter taking in the chit. She couldn't have enough blunt ter bribe them ter keep their mouths shut."

"It's possible she's hiding near the docks," Alec said. "If she had any money on her when she fled, it goes further in that part of town."

"Unless someone lightens your pockets—which is known to happen in that part of town too," Muldoon quipped.

"We'll keep searching," Sam said. "It's a bit trickier with the cold weather, and everybody bundled up these days. By the by, I spoke with Lord Westford's servants. They said their mistress left the house on Sunday by foot. I doubt she walked all the way ter Coventry Garden. She must've hired a hackney."

He took a breath before continuing, "Lady Westford's abigail admitted that her mistress was quieter, more tense than usual, in the last couple of weeks. But she didn't know why."

Kendra asked, "Did she know about Lady Westford's involvement with Mr. Goldsten?"

"Aye, but not from her ladyship. Most of the staff learned of it one evening when they overheard Lord Westford railing at her about the affair. The abigail said his rage was fierce, but her mistress never once mentioned her husband's wrath or her involvement with Mr. Goldsten."

Kendra moved back to the table. "We have to add Isabella Russo to our inquiries—" she broke off when Wakely materialized at the door.

"Forgive the interruption, my lady, but a message has come from Dr. Munroe." A strange expression crossed his face. "He requests that you come to the morgue. He said that the body that was taken has been . . . returned."

# TWENTY-THREE

The morgue was crowded—with the dead and undead. All three slabs were now occupied with bodies covered with stained linen sheets. Dr. Munroe and his assistant, Mr. Barts, stood on either side of the middle slab. The form beneath the sheet was clearly female, at least five inches shorter than the two other shrouded cadavers.

"Good heavens," Rebecca muttered, pulling out a perfumed handkerchief from her reticule and holding it against her nose. Kendra couldn't blame her. The stench of decomposition was even more pungent than the last time she'd visited.

Munroe gave Rebecca a concerned look. "Are you certain that you wouldn't prefer waiting in my office, my lady?"

Rebecca's chin jerked up a notch. "*No.*" Smiling weakly, she murmured, "Forgive me, Dr. Munroe, I was simply taken aback by the smell. I'm fine. Please carry on."

"This is quite extraordinary, doctor," said the Duke, his gaze on the middle figure. "How did she end up here? *Again?*"

Munroe hesitated, his expression cautious as he surveyed them. "I feel obligated to remind you that anatomy schools like mine face a dearth of cadavers in this country. That shortage forces those in the medical field to form alliances with unsavory characters. Those individuals supply us with much needed . . . materials."

Sam waved his hand, clearly impatient with the anatomist's careful preface. "We've known each other for too long for you ter be in a pucker, doctor. Even the Crown looks the other way when it comes ter the practice. I don't care how this woman got on yer autopsy table as much as I care about who put her there the first time around."

"You make an excellent point, Mr. Kelly. I shall be frank. The resurrectionist men that I often deal with went to a graveyard last night to dig up the recently deceased Mr. Wells." Munroe gestured to the concealed figure to the left. "When they opened his coffin, they discovered our body lying on top of Mr. Wells."

Muldoon chuckled. "I'd wager their peepers popped out of their heads when they pried open the lid."

"It certainly was a surprising development," agreed the anatomist. "Naturally, they brought both bodies to sell to me. As much as I object to purchasing the same cadaver *twice*, I decided it was the most expedient way of dealing with the situation."

He straightened, adjusting the spectacles on his nose before looking at Kendra. "I hope you don't mind, my lady, but I took the liberty of conducting the autopsy before I sent my message. I'd hoped to have a few answers for you."

"Did you find any?"

"A few. Unfortunately, I was also left with new questions." He reached for the sheet, then hesitated, his gaze cutting to Rebecca. "My lady, are you quite certain you wish to remain for this? It's not a pretty sight."

Rebecca lowered her handkerchief, her jaw tightening. "I understand, doctor. However, I like to think that I am not one of those faint-hearted, spoiled ladies of the Beau Monde." She shot a quick, almost challenging glance in Muldoon's direction. "Please continue, sir."

"Very well."

Carefully, Munroe peeled down the sheet to expose the head, neck, and shoulders. Kendra could see the Y-shaped incision peeking out like black spider legs along the collarbone. She shifted her gaze to the cadaver's face. Munroe was right; it was not a pretty sight.

More than a week had passed since the body had been pulled from the Thames, and natural gases had built up like helium in a balloon, splitting the mottled flesh and breaking down organs.

Except for her hair, which was dark and surprisingly lush, she barely looked human. Certainly, she no longer looked like the theater poster's illustration.

Her eyes were partially shut, but something was wrong. It took Kendra a moment to figure it out.

"Her eyes . . ." She swung her startled gaze to Munroe.

He nodded grimly. "Gone. Not done by animals—someone removed them." He leaned forward, lifting an eyelid to reveal the gouged-out pit.

Behind her, Kendra heard a choking sound, then a flurry of skirts heading for the door. Male footsteps followed. Briefly, Kendra glanced up to see Rebecca and Muldoon disappearing out into the hallway. She brought her gaze back to Munroe as he lowered the eyelid.

"Her eyes were intact when she was in my morgue before," he said.

"God's teeth," Sam muttered, appalled. "This was done after the lass was stolen?"

"Yes."

"But *why?*"

"Maybe the same reason her uterus was removed."

The Duke drew in deep, shaky breath. "My God. What *is* this?"

Kendra fixed her eyes on Munroe. "Can you tell me if the removal was done crudely or if it was more . . . . professional?"

She could see by the way his eyes darkened that he knew what she was really asking.

"The organs were excised neatly," he said slowly.

Kendra had to fight the chill caused by his answer. The suspicion that she'd had earlier was becoming stronger.

Stepping back from the corpse, Kendra pulled the poster out of her reticule and showed it to Munroe. "Not much of a likeness anymore, is there? But it's her."

As everyone studied the illustration, Rebecca and Muldoon returned, both flushed and tense. Kendra briefly met Rebecca's eyes before her friend averted her gaze. *Curious . . .*

*And none of my business*, she decided.

"What else can you tell me about her?" she asked Munroe.

"She didn't drown. There was no water in her lungs. And no blood in her veins. She died of exsanguination." Tight-lipped, the anatomist carefully rearranged the sheet to expose Clarice's arms. "It's difficult to see because of the advanced stage of decomposition, but there are puncture wounds here"—he pointed to a barely discernable mark first on the inside of her right arm, and then on her left—"and here."

"Can you tell if she was sick recently?" Kendra asked. "Or suffering from any disease?"

Munroe gave her a sharp look. "How did you know?"

Kendra's pulse quickened. "What did you find?"

"She was in the early stages of the French disease."

"The French Pox," Alec noted. "Also known as syphilis. It's not an uncommon illness for those who make their living on stage."

"Or for soldiers and sailors," Muldoon added.

"Is it possible someone tried to cure her through bloodletting?" Kendra asked Munroe.

He gazed at her, uneasy. "Bloodletting was done in the past for those afflicted with the disease, but it's considered archaic now. Mercury is the prescribed treatment, even though the side effects are quite devastating."

Yeah, like kidney failure, nerve damage and insanity, Kendra remembered.

"Maybe someone tried to avoid those side effects by returning to bloodletting," the Duke said.

"But why would they, when it never cured a patient?" Munroe shook his head. "Besides, no reputable surgeon would have gone so far as to take all her blood."

"What about an apprentice, someone still learning?" Kendra couldn't stop herself from glancing at Barts, who pursed his lips, but remained silent.

"No." Munroe was adamant. "Anyone with even the most rudimentary medical knowledge would never do such a thing."

*That leaves everyone without any medical knowledge*, Kendra thought. Charlatans had always existed. In another 127 years, penicillin would provide a cure for syphilis, but for now, the disease was fatal. That meant anyone diagnosed with an STD would be vulnerable to swindlers hoping to make a quick buck off their desperation. Had a con artist promised Clarice that they could cure her via bloodletting, then bleeding her until it was too late?

Kendra looked at the dead woman's wrists. The bruising from the restraints was no longer visible in the mottled flesh. "Are restraints used in the bloodletting procedure?" She recalled the leather straps that held the wherryman down while Dandridge sliced off his toes.

"No. It's relatively painless. Although, I suppose there may be a few anxious individuals that need to be kept still so as not to pull out the needles." Munroe paused. "After the body was stolen from me, it must have been stored indoors. The tearing you see is natural decomposition, not from animals. And it must have been somewhere cold, as decomposition was kept to a minimum."

"The entire kingdom is cold these days," Muldoon muttered.

The anatomist acknowledged the comment with a brief smile, then said, "She also had sediment in her hair, on her posterior side."

Sam frowned. "Aye, well, she was dug up, doctor. I'd expect she'd have dirt on her."

"She was in a coffin, not thrown into an open grave. And, as I said, the dirt was primarily on her posterior side. The body must have been placed on a surface that was covered in the sediment."

Kendra was impressed. Trace evidence involving geoscience wouldn't be recognized as a forensic tool until the early twentieth century. "Is there any way to determine the type of sediment and where it may have come from?"

Munroe looked intrigued. "I'm acquainted with a man who might be able to help. Mr. Randolph Engel is a mining surveyor. He assisted William Smith when he worked on England's canal system. He became interested in catastrophism and has made a remarkable study of geology."

"Catastrophism?" Kendra frowned at the unfamiliar word.

The Duke said, "It's an attempt to resolve the discrepancies between the biblical account of the Great Flood—basically, a sudden, cataclysmic event that created the earth's geology—and the theory that the earth was formed by a more gradual process. I have read articles penned by Mr. William Buckland, who argued in favor of sedimentary deposits left by the Great Flood."

"Mr. Engel takes an opposing viewpoint." Munroe turned to Kendra. "He lives in Cambridge. Do you want me to contact him and ask if he'd examine the sediment?"

"How long will that take?" Kendra dreaded the answer.

Munroe smiled. "If he's at home, maybe as early as tomorrow evening."

"Can you find out if Clarice was being treated by someone at St. George's?" she asked, and saw the flicker in the anatomist's eyes.

"Yes, I can do that," he said. "But if anyone at St. George's would have treated her by bloodletting, there would have been talk. And I would have heard about it."

"Would you have heard about any of your colleagues expressing an interest in curing syphilis?"

That brought a fleeting smile. "Everyone's interested in curing syphilis—or any disease that plagues humanity. We discuss these things all the time in the Metamorphosis Club—" His breath caught in his throat, his eyes flashing to hers as he realized what he'd just said. He quickly shook his head. "No member would siphon off all the woman's blood in an attempt to treat her, my lady."

"What about to experiment on her?"

Munroe's jaw tightened. Kendra thought it was telling that he didn't immediately refute what she was suggesting.

"Someone first took her blood. Now her eyes and uterus," Kendra said. Rebecca, who hadn't been in the room when that was revealed, gasped, but Kendra remained focused on the doctor. "You said the removals were done in a professional manner. Someone with medical knowledge. Even more, someone with a surgeon's skill. Could you get me a list of Metamorphosis Club members?"

"Are you planning on quizzing them all? We have nearly forty members."

"If I have to, yes. I'd like the full list, but it would be helpful if you indicated the members who've been vocal about finding new treatments for syphilis."

"Very well," he agreed, but his reluctance was palpable.

"We can narrow the list down even further if you include everyone's age. Whoever killed Lady Westford was strong enough to throw her over the railing, and young enough to chase Edwina down the street."

Munroe's eyes were shadowed as he met hers for a brief moment before he turned away. "I'll get you your list, my lady."

# TWENTY-FOUR

"Well, that was miserable," Rebecca said softly.

Kendra looked over at her friend as they walked ahead of the men, emerging from the anatomy school. "Are you all right?"

"If you are referring to my earlier . . . reaction, I apologize." Rebecca's tone was as crisp as a winter morning. "I didn't . . . I wasn't expecting what was done to her eyes."

"Don't worry about it. It's not easy to view a dead body, especially in that state."

"You mean it's not easy for me, because I'm a lady." Rebecca's jaw tightened. "You share Mr. Muldoon's belief that I'm a fainthearted, feebleminded lady, that I need to be coddled and shouldn't view such ugliness? That I'm not like *you*, and ought not try to be."

Kendra slid a cautious sidelong look at Rebecca, then glanced over her shoulder at Muldoon walking with Alec, the Duke, and Sam. Far enough behind to not be overheard.

"Is that what Mr. Muldoon said when he followed you out of the autopsy room?" she asked.

Rebecca let out a hiss. "*Yes.* He seems to think I am a chicken-hearted female prone to having vapors or hysterics. Just because I-I . . . I nearly cast up my accounts. But I *didn't.* And even if I had, I am not some silly creature that needs to be cosseted and comforted. It's insulting."

Kendra had never had any close female friends before Rebecca, but she knew there was a code. You supported your friend, especially if they were fuming against a man.

"The bastard," she finally said.

Rebecca made a noise between a gasp and a laugh. "Kendra!" She said nothing for a long moment, then went on, "He views me as part of the ton, you know. And he thinks the females of the ton are silly, timid creatures who spend their days shopping and their evenings attending balls."

Kendra actually didn't believe Muldoon viewed Rebecca in that way at all, but she wasn't stupid enough to try to defend him.

"He thinks we live our lives wrapped in cotton-wool," Rebecca muttered darkly.

"Jeez. He's never been to Almack's," Kendra said lightly. Almack's was the most exclusive social club of the day, where young debutantes put themselves on display as potential brides, to be scrutinized by society's most august ladies. Talk about nerve-wracking.

Rebecca laughed. Her amusement faded, though, as they continued to walk. "Are you really going to interview everyone on the list Dr. Munroe gave you?" she asked Kendra.

"Eventually. But right now, I want to interview Lord Westford."

"I thought you were of the mind that Lady Westford's murderer is on the list."

"Yes, but Lord Westford might know more about his wife's activities. We need to find out how Lady Westford's path crossed with Clarice's."

*And,* she added silently, *how both of their paths crossed with a killer's.*

Alec directed Coachman John to Lord Westford's black-crepe-embellished townhouse. Kendra wasn't entirely surprised to learn that the earl was not at home—and *really* not home, as opposed to being at home but refusing to see them. When she asked the butler where they could find Lord Westford, he gave her a thousand-yard stare and told her that he couldn't presume to know.

Alec suggested that she return to the carriage while he had a word with the butler.

"Let me guess—Lord Westford is at his villa in St. John's Wood," Kendra said when Alec climbed back into the carriage. "What did he think I'd do? Faint at the mention of a mistress?"

"He was being considerate of your ladylike sensibilities."

Kendra drummed her fingers on her knee. "I'm starting to understand why Rebecca was ticked off at Muldoon."

"Ah." Alec's green eyes gleamed. "Mr. Muldoon told me that he'd only tried to assure Becca that her reaction to the grisly business in the morgue was perfectly natural."

"Perfectly natural for someone like Rebecca, you mean. A lady. A fragile creature that needs to be shielded from life's unpleasantness."

"Well, she did almost cast up her accounts in the morgue," Alec pointed out mildly.

"I've seen men throw up at crime scenes too."

"He was trying to . . . never mind." He regarded her somewhat quizzically. "Are we really going to quarrel about this?"

"You think I'm being unreasonable?"

"I think . . ." He leaned back against the seat. "My wife is extremely reasonable. And I'd be foolish to say otherwise."

Kendra's lips twitched, her irritation ebbing. "You're not foolish."

Given that the future King of England had at one time stashed his mistress in a villa at St. John's Wood, Kendra had expected the neighborhood to be pretty upscale. She was not disappointed. Located a couple miles northwest of Charing Cross and a stone's throw from Regent Park, the area was a network of wide, tree-lined boulevards with neo-Palladian mansions set behind brick walls and wrought-iron gates.

It was before noon; too early for most of the Ton to be out. A milk wagon ambled down the street at a leisurely pace, along with a handful of horseback riders and one private carriage leaving a gated residence. Kendra couldn't help but wonder if the occupant of the carriage was a husband leaving his mistress to return to his legal family.

They approached an elegant limestone villa. Alec used the silver lion's-head knocker, and the door opened. A white-haired butler contemplated them with the same regal bearing and haughty expression of every butler Kendra had met in this era. For just a moment, she had the fanciful image of a factory pumping out butlers in the same mold.

The majordomo's eyes lit with recognition when his eyes fell on Alec, who had been there only the day before. "My lord, how may I help you?"

"Kirby, isn't it?"

"Yes, my lord."

"My wife and I would like to speak with Lord Westford."

"Ah . . ." The butler glanced at Kendra. "I shall inquire whether he is at home—"

"Let me be clear, Kirby. My wife and I are not leaving until we speak to his lordship. We shall wait in the drawing room."

If Kirby planned to argue, one look at Alec's set face had him nodding and hastily stepping aside so they could enter. "Yes, certainly, sir. If you would please follow me."

Kendra's gaze traveled the grand entrance hall with its potted plants and pink-hued marble columns. A footman, decked out in full livery, was positioned outside a closed door at the far end of the hall, beyond the grand staircase. There wasn't a piece of black crepe to be seen.

As the butler opened the doors to the drawing room, Kendra heard the sound of distant, childish laughter.

"I shall inform his lordship that you are here," Kirby stated, stepping back and closing the doors.

Kendra turned to survey the elegant room, done in butter-soft hues. Chinese vases were positioned around the room, exploding with colorful flowers. "Don't you find this odd?" she asked. "The man's wife was murdered four days ago, and it's like she never existed."

"I doubt she ever existed here. This is a world apart from the one that Lord Westford created with his wife." He eyed her curiously. "You've never encountered arranged marriages like this in your America?"

That gave her pause. "Well, yes. I suppose there are wealthy, high-profile couples who stay together for political ambitions or because they don't want to split up the family fortune. Or they have an image to protect," she admitted. "But if a wife—or husband—found out their partner had a secret family, they tended to get seriously pissed. Then they called their divorce attorney to take their ex for every dime they can get."

*Except for the spouses that don't—the spouses who choose to kill their partner rather than get a divorce.*

But she no longer believed that was what they were dealing with here. This was bigger, more insidious.

She heard the heavy thud of footsteps before the door burst open, and Lord Westford strode through in an agitated rush.

"What is the meaning of this?" he demanded. His face was red, his eyes burning with fury. It gave Kendra a moment of déjà vu from the first time she'd met the earl.

"We have a few more questions about your wife's murder," she said, but was momentarily distracted as a woman glided into the room after him. *The mistress.* Kendra had to admit that she was surprised. She had expected the "other woman" in Lord Westford's life to be younger and prettier than his wife. Mrs. O'Leary was around the same age as Lady Westford, with a figure that could be best described as pleasantly plump. Or, less charitably, frumpy. Her hair, under the heavy lace cap, was a graying mouse-brown.

Lord Westford's left-handed wife was unremarkable, Kendra thought, but revised that opinion when the lady smiled. There was something winsome in the curve of her lips that invited shared laughter, a light in her eyes that indicated kindness.

Or maybe her smile stood out because it was in stark contrast to Lord Westford's hostile glower.

"Good morning. Lord Sutcliffe, isn't it?" Mrs. O'Leary had a lovely, musical voice. She dipped into a pretty little curtsy, her sparkling hazel eyes cutting over to include Kendra as she rose. "And Lady Sutcliffe. Forgive me for being so bold as to force an introduction; I am Mrs. O'Leary."

The woman thread her arm through Lord Westford's. *A united front.*

"Heather," Lord Westford muttered, half embarrassed.

Mrs. O'Leary ignored him. Keeping the smile pinned to her face, she gestured toward the two pale yellow Chippendale sofas facing each other. "Let's sit, shall we? I hear congratulations are in order." They did so, and her pale fingers plucked at her skirt, carefully arranging the material around her. "Westford tells me that you were recently wed."

Alec nodded. "Yes, a few days ago."

"He also told me about this terrible business with Lady Westford." She pressed a hand to her chest as she glanced first at Alec, then at Kendra. "Westford would never harm his wife. I cannot bear anyone thinking him such a fiend."

"Heather—"

She patted his hand. "No, Westford. We must discuss this. I sent the children to the schoolroom, so we shan't be disturbed. When we heard the news, Westford thought . . . well, we both thought Lady Westford had done something dreadful."

Kendra eyed the woman curiously, then looked to Westford. "Why? Did your wife say anything to make you think that she was depressed? Suicidal?"

"No." He frowned a bit uncertainly. "At least, I don't think so. Grace was, as I already told you, preoccupied."

"You never saw her weeping?"

"No."

"She never indicated to you that she was afraid?"

"Afraid?" Now he looked baffled. "Afraid of what?"

"Maybe of you," Kendra said bluntly, studying him closely.

The earl sucked in a shocked breath. "Balderdash! I—"

"Was overheard threatening to kill your wife after you learned about her involvement with Mr. Goldsten," Kendra interjected. "Why don't you tell us about that?"

"I . . . well, for God's sakes, I didn't mean it *literally*. Grace and I had a cordial relationship. If you must know, I was quite fond of her." He licked his lips nervously. "I would never kill her! What kind of monster do you think I am?"

Mrs. O'Leary laid a comforting hand on the earl's arm, locking her steady gaze on Kendra. "Lady Westford has had several liaisons over the years once the line was secured, and Westford voiced no objections."

"Until Lady Westford's affair with Mr. Goldsten."

"Well, of course!" Westford exploded. "He's a *Jew*! Who would not be upset? Especially when I was being made sport of!"

Mrs. O'Leary patted his arm again, but kept her gaze on Kendra's face. "Lord Crawford approached Westford about it one evening while he was at White's," she explained. "He taunted Westford in the most insulting way. Odious man! 'Tis little wonder Westford was distraught about the situation. He spoke unthinkingly."

"Did you ever talk to your wife about her relationship with Mr. Goldsten?" Kendra asked.

"Of course!" Westford's chest swelled in his indignation. "I told Grace that she needed to end it quickly. Not only for the Westford name, mind you, but also because she had a duty to the Queen as her lady-in-waiting. I can't imagine Her Royal Highness being tolerant of the relationship either."

Alec's green eyes were cool as he regarded the earl. "I wouldn't be too certain of that, Westford. Our Queen is an intelligent woman, and well aware that it was Nathan Mayer von Rothschild who funded Wellington's campaign against the French. We ought to thank God that he was on our side, not Napoleon's."

Westford's face reddened, but he waved his hand dismissively. "I think we would've won the war regardless, my lord."

"Doubtful," Alec countered drily. "Every war needs to be financed, its troops funded. Soldiers are always full of patriotism, love of God and country when wars begin, but without food in their bellies, fresh horses and ammunition, armies fall, campaigns fail."

Westford scowled, his chin lifting at a mutinous angle, but he didn't reply.

"When did you speak to your wife about Mr. Goldsten?" Kendra asked, refocusing the conversation.

"I can't be expected to know the exact date, can I?" Westford grumbled.

"Before or after you spoke to Lord Crawford?"

"I spoke to her before—a word of caution. Then I spoke to her again after Lord Crawford brought home to me how much she was making a cake of herself."

"You were angry. You argued." Kendra paused. "How violent was your argument, sir?"

Westford's nostrils flared. "I did not harm Grace! How many times must I tell you? For heaven's sake, I did not throw her over the balcony in some shabby theater!"

Mrs. O'Leary said, "This is getting redundant, my lady. Westford is not responsible for his wife's death."

"Lady Westford had bruises on her that had nothing to do with her murder," Kendra said. "It looks like someone grabbed her, maybe shook her."

Westford turned a deeper red, shaking his head. "I swear, I did not lay a finger on her!"

Kendra noticed Mrs. O'Leary squeeze Westford's arm. Trying to comfort him? Or a cautionary gesture?

Mrs. O'Leary smiled at Kendra. "Westford would not harm a fly. I can vouch that he was here all day on Sunday. The weather was nice enough for us to take the children to Regent Park to feed the ducks. This summer has been dreadfully cold."

"How many children do you have, Mrs. O'Leary?" Alec inquired politely.

She smiled at him. "Six. Our eldest, Charles, is a barrister in the House of Commons. Blythe married last year, which makes her two sisters, Fanny and Sarah, frightfully jealous. They will soon be out of the schoolroom, finding beaus of their own. Thankfully, I have Robert and Cecil for a few more years, even though they are a bit of a handful."

"Did your wife ever mention a woman named Clarice? Clarice Chapman?" Kendra asked Westford.

He appeared confused by the abrupt change in topic. "No. Who is she?"

Kendra shifted her gaze to Mrs. O'Leary. "Do you know Clarice Chapman?"

"No. Who is that?"

Kendra fished the poster out of her reticule. "She was an actress at the Bowden Theater. Do you recognize her?"

"Westford and I enjoy the theater and have been to the Bowden Theater a time or two." She frowned as she studied the illustration. "I don't recognize her, but that isn't entirely unusual with the greasepaint one wears on stage."

"You don't keep in touch with anyone from the theater?"

"Oh, good heavens, no! It's been decades since I was part of a troupe. After I met Westford"—she beamed at the earl—"I never considered continuing on stage. My fellow thespians move around so often, 'tis difficult to keep up a correspondence."

Kendra replaced the paper in her reticule. "Lord Westford, did your wife ever say the phrase, '*Exitus acta probat*' to you in conversation?"

"No." Now his frown was more puzzled than angry. "It's Latin, isn't it? I was never good at foreign languages. Waste of time, as far as I'm concerned. The King's English is good enough for me. What does it mean?"

"'The outcome justifies the deed,' or 'the end justifies the means.' Maybe she said it to you in English."

"No. Why would she?"

"Did she talk to you about St. George's Hospital?"

His brow cleared, seemingly relieved to be able to answer in the affirmative. "Yes! She was concerned about its state of disrepair. My wife enjoyed playing Lady Bountiful. She was drumming up interest with likeminded ladies to raise funds to build a new hospital."

"Did she ever speak about the physicians or surgeons that worked there?"

Lord Westford's jaw tightened. "I am aware of Grace's fascination with medicine and natural philosophy. Even when we were children, she expressed curiosity in such matters. We did not share the interest, so we never discussed it. Her sister died from typhus. I believe that's where her obsession came from."

"Obsession is a strong word, my lord."

"She was always reading books and journals on the subject, and going to St. George's and lectures at the Royal Society. What would you call it?"

Before Kendra could reply, the door suddenly flew open and two young boys, about nine or ten, sprinted into the room.

"Papa! Papa!" they shouted, diving toward their father.

"Cecil kicked me, Papa—"

"I did *not!* You kicked me first!"

The younger boy scowled at his brother. It made his small, chubby face look oddly like his father's. *In another forty years,* Kendra thought, *he'll be a replica of Lord Westford.*

"Children, children!" Mrs. O'Leary clapped her hands to gain their attention, then shot an apologetic look at Kendra and Alec. "We have guests. Bow to Lord and Lady Sutcliffe."

The boys immediately fell into quick, sloppy bows.

"Ma'am, I do apologize!" exclaimed the harried young woman who materialized in the doorway. "They got away from me."

Mrs. O'Leary rose, herding her boys to the door. "Don't fret, Lauren. Come on, bratlings. You're going back to the nursery." She paused to glance back at Kendra. "We've told you everything. Westford was with me on Sunday. I will swear that under oath if I have to."

Kendra nodded. "Thank you, Mrs. O'Leary. I have one more question for his lordship."

"Go on, Heather," Westford said, shoving himself to his feet, a signal that the interview was at end. "This won't take long."

Kendra and Alec stood, as well. Mrs. O'Leary and Lord

Westford exchanged a look, and she reached out to capture his hand, giving it a reassuring squeeze. Westford's face softened.

The look disappeared as soon as he turned to face them. "Well? What else do you want to know?"

"I want to know why you ordered Dr. Thornton to declare your wife's death an accident?"

"What?"

"You interfered with an investigation, my lord. I want to know why."

Kendra expected him to give the typical speech: how families were tarnished if it became known that their loved ones had committed suicide, how anyone who committed self-murder could not be buried on church grounds, and their souls were damned for eternity. She certainly expected him to justify pressuring Thornton to shut down any investigation.

But she was wrong.

Westford stared at her, mystified. "What the devil are you talking about? I told Dr. Thornton no such thing! *He* was the one who informed me that Grace had killed herself. To save our family from disgrace, he offered to declare the death an accident and even said that he could shut down the inquest. He never once mentioned the possibility that she could've been murdered. *Never once.*"

# TWENTY-FIVE

Alec used the brass knocker when they arrived at Dr. Thornton's townhome. After two rounds of polite knocking, Kendra used her fist to not-so-politely bang on the door.

"Damn it, where is he?" she muttered, tapping her foot impatiently.

"He could be making house calls," Alec suggested.

"Where's Jenny?"

"The market? Or her day off? Or she peered out of the window, saw your face and is now hiding under the bed rather than risk your wrath. You are a fearsome creature, my love."

"Ha-ha. Very funny."

Kendra took a step back to scan the house's windows. Around them, the neighborhood hummed with quiet activity, but there was only stillness from Thornton's townhouse. A sense of disquiet crept down Kendra's spine.

"Let's try the servant entrance," she said, moving off the stoop and down the path.

Alec gave her a sidelong glance. "You think that Thornton has fled, don't you?"

"No. Or if he has, it's only temporary," she said.

They walked the length of the townhouses, eventually turning to find themselves in the narrow alley behind the houses.

"He kept the drawing room exactly how his late wife decorated it," Kendra went on. "Her portrait is in there, and in his study, like a shrine. He's not going to abandon the home that he built with her."

Counting the houses, Kendra located the servant's entrance to Thornton's townhouse. There was no brass knocker here, so Kendra used her fist again to thump against the panel.

A door in the adjacent house opened, and a middle-aged woman, bundled in a coat and bonnet and carrying a canvas bag, stepped onto the stoop. She paused when she spotted them.

"Are ye needing Dr. Thornton?" She cocked her head as she surveyed them, clearly pegging them as upper class from their clothing. "What are ye about, using the servant's entrance?"

"We tried the front door, but no one answered," Kendra replied. "We thought Dr. Thornton's cook or maid might be in the kitchens."

"He ain't got a cook. He's got a maid-of-all-work. Jenny. I haven't seen her today."

Kendra asked, "How about Dr. Thornton? Have you seen him?"

"Nay. It's been quiet."

"Is it normally quiet?"

The woman shrugged. "Quiet enough, I reckon. His patients are respectable folks. Not like they're gonna make a ruckus. Sometimes he has his fellow physicians for dinner. Some kind of group, it is."

Kendra thanked the woman for her time and received an uncertain nod in reply. When she reached the mouth of the alley, the housekeeper cast them another glance over her shoulder. Kendra waited for her to disappear from view, then reached out to test the knob. Locked.

She considered her options, then removed her bonnet and extracted two long pins from her hair. Pushing the tumbling curls away from her face, she knelt down.

Alec sucked in a breath. "Are you doing what I think you're doing?"

She shot him a quick grin as she inserted the pins into the lock. "I can't pull anything over on you."

"Do you really think—"

"Sh-sh. I need to concentrate."

It took her almost two minutes. "Damn. I'm getting rusty," she muttered, straightening.

"At what? Being a housebreaker?"

"These skills have saved my life, you know," she reminded him, and saw his eyes darken as he recalled the horrific time. She deliberately lightened her tone as she pushed open the door and added, "Consider this a welfare check."

"And what, pray tell, is a welfare check?"

"Exactly what it sounds like. If there's a concern, police can check on someone's welfare, to make sure they're okay."

"We're not police."

Kendra didn't reply as they stepped inside. She looked down the long hallway that ran the length of the townhouse. The fan window above the door let in the soft light of the day. The candles in the wall sconces and candelabra on the walnut cabinet were gutted. The house was eerily silent, as though the building was holding its breath. Kendra's sense of disquiet intensified. She reached into her reticule to retrieve her muff pistol.

Alec said nothing, but brought out a gun of his own from the pocket of his greatcoat. Catching her astonished look, he grinned.

"Married to you, I thought I ought to come prepared."

Sounds drifted in from outside: the clatter of wagon wheels; the clip-clop of horse hooves; the jingle of reins; the sporadic tweeting of birds; the occasional gust of wind.

But inside the house . . . nothing.

Nerves tightening, Kendra moved quickly to the stairs. Alec was on her heels as they climbed the steps. Reaching the landing, she stopped so abruptly that Alec bumped into her.

"What—?" he began, but she was already dashing down the hall.

The door to Thornton's study was open. Jenny's body lay across the threshold, face down in a pool of dried blood.

"Bloody hell," Alec cursed as he came to a halt next to Kendra, his gaze locked on the young maid.

Kendra moved into the room, careful not to disturb the blood or the body. A silver tea tray was overturned about a yard away from the maid. A porcelain teapot lay on its side, cracked. Tea had soaked into the area rug. Two cups and saucers, plus bowls for sugar and milk, were part of the debris, scattered around the tray. Milk and tea mixed with blood. There was blood spattered on the wall.

Kendra's eyes fell on the other body in the room, sprawled in front of the fireplace. Dr. Thornton was lying face up, his eyes open and filmy. His mouth was slightly agape, giving him a surprised look. His cravat, shirt, and vest were black with his blood.

Alec lifted his gaze from Thornton to Kendra's eyes. "My God . . . why?"

"Because he was the weak link," she said softly. "Thornton may have told Lord Westford that his wife killed herself, but it wasn't his idea. Someone told him to do it."

A wave a guilt washed over her. "I knew he was involved; I could tell when I talked to him yesterday. He was sweating, nervous. If I'd pushed him more, he would've given me the person who told him to shut down the investigation into Lady Westford's death. I should've pushed him."

"Stop it," Alec said firmly. "This is not your fault, Kendra. You couldn't have known this would happen."

"I should have known it was a possibility."

"Kendra—"

"Okay." She held up a hand. "Give me a minute, okay?"

She drew in a deep, shaky breath, counted to three, and let it out slowly. This wasn't the time for self-recriminations. That could come later. Now was the time to focus.

"All right," she finally said. Shoving her pistol back into her reticule, she squatted down to study Thornton. Using one finger, she carefully pushed down the cravat. The material was stiff with dried blood, but she managed to expose a deep slash across Thornton's throat.

"His vocal chords have been cut," she said, and met Alec's eyes. "Expedient or symbolic? Someone made damn sure Thornton would never talk."

"God's teeth," said Sam Kelly, his gold eyes hard as he stared down at the carnage in Dr. Thornton's study. "What madness is this?"

Kendra shook her head. "It's not madness. The killer is covering his—" *Ass*, she nearly said, but caught herself. "He's eliminating threats."

"Dr. Thornton was a threat?"

Again, she had to take a moment to battle back the guilt. "I came here yesterday to talk to him. I knew he was hiding something, and I thought it was that he'd let Lord Westford pressure him into having Lady Westford's death declared an accident. But we spoke with Lord Westford today. He said that Dr. Thornton was the one who told him that his wife's death was a suicide and offered to cover it up."

The Bow Street Runner let out a low whistle. "So, Dr. Thornton was deliberately shielding the murderer. And the villain paid him back by killing him." His gaze moved to Jenny. "And his servant. Why now?"

Bile rose in Kendra's throat. "I pushed him hard. He must have contacted the killer. Either he was seeking reassurance or he wanted to warn him. Maybe both."

Sam shook his head. "Can't blame yourself, lass. He made a choice. He might not have killed Lady Westford, but he made damn sure ter cover for the monster. He would've gotten away with it, too, if the Queen hadn't asked you ter inquire into the matter."

"Jenny didn't make a choice," she said softly.

Sam said nothing.

Kendra forced herself to concentrate on the crime scene. "The postmortem will give us the full story on what happened," she said, careful to keep her tone brusque. "Based on my visual examination, the only injury that Thornton appears to have sustained is the slash across the throat. It looks deep, from ear to ear. I believe he was facing his killer when his throat was cut." She surveyed the blood spatter on the wall and fireplace. The arterial spurt pattern showed the last beats of Thornton's heart.

She brought her eyes back to the dead man. "He doesn't have

any defensive wounds, but his palms are bloody. He brought his hands up to his throat to staunch the flow of blood."

"The poor bastard must've known he was dying," Sam said.

"Oh, yeah. He had a minute, maybe two."

"That's an eternity for someone feeling their life's blood seeping away," Alec said grimly.

"It could've been quicker if an air bubble entered the jugular vein, causing an embolism," Kendra said. "Same with Jenny. Her throat was slashed too."

Everyone's eyes tracked across the room, to where the maid lay sprawled.

"Thornton invited his killer into his inner sanctum," Kendra said slowly. "He asked Jenny to bring tea . . . or, more likely, the killer asked for it."

Alec frowned. "Why do you say that?"

"The murders happened sometime last night. The candles in the hallway are burnt down," Kendra added, anticipating the question she saw in Sam's eyes. "The killer didn't think to put them out before he left. Why bother? And since it was evening, Dr. Thornton would be more likely to offer his guest something stronger than tea." She flicked a hand at the decanters on the side table. "Jenny was a witness. As soon as she opened the front door . . ." *She was as good as dead.* "The killer knew she had to be eliminated. That's why he turned down an offer of brandy or whisky in favor of tea. He needed Jenny to go down to the kitchen to make it."

"Giving him time ter slit the doctor's gullet." Sam pressed his lips together in a tight, grim line. "Cold-blooded bastard. Beggin' your pardon, lass."

"He *is* a cold-blooded bastard. He stood facing Thornton—a man he called a friend, I think—and he slit his throat in a quick, violent attack. Then he waited . . ." *Waited while Thornton's blood pooled and cooled around him.* "When Jenny returned, she saw what happened and threw down the tray. She tried to run."

Alec said, "She didn't have a chance."

"No." Sadness rose inside Kendra as she contemplated the

young woman. Girl, really. What was she, seventeen? Eighteen? Murder was wrong on any level, but Thornton wasn't completely innocent. He'd waded nose-deep into danger. Jenny, on the other hand, *was* innocent.

"Her wound is consistent with the killer coming at her from behind," Kendra said. "He grabbed her hair and yanked her head back to expose her throat before slashing it."

There was a brief silence, weighed down in horror as they imagined the scene. Kendra was aware of the noises outside the window, the earth continuing to spin.

She cleared her throat. "There's no way the unsub wouldn't have gotten blood on him. He probably removed his outerwear at the front door and handed it to Jenny. Before he left, he would have put his coat on, covering the blood. Maybe he walked home or got a hackney. If he has a carriage, he wouldn't have used it. His coachman would be one more witness."

"I'll have me lads inquire around the neighborhood," Sam said. "Maybe someone had their peepers out and saw him arrive or leave. He ain't a ghost."

"We spoke to the housekeeper next door. She was the one who told us that she hadn't seen Jenny or Dr. Thornton at all today."

Sam frowned. "If she thought something was wrong, why didn't she find a watchman or constable, raise hue and cry?"

"It was more subliminal than that," Kendra said. "It struck her as odd, but I don't think she really had any idea what had happened."

Alec looked at Kendra. "Who will do the postmortem?

The question was a good one. Munroe was a friend of Thornton's. If this were the twenty-first century, another ME would be called in. The problem, at least from her perspective, was that she didn't trust anyone else.

Especially now, when she was starting to suspect that the person responsible was in the medical community: one of Thornton and Munroe's colleague's.

She blew out a breath. "We have to let Dr. Munroe know. Then we'll go from there."

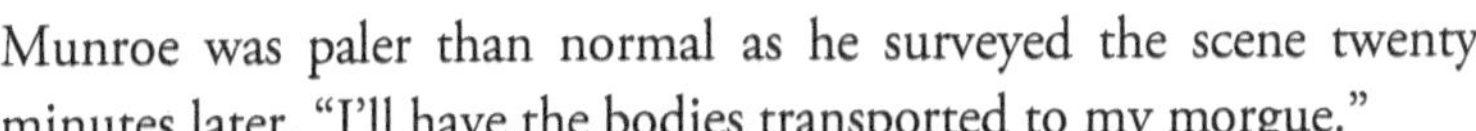

Munroe was paler than normal as he surveyed the scene twenty minutes later. "I'll have the bodies transported to my morgue."

Kendra regarded him closely. "I don't think it would be wise for you to do the autopsies, Dr. Munroe. You knew the victims. But I was hoping you'd recommend someone else?"

"No. I want them done under my supervision. I won't do the actual postmortem. I'll have Mr. Barts do it."

"Mr. Barts? Is he . . ." She didn't know how to ask about the apprentice's competency without it sounding insulting.

A small smile flickered on Munroe's face. "I can set your mind to rest, Lady Sutcliffe. Mr. Barts has been my apprentice for five years now. I can assure you that he is good. Quite good, in fact. He ought to be striking out on his own, but he's a retiring sort of fellow, and is more comfortable working under my management."

The sound of heavy footsteps trudging up the stairs reached them. Sam appeared in the doorway, followed by several men carrying a canvas shell for the body.

"I've got me lads knockin' on doors ter find out if anyone saw or heard anything last evenin'," he informed them briskly. "A wagon is downstairs for . . ." He gestured toward the two bodies, then looked to Kendra. "Where'd you want them transported?"

"My morgue, Mr. Kelly," Munroe answered. "Mr. Barts will take over the postmortem, but I want to be close by if any questions arise."

They watched in silence as the men loaded the bodies. They weren't exactly gentle, but they were efficient. Within minutes, they were carrying the bodies out of the room, footsteps reverberating as they descended the stairs. Without the bodies, the blood spatter around the study seemed more pronounced, more garish and ghastlier.

"I was teaching a class when I received your message, my lady," said Munroe, digging out his timepiece. "Mr. Barts stepped in, but he ought to be able to conduct the postmortem afterward. Would two o'clock be sufficient?"

Kendra nodded. "I'll be there."

# TWENTY-SIX

Later that afternoon, Kendra sat alone in the library, Alec having accompanied the Duke to view a possible business venture. Munroe had sent her the list of Metamorphosis Club members, and she was now carefully perusing the names.

Without Munroe or Barts's names on the list, the club's members totaled thirty-eight. However, Munroe had put a line through twelve names, with a helpful notation to explain those gentlemen were either out of the country or had retired to the country for the summer months.

Kendra went down the twenty-six remaining names and began crossing off everyone Munroe identified as sixty-five or older. Sir Preston was in that group. She might even be able to go down another decade, given that Bridget had claimed the man she'd seen was younger.

That left her with fourteen names. More could be eliminated once they factored in physical description—average height and weight—and verified alibis.

Still, fourteen names out of thirty-eight wasn't bad.

She went to the slate board, grabbed a rag she'd wetted earlier, and scrubbed off Lord Westford's name. She could envision him being angry enough to put bruises on his wife because of her involvement with Goldsten, but he was a piece that no longer fit the rest of the puzzle.

Goldsten, however, remained on the list.

She began to pace. The man checked all the boxes, didn't he?

He'd dedicated himself to medicine, working at both his own clinic as well as St. George's. He was intimately involved with the victim. He'd *lied* about the last time he'd seen her. And—this was the kicker—he'd been seen by Lady Westford with a younger, prettier woman.

Before death claimed her, Clarice had been younger and prettier.

Clarice was the key. The *reason* Lady Westford was murdered.

Kendra stopped pacing to read the words she'd written about the actress: *Clarice Chapman (now confirmed) – exsanguinated, body stolen, body recovered, eyes and uterus removed.*

Why remove the eyes and uterus *after* the body was stolen from the morgue? If the killer had wanted them, why not remove them at the time the victim's blood was drained? For that matter, why remove them at all?

She understood the Duke's fear that they were dealing with a serial killer—they were known for taking trophies off their victims. The infamous murderer Ed Gein had decorated his Wisconsin farmhouse with a macabre collection of severed noses and heads, bowls fashioned from skulls, and even a lampshade made from the face of one of his victims. Most serial killers felt compelled to take souvenirs because they wanted to maintain an intimate connection to their victim, to relive the murder over and over again in their minds.

But a serial killer would have removed the eyes and uterus the first time. The only thing taken from Clarice before she'd been dumped in the Thames had been her blood. No torture, except for the puncture wounds and chafed skin where she'd been restrained.

No, they weren't dealing with a serial killer. She'd stake her reputation as an FBI agent on it—even if that reputation wouldn't be made for another two-hundred-plus years.

"My lady."

Wakely stood in the doorway with a look on his face that suggested he'd been trying to get her attention for a while.

"Sorry, I was lost in thought," Kendra said. "Can I help you?"

"Mr. Kelly is at the door. Are you at home?"

"Yes. Show him up." When the Bow Street Runner appeared, she said, "Mr. Kelly, please tell me that you've learned something."

He removed his tricorn hat. "A maid across the street saw a carriage outside Thornton's last night, and a gentleman went inside. She didn't think he was a stranger, as Jenny invited him in immediately. Unfortunately, she couldn't give a description, as he and his coachman were bundled up because of the rain. She didn't see a crest on the carriage, but it wasn't a public hackney."

Kendra bit back a sigh. Of course, it couldn't be that easy, could it? She brought the list of names over to Sam. "This is the list of Metamorphosis Club members that Dr. Munroe sent me. He eliminated everyone who's not in town. I crossed out those that are too old."

Sam's eyes were troubled as he took the paper. "These men . . . physicians, sawbones, surgeon apprentices and apothecaries. They're dedicated ter healing."

"You know as well as I do that murderers come in all forms and classes, Mr. Kelly."

He exhaled a long breath. "Aye, I do. It don't make much sense, though. These are clever men. Why would one of them kill Lady Westford in a way that was bound ter attract attention?"

*A very good question.*

"It wasn't very clever, was it?" she murmured, her eyes on the slate board as she let the possibilities run through her head. "And we are dealing with intelligent men."

Sam regarded her intently. "What are you thinking, lass?"

"I'm thinking . . . it would make sense if Lady Westford's murder wasn't premediated."

The Bow Street Runner lifted a skeptical eyebrow. "He just happened ter followed her ter the theater? What did he want? Ter talk?"

"Yes. That's exactly what I think." She turned back to Sam. "Remember Lady Westford's reputation. She was interested in finding cures to diseases. She even corresponded with Edward Jenner about his smallpox vaccine. Somehow, Lady Westford learned about the experiments being done on Clarice. *Exitus acta probat.* The end justified the means."

"Aye, but the means resulted in the death of a girl."

"If Clarice's death was an accident, our killer might have believed he could talk Lady Westford into . . . understanding what he was trying to accomplish."

"He expected her ladyship ter ignore Clarice's murder?"

"In his mind, Clarice wasn't murdered. She was an experiment that went wrong. And, yes, I think that's what he hoped for when he approached Lady Westford. When she didn't get onboard, he knew he couldn't let her leave the theater alive." Kendra tapped the piece of slate against her chin. "He had to think fast. He didn't want her death to look like murder. That would mean an investigation. Scrutiny. So, he forced her up the stairs and threw her over the balcony.

"He then made certain that Dr. Thornton oversaw the postmortem and planted the seed that the victim had killed herself while he ruled her death an accident. Who wanted to be the person to suggest someone like Lady Westford, a lady-in-waiting to the Queen, had committed suicide?"

"God's teeth, I take back what I said. The fiend is clever. No one in Bow Street would raise doubts. Certainly not Parker. It would've been left alone—if not for the Queen." He shook his head, then scanned the list in his hand. "Dr. Thornton must have known the truth. Was he part of this experimentation?"

"I don't know. His wife died from diabetes, and he still mourns her. I don't think it would've been too difficult to get him to look the other way if someone was trying to cure diseases with unethical research."

"Even if it caused a girl to die?"

Kendra shrugged. "There are winners and losers in all medical research." Even in her own time, sick people were given placebo treatments while others were given experimental drugs. Both could die. Or be saved. It was the price of research. The difference was that the participants in medical trials knew the risks.

Not always, though. History echoed with unethical experiments. One of the more infamous was the Tuskegee Experiment, which, ironically, was also an attempt to cure syphilis. Beginning in the early 1930s, researchers enlisted more than six hundred Black men from Alabama's Tuskegee College. Four-hundred-thirty-one men had syphilis, and were studied as the disease developed. When penicillin became available to treat the disease in 1947, the doctors chose to supply the men with placebos in order to study how the disease progressed. Doctors—scientists—allowed the men to go blind and insane—and give birth to nineteen syphilitic children. It took decades before the experiments were halted, thanks to a whistleblower.

Lady Westford would have been a whistleblower if she hadn't been killed.

"Why did the fiend murder Dr. Thornton, then?" Sam asked.

"Clarice died in a treatment. In his eyes, it was for the greater good. But Lady Westford . . . that crossed a line."

"He still ruled it an accident."

"He was an accessory after the fact," Kendra agreed. "Probably hoped the whole thing would go away. The investigation forced him to think about his actions. If he showed any doubt, he became a threat. And just like Lady Westford, he needed to be eliminated."

"The villain is bloody ruthless."

"Yes. He also thinks he's the smartest person in the room. Do you know who thinks they're smarter than everybody else, Mr. Kelly?"

"The French, the royals, most noblemen and women, the clergy—"

Kendra had to laugh. "Point taken. You can add to that list: doctors. Surgeons, physicians. They tend to have a god complex."

"They think they're God?"

"Sometimes." She remembered Dandridge arguing that surgeons played God every time they operated on a patient. "Or they consider themselves superior to other men. Infallible in their thinking, their decision-making, their feelings."

*Like my father.*

"We know the why—his motive for killing. Now we need to find out the who." Kendra gestured to the sheet of paper that Sam held. "He's one of the names on that list, Mr. Kelly. I'd bet my life on it."

# TWENTY-SEVEN

At two o'clock, Kendra entered Munroe's shadowy subterranean morgue to find Munroe and Barts flanking the middle slab that held Thornton's mortal remains. They'd lit all the candles in the room—including the lanterns hanging from the wagon wheels above each slab—and the flickering light spotlighted Thornton's ashen face bracketed by his bushy muttonchops. A dirty linen sheet covered the rotund figure, tucked almost modestly under the physician's chin. The physician would've looked as if he'd laid down to take a nap, if it wasn't for his milky, sightless eyes.

On the slab to the right was a small, shrouded form. *Jenny*.

Kendra's stomach knotted. She ripped her eyes away from the dead maid to look at Munroe's grim face and that of his apprentice. "You've completed both autopsies, Mr. Barts?"

"Yes. A few minutes ago."

"What can you tell me?"

Barts waited for Munroe to nod before saying, "I estimate the time of death to be less than twenty-four hours ago, as rigor mortis is still evident. Also, there is no reddish-green discoloration around the head and neck, which normally takes place after twenty-four hours."

Kendra eyed the apprentice. He was coming across far more confident than she'd expected. "That fits with my assessment of the crime scene," she said. "What can you tell me about the injuries themselves?"

"Both victims died from having their internal and external

jugular veins severed. There were no other injuries on the bodies. The blade itself is relatively small, but extremely sharp. The lacerations indicate . . ." Now he faltered, his eyes flicking again toward Munroe.

"Go on, Mr. Barts," ordered the anatomist.

Barts nodded. "Yes, well . . . the instrument is a single blade with a slight curvature. Sharp on one side, flat on the other. The blade itself, based on the depth and angle of the injuries, was approximately three inches in length and slightly less than an inch at its widest point before tapering to the tip."

The apprentice was holding something back. Kendra frowned at Munroe. "What aren't you telling me, Dr. Munroe?"

Munroe sighed heavily and picked up a scalpel, holding up the blade so the light from the candles glinted off the steel. "This is the instrument used to slice both throats. Exactly like this."

Kendra said nothing as Munroe set the scalpel down again.

"I would like to point out that anyone with a few coins can buy a scalpel," Munroe said. His tone was careful, measured. "Also, it wouldn't be unusual for Lucien to have several scalpels lying about in his study, this particular blade being one of them. The monster could have used whatever was at hand."

Kendra shook her head. "The crime scene indicates premeditation. If it had been impulsive—something that occurred in a rush of anger—it would have been . . . messier." She glanced at Barts. "Were there any hesitation marks?"

"Not on the maid. The injury was one single cut—long and deep. However, there were a few lacerations on Dr. Thornton's throat."

Kendra reached for the sheet tucked under the physician's chin, then hesitated, glancing at Munroe. "Do you mind?"

"No, of course not."

She peeled the sheet away to expose the gaping wound at Thornton's throat. They'd cleaned up the blood, allowing her to examine the ragged flesh.

"These aren't hesitation marks," she said after a moment.

Hesitation wounds were usually shallow slashes, a natural repugnance to the act that was being done. She looked at Munroe. "It's rare to cut someone's throat when you're facing them. When it happens, usually there is more than one laceration. They also tend to be shorter in length."

"Those are the injuries we see here." Barts pointed out the direction of the slashes. "The wounds are short and angled. Deeper on the left, shallower on the right."

"Left to right. Our killer is righthanded."

"Most people use their right hand. It's the mark of the devil to be left-handed." Barts flushed when they stared at him. "My brother had a propensity to use his lefthand when he was an infant. Our mother bound his left hand, forcing him to use his right. He's now quite adept at using both hands, but always favors his right, for fear of the stigma."

Kendra shook her head. "How does anyone know what hand the devil uses? Has anyone seen the devil?"

Munroe yanked the sheet over Thornton before he turned to the small body on the next slab. Pulling down the linen, he exposed Jenny's slack face and neck. The slash across the throat was grotesque, and pity surged through Kendra. Her stomach twisted as she remembered another young maid who'd died at the hands of a killer, more than a year ago. Regret tasted like vinegar on her tongue. She'd failed Rose, and now, she felt like she'd failed Jenny too.

"The victim sustained only one injury—a single incision done in a continuous motion," the apprentice explained, unaware of Kendra's distress. "Dr. Munroe and I are in agreement that the fiend was behind her when he slashed her throat."

"From ear to ear," Kendra said softly. He wasn't telling her anything that she didn't already know from her own observation, but now it was official. She let out a weary sigh. "Thornton was the target. Jenny just happened to be there. Our killer isn't concerned that innocent people die."

Kendra thought about Edwina. Another innocent. And if she

didn't stop him, the girl would be the next body lying on the slab, if she wasn't already dead. *Where was she?*

Munroe cleared his throat, drawing her attention. "The Metamorphosis Club will be meeting tonight at Sir Preston's. Word has spread about Lucien. We want to pay our respects."

"Are you inviting me?" Kendra asked.

"Yes." He let out a long sigh. "I can't ignore the fact that Lady Westford, and now Lucien and Jenny, may have been murdered by a colleague. Maybe even someone I consider a friend. I hope you're wrong. But I won't play the fool any longer." He drew a scrap of paper from his pocket and handed it to her. "The details for tonight."

"I know this is difficult for you, doctor. I appreciate your help." Kendra hesitated, but there was nothing more to say.

"In answer to what you said about no one ever having laid eyes on the devil, Lady Sutcliffe," Munroe said. "I haven't seen the devil himself, but I see his handiwork." He spread his hands to indicate the dead around him. "Every day."

# TWENTY-EIGHT

Human beings didn't need the devil to commit evil. They were quite adept at doing it all on their own.

Kendra left Munroe and Mr. Barts, ideas, theories, and conjecture spinning in her mind like bits of flotsam caught in an eddy. She liked Dr. Munroe. Hell, she respected him as much, if not more, than any M.E. she'd dealt with in the twenty-first century. But she had some reservation over his ability to think objectively when his colleagues and friends were the prime suspects.

On the landing, she began opening and closing the doors in the long hallway. It took a few minutes to find what she was searching for: an exit that dumped her into the narrow alley, which smelled of urine and rotting vegetation. She saw movement out of the corner of her eye and turned quick, muff pistol ready . . . as two small pigs darted out from under a pile of trash, snorting and squealing down the narrow lane.

A single gust of wind whipped her skirts around her ankles and sent a few bottles rolling noisily as she followed in the pigs' wake. Emerging from the alley, she joined the pedestrian traffic. She could see Coachman John waiting next to the carriage, his attention on the street vendors and scantily clad women who were beginning to congregate in the shadows of the Theater-Royal.

She wheeled in the opposite direction, scanning the street as she walked. A few roughly dressed men eyed her. Coventry Gardens was the kind of neighborhood that became increasingly more dangerous in the evening. Midafternoon was iffy enough for her to keep her hand in her reticule, around the comfortable weight of her muff pistol.

Deliberately, she made eye contact with the more nefarious individuals. Attitude always helped. Predators, human or animal, preferred meek prey. Whether it was the attitude she was projecting or it wasn't dark enough to cover their criminal activity, Kendra arrived unmolested at a hackney parked along the curb.

She told the driver where she wanted to go, then signaled to one of the street children.

"There's a carriage down the street with a coachman—Coachman John. Tell him that he can return home. I have an errand to do and will return later."

The boy gave her a suspicious stare. "An' who might ye be?"

"The Marchioness of Sutcliffe." It was the first time she'd used her title, and it made her feel strange. Like there were too many words in her mouth. Pulling out a coin, she pressed it in the grubby palm. "Can you do that?"

"Aye, me lady!"

After watching the kid scamper away, she climbed into the public coach and was immediately assaulted by the smells of bad body odor and cheap perfume. It made her appreciate Alec and the Duke's private carriages all the more.

Chewing on her bottom lip, she gazed out the window as hackney barreled down the street. Her stomach coiled itself into greasy knots. Not because of what she was doing—damn it, she was a trained FBI agent. She could take care of herself.

Her nerves came from anticipating Alec's reaction when she eventually told him what she'd done.

She'd never had to worry before about taking action in an investigation. She had to report to her supervisor, sure, but not about something like this. Besides, Alec wasn't her boss; he was her husband. They were equal partners. She refused to feel guilty. Yet her head was beginning to throb with not feeling guilty.

The streets changed from cobblestone to gravel, from gravel to muck and dirt. She'd visited the neighborhood of Cheapside before.

The area hadn't improved. Poverty clung to the smudged shops, businesses, and tenements like moss on a tree. The residents of Cheapside ranged from the tattered poor to the rough working class. And criminals.

When the hackney pulled up outside its destination, Kendra pushed open the door and leapt down.

"Wait here," she ordered the driver, then flagged down another young boy flitting about the street. *School, what school?*

Pointing at a half-timbered Tudor building that housed a pub that went by the name of Ye Old Beelzebub, she gave the kid a coin to find out if the person she wanted was inside, and to deliver the message that she needed to speak to him immediately. She promised another coin after he delivered the message.

The kid's eyes widened at the name she gave, but he looked more excited than scared about his errand. She watched him sprint away and disappear inside the tavern.

A prickly sensation on the nape of her neck warned Kendra that she was attracting unwanted attention from at least a dozen men on the street.

The hackney driver shifted in his seat uneasily. "Miss, maybe ye ought ter get inside the carriage—"

"Maybe ye ought ter shut yer mouth and let the lady be," said a man, advancing toward her with the slinky slyness of a tomcat. "The lady came ter ol' Cheapside for a reason."

Not taking his eyes off Kendra, he stepped close enough for Kendra to smell his fetid breath. "Only right ter give her a proper welcome."

Kendra narrowed her eyes at him, shifting subtly. "I appreciate the welcome, but I've got business with someone. I suggest that you move along."

The man's face hardened. "Aw, now, that don't seem friendly. Looks like you need ter be taught some manners, yer ladyship."

He reached for her. She didn't hesitate, whipping her pistol out of the reticule and drilling the muzzle into the man's forehead. His eyes bulged and his mouth dropped open, and he scrambled back a step. She followed, her hand rock-steady, finger on the trigger as she pinned her eyes on his.

"Eh, now, ye be careful with that barkin' iron. It could go off!"

"Yes, it could. And if it does, you're going to have a hole in your head. But, hey, look on the bright side. There's a good chance the bullet will miss your brain, because it's so damn tiny. Hands up! Lace your fingers together at the back of your head. *Now.*"

"Damnation." But he obeyed.

The other men circling them stared at her with wide eyes. But they didn't advance. Yet.

"Fokking hell!"

Kendra looked up at the reason for her visit here: Bear, aka Guy Ackerman, aka London's most infamous crime lord. She'd forgotten how enormous he was: at least six-five, with a massive chest and bulging muscles. He had the kind of face only a mother could love, and even that was debatable, given how soulless his mud-brown eyes were at times.

Those eyes were now staring at her in amazement.

"What are ye doin'?" he demanded.

"Getting to know the locals. What the fuck does it look like I'm doing?" she shot back, glaring at him.

"Ye're a bloodthirsty wench," Bear muttered.

Kendra ignored the insult, instead focusing back on her captive. "I'm going to let you go, but the next time you decide to be *friendly* to a woman, make sure she wants your attention. Do you understand?" She pressed the gun's muzzle into his forehead, hard enough to leave an indentation, when his lips started to curl in a snarl. "I'll ask you again. Do. You. Understand?"

"Aye, aye!" he gulped. "I understand!"

She kept the gun aimed at him but took a step back, then another. His eyes burned with fury, hatred, and humiliation. She braced herself for retaliation, but the man blanched when Bear growled, "Get off with ye, ye stupid scum!"

Kendra wasn't surprised when the man took off running. The crowd around them melted away just as quickly.

Bear planted his hands on his hips and declared, "Ye're as mad as a fokking hatter." Then his lips trembled and he began to laugh, a big, booming sound that drew the attention of passers-by, who just as quickly averted their eyes as soon as they realized who was laughing.

She didn't blame them. She'd had an odd relationship with Bear ever since he'd kidnapped and tried to kill her and Alec the year before. The way she saw it, she'd threatened to blow the criminal's balls off, so they were even. Unfortunately, Alec didn't see it the same way.

"I'm glad you think this is funny." Kendra pulled a coin from her purse, pressed it into the kid's palm, then turned back to Bear. "I need to talk to you."

"Aye, so I was told." He folded his arms in front of his immense chest. "This is about the gentry mort that offed herself at Bowden's?"

Kendra couldn't hide her surprise. "How'd you know?"

He snorted. "'Cause it sounds like somethin' ye'd get tangled up in. Why d'ye care that she brained herself?"

"She didn't kill herself. She was murdered."

"Wot's it ter do with me if me betters kill each other off?"

"How do you know the killer is . . . one of your betters?"

"Who else would kill some uppity gentry mort but one of their own?"

"Have you heard about anyone being contracted to kill her?"

Bear cocked an eyebrow at her. "Now, why should I tell ye?"

"Aside from being a good citizen? Queen Charlotte asked me to personally look into the matter."

Kendra had introduced the Queen's name to emphasize the importance of the investigation, but was astonished to see real fear flash in Bear's eyes.

He lifted his hand, as if to ward off something evil. "I don't know nothin'."

"You haven't heard, or you don't want to say?"

"Both," he retorted, then hesitated. "I ain't heard nothin'," he admitted. "And I would have, if someone was hired ter stop a noblewoman's claret. Word gets around in the stews. Particularly word like that."

"I believe you. How about word on the street about an actress named Clarice Chapman going missing?"

He scowled. "Nay."

"Another actress—Isabella Russo? Or any other women missing? Actresses, prostitutes?"

Bear rolled his eyes. "Blimey, who do ye think I am? Chits come and go all the time. I ain't their keeper."

"How about women found drained of their blood?"

"W'ot?" His eyes widened, and Kendra thought she saw a flicker of interest stir behind his flat gaze.

"Clarice Chapman's body was pulled from the Thames. They called her a mermaid in the papers." Kendra watched him closely, saw recognition flash briefly across his face. "She didn't die of drowning, though. She died of exsanguination—someone drained all her blood."

"Christ. Why'd they do that?"

"She had syphilis. I think someone was experimenting with ways to cure her."

"What kind of ningimmer would bleed anyone dry?"

Kendra had to ask: "Ningimmer?"

"A leech that treats someone with the French Pox."

"That's what I need to find out," she said. "You're in a position to hear things, Bear. I'd appreciate it if you let me know if you hear about any other women . . ." Was there politically correct language to describe a woman in the lower classes? "Women who are *not* gentry morts disappearing or being found dead under suspicious circumstances. Or if you hear about anything odd going on."

He gave her a quizzical look. "Odd, how?"

"Maybe someone promising to cure syphilis or some other disease."

"There's no cure for the French Pox."

"That doesn't mean someone isn't promising one," she said. "I'm just asking you to keep your eyes and ears open. Also, there's another girl—Edwina. A seamstress from the Bowden Theater. Young, with a scarred face from a fire. We had reports that she might be somewhere on the docks. I'm looking for her, but so is the killer. I'd appreciate you letting me know if you hear anything that could help find her." She swung herself up into the hackney. "Send word to Number 15 Bedford Square."

She shut the door, only for Bear to knock on the window. She fumbled with the latch, finally dropping down the glass pane.

"What?"

"Ye still with yer tulip?" he demanded.

"I am." She rapped on the ceiling and the hackney started to pull away from the curb. She popped her head out the window to flash the crime lord a grin. "I *married* the tulip."

# TWENTY-NINE

And she had to admit that she was a little bit nervous how that tulip would react to her meeting with Bear. The relief that rushed through her was almost embarrassing when she returned home and learned that Alec hadn't yet arrived. She had every right to pursue the investigation as she saw fit. And how many criminals had she pumped for information in the twenty-first century? If Alec didn't understand that . . . well, she'd deal with it.

And she'd have to deal with it. The servants clearly already knew about her errand. She could see it in Wakely's face, although he'd never question her about her decision to send Coachman John home without her. But that didn't mean they didn't talk.

Needing a jolt of caffeine to shake off the afternoon slump, Kendra ordered coffee for the library. Ten minutes later, she was drinking it while she considered the Metamorphosis Club.

Metamorphosis meant change, transformation. Its members believed that science and medicine needed to evolve. Most were satisfied to keep their ideas to the theoretical realm, gathering to puff on cigars, drink brandy, and discuss possibilities. What if at least one member wasn't content to simply *talk* about what could be done? It wasn't too much of a stretch to think they'd transformed talk into real-life research, using human beings as guinea pigs.

She knew what it was like to be a guinea pig.

She took a swallow of coffee and forced herself to consider Clarice. She hadn't been snatched off the streets. She'd volunteered for the experimental treatment. Why wouldn't she? People trusted doctors. And she had a fatal disease. What did she have to lose?

Nothing, except her life.

Syphilis would eventually kill her, but a person could live with the disease for years, even decades. The killer had robbed her of that time.

*The killer . . . or killers?* Kendra had to consider the possibility that more than one member of the Metamorphosis Club was involved.

"Once again, I find my wife in fierce concentration."

Kendra didn't exactly jump, but she certainly started and spun around to find her husband walking toward her.

"You remind me of Duke when he's in his laboratory," Alec went on, taking the cup out of her hand and stealing a sip. "Care to tell me what you did this afternoon?"

Kendra searched his face, but it was unreadable. "You first. What was the business venture that His Grace wanted you to look at?"

He didn't answer immediately as he strolled to the sideboard. "Intriguing," he finally said, topping off her cup with fresh coffee from the pot. "Mr. Ronalds has a new invention that uses iron wire to conduct electrical signals. He actually managed to send a signal eight miles away."

"Wow. A whole eight miles?"

He grinned, handing her the coffee cup. "Minx. Whilst such technologies seem archaic to you, I can assure you, it is quite innovative. Mr. Ronalds is trying to drum up support for his invention, especially after Mr. Barrows dismissed it as frivolous."

"I see. Who is Mr. Barrows?"

"Second Secretary of the Admiralty. Mr. Ronalds believes we can free ourselves from pen, paper, and post by sending communications electrically instead."

"Morse code," Kendra murmured, and then her eyes widened. "Are you talking about Sir Francis Ronalds?"

Alec studied her. "Fascinating. He hasn't been knighted—yet, apparently. You've heard of him then? In your America?"

"Well, he's not exactly a household name," she admitted. "I took a few engineering courses when I was at Princeton, and there was a debate over whether Sir Francis Ronalds should be considered the first electrical engineer."

She sucked in a breath, suddenly feeling unsteady, and moved to the desk to set down her cup. "It's so weird. Sometimes I feel like I'm living two lives," she whispered, "one overlapping the other."

Alec came to her and put his hands on her shoulders. "No," he said when their eyes met. "You're living one life, Kendra. *This* life, with me. The other is just memories."

"Memories of things to come."

He rubbed her shoulders. "I can understand how your unique experience may be distracting at times."

She laughed, but there was no amusement in the sound. "It's damn distracting. You just viewed an experiment that will eventually lead to technologies that I use—I *once* used—in my daily life. It's . . ."

"Weird," he finished for her.

For some reason that made her laugh, and this time the laughter was genuine. "Yes. It is. And it's very short-sighted of your Mr. Barrows to reject it. I wonder how much more advanced the world would have been if England had financed the project?"

"Based on what little you've told me about the innovations in your America, I'd say civilization hasn't suffered unduly by having to wait. My uncle is interested in investing in Mr. Ronalds' invention."

She bit her lip with worry. "Don't do it because of what I just told you. As far as I know, this experiment will fail and his investors will lose all their money until he finally strikes it rich decades from now."

"All investments are a gamble, Kendra. There was no guarantee when Duke and I invested in Richard Trevithick's steam engine or countless canal projects in the last decade that they'd be successful." He smiled at her. "Don't worry, sweetheart. We shan't be punting on the River Thames anytime soon. Most of our investments are in our estates, the land, from which we derive a steady profit—although this summer has been so cold that the harvest has been bloody miserable." He skimmed his fingers down her arms in one, long caress. "Now, if you tell me that they've invented a machine to control the weather . . ."

She gave a quick laugh. "Not in my time. Nothing like the weather to make human beings feel powerless."

"Very true." He released her to pour himself a brandy at the sideboard, then glanced at her over his shoulder, one dark eyebrow lifting. "Well, I've told you how I spent my afternoon. Do you want to tell me why you disappeared after the postmortem, only to return home in a hired hackney?"

She hunched her shoulders in a defensive posture. "Wakely's a tattletale."

"Actually, Ramsey told me. Was it your intent to keep it a secret from me?"

She blew out a breath. "No."

"Well, then . . ."

"You know that you married a woman who is smart and capable and very good at her job, right?"

"I count my blessings for it every day."

Her eyes narrowed. "Do I hear sarcasm?"

"Are you stalling?"

"Okay, okay. I went to talk to Bear." Despite her best efforts, the words came out in a rush. She kept her gaze on Alec's impassive face. "He might hear talk on the street about the disappearances of actresses or sex workers. Or if there's buzz about someone claiming to have a cure for syphilis."

"Bear," was all he said, without any inflection.

"I need information, Alec." She gestured to the slate board. "I can't afford to turn down any resource, and Bear is a valuable one."

"He's a bloody criminal."

"Well, yeah. I've dealt with criminals before, you know. It's standard procedure. Work with a smaller fish to catch the bigger fish."

"Bear *is* the bigger fish."

"If my goal was to take down his criminal enterprise, yeah, he would be. But I'm not interested in him or what he does. I'm looking for a murderer, Alec. And I need answers."

"Why do you think that man can provide you with answers?"

She took a moment to consider her answer. "Your world has a class system—"

He paused in taking a sip of his brandy. "And yours doesn't?"

"It absolutely does. But people can move more easily between the classes. Here, it's more rigid, and I need to be able to go to every level, to question everyone. Bear knows what's happening on the street, in the rookeries and flash houses. He knows things that you or the Duke won't hear in your clubs, and that I can't learn from Lady St. James or even Lady Harrington."

She walked over to him and captured his free hand, lacing their fingers together as she met his eyes. "I've dealt with a lot of Bears in my life, Alec. You need to trust me to do my job, to be able to handle myself."

She waited for what seemed like an eternity. She couldn't read his expression.

"I do trust you," he finally said.

"Good."

"I also think that Mr. Kelly could have spoken to Bear. You didn't have to do it."

"Alec—"

"And you don't trust me."

She jerked back. "That's crazy! Of course, I trust you."

"You don't, otherwise you would have confided in me what you planned to do. Instead, you snuck away from the anatomy school and sent Coachman John home without giving him an explanation."

She said nothing for a beat, then, "Point taken. But it's not because I don't trust you. I didn't trust your coachman to take me where I needed to go. I didn't want the argument. But I promise you that I didn't do it with the intention of hiding it from you." She searched his eyes. "Do you believe me?"

He brought their laced hands up and brushed a kiss along her knuckles. "I believe you." He gave her a crooked smile. "I always knew that marriage to a woman from the future wasn't going to be easy."

Kendra slowly released her breath. Marriage, she decided, was a mysterious landscape, with continually shifting boundaries.

He said, "Promise me, though, that in the future, you will use our carriage, not a public hackney, when you go about town. No sense spending money on public transportation when you've a perfectly good carriage at your disposal."

She gave him a pointed look. "And a coachman with a blunderbuss at *his* disposal."

"Does he? Why, yes, I believe he does."

Kendra laughed, then sobered instantly, fixing her gaze on his. "Are we good?"

"We're better than good, my love." He leaned down and kissed her. "By the by, the inquest is tomorrow morning at nine. As I discovered the body, I'll need to testify."

"*We* discovered the body."

"Yes, but since we were together, you aren't required to attend. The magistrate is no doubt protecting your ladylike sensibilities." He grinned at her and gave her another kiss, slower this time. She tasted the brandy on his tongue.

"He doesn't realize you are a ferocious creature," he added when he released her.

Her chin jerked up. "I'm going."

"I had no reason to think otherwise. Did you learn anything from the postmortem?"

Maybe because she'd expected more of an argument, she had to take a moment to recalibrate. "Thornton's and Jenny's throats were cut using a scalpel."

He threw her a startled look. "Well, that certainly supports your hypothesis that a physician or surgeon is responsible. Unless that's the fiend's intention."

Kendra had to grin. "You've got a very suspicious mind, my lord. I like it."

He chuckled. "But you don't believe the fiend was trying to deceive authorities?"

"No. There were no hesitation marks. Who uses a scalpel with such comfort, such confidence and ease, that they can slice through flesh and muscle on the first try?"

"I imagine that's a rhetorical question, but I'll say it—a surgeon."

"Oh, yeah."

Kendra ran through her theory that they were dealing with a rogue doctor—or doctors. When she was done, Alec eyed her over the rim of his glass. "You believe we're dealing with more than one killer?"

"Not necessarily," she said slowly. "I'm talking about the experiments. Dr. Thornton knew about them, or suspected. It's not difficult to believe that a few like-minded individuals decided to work together in their research."

"Good God. You could be talking about the entire club."

"I think we're dealing with two people, maybe three. I don't see many more than that."

"Why?"

She smiled. "To quote Benjamin Franklin, 'Three can keep a secret if two are dead.' People talk. It's human nature. The more people involved, the more likely that word would've gotten out, especially if they're excited about their research."

He shook his head. "You say research like it didn't involve killing a young woman. Maybe more women, seeing as Isabella Russo has disappeared."

"Whatever happened to Clarice—or Isabella—I don't think they considered it murder. *Exitus acta probat*—any death is justified by the end result of what they're hoping to accomplish."

But how, Kendra wondered, could they think draining Clarice of all her blood would save her? Even quack doctors in this century had to know that a human couldn't live without blood for any length of time. Unless . . .

"Was it supposed to be a transfusion of some kind?" Kendra asked aloud. She locked eyes with Alec.

"If so, they forgot to replace it," Alec said dryly.

"The Metamorphosis Club is meeting tonight at Sir Preston's," she told him. "They'll be honoring Dr. Thornton, raising a toast in his memory. Hopefully we'll be able to figure out more from that."

And she knew deep in her gut that there would be one member lifting his glass to honor the man that he'd murdered.

# THIRTY

At 8:00 p.m., a long-faced butler escorted Kendra, Alec, and the Duke through Sir Preston's neoclassical mansion in the fashionable Portman Square. It felt like walking through a museum rather than a home, with the gray-veined marble floors; Ionic columns framing wide doorways; life-sized, exquisitely carved Hellenistic sculptures; rococo artwork hanging on the walls.

In the drawing room, a footman came forward carrying a silver platter. Instead of drinks, though, it held black strips of fabric: mourning armbands. While the Duke and Alec put them on, Kendra surveyed the room. Area rugs in burnished gold, muted greens, and grayish-blues softened the space up a bit, as did the sofas and chairs arranged in conversational pockets. Twenty-plus men, all wearing black armbands, were talking in low voices around the room. A few occupied chairs; others stood in front of the enormous fireplace with a marble-and-wood mantle, taking advantage of the warmth of the fire raging in the grate. Most of the men, however, were crowded in front of the long buffet, which carried an assortment of drinks on one end and platters of food on the other.

Kendra noticed Dr. Munroe in the group near the fireplace, while Dandridge, Goldsten, and Burnell were near the buffet table. There were other faces that were familiar—from Goldsten's surgery and St. George's. She recognized Mr. Barts, Mr. Dawes, and Mr. Beane among the apprentices.

The only other woman in the room was a frail old woman wearing a gown the color of a ripe eggplant, sitting in one of the chairs. No one was talking to her, leaving her to quietly observe the circulating men as she sipped her sherry.

Sir Preston, his age-speckled hand curving over the silver handle of his walking stick, ambled over to greet them. "Lord and Lady Sutcliffe. And Your Grace!" His wrinkles deepened with his smile. "Delighted to see you again, sir. When was the last time? The lecture on astronomy that Mr. Herschel gave at the Royal Society, I believe?"

The Duke inclined his head. "Yes, and I would wish for a happier reason to meet again, Sir Preston. My condolences on the loss of your colleague."

"Thank you. Lucien was a friend as well as one of the finest physicians in London." He glanced away and sighed. "I confess, I'm still in shock about this whole business. Who would do such a thing? What possible motive could they have? 'Tis madness."

Kendra studied their host. "How long did you know Dr. Thornton?"

He blinked at the question. "Oh, goodness. Forty years, at least. He was actually my apprentice when he was only a young pup starting out. Brilliant mind. I recognized it the instant I met him."

"You must have known his wife."

"Yes, indeed." His lips compressed into a tight seam of sorrow. "Another tragedy. Lucien was a young physician at that point. Not afraid to get his hands dirty, as it were, unlike those who aspire only to coddle the wealthy by handing them tonic water and tinctures. When Elizabeth was diagnosed, Lucien knew . . . well, we both knew. Still, he tried everything. Those are the times that remind us how limited our medical knowledge is."

"Ah, beating a familiar drum, Sir Preston," said Burnell, as he and Dandridge strolled over to join them.

"It's a drum you beat loudly yourself, sir."

"Yes, indeed. And I will continue to beat it until real reform is done. Lord and Lady Sutcliffe." Burnell acknowledged them with a slight bow, then turned to the Duke. "Your Grace. You probably don't remember, but we were introduced at the London Institution a few years ago."

"'Tis good to see you again, Mr. Burnell," the Duke said politely.

"Do you specialize in any particular disease, Mr. Burnell?" Kendra asked.

He gave her a strange look. "Specialize? No. I can't imagine anyone limiting their skills or interest to only one illness."

"Sir Preston."

At the high-pitched, croaky voice, the group of men parted to allow the old woman Kendra had noticed earlier to join them. She followed protocol, waiting for her husband to introduce her as Lady Maude, then said, "This is an informal gathering to pay respects to Dr. Thornton, but please avail yourself of refreshments and food."

Lady Maude skillfully ushered them to the buffet table. Kendra got the impression that the woman had been playing hostess to her husband's colleagues for decades. Maybe half a century, based on her wrinkles and the hairs sprouting from her chin.

After accepting a glass of wine, Kendra somehow found herself culled from the men, sitting in a chair opposite Lady Maude.

"I confess, it's rather nice to have another lady present at these soirees," Lady Maude said, taking a sip of her sherry before pinning Kendra with an intelligent gaze. "However, you're not here to simply pay your respects, are you? Sir Preston tells me that you are investigating Lady Westford's death."

"I am. Did you know her?"

"Oh, yes. We worked together on several committees at St. George's. I wouldn't say we were friends, but we had our mutual passions. I quite liked her. And I never believed the fustian that she threw herself off that theater balcony. Nor could I imagine her being so butter-fingered to accidentally fall off, no matter what Lucien said."

Kendra regarded the old woman. "Why do you think he made that determination, then?"

"Lord Westford, no doubt. Trying to stop the investigation."

"You think Lord Westford killed his wife?"

"Oh, good heavens, no! He's a lord of the realm. No, no. I

expect he simply didn't want the gossip associated with an investigation."

Kendra didn't understand why a lord of the realm would get a pass on murder any more than why gossip was more important than getting justice. But since she was no longer focused on Lord Westford as a suspect, she let it go.

"When was the last time you saw Lady Westford?"

Lady Maude took another swallow of her sherry. "Our last meeting at St. George's. Monday afternoon—a week before her death."

"What was the meeting about?"

Lady Maude raised her eyebrows a fraction, as though surprised to be asked such a question. "Whether we ought to use the funds we'd raised for repairs, or wait until a decision was made to tear down the hospital. Grace—that is, Lady Westford—and I were in accord in not wanting to throw good money after bad."

"Did she appear worried or upset to you?"

"I don't recall her being blue-devilled. She wasn't in high spirits or particularly happy, but she was never a flighty, frivolous creature."

"Did she talk to you about anything aside from hospital business?"

"Not then."

"She did other times?"

Lady Maude gave a delicate shrug. "She was an intelligent woman. Of course, we spoke about different subjects. She had a passion for natural philosophy, and while I can't say that I share it, I've certainly been exposed to it through my husband."

"Did she talk to you about her interest in advancing medicine— coming up with new treatments, curing disease?"

"Well, yes. She and Mr. Jenner were engaged in a lively correspondence. She was quite fascinated by how he first began experimenting with cowpox. He also conducted experiments with human blood that quite intrigued her."

Kendra found herself leaning forward. "What kind of experiments?"

"Oh, goodness, I don't know. You ought to ask my husband . . . or anyone else here."

"Has anyone here experimented with human blood? Maybe bloodletting or transfusions?"

"Bloodletting, yes. What reputable physician or surgeon has not? But blood transfusions are illegal in this country, my lady. Though I expect, as an American, you aren't familiar with English law."

Lady Maude lifted the wineglass to her lips, then paused and eyed Kendra. "That's not to say there aren't many discussions at my husband's meetings on how to treat and even cure illnesses by introducing a vaccine into the bloodstream or purifying the blood in some fashion."

"Purifying the blood how?"

"Oh, that I can't tell you. I don't actually attend the meetings when Sir Preston is the host. I've helped as hostess and have overheard a few things."

"Sir Preston founded the club, didn't he?" Kendra asked politely.

"Yes, along with Lucien—Dr. Thornton—and Mr. John Hunter." Lady Maude tilted her bristly chin up, her eyes glowing with pride. "He was renowned in the medical circles here. Unfortunately, the club was still new when he had his seizure and died."

Kendra made a sympathetic noise.

"Sir Preston and Lucien paid tribute to Mr. Hunter by continuing his practice of allowing members to join based on merit and experience, rather than following a patronage-based system. Oh, I know what you are thinking, my lady." The matron smiled at her. "My husband is a baron, and some might say he's benefited from the patronage-based system, but he's never relied on it. He is a strong believer in medical knowledge and skill."

Kendra hadn't been thinking anything of the sort, but now asked, "He believes in pushing the boundaries of science?"

"Every Metamorphosis Club member believes true discovery comes only from pushing boundaries."

"Is there anyone in the club more likely to try it?"

Lady Maude's eyes narrowed a fraction. "What an odd question, my lady. Whatever do you mean?"

"I was just wondering if anyone had been particularly vocal about the rules and regulations that keep medicine from advancing. I can imagine that would be frustrating."

Lady Maude pursed her lips. "Well, all the members find that quite vexing."

"Is anyone here known for bending the rules for the sake of medicine?" Kendra asked.

The old woman studied her carefully. "Yes," she replied. "Dr. Munroe. The law is quite strict in the use of cadavers for medical examination. Sir Preston says it's impossible to treat the body when one doesn't even know how it works."

"He's right." Kendra summoned a smile, even as she believed that Lady Maude knew a lot more than what she was letting on.

～

After extracting herself from Lady Maude's company, Kendra joined a circle of men that included Burnell, Dandridge, and Goldsten's two apprentices, Mr. Beane and Mr. Dawes.

"My lady." Dandridge smiled in greeting, but it vanished when he said, "Ethan told us that you found Thornton's body. That must have been a shock."

"It's not something you want to find," she acknowledged.

Burnell scowled. "I'm beginning to agree with those who want to set up a police force like Glasgow's. God-fearing citizens in their own homes shouldn't fear common filth from the stews."

Kendra eyed him. "You think Dr. Thornton and Jenny's murders were random crimes?"

"What else could it have been? Clearly, housebreakers didn't realize Lucien was at home."

She could give him a long list of reasons why that theory didn't hold water, but she kept it simple: "Nothing was stolen."

Burnell pursed his lips. "Alarmed, no doubt, by their own act of violence. Criminals are, at heart, cowardly creatures."

"Not so cowardly that they wouldn't have grabbed a few valuables on their way out the door. And,"—Kendra paused, watching Burnell closely—"they wouldn't have chosen a scalpel as their murder weapon."

Dandridge looked shocked. "How do you know that a scalpel was used?"

"Mr. Barts did the postmortem," Munroe said as he and Alec joined the group. "I supervised. Lady Sutcliffe is correct—a scalpel was the murder weapon."

Burnell's lip curled. "I suppose you'll now be quizzing us on where we were last night?"

Dandridge's mouth dropped open. "You can't possibly think one of us would harm him?"

"It's a routine question."

"Well, it's insulting." But then Dandridge seemed to take a beat and reconsider. "What time did it . . . did it happen?"

"Let's say sometime between six and twelve that night."

"I was at St. George's until half-past seven. Then Andrew—Mr. Dawes—and I had dinner together. We were together until nearly ten. Isn't that right, Mr. Dawes?"

Dawes looked a little startled to have been spoken to, but quickly nodded. "Yes, sir. We dined at the Gray Goose Inn, near St. George's."

"And after ten?" Kendra asked.

"I went home. Had a nightcap and went to bed. It'd been a long day." Dandridge looked at Dawes. "Andrew?"

"I met Mr. Beane and Mr. Sumner at the Swan—it's a pub on Piccadilly. We had a few rounds there, then went to one of the gaming clubs." Dawes threaded his fingers through his ginger hair, a nervous gesture. "I lost," he admitted. "My stepfather shall ring a peel over my head when he finds out."

Mr. Beane nodded. "I was with Mr. Dawes. We didn't leave the gaming tables until well after one in the morning."

Burnell blew out a breath. "To be young again, when one could burn the candle at both ends. I left St. George's shortly before five and was at home for the rest of the evening. Unfortunately, I was alone."

Kendra regarded him steadily. "You seem to spend most of your free time alone, Mr. Burnell."

"I'm of an age at which I prefer my own company to being forced to make tedious conversation with others," he said, with a smile that reminded Kendra instantly of her father. *Arrogant asshole.*

"The conversations that you've had with your fellow members in the Metamorphosis Club aren't tedious, Mr. Burnell," she shot back. "There's been talk of curing diseases through the blood, by introducing a vaccine or purifying the blood itself in some way. Interesting stuff."

Burnell's gaze sharpened. "We've discussed many theories on how to use the circulatory system to treat illnesses."

"We have so much to learn," Mr. Beane spoke up. "We haven't had any advancement in that area since William Harvey's theories on blood flow."

"And Harvey was roundly trounced by the medical establishment in his time," said Sir Preston, walking over with the Duke. The circle opened to include them.

"Forgive me, I couldn't help but overhear your fascinating discussion," Sir Preston said, offering Kendra a benevolent smile. "The reason the Metamorphosis Club was formed was to introduce any and all ideas without fear of being disparaged."

Kendra took a sip of her wine as she surveyed the men around her. "Do you think a person's blood can be removed and purified in some way?"

"Are you, perchance, referring to the body stolen from Munroe's morgue?" Burnell guessed.

"Blimey," said a pimply-faced young man standing with three other youths in their own cluster. They'd clearly been eavesdropping and now inserted themselves into the circle. "My uncle owns a plantation in the Caribbean. There are stories of a *soucouyant*," he went on. "It's a demon that disguises itself as an old woman in the day, and at night, it slips out of its human skin and becomes a fireball, invading bedrooms and sucking the blood out of its victims."

Kendra was reminded of Muldoon's *Dearg-due*.

"Another reason to avoid the company of old women," laughed one of his cohorts. His friend gave him a warning nudge, shooting a glance at Lady Maude, still in her chair and now chatting with Goldsten.

"I'm looking for a more scientific explanation," Kendra said dryly.

Sir Preston shook his head. "There can be no scientific explanation for draining someone completely of their blood supply, madam. At least not in our modern age."

"No, but using blood as a cure for ailments is not new," Mr. Beane said, his dark eyes serious. "In ancient Rome, the blood of gladiators who'd been defeated in the Coliseum was used to treat disease. There are tales that the sick would rush the arena to drink the fallen gladiator's blood while it was still warm."

Burnell looked amused. "Where did you hear of such barbarism, Mr. Beane?"

The apprentice's chin jerked up. "The Roman physician Scribonius Largus wrote about the practice. It wasn't just drinking the blood either. Spectators would dig out and consume the gladiator's liver, believing it would cure them of any disease with which they were afflicted."

Dawes nodded. "I read that a couple of centuries ago, a Franciscan apothecary made a jam mixture from blood, which he sold to those wishing to increase their vitality."

"And there are reports of bystanders consuming the blood of those executed by *La Guillotine*," added another young man. "That wasn't very long ago."

"Ignorant peasants," Burnell snorted.

"It's been said that King Louis XI and Pope Innocent VIII both were known to consume the blood of young boys to give them back their strength," said Sir Preston mildly.

"What can you expect from the French and Catholics?" a man named Tyson muttered.

"The Catholic Pope didn't consume blood like your mythical *soucouyant*, Mr. Tyson," Dawes argued. "He was given a transfusion while on his deathbed, in the hope that it would rejuvenate him."

Mr. Tyson's lip curled. "Not only barbaric, but foolish too."

Burnell's mouth thinned. "We are practicing our own barbarism by not allowing scientific exploration when it comes to our life blood. We know so little and are hamstrung in every way from pursuing what could be life-saving knowledge."

That declaration received vigorous nods and a few frowns. Their group had grown to include everyone in the room, with the exceptions of Goldsten and Lady Maude.

"From my understanding, safeguards were put into place after the disastrous experiments in the seventeen-hundreds," the Duke said quietly. "King Louis XIV's physician, Jean-Baptiste Denis, killed a man by giving him a transfusion."

"Yes, but that was after several *successful* transfusions," Burnell pointed out. "Denis gave a fifteen-year-old suffering from fever and excessive bloodletting a transfusion of sheep's blood, and the boy lived. One might even say it saved his life."

"The French were only replicating what we English were doing at the time," Dandridge said, taking a sip of his drink. "It was Richard Lower who documented his experimental transfusions with dogs, which eventually led him to give a patient a transfusion of lamb's blood."

Kendra stared at the surgeon. "And the patient lived?" she had to ask.

Dandridge nodded. "He did, indeed. He even had another transfusion, with no ill effects."

*Holy shit.*

"That's true, but as Denis continued to experiment, more people died from the procedure," Munroe interjected. "He was eventually tried for murder when the wife of one of his patients died. He was acquitted, but the French government then banned the practice. The Crown and the Pope followed suit."

"As if it matters what the Papists do," Mr. Tyson sniffed.

Dandridge narrowed his eyes at the young man. "It matters when those in power restrict natural philosophy from advancing. Burnell is right. Think of all we have lost! Denis had only just begun to discover that certain bloods ought not be mixed. But why? What makes one person's blood different from another? How can we ever know without conducting research?"

After listening quietly, Kendra asked, "What about syphilis?"

That stopped the discussion, and everyone turned to look at her.

"What of it?" Burnell finally asked.

"Could someone be cured of syphilis through a blood transfusion?" She expected them to scoff at the idea, but several of the club members nodded.

"We discussed the possibility at one of our meetings," Sir Preston said. "And not only the pox. Any number of diseases."

Alec asked, "Did you reach a consensus?"

Burnell laughed. "In the Metamorphosis Club, there is no consensus, my lord. We discuss, challenge, theorize, and hypothesize. Alas, we do not agree."

"Yes, but we had many in agreement that the French pox is caused by some sort of blood mutation," said Mr. Tyson. "The mutation is no doubt caused by the poor living conditions of women of ill-repute." He cast Kendra an apologetic glance. "Begging your pardon, my lady."

"We cannot assume that," Sir Preston argued. "We need more research—"

"And how do we conduct research when we aren't allowed to test our theories?" Dandridge interjected. The surgeon sounded exasperated.

Munroe offered Kendra a wry smile. "This is a common theme among our members, my lady: frustration."

Sir Preston chuckled. "Ethan is right, and I suggest we put it aside—at least until our next meeting. Tonight is not about scientific inquiry, but to remember our colleague and friend. Let's raise a glass to his memory."

Kendra lifted her glass and let her gaze skim over the faces around her. Cold washed over her. Because she knew, absolutely *knew*, she was drinking with a murderer.

But who was it?

# THIRTY-ONE

The question haunted Kendra throughout the evening, as she maneuvered around the room, asking questions of each conversational group she entered and keeping thorough mental notes. She could eliminate some suspects easily, but others needed a deeper dive.

Goldsten eluded her. She wasn't sure if it was deliberate or not, but every time she joined a cluster that he was a part of, he managed to slide away. When she spotted him alone at the buffet, she abruptly left the trio of surgeons who'd been talking to her.

"Mr. Goldsten," she said.

He paused topping up his brandy to glance at her. "My lady," he said, and set the decanter down. "Would you like more wine?"

The lines of worry and fatigue that she'd noticed when she'd first met him had deepened into craters. He looked twenty years older than the last time she saw him.

He looked, she decided, like a man with a lot on his mind.

"No, thank you. I was hoping for a moment of your time."

Wariness flashed in Goldsten's eyes. "I was about to take my leave."

"This shouldn't take long." She gave a pointed look at the brandy he'd just refilled. "You'll be able to finish your drink."

His mouth turned down. "Very well."

"Why don't we step into the hallway? It'll give us more privacy."

In the marble hallway, Kendra stopped next to the sculpture of Tyche, the Greek goddess of prosperity and fortune. "You lied to me, Mr. Goldsten," she began.

Goldsten's nostrils flared at the blunt accusation, and something flickered behind his eyes. Fear? Or fury?

"What—"

"You told me that you hadn't seen Lady Westford since the lecture you attended, but that's not true, is it? You were seen together at St. George's last week—shortly before she died. You were arguing. Why did you lie?"

Goldsten's lips tightened, and he looked away for a long moment. "I did not murder Grace," he said finally.

Oddly enough, she believed him. "That's not what I asked. I want to know why you lied about the last time you saw her."

"Because I knew how it would appear. And I . . . I was ashamed."

"Ashamed of what?"

He sucked in a shaky breath, his lips twisting into a sad smile. "I shall rue my last moments with Grace until the day I die. I was upset and rough with her."

"You grabbed her?"

"I only touched her to emphasize my point."

*That explains the bruises on her arms*, Kendra thought.

"If I'd known that would be our last encounter . . . 'Tis a pathetic lament. One cannot wish away one's regrets."

"What were you arguing about?" she asked.

He averted his gaze. "Lady Westford was always passionate about her causes. She believed that St. George's was too far gone to be saved. I did not agree."

Kendra didn't bother to hide her skepticism. "Please. You're telling me that you were arguing about the hospital's future so passionately that you left bruises on her arms?"

He pressed his lips together and fixed his gaze on Tyche.

"*Exitus acta probat*," she said softly, and watched Goldsten's face pale. He looked back to her.

"W-what?"

"Did Lady Westford ever say that to you?"

"No. Why would she?"

Kendra ignored the question. "Did Lady Westford talk to you about meeting Clarice?" .

"I . . . no."

"Clarice had syphilis. Have you treated that disease?"

"Most of my patients are dockworkers and sailors. Of course, I've treated the French pox," he snapped.

"Have you heard anyone claim they found a new treatment or cure for it?"

"The treatment is almost as worse as the disease. There's no cure, other than those promised by charlatans seeking money. They're always claiming to cure diseases for the most gullible."

"Why would someone remove all of Clarice's blood?"

"Good God. How would I know?"

"I'm asking you as a surgeon, Mr. Goldsten. Could it be for a transfusion of some kind?"

"Transfusions are prohibited," he said stiffly. "And it involves an exchange of fluid. What is removed must be replaced."

"Dr. Munroe was given the body, and then it was stolen. But by a strange bit of luck, the body was found again. Except someone removed the corpse's eyes and uterus. Why would they do that?"

"Why are you asking me this?"

"I'm asking you for your medical opinion. To help me understand."

"I don't know. I can't help you. Clearly, those are the actions of a madman."

"Or someone conducting medical experiments." She kept her gaze locked on him. "Have you heard of anyone conducting experiments to treat syphilis or any other diseases?"

"No."

"*Exitus acta probat*," she repeated, and noticed this time that he was a little steadier. "If Lady Westford heard about someone conducting unorthodox medical tests, I can see where that would put her in a difficult position. She believed in advancing science, trying to find cures. Her sister died from typhus. If an experiment showed promise in curing that disease, even if there was a fatality, she might wonder if the end justified the means."

She paused. When Goldsten said nothing, she continued, "Dr. Thornton probably thought the same. He lost his wife to diabetes. What would he have given to find a cure? What would he overlook? What about you, Mr. Goldsten?"

He gave a small jerk. "What about me?"

"Did you lose someone to a disease that you would have given anything to find a cure for? Is that why you became a doctor?"

"I'm not a physician. I'm a sawbones. And most people—rich and poor—have known someone who has perished from an illness. Humanity is remarkably frail. Whoever discovers cures to the sickness that plague us will not only be honored, they'll be revered."

"Even godlike," Kendra said quietly. "That prospect might be enough to make a person kill anyone who stands in their way."

He took an unsteady breath. "I must go—"

"You need to *talk*, Mr. Goldsten." She stepped forward. "A woman you know, a woman that I think you cared for, maybe even loved, was murdered. She was chased—*stalked*—up four flights of stairs and thrown over the railing to her death. In her final moments, she would've known absolute terror. If you know who did that to her—"

"I *don't!*" The fury erupted, hot enough to scorch. His hand shook so badly that brandy threatened to spill out of his glass. He set it down and then turned back to her, a muscle pulsing in his jaw. "You don't know what you ask of me!"

"I'm asking for the truth."

"You're asking me to destroy my life!" He pointed to the drawing room's closed door. "Do you think it's easy for me, a Jew, to be accepted in there? I set my clinic up in the stews because those men don't care what I am when I'm removing balls of lead from their flesh or mending their broken bones. I've fought hard to practice medicine in London, much less at St. George's. I will—"

"Not get justice for Lady Westford, apparently," Kendra

snapped, cutting him off. He flinched as though she'd slapped him. "You pay a heavy price, Mr. Goldsten, for keeping secrets."

"I don't know who killed her!" he hissed, nostrils flaring. "I swear, I don't. I thought she'd killed herself. She'd seen—" He stopped suddenly and glanced uneasily at the door.

"What did she see? What do you *know*?" Kendra pressed.

Emotions, too fast to decipher, flickered across his face.

"Lady Westford isn't the only victim," she reminded him softly. "Thornton and Jenny are dead too. Not to mention the patients being treated. How many more people are going to die because you kept silent, Mr. Goldsten?"

Kendra could see him waver and felt a moment of triumph. Then the door to the drawing room opened, and Burnell, Dawes, and Beane poured out. They stopped in surprise when they saw Kendra and Goldsten in the hallway.

"Continuing your inquiries, my lady?" Burnell wondered.

Kendra didn't answer him. Instead, she asked, "You're leaving? It's a little early, isn't it?"

"I can't speak for these young bucks, but my day begins early tomorrow. Good evening, my lady." His expression was unreadable as he looked to the surgeon opposite her. "Mr. Goldsten."

The two apprentices muttered their goodbyes, as well, and hurried to catch up with Burnell. Dawes and Beane both cast curious glances over their shoulders, but Burnell never looked back.

Kendra waited for them to disappear from view before saying, "Mr. Goldsten—"

"I can't speak to you here." He licked his lips uneasily. "Tomorrow. Can you come to my clinic tomorrow morning? Or we could meet—"

"No. I'll come." She kept her tone neutral. "What time?"

"Ten o'clock?"

The inquest was scheduled for nine, but she didn't dare try to negotiate for a later time. She could tell that Goldsten was already regretting their appointment. "I'll be there. Thank you, Mr. Goldsten."

A muscle in his cheek jerked, and he looked as if he was going to say something. But in the end, he simply shook his head, turning to walk down the hallway.

232

# THIRTY-TWO

Kendra woke early the next morning. She cycled through her yoga routine as the sun—a rare sight—streamed through the bedchamber windows while Alec left for his morning ride.

Life was about patterns. She and Alec were finding their own, as they built their life together. There were a few bumps (Bear came to mind), but overall it felt good. Damn good.

Rising from the corpse pose, Kendra donned a robe and slippers and made her way to the library. In the hallway, a maid gave her a strange look, clearly not accustomed to encountering ladies running around before seven o'clock, and certainly not in dishabille with their hair tumbling down their back.

"My lady. A-are you looking for your maid?"

"No, I'm sure she's still sleeping. But I'd like coffee to be sent to the library, if it isn't too much trouble."

Another strange look. "No trouble at all, ma'am."

Kendra spent the next fifteen minutes reworking the slate board to her satisfaction. The coffee arrived and she held a cup, sipping occasionally as she studied the new information.

Murder investigations, she reflected, were a little like the embroidery upon which Lady Atwood spent so much time. You began with dozens of colorful skeins that needed to be separated into individual threads. Each thread was then applied to cloth, and slowly, slowly, a picture began to emerge.

The analogy reminded Kendra of Edwina. Clever with the needle, Prudence had said. Where was the girl? Was she even alive?

Edwina had worked with the theater's seamstress, Old Beatrice, who had insisted to Sam that she didn't know anything. But was that true? Maybe she was like young Bridget, and didn't want to talk to law enforcement. Or maybe she needed time to think, to remember something that might help them find the girl.

After she met with Goldsten, Kendra would pay Old Beatrice a visit.

Kendra looked back to the slate board. Less than a dozen names now. Burnell's was at the top of the list. She didn't like him; he reminded her of her father. But that wasn't the reason he was the top suspect—was it?

She reviewed the evidence. He didn't have an alibi, had been home alone for both murders, for Christ's sake. But that bothered her. Burnell wasn't stupid. If he was going to kill someone, wouldn't he have a ready-made alibi in place?

Of course, he was also an arrogant prick. Maybe he was egotistical enough to think he didn't need to.

The library door sprang open and, with some surprise, Kendra watched Molly barrel into the room in a flurry of skirts.

"Miss—Oi mean, milady!" The maid put her small hands on her hips and glared at Kendra. "Ye can't go about lookin' like that! It ain't proper! Ye 'aven't even brushed yer 'air!"

Kendra glanced at the clock on the fireplace mantel. Time, she was shocked to see, had slipped away from her—it was close to eight-thirty.

"I was up early and wanted to work on a few things. I didn't want to wake you." Why was she apologizing? She was pretty sure there were rules in this era that ladies did not apologize to their maids and maids did not lecture ladies.

Molly's freckled face scrunched up in a scowl. "'Tis me job! If'n ye wander about 'alf-dressed, w'ot does that say about me?"

"So, what you're really concerned about is your reputation as a lady's maid?"

"It's the only reputation Oi 'ave, my lady," she sniffed. "It means somethin' ter me, even if ye don't care if Oi'm a laughingstock."

Kendra could deal with Molly's irritation, but not the hurt she heard in the girl's voice. "I'm sorry," she said—rules be damned. "I was trying to be considerate. It won't happen again."

Good grief, did she really just promise to *not* be considerate?

Shaking her head, she started for the door. "Let's go. I've got an appointment at ten. I don't want to be late."

Molly sniffed again, scurrying after her. "If ye'd 'ave waken me like a proper mistress, ye wouldn't 'ave ter fret about being late for yer appointment, now would ye?"

Though in the end, she didn't have to worry about being late for her appointment with Mr. Goldsten. Molly was putting the last touches on Kendra's hair when a note arrived from Sam Kelly: The surgeon had died at his clinic from a self-inflicted gunshot wound.

# THIRTY-THREE

Throngs of men—apprentices and patients alike—were huddled outside the door to Goldsten's laboratory. Kendra bulldozed her way through, earning a few grunts and annoyed exclamations.

"*Son of a bitch.*" The profanity was torn from her as soon as she crossed the threshold and her gaze landed on the surgeon sprawled on his back on the floor. Goldsten's eyes were open and glassy. A pistol lay at least a foot away. A black hole drilled into his right temple. Blood congealed on the floor and spotted Goldsten's cheek.

Sam was standing with two other men in front of a seated man. Kendra glimpsed red hair and a face pale enough to fit in with the patients in the ward. The man's expression was blank, his eyes pinpricks of shock.

"What the hell happened?" she demanded furiously.

Sam stepped over to her. "Self-murder."

"No fucking way! The gun is more than a yard away from him."

"Mr. Dawes came in when Mr. Goldsten was about ter pull the trigger. He ran over ter stop him, ter knock the gun out of his hand—but he was a second too late."

"Shit, shit." She couldn't seem to catch her breath. *Did I do this? I pushed and pushed . . .* "Mr. Dawes saw Goldsten kill himself." She looked at the apprentice. He'd buried his face in his hands, his shoulders shaking.

"Aye. The poor lad's torn up. Terrible thing ter witness."

Kendra pinched the bridge of her nose, trying to think. "He— Goldsten told me to meet him here at ten," she said, lowering her hand to level a hard look at the Bow Street Runner. "He was ready to talk!"

Sam said nothing.

She turned to the apprentice. "What happened, Mr. Dawes?"

"I told Mr. Kelly everything," he mumbled without looking up.

"You need to tell me." She realized Dawes was still wearing his heavy wool greatcoat. "When did you arrive, Mr. Dawes? Did Mr. Goldsten say anything to you when you came in?" She waited. Impatience sharpened her tone as she prompted, "Mr. Dawes?"

"Lass, he's in shock—"

"He's training to be a surgeon!" she snapped. *Damn it.* She forced herself to take a breath. "I'm sorry, Mr. Kelly, but if he can't handle what happened, I'd hate for him to operate on me in an emergency."

Dawes lifted his head to glare at her. Tears ran down his face. "He was my *friend*!"

"Then tell me what happened." But she softened her tone. "When you arrived this morning, what was Mr. Goldsten doing?"

"H-he just finished operating on a midshipman that had been shot in the leg. I went over to observe the procedure . . ." Dawes gulped, more tears spilling over. "This is terrible. A terrible loss."

"How was he? Was he behaving oddly? Was he upset?"

"He must have been. Oh, God, he must have been. He wouldn't have done what he did otherwise." He wiped his eyes with his coat sleeve. "I-it was terrible. More terrible than I could ever have imagined."

Sam rummaged through the desk and found a bottle of gin. *Secret stash?* Kendra wondered. More likely, the nineteenth century's answer to anesthesia.

Uncorking the bottle, Sam brought it over to Dawes. "Here, lad."

"Tell me what he did when he finished the surgery," Kendra said.

The apprentice took a swig of gin, choked and gasped, bringing fresh tears to his eyes. "He stopped to examine a few more patients and gave us instructions . . . . He told us that he needed a moment. He came in here, shut the door. I-I was . . . I couldn't believe it when I followed him in and saw the gun in his hand. Then—oh, God—he . . . h-he pressed it to his head." Dawes squeezed his eyes closed, sucked in a long, shuddery breath. "He looked at me. I think I shouted. Told him to stop. Stop! It happened so fast. I ran toward him. I ran, dear heaven. And he shot himself."

"Did he say anything to you when you opened the door?"

"I . . . no. I don't think so. I was so shocked. I tried to get to the weapon. That's all I could think. *Get the pistol.*" Dawes opened his eyes and lifted the bottle of gin, grimacing as he took another gulp. His face was no longer deathly pale, but flushed a rosy pink.

Kendra asked, "Why did you go after him, Mr. Dawes?"

The apprentice did a slow blink. "What?"

"He asked for a moment of privacy, but you didn't give him that moment. Why?"

"I . . ."Dawes' gaze slid over to where Goldsten's body was sprawled. He visibly shuddered. It seems so ridiculous now."

"What's ridiculous?"

"I wanted to do a rotation at St. George's this afternoon. I needed Mr. Goldsten's permission. I was scheduled to work here."

Kendra kept her gaze on him. "It's normal for you to do rotations at St. George's?"

He frowned. "Yes, of course. Everyone here puts in time at St. George's, including Mr. Goldsten."

"Are you assigned to a particular doctor when you do your rotations?"

"What does that have to do . . . with this?" His hand trembled as he gestured to the body.

"Do you have a problem answering the question, Mr. Dawes?"

A spark of annoyance lit his eyes. "Of course not. I usually assist Mr. Dandridge, Mr. Burnell, and Sir Preston. But it depends on what is happening at the hospital, and who requires assistance."

She waited a beat, then said, "You have blood on your hands, Mr. Dawes."

He lifted his palms, surveying the specks of blood like he'd never seen them before, and shivered. "Hazard of this profession, I'm afraid." His breath hitched a little. "I knew he was gone, but I still tried to . . . tried to save him."

The door opened, and Kendra glanced at Alec and Dr. Munroe as they came into the room. Alec walked over to her, placing a hand on her shoulder. "Dr. Munroe and I had just finished at the inquest when he got Mr. Kelly's note." He took in the scene. "Suicide?"

"Aye," Sam answered, and looked at Munroe with concern. "I didn't think before, but maybe we should call in someone else—"

"Nonsense." Munroe's tone was brusque. Kendra saw more than grief on his face. Anger tightened his features, burned in his eyes. He hunched down to examine the dead man. "I want to be involved, Mr. Kelly."

Sam shifted uneasily on his feet. "Aye. Well, it's pretty clear what happened, even if we didn't have an eyewitness to confirm it. But we'll need you for the inquest, doctor. And you, Mr. Dawes."

Munroe pointed at the ugly bullet hole. "The stellate shape around the wound indicates that the barrel was pressed directly against his skin when the gun was fired."

Kendra nodded. She'd already noted the injury's star-burst pattern.

"I don't understand this." Munroe slowly rose to his feet and looked to Kendra. "Why would he kill himself?"

Kendra had one answer, and it made her feel sick.

"May I . . . go?" Dawes ran a trembling hand through his red hair, leaving it in unruly tufts. "I've told you everything . . ."

Sam nodded. "Aye. I'll let you know when the inquest is."

Dawes nodded as he pushed himself to his feet and shuffled unsteadily to the door. Kendra felt a little unsteady herself.

"Kendra—" Alec began, but she put up a hand to stop him.

"It's my fault," she whispered. Bile rose up in her throat, leaving a bitter taste in her mouth. "I pressured him last night. He wasn't ready to talk, but I wouldn't listen. I didn't care."

"You think he knew who killed Lady Westford, but never said anything?" Sam asked.

Kendra shook her head. "I think he *suspected*, and was doing his best to pretend otherwise."

"But why?" the Bow Street Runner insisted. "And why would he blow out his brains before talkin' ter you, lass?"

Kendra pressed a fisted hand to her roiling stomach as she answered, "Last night, he told me how difficult it's been for him to become accepted in the medical community because he's Jewish. He was afraid he'd be ostracized and lose everything he'd worked for."

"His fear was justified." Munroe sounded weary. "Many voiced their reservations about allowing Mr. Goldsten into St. George's. Dr. Carter was the loudest in his objections. He's fond of saying that if the hospital lowered its standards to permit Jews to practice medicine, then we might as well open the doors to women."

Kendra wasn't surprised. The old geezer was against the freaking stethoscope.

"Sir Preston advocated for Mr. Goldsten to join both St. George's and the Metamorphosis Club," Munroe continued. "Mr. Goldsten never gave into the naysayers. How could he have done this? *This?*"

"I've known men who put a bullet in their brain after losing everything at the gaming tables," Alec murmured. "They couldn't face their families after what they'd done. If Mr. Goldsten truly believed he'd lose everything . . ."

That brought up an excellent point. Kendra turned to Munroe. "Does Mr. Goldsten have family?"

"He has a mother and a sister. They live in Fulham "

"They'll have to be notified and questioned," Kendra said as she crossed the room to Goldsten's desk. "Maybe he said something to them recently about his suspicions."

"I'll do it," Sam said, watching her as she sifted through the papers and books. "What are you doing, lass?"

"Looking to see if he left a note."

In truth, suicide notes were rare and never gave the family

closure. More often than not, the notes involved only instructions to mundane chores. But it could be useful.

Slamming a drawer shut, she sighed. "It doesn't look like he did."

"Maybe he left it in his home," Sam said. "We'll keep our peepers out."

Kendra nodded, and let her gaze drift back to Goldsten's body and the gun that lay a few feet away. She had to fight against another wave of nausea, and the rush of guilt that came with it. *What have I done?*

"Kendra," Alec murmured, touching her arm again.

"I'm okay." She wasn't. But this wasn't the time to fall apart.

She steeled her spine and followed Munroe and Sam out of the laboratory. In the ward, the handful of apprentices looked lost, baffled, and scared. Dawes, she noted, was gone. Mr. Beane had taken charge, issuing orders and hurrying from patient to patient. When he spotted them, he jogged over.

"This is dreadful, just dreadful," he said, shaking his head. "I don't know what to do. Andrew—Mr. Dawes and I are the senior apprentices here, but we're still learning from Mr. Goldsten." He swallowed and looked at Munroe. "What do I do?"

"Continue as you are," Munroe replied. "After I'm done at Bow Street, I shall go to St. George's and see if I can find another surgeon to offer you instruction and guidance. If no one is available, I shall do it myself."

Relief flooded the young man's face. "Thank you, Dr. Munroe."

Kendra asked, "Were you here when Mr. Goldsten arrived this morning?"

"Yes. I assisted him in removing a lead ball from a patient's leg. Nothing seemed amiss. I cannot believe he . . . he did what he did!"

"Did he say anything to you?"

"He certainly didn't say what he planned to do!" Mr. Beane scrubbed his palms over his face. "My God. We were shocked when we heard the gunshot."

"What did you do then?"

"What did we do? We—all of us—ran to the laboratory and . . . and saw what we did."

"What exactly did you see?"

"Mr. Goldsten on the floor. Andrew was down beside him. He was shaking, crying. He said . . . he said that he tried to stop him. It was awful." Mr. Beane blinked, then glanced away for a long moment.

"It was all so normal," he whispered on a ragged breath. He brought his gaze back to them, the expression in them dark and shattered. "I swear everything was normal . . . until it wasn't."

# THIRTY-FOUR

"You are not responsible for Mr. Goldsten's death," Alec said quietly as he walked Kendra to the carriage.

"Aren't I?" Her throat burned. She lifted her face to the sunshine, but felt cold. *So cold.* "I saw his desperation, but I kept pushing him. *Exitus acta probat.*" Her lips twisted in a humorless smile as she met her husband's eyes. "I didn't care about Mr. Goldsten's state of mind, even when he tried to tell me how difficult this would be for him."

Alec took her hand and squeezed it. "You weren't trying to satisfy your own morbid curiosity, Kendra. You're trying to identify a fiend who has killed at least three people. Maybe more, with these experiments."

"I know what it's like to be an outsider, Alec. To be watched and to worry that everything you've worked for might be taken away."

His green eyes were cool as he regarded her. "And what would you do if someone threatened to take it away?"

She frowned. "I don't know."

"*I* know. You would have fought. You certainly wouldn't have looked the other way while someone was harming people in order to preserve your bloody reputation. You're not a stupid woman, so, pray, don't act like one."

Kendra sucked in a sharp breath. "Wow." She tried to remove her hand from his, but he only tightened his hold. She glared at him. "Thanks for being *so* understanding."

"Do you want me to coddle you?"

She finally managed to yank her hand free. "No. Call me crazy, but I don't want the man's death on my conscience."

"You didn't put a gun to his head or in his hand—"

"Not literally, but figuratively—"

"Bugger that! He was a grown man, and he made a choice. I don't bloody well care if he thought his world was crumbling down around his ears. What he did was cowardly. It's the same cowardice I've seen with gamesters who couldn't face their wives and children after losing their homes. It has nothing to do with you."

"I failed to see how fragile his mental state really was."

"He cared more about his standing in the medical community than justice for a woman with whom he was involved."

Kendra pressed her fingers against her eyes as she considered Alec's words. "You're right," she finally said, dropping her hand. "I know you're right. But . . . this has messed me up. I don't understand why he did it."

"It's a senseless act, beyond comprehension."

She nodded, meeting his gaze. "You're right about that too. Thanks for giving me a kick in the ass."

Alec grinned. "A unique way of expressing gratitude, but you're welcome, darling." He took her hand again. "You're all right?"

"I will be."

"I'll see you at home?"

"Not yet. I want to stop at the Bowden Theater and interview the seamstress that Edwina worked with. Old Beatrice."

"Didn't Mr. Kelly interview her?"

"Yes, and she told him that she didn't know anything. But . . ." She lifted her shoulder in a half-shrug. "You know how people can be with law enforcement. Or maybe she's had a chance to think and has an idea where the girl might be hiding."

"Kendra—"

"I know—Edwina's probably dead."

"I was going to ask if you want me to go with you."

"Thanks, but it might be less intimidating if it's just me."

Alec smiled as he ran a gentle finger along her jaw, the gold flecks in his eyes brightening with his laughter. "No one could ever believe that you are less intimidating than me, my love."

It may have been before noon, but the Bowden Theater already had the same chaotic energy that Kendra had witnessed on her first visit. While there were no actors rehearsing lines on stage at the moment, stagehands sawed and hammered backdrops and several acrobats practiced their flips and rolls. The smell of sawdust tickled her nose as she mounted the steps to the stage. Mr. Myott was absent, she noted.

One of the workers paused when he spotted her. "Can Oi help ye, miss?"

"I'm looking for Old Beatrice."

"Backstage." He pointed to a hallway next to the stage. "Thatta way."

The hallway branched into a labyrinth of narrow, low-ceilinged corridors. Empty, but Kendra heard the murmur of voices and laughter behind one of the closed doors. She knocked, and the door opened inward abruptly to reveal a scantily dressed, raven-haired beauty who glared daggers at her.

"Go away, ye bloody git— Oh, bugger! Pardon! I thought . . . well, never mind what I thought." She grinned. "Ye're early. Mr. Myott ain't here yet. Want a drink?"

Kendra's gaze moved past her to the four other young women wearing only shifts and robes—or nothing under the robes— lounging in a room that looked like a college dorm in the midst of a raging party. Clothes were everywhere—on chairs, puddled on the floor, balled up on the mirrored vanity around the grease paint pots, hairbrushes, wigs, and hair ornaments. Bottles of gin and whisky poked through the piles. The women were drinking out of tin cups. Given their flushed faces and foolish grins, Kendra was pretty sure it wasn't tea. A girl with strawberry blonde hair pushed herself up from a worn settee and weaved across the room to grab a bottle.

"There's another cup around here somewhere," she said, casting a vague glance around the mess.

"Thanks, but I'm looking for Beatrice," Kendra said.

The raven-haired woman who'd opened the door now cocked her head, eyeing her curiously. "Yer a Yank. Thought Mr. Myott was gonna interview a chit from Cornwall."

"I'm not here to be interviewed." *I'm the interviewer.* "I'm Kendra—Lady Sutcliffe."

"Gor! *Lady* Sutcliffe, you say?"

"Oy! You're the lady that was here the other day about the gentry mort that cocked up her toes," said Strawberry Blonde. "Prue told me that Mr. Myott was in a pet 'cause you interrupted rehearsal."

"Yes." Kendra eyed the women. "Who are you?" The question opened the floodgates, with everyone giving their name at the same time. Leeza. Anne. Selena. Alberta. Penelope.

"Did you know Clarice?" Kendra asked.

"Course we did," said Penelope, the raven-haired woman. "She was an understudy, like us, but Mr. Myott was gonna let her play Portia in *The Merchant of Venice.* Even though the bitch didn't deserve it—"

"Catty!"

Penelope whirled to glare at Leeza, a languid stunner with titian hair. "I'm speakin' the truth, and ye know it! Then she took off, didn't she? Threw it all away 'cause she thought she was one of our betters, la-tee-dahing it over us."

"She's dead," Kendra said bluntly. The women gaped at her with varying degrees of surprise and horror. "She was pulled from the Thames about a week ago."

"Lawks!" Leeza exclaimed. "Drowned?"

"Not exactly. But she was ill. Did she talk about being in treatment for syphilis? Or someone offering to cure her?"

"Aye," Leeza admitted, dislodging her silky robe with a shrug and revealing that she wore nothing underneath. "She had the pox. I thought that's why she left."

Penelope frowned. "Ye're certain? I never saw her fretting about a thing."

"Oh, she was worried," said Leeza, adjusting her silk robe to cover her breasts again as she looked at Kendra. "But she said Isabella found a cure—"

Kendra said sharply, "Isabella Russo?"

"Aye, she used ter work here. She and Clarice were friends. Isabella had the pox for years."

"And she said that she found a cure?"

"Aye, but that was a Banbury tale. There's no cure."

Kendra eyed the actress. "Why would she lie to Clarice?"

"Not sure that she did. I think she believed she *was* being cured." Leeza's gaze dropped to her tin cup. "There is no bigger fool than the dying," she said softly, her lush mouth twisting into a bitter knot. "They're ripe for the plucking for every wisewoman and trickster that offers tinctures and cordials to save them."

"Did Isabella tell you who she was going to for this cure?" Kendra asked.

"Nay." Leeza took a gulp of gin.

Kendra tried a different tack. "Did any of you see Isabella or Clarice talking to a gentleman—or gentlemen—before they left? Maybe after a performance?"

"We always have blokes coming backstage to talk to us." Penelope lifted her tin cup in a mocking salute. She laughed and gave Kendra a wink. "Course, they don't want to *talk*."

The women tittered, clearly happy to move away from such serious topics of conversation.

"But no one in particular?" Kendra pressed, and was disappointed when they shook their heads. "Where can I find Beatrice?"

"Down the hall. I'll show you." Penelope opened the door and shrieked at a bulky figure looming in the hallway. Kendra whipped out her muff pistol, and Penelope's eyes went wide.

"Bloody hell," she breathed. "Don't shoot the wanker! Caleb's a letch, but he ain't worth the bullet."

"I was jest comin' ter see if ye needed more gin, Penny." He lifted a beefy hand clutching a bottle of gin, although he kept a cautious eye on Kendra. "Din't know ye had company."

Penelope sniffed. "Aye, and fifteen minutes ago, ye were knocking ter see if we needed coal for the fire. And twenty minutes before that, ye wanted ter see if we needed a bite ter eat." Stepping forward, she drilled a finger into his flabby belly. "Ye're a lustful shit-sack, Caleb Sands!"

"Oye!" Caleb yelped, retreating. "I'm jest tryin' ter help."

Keeping her eyes on the man, Kendra returned the pistol to her reticule. Now she understood Penelope's hostile greeting.

"Bugger off! And if ye keep knockin' on our door, I'll box yer ears and then take me knife out and carve ye up and feed ye to the dogs."

Kendra raised her brows. And Bear thought *she* was a blood-thirsty wench.

Caleb threw up his free hand as if to ward off a demon, wheeling backward. "Fine. Don't be beggin' me for anything, Penny-girl."

"I won't. And don't call me Penny, ye bloody oaf." Penelope followed him out into the hall and kept her eyes on him as he fled. "The bastard's always trying ter get under our skirts," she explained to Kendra, gesturing for her to follow in the other direction.

"Have you complained to Mr. Myott about his harassment?" Kendra asked.

"Are ye touched in the head? Mr. Mylott would tan our hides good if we started complaining. Don't matter anyways. Me knife does the trick."

Kendra had to smile. "I'll bet it does."

"Guess your little pistol does the same. Would ye have shot the bugger?"

"I guess we'll never know."

Kendra was aware of Penelope studying her out of the corner of her eyes as they walked down the shadowy corridor. "Ye're not like most ladies," the actress finally remarked. "Must be because ye're a Yank. English ladies treat us like we're dirt on their dainty slippers."

Penelope stopped to knock at a door. She didn't wait for an

answer, twisting the knob and pushing open the panel. "Old Beatrice," she said, "I gotta lady ter see you."

Old Beatrice was an appropriate appellation, Kendra decided. She had to be in her nineties. Gray hair stuck out like barbed wire from beneath the beige mobcap she wore. She had lashless brown eyes behind round spectacles. Her skin was creped, sagged, and spotted. But her hands were quick and steady as she stitched the hem of a crimson satin gown that shimmered across her lap while she rocked in a chair.

The room was small, almost claustrophobic, thanks to the fabric shoved into every nook and cranny: bolts against the wall, swatches scattered across a cabinet, stacked in shelves. A table held dressmaker tools—scissors, tape measures, spools of thread, pincushions stuck with pins, and muslin pattern pieces—while another cupboard held baskets brimming with buttons, trimmings, and other odds and ends. Four wicker dressmaker dummies stood like headless sentries in a corner.

"Lady Sutcliffe, this is Old Beatrice," Penelope introduced.

Old Beatrice didn't stop her sewing as she looked at Kendra. "Come ter ask me about Edwina, then?"

A little surprised by the old woman's bluntness, Kendra nodded. "Mostly. Do you mind?"

"Nothing's stopping you from asking."

"I'll leave ye to talk, then." Penelope's silk robe fluttered as she made her exit.

"There's a chair under those gowns and breeches," Beatrice said.

Kendra took that to mean she could remove them, so she scooped up the mounds of clothes, then stood there, not really sure what to do with the armload.

"Just drop them," Beatrice instructed.

Kendra obeyed, then sat down across from the seamstress. The old woman had the composure of someone who'd lived long enough to have heard and seen it all.

"Do actresses talk to you when they're being fitted?" Kendra asked.

If Beatrice was surprised that Kendra didn't bring up Edwina, she didn't show it. "Some are chattier than others."

"What about Clarice and Isabella? Were they chatty?"

"Sometimes."

Old Beatrice was clearly *not* chatty. "Did they tell you that they were ill?"

The old woman didn't answer immediately. Her silence was contemplative as she hemmed. The thimble on her thumb glinted gold in the candlelight as she pushed the needle in and out of the satin material in a gentle rhythm.

Finally, she huffed out a sigh. "Aye. They both had the pox. I told them to use the condom, but these girls . . . . They come here young and pretty, thinking they'll be the next Sarah Siddons." The old woman deftly knotted the thread and snipped it with tiny silver scissors. "They have such dreams, and are wooed by every manner of man. They never think they'll grow old or fall out of favor. Too many end up as Haymarket Wares."

Haymarket Wares, Kendra knew, were streetwalkers, considered the lowest in the sex worker trade.

"Did Clarice or Isabella tell you that they were receiving treatment for the pox?" she asked.

"Aye." The seamstress removed the remaining thread from the needle, then slid the needle into her pincushion before hunting through the wicker basket next to her for another spool. "Isabella said that she'd learned of a cure. Silly cow." She found a spool of gold thread and measured what she needed before cutting it. "Then she was gone. Dead, most likely. But not before she filled Clarice's head with her tomfoolery."

Beatrice's tongue flicked out to wet the thread's tip, then she drew it through the needle's eye.

"Now Clarice is gone," she continued. "Probably dead too."

"She is. But not because of her illness. She was found in the Thames, no blood in her veins."

Beatrice picked up another dress and inspected the torn seam. The old woman's weathered face remained impassive.

"Did they tell you who was helping them?" Kendra asked.

"Nay. They didn't say and I didn't ask." She raised her gaze to Kendra. "Sometimes it's best to mind your own business, my lady."

Was that a warning? Kendra wondered. She asked, "What did Edwina know?"

"Why do you think she knew anything?"

"Because Lady Westford was asking about Clarice on Saturday, and then she came back on Sunday. Edwina would be the only one here to meet her."

Old Beatrice kept her eyes on her stitches. "If she did, she didn't tell me."

"Edwina was here," Kendra repeated. "She witnessed Lady Westford's murder and was seen running from the theater with a man chasing her. Do you know where she is?"

"No."

"She never talked to you about her friends? Somewhere she might seek shelter?"

Beatrice's busy fingers stilled, and she slowly raised her eyes again to lock on Kendra. "Edwina's a good girl. She don't need no trouble."

Kendra studied the old woman. "She's in trouble, Beatrice. She witnessed a murder and can identify a killer. That killer is trying to find her. Maybe he already has."

"He hasn't."

Kendra stared at her. "You sound certain of that."

Beatrice said nothing.

"I'm not the enemy, Beatrice. If you want to help Edwina, you'll tell me what you know."

Beatrice tilted her head, regarding Kendra thoughtfully. "And how can you help her, my lady?"

"By catching the person who killed Lady Westford. Edwina witnessed her murder; she can provide a description of the man who did it. I'll make sure she's safe. I'll protect her."

"Seems to me that she's been protecting herself well enough without your help, ma'am."

"The murderer isn't going to stop. He's killed two more people since Lady Westford. He killed Clarice and Isabella." *And how many more?* "Don't let Edwina become another victim."

Beatrice continued to study her. "How will you protect her, my lady?"

"I can send her to Aldridge Castle. She'll be safe there." Kendra waited a beat. "I promise to keep her safe. Please tell me where she is, Beatrice."

"I don't know where she is."

Kendra let out a frustrated breath. "You didn't ask her where she's been hiding when you saw her?"

"I never saw her."

"But . . ." Kendra frowned. "I don't understand. Did she send you a note?"

"No. She was here—but I never saw her."

"Then someone else saw her?"

"No." Beatrice slipped the needle into the gown she'd been sewing, and set the bundle aside. Slowly, she hoisted herself out of the rocking chair. "Edwina slept in the theater," she told Kendra as she walked to the shelves. "Sometimes in this room, sometimes others. Like a little mouse, she was. But she kept the few things she owned in a basket. This basket."

Beatrice brought down one of the baskets woven out of straw. "Weren't much, but they were dear to her," she said, lifting the lid. "Yesterday morn, I noticed the basket had been moved. When I looked inside, Edwina's things were gone. This was left in its place."

She reached inside, and brought out what looked like a large, copper bullet.

"What is it?" Kendra asked, puzzled, when Beatrice gave it to her. On closer examination, Kendra saw dimples, like a golf ball, hammered around the middle, and an intricate scrolled pattern carved into metal at is base. The object tapered to a smooth pointed tip and was hollow on the inside.

In answer, Beatrice took back the item and slipped it on her left thumb. She held up both hands, each thumb now covered.

"Ah. A thimble," Kendra said.

Beatrice nodded. "Yes, but I've never seen the likes before. It's old. Looks foreign."

"May I?"

Beatrice plucked the old thimble off her thumb and dropped it into Kendra's open palm.

"Why would she leave you a thimble?" Kendra asked, sliding her own thumb into the cylinder.

For the first time, the old woman cracked a smile. "She knows I can always use more thimbles. Edwina and I shared this one." She wiggled her other thumb. "We always complained about Mr. Myott's cheeseparing ways. I reckon she came to collect her things, and left this behind to let me know she was all right."

Kendra took the thimble off. Grit coated her skin and thumbnail. She rubbed it curiously with her index finger.

"I didn't have a chance to clean it proper," Beatrice said, watching her. "I'm going to soak it in water and lye to get some of the crusty spots clean."

"Do you mind if I take it with me? I promise to bring it back."

"Why? How's it going to help you find Edwina?"

"She got it somewhere. Given its age and the grime on it, maybe a used clothing shop. Or a pawn shop. If I take it around, maybe someone will remember it." Though why would Edwina spend her coins on an old thimble? Most likely, she'd found it on the street.

Still, it was *something*.

"I'll bring it back tomorrow," Kendra repeated. "I promise."

Beatrice pressed her lips together for a long moment, then nodded. "If that thing can help you find Edwina, keep it. And when you find her, I expect you to send her to your castle, where she'll be safe. I have your word?"

"Yes," Kendra said simply. And prayed that she wasn't making a promise that she wouldn't be able to keep.

# THIRTY-FIVE

Kendra noticed the nondescript black carriage parked down the street as soon as Coachman John let her out in front of 25 Bedford Square. She wasn't surprised when a grubby street urchin raced over to her.

"Oye, there. Bear wants ter speak with ye!'"

The boy didn't wait, darting back to the carriage. Kendra followed, keeping her expression neutral as the kid opened the door.

Kendra peered into the shadowy interior. "I hope this isn't a social visit," she said, mounting the steps and dropping into the seat opposite Bear. "Tell me you got something."

The crime lord grinned. "I got news about the lightskirt. Isabella Russo."

"I already know she had syphilis."

"Aye, and it's made her addlepated." He tapped a thick finger against his temple. "She don't have long for this world."

"You're saying . . . she's *alive?*"

"Didn't know that, did ye?" He looked pleased. "Her sister's been takin' care of her in Soho."

"What about the medical experiments to treat syphilis, and other missing women?"

"I told ye, I can't be knowin' what happens ter every trollop in London. As for the other, there's always gossip and canny folks tryin' ter make a profit by offering remedies ter the dying."

"Speaking from experience?"

He let out a booming laugh. "I might have a finger or two in those games. But trollops don't have the kind of blunt that gets me interested. Would be a waste of me time ter scheme them out their coins. Can't imagine why anyone would."

"It's not about money." At least not in the short term, she reflected. In the long term, though, if you found a cure to one of society's deadly diseases? Well, that would come with money, prestige, and the kind of fame that is written into the history books.

Names that she would know centuries later.

Bear frowned. "If it ain't about money, w'ots it about?"

"Becoming a god," she said softly. She leaned back in her seat. "Can I ask one more favor?"

"W'ot?"

"Can you give me a ride to Soho?"

<hr>

Soho was only a ten-minute drive from Bedford Square, but the neighborhoods were vastly different. At one time, Soho had been home to aristocrats and the affluent. Yet the influx of immigrants—French, Italian, German—had the nobility fleeing to other, more fashionable enclaves. Former mansions were now divvied up into apartments, businesses, and shops. Savvy landlords had developed neighborhoods with small houses and cottages for the new arrivals.

Kendra knocked on the door to one of those cottages, a pretty, white-washed stucco with blue-trimmed sash windows and planter boxes exploding with colorful flowers, located on a quiet, dirt lane off St. Peter's Street. An attractive, dark-haired woman in her late thirties opened the door.

"Yes? May I help you?" Her voice was musical, with just a trace of an Italian accent.

"Mrs. Chirone? I'm Lady Sutcliffe." It was, she decided, becoming easier to use the title. Especially if it got her what she wanted. "I've come to talk to your sister."

Mrs. Chirone's lips parted in surprise. "You know my sister?"

"No, but I need to see her."

The woman frowned. "*No, mi dispiace.* It is quite impossible, my lady. My sister, she is . . . she's indisposed."

"I know she's ill, Mrs. Chirone, but it's important that I speak with her."

"You don't understand." She let out a heavy sigh. "Isabella won't be able to talk to you. She is very ill. She is . . . she's dying, if must know."

"I know, and I'm very sorry. I promise you that I'll only be a moment. I won't tire her."

"I don't know what she'll be able to tell you, my lady. She is not always lucid. And"—her breath hitched—"she is no longer the beautiful girl she once was."

"I understand. I'll only take up a few moments of your time."

Mrs. Chirone hesitated, but finally acquiesced, stepping back to allow Kendra to enter the tiny foyer. "May I ask what this is about?"

"I'm hoping she'll be able to give me information that I need in another matter." Kendra followed the woman to the staircase at the end of the hall. It was so narrow that they had to ascend single-file. "How long have you been taking care of your sister?"

"All her life." That was said with a sad smile. "She's my youngest sister. It was very hard to deny her anything, even when she dreamed of the stage. Opera," she added, pausing to wait for Kendra on the landing. "Isabella has . . . had the voice of an angel."

Kendra didn't know how to respond to that—offering her sympathy again seemed pointless—so she said nothing.

The upstairs hallway was a skinny strip with two closed doors on either side of the stairs. Sunshine fell from a window on the opposite wall.

"She may be asleep," Mrs. Chiron cautioned, moving to the door on the right. "I give her opium. To ease the pain."

They entered a tiny room dominated by a single cot and a nightstand with a candle, a glass of water, and a vase with several roses. A chamber pot was under the window. Kendra took in the figure in the narrow bed. The sun's rays were merciless as they illuminated the woman's face. Boils and raw lesions pitted Isabella's forehead and chin. Horrific, but not as horrific as her nose—or, rather, the place her nose should have been. The disease had eaten away the flesh and cartilage, collapsing the bridge, leaving a gruesome, skeletal gap in the middle of her face.

Kendra believed Mrs. Chirone when she said that her little sister had been beautiful. Unfortunately, the only thing left of her former beauty was her dark mane. It had been cut short, but it was still thick and vibrant, curling around the ravaged face.

Isabella's eyes were closed, and she was breathing heavily.

"Isabella," Mrs. Chirone crooned softly, moving to her sister's side. "Wake up, *cara*. A lady has come to visit with you."

Stepping closer, Kendra had to brace herself against the smell. The roses couldn't cover the stench of rotting flesh, urine, defecation, and impending death.

"Isabella?" Mrs. Chiron said a little louder.

Isabella's eyes fluttered, then opened. Blue eyes filmy with encroaching blindness searched for her sister. "Bianca?"

"*Sì*. I'm here, *cara*." She darted a quick, agonizing look at Kendra. "And Lady Sutcliffe. She would like to speak with you."

"Lady, my lady . . . oh, to be addressed by the high-born," Isabella smiled mistily in Kendra's direction, then frowned. "Ladies don't know women like me. Is she a spirit, Bianca? Come to take me away?" Skeletal fingers clutched at the quilt covering her. "Take me to the heavens to soar with the angels?"

"No, no, *cara*. Lady Sutcliffe is real. She is here."

"The lords like me. Not the ladies. Nine ladies leaping . . . no, that's wrong. Nine ladies dancing. Yes, that's right!" She giggled. "Ten lords a-leaping."

Kendra stepped closer. "Isabella, I need to ask you a few questions."

Isabella frowned. "How can there be nine ladies and ten lords? There are too many lords. They need to match. How can the lords and ladies dance if they don't match?"

Mrs. Chirone shot Kendra an apologetic look. "This is the way she's been for the last several weeks, my lady."

Kendra nodded, but kept her eyes on Isabella. "Do you remember Clarice, Isabella?"

"Clarice isn't a lady dancing. She isn't a lady. She's my friend. We will perform on stage. White roses will be thrown at our feet. The lords will be a-leaping then." She threw her head back and laughed. In that joyous sound, Kendra could almost imagine the flirtatious girl that Isabella must have been. "We will be the sun and the moon. Glory be . . .

"Gloria. Glo-ri-a, glo-ri-a," she began singing. Her voice was hoarse and thready, but again Kendra caught the echo of another Isabella. "*Glo-ri-a in excelsis De-o.*"

"*Cara—*"

"*Sposa son disprezzata.*" Isabella's voice gained in strength as she switched from Vivaldi's famous church hymn to an aria written by Geminiano Giacomelli. "*Fida, son oltraggiata…Cieli che feci mai? Cieli che feci—*"

"*Silenzo!*" Mrs. Chirone snapped, rubbing her temples. "*Per amore di Dio. Mi scuso*—I apologize, Lady Sutcliffe, but my sister's wits have fled. She can be of no help to you."

Kendra was beginning to think Mrs. Chirone was right, but she had to try. "Isabella, did you help Clarice when she told you that she had the pox?" she asked. "Did you send her to someone who might cure her? The same person who promised to cure you?"

Isabella had stopped singing at her sister's sharp rebuke. Now she whispered, "They will save us. They will clean our blood and make us whole again. And we will save the world."

"Who, Isabella? Tell me who told you that you'd save the world?"

"God spoke through Vivaldi," she murmured dreamily. "*Glo-ri-a in excelsis De-o—*"

"How were they going to save you?" Kendra tried again. "How were they going to clean your blood?"

"*Sposa son disprezzata . . . Fida, son oltraggiata . . . Cieli che feci mai?*"

"Where did they give you treatments?"

*"Cieli che feci mai?. . ..E pur egl'è il mio cor . . . Il mio sposo."*

Kendra struggled to contain her frustration. "Who tried to save you, Isabella? Give me a name."

"I told you." Isabella's eyes fluttered shut. "Vivaldi and the saints."

*Saints.* "How many saints, Isabella?"

She smiled but didn't open her eyes. "The heavens are filled with saints. Bianca, are you there?"

"*Sì, cara.*" Mrs. Chirone touched her sister's hand.

"I'm so very tired," Isabella whispered. "So very cold."

"Go to sleep, *cara.* Rest now."

Kendra watched tears gather in Mrs. Chirone's eyes as she leaned over to smooth the quilt. Isabella was already slipping into slumber. After a moment, Mrs. Chirone straightened, lifting her watery gaze to Kendra.

"She cannot help you, Lady Sutcliffe," she said quietly, moving to the door.

In the hallway, Mrs. Chirone fished a handkerchief out of her sleeve, dabbed her eyes, and blew her nose.

"She didn't mention anything to you about being treated for syphilis before . . . ?" *Before disease rotted her brain and insanity took over?*

"No. I wasn't aware Isabella was sick until recently." She sniffed and blew her nose again. "We grew apart when she joined the theater troupe. She always wanted to be an opera singer. She dreamed of performing at the Teatro alla Scala and dazzling Europe with her voice. I think . . . I think there was a time when she might have accomplished it too."

They fell silent as they descended the staircase.

"Thank you, Mrs. Chirone," Kendra said when they reached the bottom. "I know this has been difficult for you. I appreciate you letting me talk to her."

"I'm only sorry you didn't learn anything, Lady Sutcliffe."

She was wrong, Kendra thought, stepping outside. Isabella had confirmed her suspicions when she'd spoken of the saints—plural.

The killer had at least two partners.

# THIRTY-SIX

The Duke contemplated Kendra across the dining room table where he'd joined her and Alec for a late lunch. "You think there's been a conspiracy to commit murder? Because Isabella spoke to you about Vivaldi and the saints? My dear, the creature's mind is hardly sound."

Kendra speared a boiled potato. "It's about seeing the world through Isabella's eyes. She wanted to be an opera singer and seems to have idolized Vivaldi. It's not too much of a stretch to have her look at the group's leader as a composer like Vivaldi."

"And the saints are his followers?" murmured the Duke. "I suppose that's possible."

"We've got a leader and at least two others. Maybe three. Four—if Thornton was part of the group or loosely connected."

The Duke's blue eyes took on a grayish cast that indicated he was disturbed. "Or more. Who knows how many are part of this conspiracy?"

"She's going to quote her fellow countryman, Benjamin Franklin," Alec warned, and smiled crookedly at Kendra.

"It holds. The group has to be limited to only a few trusted individuals to remain a secret. Otherwise, you open yourself up to that human failing that Lady St. James relies on—gossip."

"Transfusions are a crime," the Duke reminded her. "They're hardly going to gossip about that."

"These men think they've come up with a way to purify blood. That's thrilling stuff. It's hard to keep thrilling stuff to yourself."

"Not so thrilling when their procedure resulted in the death of a woman," the Duke said softly. "Which brings up another point. If they've come up with a process to purify the blood, why is Isabella alive and Clarice dead?"

"I don't know," Kendra admitted. "Isabella was treated before Clarice. Obviously, she wasn't cured. Maybe they became more aggressive with Clarice."

The Duke's mouth formed a grim line. "And murdered the poor creature."

"I doubt that they'd view it like that. She was an experiment that failed."

"She was a human being. How could they look at her as…as something to be discarded?"

Kendra understood the Duke's horror, but shrugged. "A certain cold-bloodedness—or, at least, detachment—is necessary when you're conducting medical research. People die in drug or medical device trials. It's part of the learning process. All advancements come with a cost."

Alec's eyes narrowed. "They murdered Lady Westford, Dr. Thornton, and his maid to keep their experiments a secret."

"One could argue that Mr. Goldsten was also their victim," the Duke added. "He may have committed self-murder, but only because he felt he had no alternative. You're right, Kendra, about these men—Vivaldi and the saints. They're powerful enough that Mr. Goldsten believed they could destroy everything he's worked for—his reputation, his practice."

They fell into a thoughtful silence. Alec and the Duke finished their meal, while Kendra pushed away her plate. She was no longer hungry.

"Did the seamstress at Bowden Theater tell you anything?" Alec asked.

The change of subject snapped Kendra out of her brood. "Yes. Edwina's alive. Or, at least, she was a day ago. Just a minute." She jumped up from the table and ran out of the room. A maid and footman gaped at her as she bolted up the stairs. Their mouths dropped open again when she raced back to the dining room.

"Here," she said, opening her hand to show them the thimble that Edwina had left for Old Beatrice.

"It's a thimble," the Duke observed, taking the sewing tool from Kendra.

"I have to admit that I had no idea what it was when Betrice showed it to me."

"Why is a thimble so important?" Alec wondered. "The woman is a seamstress, isn't she?"

"It's a very old thimble," the Duke said. "Maybe Greek or Roman?"

"Edwina left it for Beatrice when she retrieved her possessions. I'm hoping it will help us find her. Maybe Edwina bought it, although it seems a strange thing to spend money on, especially if she has limited funds."

"She didn't buy it."

At the certainty in the Duke's voice, she turned to him. "How do you know?"

"Because I've seen similar items. She found it—one of the Thames's treasures."

"Ah, of course," Alec said.

Kendra glanced between the men. "What do you two know that I don't?"

The Duke said, "Mudlarks pick up things like this all the time."

"Mudlarks?"

"Scavengers," Alec answered. "They wait for the Thames's tide to go out, then they mine the mudflats for coal, coins, anything that they can use or sell to survive."

"Edwina was seen around the docks," Kendra said.

"It would be clever of her to join the mudlarks." The Duke picked up his ale and took a swallow. "They're around, but no one pays them any attention. Unless they misjudge the tide and drown, which is an all-too-common occurrence, I'm afraid."

"So, they go out every time the tide is low?"

Alec said, "If they want to eat, they do."

"When's the next low tide?"

"Later this afternoon." Alec regarded her. "I guess we're going mudlarking."

Kendra's palms tingled in anticipation. "It's a chance. Our best chance of finding Edwina. We're going to take it."

Dark clouds began blowing in around two-thirty. Kendra prayed the rain that might come with them would hold off until after they'd conducted their search for Edwina. They were getting close.

A message arrived from Munroe to let her know that his geological expert, Mr. Engel, was at the anatomy school.

"You don't think he'll give you anything useful for the investigation," Alec guessed, watching her from the seat on the other side of the carriage. "Finding the location of where a body had been based on dirt seems a bit fanciful."

"Not in another couple of decades it won't be. But because we're not there yet . . . yeah, I guess I don't think he'll be that useful."

"Why are we wasting time speaking to him then?"

"I don't know if it is a waste of time—yet. You have to explore an angle before you know if you've wasted your time exploring it, if that makes sense."

"Oddly enough, it does. No one can predict the future." He flashed her a wicked grin. "Even a time traveler."

Kendra was a little surprised to find Munroe's anatomy school humming with activity, as most of her visits had been conducted after school hours. Today, the wooden bleachers in the operating theater were filled with medical students, while Mr. Barts lectured, standing next to a table upon which lay a naked male cadaver. A few men in the audience shouted ribald remarks, prompting an astonishingly stern rebuke from the weak-chinned apprentice.

Kendra and Alec continued down the hall to Munroe's office. Inside, the anatomist was sitting behind his desk, talking to Sam, the Duke, and another man—Mr. Engel, Kendra presumed. At Kendra and Alec's entrance, all three men stood.

"A pleasure," Mr. Engel said, beaming and bowing as

introductions were made. He was a short, spare man clothed entirely in black except for his snowy white cravat. Kendra thought he might be a Quaker, but he wore an ornate gold-and-ruby pin fastened to the folds of his cravat. Early sixties, Kendra estimated. The sun had permanently browned his complexion and bleached his hair into a silvery-sheened blond.

"Thank you for coming, Mr. Engel," Kendra said once they'd settled into chairs again.

"Well, I have to say this has been quite exciting, my lady," he replied. "I'm a surveyor by trade, but the study of geology is a passion of mine. The two, of course, intersect. There is so much to learn from Mother Earth."

Kendra caught Sam's dubious expression.

Mr. Engel leaned forward, eyes twinkling. "I must say, I've never been asked to identify sediment off a corpse before. Naturally, when I received Dr. Munroe's letter, I was *quite* intrigued. I wanted to come straightaway, but my sister—she keeps house for me in Cambridge—reminded me that it's not safe to travel at night. I waited until dawn and came as soon as I could."

"We appreciate your speed," said the Duke.

"Well, I confess, I was fascinated. Examining soil and sediment on a corpse to help in a criminal investigation is a novel idea. I simply couldn't pass up the opportunity."

Kendra had to suppress a smile. Mr. Engel was eerily accurate— it *was* a novel idea. Forensic geology would first be envisioned by the novelist Sir Arthur Conan Doyle, whose most famous character, Sherlock Holmes, was able to identify where suspects had been based on the dirt on their shoes. A few years later, fiction would become fact when German scientist George Popp analyzed soil samples in an effort to solve crimes, and a new branch of forensics was born.

"Have you examined the sediment on the body, Mr. Engel?" Kendra asked.

Munroe spoke up. "I brought Mr. Engel to the morgue as soon as he arrived to conduct the examination." He gestured to the counter holding one of his old-fashioned microscopes. "We brought the samples here, if you would care to view them yourself, my lady."

"I'm not sure I'd know what I was looking at," she admitted, but stood up and moved over to the counter. "Why don't you explain what you found."

Mr. Engel joined her. "London has a complex geology, my lady. There is much discussion about how this came to be." He paused and smiled. "Which is neither here nor there. My passions often get the best of me. My sister is always reminding me that few people appreciate long, tedious lectures on how the earth may have been formed."

"I'm actually interested," said the Duke, peering through the microscope. He raised his head to look at the surveyor. "Would you be available for dinner tonight to discuss the subject at length?"

Mr. Engel seemed dazzled by the invitation. "Oh, my. Yes, Your Grace. I would be honored."

"What did you find, Mr. Engel?" Kendra asked again.

The surveyor cleared his throat. "Ah, yes. The sediment on the body is alluvium, which is a mixture of clay, sand, silt, and gravel, deposited by running water."

"Like a river? The Thames?" Kendra wondered.

"Yes, but not only the Thames. London is built on a network of tributaries. Over the years, we've built over rivers and streams, forcing them mostly underground or to disappear altogether. Sadly, they've become riddled with refuse, little more than sewers—even River Fleet, which is the most famous. That's the one I think we're dealing with, given the dominance of London clay in the alluvium."

Kendra recalled her first visit to Goldsten's clinic in Blackfriars. She'd seen portions of the River Fleet aboveground where it wouldn't be in the twenty-first century.

"London clay?" Sam asked.

"'Tis seabed sediment layered above chalk below. Typically, London clay is too dense for proper agriculture. However, it's easily tunneled and is an excellent source for brickmaking. You see it used in buildings all over the city."

"Is there any way to pinpoint where the victim may have been in order to be covered with that sediment?" Kendra asked.

"Not specifically, no. But . . ." He dashed over to a leather satchel on the floor near the chair and drew out a rolled parchment, unfurling it on Munroe's desk to reveal a map of London.

They gathered around as he used his index finger to trace the heart of London. "London clay is found in the soil north of the River Thames. In this section here. As you go south of the River Thames, sediment becomes more sand and gravel."

Sam tapped the map. "So the chit would've had ter been kept in this area."

"Yes, if she was kept in the city," said Mr. Engel.

"She was." Kendra had no doubt about that. "They need a place easily accessible to them to conduct their experiments." *Easily accessible to St. George's,* she thought but didn't say. "If they were outside the city, in the countryside, the body would never have been found. It's easier to dispose of a corpse by digging a grave or dumping it where the animals can get to it. In London, space is limited. The Thames is the easiest way to get rid of a body."

Mr. Engel's lips parted in shock as he stared at her.

Sam frowned, studying the map. "That's a lot of ground ter cover."

"Very true," Mr. Engle agreed, tearing his gaze away from Kendra. "However, you need to factor in other elements. Your victim was definitely stored belowground, which is how she came into contact with London clay. You ought to look for running water—a river or a stream. Not a pond or lake. And because the woman was kept underground, I'd say you are dealing with one of London's lost rivers."

"In this area." Kendra retraced the section of the map that he'd identified. Sam was right; it was a lot of ground to cover. She looked at Mr. Engel. "Could it be an icehouse of some kind?"

He put his hands in his pockets, rocking back on his heels as he contemplated the idea. "Ice houses *are* built near rivers and lakes. It's possible, I suppose. However, I imagine it would have to be a defunct ice house. Servants would be constantly retrieving ice or whatever is being stored in it." He gave a laugh. "One hopes they'd notice a corpse."

"Any other ideas?"

The surveyor pursed his lips. "An older structure that has been built over an underground river, and still has a subterranean chamber." He sighed. "I wish I could be more help in finding where your body was before she came to you."

"Cold, underground, near one of London's underground rivers, north of the Thames. You've actually been very helpful, Mr. Engel. Thank you." Kendra glanced at Sam. "Mr. Kelly, will you walk with us to the carriage?"

Once they left Munroe's office, Sam grumbled, "North of the Thames is still a lot of ground ter cover."

"Yes, but now we've got a starting point. Pull in Muldoon. He may be a pain in the ass," she stated, which made Sam grin, "but he knows how to do research. We need to cross-reference our suspects with property they might own or rent—"

"Own," Alec put in. "They wouldn't want a nosy landlord stumbling across what they're doing."

Kendra nodded. "Right. It needs to be private. Then we narrow it down by looking for property with an underground chamber or an ice house, with one of the lost rivers running through it."

"I'll tell Muldoon, but if we find Edwina, we won't need the location. We'll have our witness." Sam glanced at Kendra. "You really think she's been mudlarking all this time?"

"I can't say with one hundred percent certainty, but the probability is high."

Sam scowled when he opened the door, his gaze going to the ominous clouds on the horizon. "It's gonna rain."

"Will that stop the mudlarks from showing up?" Kendra asked.

"Don't worry. They'll be there," Alec assured her.

"Aye. Rain ain't gonna stop them." Shoving his tricorn hat on his head, Sam sighed. "It'll just make it miserable for us."

# THIRTY-SEVEN

Kendra prepared for the miserable. A light rain pinged against the windowpanes as she dressed in her warmest gown and wool coat, her thickest tights, and her sturdiest leather half-boots. Not fashionable, which Molly lamented, but functional. Or as functional as it could be for the era. Neither the gown nor the coat had pockets, so Kendra still had to keep her pistol in the dainty reticule dangling from her wrist.

Alec was waiting for her by the door. Like her, he'd dressed for the cold. She was sure he also had a gun on him, but he had plenty of pockets to keep it in. While Kendra didn't anticipate any problems with the mudlarks, the docks were a high-crime area. One of the reasons, she remembered, why Goldsten had set up his practice nearby.

Briefly, she wondered what would happen to the clinic now.

When they climbed down from their carriage, Sam was waiting for them on the embankment with six other Bow Street Runners. Kendra recognized a tall, lanky figure staring out the receding waters of the Thames as Muldoon.

"I spoke ter Mr. Goldsten's ma and sister an hour ago," Sam told Kendra. His golden eyes were shadowed and a muscle twitched in his stubbled jaw.

"I'm sorry." She understood what it meant to be the messenger that brought grief to a family.

The Bow Street Runner moved his shoulders as if he was trying to dislodge a weight. "Aye, well. They were shocked. Refused ter believe he killed himself. I reckon that's natural. No one wants ter believe something like that."

Kendra acknowledged that with a nod. "When was the last time they saw him?"

"A week ago. Last Friday, for something called Shabbat."

Kendra hunched her shoulders against a gust of wind and rain. "They didn't think it was strange that they hadn't seen him for over a week?"

"Wasn't peculiar for him. Mrs. Goldsten said he spent most of his time at his clinic and St. George's."

"Did he seem troubled or worried about anything the last time they saw him?"

"According ter Miss Goldsten, her brother was always serious-minded. Fretting that he'd lose status or have his clinic shutdown if he stepped out of line."

Muldoon joined them. "I quizzed the sisters at St. George's and learned that Sir Preston and Dr. Carter have treated the most syphilis patients over the years, but that could be because they're the oldest physicians in residence. Everyone has treated the pox at one time or another."

"Anyone with a personal connection to the disease?" Kendra asked.

"There are some whispers that Mr. Beane's brother died of the disease, but I haven't been able to confirm that. I thought that if I don't drown tonight, I'll ask him directly tomorrow morning." Muldoon grinned at her.

"They're coming now," Alec said.

Kendra's gaze traveled to the shoreline below. Black patches of mud, rocks, and rubble were slowly exposed as the tide receded, and dozens of shadowy figures crept out onto the sludge. The old and disabled used long sticks to poke through the mud and navigate the shifting sands. The children used their hands to dig through the debris. They all wore long coats, bulky, with multiple pockets that they stuffed with the objects they found. A few carried burlap sacks as well.

Kendra turned her attention back to Sam, Muldoon, and the other Runners. "We want Edwina, but if she's not down there, maybe someone knows where she is. If you don't see her, interview as many mudlarks as possible."

She saw Muldoon's quick grin, and half-expected him to give her his mocking salute like he had before.

"Do I sound imperious?" she asked Alec as they made their way down the embankment.

"Darling, you sound like a leader. Mind your step."

Her boots skidded across the slick, seaweed-covered rocks, and Alec's hand shot out to steady her. She gave a relieved sigh when she finally landed on the shore, even if her half-boots sank into the mud.

Kendra surveyed the newly exposed beach, with its long patches of mud, clumps of seaweed, rocks, and swirling tidepools. The world was different down here, almost apocalyptic. A one-armed man struggled to yank a tin box out of a tangled pile of kelp and muck. Nearby, an old woman, spine curved into a large dowager's hump, combed the sand with her fingers. Children as young as four were rooting around for any meager scraps. *Society's abandoned*, she reflected sadly.

"We're being watched," Alec murmured beside her.

"I know." Kendra nodded, her gaze drifting over several young mudlarks.

"Not by them. Him." Alec inclined his head in the direction of the embankment.

Kendra turned slowly, careful not to draw attention, and glanced up the rocky incline. The man had chosen his position well, standing between two warehouses, leaving him in shadow. That, along with the gray drizzle, made it impossible to discern anything about him, except that he was wearing tricorn hat and a caped greatcoat.

"He could be a dockworker—"

"They don't wear greatcoats. I noticed him when we were on the embankment. He pretended that he was part of the group of men working near one of the warehouses, but he was watching us. He wasn't subtle, but I put it down to curiosity."

Kendra studied Alec. He'd been a spy on the continent during the Napoleonic Wars. If anyone would recognize surveillance, he would.

Now he said, "Why don't I go and have a word with him, shall I?"

A frisson darted down her spine, and she grabbed his arm before he could turn away. "Be careful, Alec."

His teeth flashed in a crooked smile. "Don't worry about me, sweet. You'd better worry about catching your quarry. It looks like they don't want to be interviewed."

"Damn!" she cursed, when she saw that the younger mudlarks had begun running, scattering in all directions. Hiking up her skirts, Kendra chased after a handful of the children running north. Sam, Muldoon, and the other Bow Street Runners were yelling and racing after the other kids. The mud sucked at her boots, hampering her progress. In contrast, the kids seemed to fly across the beach, as fleet of foot as a herd of gazelles.

To think she'd once prided herself on her speed at Langley's racetrack and the laps she'd made around the FBI Hoover Building in DC. But a year of not running had taken its toll. The muscles in her legs burned as she sprinted after the mudlarks. Wind and rain slapped at her.

"Stop!" she shouted.

Several in the pack glanced over their shoulders, squealing. Smaller children peeled off from the older kids. Kendra made a split-second decision to go after the older children. She didn't know how it was possible, but they seemed to increase their speed, lengthening the distance between them.

Gritting her teeth, she bore down and found a spurt of energy as the children ran toward a rocky formation that jutted like a finger from the embankment. She gained a few feet, but had no breath left in her lungs to order them to stop again. They were twenty yards ahead. Her heart felt like it was going to explode. Her calves screamed. Still, she gulped air and barreled forward, shrinking the distance to fifteen yards.

Then the kids disappeared around the jagged outcrop.

Kendra was running so fast that she nearly collided with a large boulder. Skidding, she corrected course around the stones. On the other side, she saw the mudlarks vanish into a yawning black hole cut into the embankment.

Ignoring the painful stitch burning in her side, she jogged the last few feet to the opening. It was a stone tunnel, at least seven feet high, five feet across. Large enough to accommodate her without forcing her to bend over.

She paused to catch her breath. Her ears were still roaring with her blood, but her heart was beginning to settle. Cautiously, she moved forward. The gray light outside rapidly diminished, and she stepped into the pitch-black. Did she hear the scurrying of running feet?

She stopped. Listened. Heard nothing except for the drip-drip-drip of rain outside the tunnel entrance. Either the children had stopped running or there was an escape hatch somewhere.

Lichen and seaweed crawled up the stone walls around her, hung from cracks on the arched ceiling. This had to be one of the abandoned aqueducts built by the industrious Romans when they ruled England. She walked another foot, glass, seashells, and gravel crunching under the soles of her half-boots. The strong smell of sea, sewage, rotting vegetation, and decaying flesh—animal, she hoped— felt like a punch to the throat.

She stopped again. "Hey!" she yelled. Her voice echoed back to her. "I'm not going to hurt you! I just want to talk!"

Nothing.

"I'm looking for Edwina!" she shouted into the abyss. "I need her help! I'm offering a reward!"

Straining her ears, she thought maybe, just maybe, she heard movement somewhere in the endless darkness. "I'll protect her!" she tried again. "I promised Old Beatrice that I'd protect her!"

She took another step.

"My name is Kendra—Lady Sutcliffe. Twenty-five Bedford Square. Tell Edwina! Tell her that I will protect her!"

She held her breath. Silence.

*Damn.* She couldn't advance farther without a lantern. She already felt like she'd been swallowed by the darkness.

She wheeled around and began walking back to the tunnel's exit. It was darker now; she could barely see. Her boots splashed through a puddle. She froze. The tunnel had been dry when she'd come in—there should be no *splashing*.

She picked up her pace. As she hurried forward, the light from outside pierced the gloom and she could see the rivulets surging between the rubbish and seashells that littered the tunnel's floor. The rising water lapped at her half-boots.

Heart pumping wildly, she sloshed her way to the tunnel's opening.

*Holy shit.* She stopped abruptly, her stomach dropping in dismay as she stared.

The tide had come in.

# THIRTY-EIGHT

The Thames' icy water stole Kendra's breath as it surged and swirled, twisting her skirts around her legs. Rain pelted her as she scanned the nearest embankment, the rocky outcrop that cut her off from everyone else, making her feel like she was completely alone in a desolate world.

*Too steep.* Unless she turned into a billy goat, there was no damn way she was going to scale those rocks. Her best bet, she decided, was to get to the end of the rugged outcrop, where the incline sloped downward.

The day's light was fast disappearing. She had to move.

She yanked up her waterlogged skirts and struck out toward the most accessible point of the rocks, gasping as the murky water gushed above her knees. Her legs were already numb, making her stumble as the river's current tried to drag her down with greedy hands. She staggered and fell, tasted the brine of the Thames. Choking and wheezing, she thrust herself up again. The water swelled to her waist. The cold of it sapped her strength.

Clenching her jaw, she forced herself to move toward the craggy boulders which were mere shadows now on the embankment.

"Kendra!" Alec's voice came to her over the rush of water.

"Here!" she shouted, using her hands to slice through the freezing water and propel herself forward. One foot. Another. "I'm here!"

She focused on each movement, determination gritting her teeth.

Then Alec was before her, his hands clamped around her waist. She found herself floating as he towed her toward the shoreline, barely visible in the rain and darkness.

"I-I can w-walk," she said through chattering teeth as they reached shallow waters.

"Of course, you can." He swung her up into his arms, carrying her up the rocky incline.

Once they were clear of the rising tide, Alec set her down and whipped off his greatcoat. Grim-faced, he wrapped the wool coat around her, then ran his hands up and down her arms to warm her. Stones clattered as Sam and Muldoon skidded down the incline toward them. Both were carrying lanterns.

"God's teeth, lass, you gave me a fright when you disappeared and the tide came in," Sam said when he stopped in front of her.

"I g-gave myself a fri-ight. T-tried to follow k-kids. They d-disappeared in a tunnel. Couldn't c-catch them."

"Those little devils are fast." Muldoon held up his lantern and studied her face. "Your lips are blue, my lady."

"T-thanks for the o-observation. D-did you get any-anything?"

"We're not going to have that discussion now," Alec snapped, and hauled her up again. "You're going home and into a hot bath before you catch your death."

Kendra scowled at him. "I-I'm fine."

"I could use a hot whisky meself," Sam put in. "Me bones are brittle with wet and cold."

"W-we need t-to have a brief—a b-briefing."

"Two hours. She'll be ready for you then." Alec didn't wait for Sam to respond, carrying Kendra up the rest of the incline. Spotting them, Coachman John rushed to open the door and pull down the steps.

"Get us home," Alec ordered, climbing into the carriage and lowering Kendra to the seat.

Reaching into a small cubbyhole under the seat, he withdrew a heavy wool blanket, which he tossed over Kendra. Between the blanket and Alec's greatcoat, Kendra felt marginally warmer.

Alec settled in the opposite seat, and Kendra raised her eyebrows when he leaned forward and pushed up her wet skirts.

"I-I'm really not in the m-mood, darling," she managed to say through her chattering teeth, and tried to smile at him.

He leveled a grim look at her. "Rest assured, I shall not be exercising my husbandly rights at this precise moment. You don't exactly smell of roses, sweet."

She sighed. "You're pissed."

Alec said nothing as he lifted her legs across his lap and worked to untie the soaked shoelaces.

"Bugger it," he muttered, and produced a small knife from his pocket. In a deft move, he sliced through the knots, then tugged off her boots and tossed them to the floor. Next, he stripped her of her stockings and garters.

Kendra allowed herself to burrow down in the blanket and coat while Alec massaged her feet and kneaded her calves.

"That feels . . . *shit!*" She sat up straighter as the sensation of sharp needles seemed to score her flesh. "That feels like I'm in a medieval torture machine."

But the pain was already receding, replaced by glorious warmth. After a tense moment, she relaxed. "Okay. Okay, this is good."

He released her legs and switched seats, then pulled her onto his lap and wrapped his arms around her.

"This is better," she murmured, snuggling against him as the violent shudders dissipated.

"I need to take a moment, one moment . . ." Alec pressed his lips into her hair, his arms tightening around her.

Kendra laid her head on his chest and slid her arms around his waist. Outside, the rain drummed and splashed, but all Kendra heard was the steady beat of Alec's heart.

Deep inside the ancient stone aqueduct, Edwina huddled with the rest of the mudlarks, hands outstretched to capture the warmth from the fire. Not enough to dispel the damp and cold, but Edwina no longer felt discomfort. Instead, she felt . . . safe.

Or, rather, she *had* felt safe. The woman—Lady Sutcliffe, she called herself—had changed all of that. Edwina licked her dry lips as fear churned her stomach. If the lady could find her, what was stopping the devil?

"'Ere ye go, Edie. It'll warm ye up."

Edwina glanced at the tin cup clenched in a grubby hand. The hand was attached to an equally grubby boy of about fourteen, who went by the name of Fish.

"Thank you," she whispered, and took a cautious sip, no longer surprised to taste gin. Fish had probably filched the bottle. He had been a Little Snakeman at one of the rookeries, until he'd gotten too big to slither through pipes and down chimneys to open doors for his gang of housebreakers. He'd been forced into stealing and begging on the streets before he'd taken up mudlarking. He was good at scavenging, always digging out the biggest lumps of coal or finding the most interesting artifacts and old coins—coins used by the same folks that built these tunnels. He supplemented his finds with a fair amount of pickpocketing and thievery, which kept their small group from starving.

Fish had been the one to find her after she'd fled the devil.

She drew in a ragged breath as she thought about how she'd wandered the streets of London. Fear and horror had gnawed a hole in her gut. She hadn't known what to do, other than return to the Bowden Theater later that night. It was only by the sheerest of luck that she'd seen the man leaning against the streetlamp, watching the theater from across the street. He wasn't the same man who'd killed the lady and chased her, but she *knew*. She knew he was waiting for her.

And she knew then that she could never return to her old life.

Despair and hopelessness had flooded her as she retreated to the streets. She'd briefly considered going to the magistrate. But her past experiences with Charlies had never ended well. They might even accuse *her* of pushing the lady off the balcony.

Edwina had bitterly regretted leaving behind the loaf of bread she'd purchased only that morning, especially after a meager early meal and a growling stomach that evening. She had sought refuge from the plunging temperatures in the doorway of a church, curling up into a tight ball, tears freezing on her eyelashes and face.

She couldn't remember hearing a sound, but when she'd opened her eyes, Fish had been looming over her.

Later, he confessed that he'd intended to nick her reticule, but for reasons that weren't even clear to him, he'd changed his mind when she'd opened her eyes. Instead of robbing her, Fish had brought her to his gang of raggedy mudlarks.

Most were children, the youngest being five and the oldest fifteen—just two years younger than her. Abe was the old man in their group, older, she thought, than Old Beatrice. His right hand was a stump, as he'd lost it fighting Boney in the war.

"Who's the gentry mort?" A querulous voice broke the silence. "She knew yer name."

Edwina looked to Raven—a nickname, Edwina suspected, derived from the dark locks that tumbled around a plain, pinched face. At fifteen, Raven was closest in age to Edwina, but that didn't mean they were friends. In fact, the other girl had taken an active dislike to her.

"Lady Sootcliffe, she said she was," said five-year-old Peter.

"How'd she find ye?" Raven demanded, her eyes locked on Edwina.

"I don't know." But Edwina averted her gaze as guilt assailed her. She'd only returned to the Bowden Theater once—*once*—to collect a few things and leave an old thimble she'd dug out of the mudflats for Beatrice. It was too old fashioned to be of much use or any value, but she'd thought Beatrice would enjoy the artifact.

"Don't matter how she found 'er," Fish snapped, his chin jutting up belligerently. "We protect our own."

Raven's mouth knotted. "She ain't our own!"

Edwina swallowed, the gin she'd drunk earlier threatening to come up.

"Stop yer bickerin'," Abe muttered, shifting. "We need ter eat a bite and rest. We barely got a haul 'cause of the nobs. The tide'll be goin' out again soon enough."

Edwina opened her mouth to apologize, but Fish shot her a warning look and shook his head. No one spoke as oranges—again, thanks to Fish's nimble fingers—were passed around and eaten. Afterwards, each mudlark found their space, as near the fire as they could manage, and curled up to sleep.

Edwina did the same. She'd become used to the mudlarks' odd sleeping habits. Life revolved around the River Thames' tide. In the beginning, she'd lain awake and counted the breaths rising and falling around her in the small space. The scurrying of mice and rats never bothered her, as they were familiar sounds in the theater. Now the soft huffs of breaths around her lulled her into sleep within minutes.

No one heard the mudlark rise and slip out of the tunnel.

# THIRTY-NINE

Kendra felt human again after the hot bath, although she had to endure Molly's lecture about ruining her half-boots and risking her life. Both seemed to be of equal concern to the maid.

Dressed in a velvet gown of deep indigo with a cashmere shawl for extra warmth, Kendra made her way to the library. She found herself appreciating the lemon and beeswax scents of furniture polish after the drainage systems of London.

She heard voices before she entered the library. Alec was leaning against the fireplace, and God, the man was gorgeous. He'd changed into an exquisitely tailored black jacket, burnished gold vest, and beige pantaloons tucked into a fresh pair of boots. She tore her gaze from his to scan the other occupants in the room. She'd expected Sam, who had a glass of whisky in his hand, but she was surprised to see Rebecca and Muldoon sitting on the sofa.

"You're looking better, sweet," Alec remarked, peeling himself away from the mantel to move to the sideboard. He poured her a glass of wine and brought it over with a smile. "Smell better too."

"I should. Molly threw in enough bath salts and oils to make the Thames smell like a garden. Thanks." She took the wineglass and looked to Rebecca. "I didn't realize you were here."

"I'm on my way to a musical recital at Lady Chevallier's and thought to persuade you to accompany me. Of course, that was before I found out you nearly drowned." Concern darkened her eyes. "Dear heaven, Kendra. How are you?"

Kendra thought she saw something else in Rebecca's eyes—a

remembered horror. Almost a year ago, the aristocrat had nearly drowned in the Thames.

"I'm fine," she assured her. "But I don't think I'm up for a musical recital."

"Mr. Kelly was telling us that you may have found Edwina," Rebecca went on.

Kendra took a long sip of her wine. "I never got close enough to identify her. I'm hoping she was part of the group of kids that I chased into the aqueduct. I could only give them my name and address. If she wasn't with them, I'm hoping they know her and pass on my information."

Sam looked at Alec. "Who was the bloke spying on us?"

"I wish I knew." Alec's face hardened. "The blasted man ran off before I could get to the top of the embankment. I was never close enough to get a proper look at him, although he appeared to be the same height and build as the man Bridget saw running after Edwina."

"I can't imagine he's one of your suspects," Muldoon said, glancing at the slate board. "They're all physicians, sawbones, and apprentices. I'd think they're too busy to be following you. Most likely, he was someone hired to keep an eye on Lady Sutcliffe. Everyone knows she's the one leading the investigation. Would make sense to watch her, like they were watching Lady Westford."

Kendra shook her head. "They probably have someone watching me, but not someone off the streets. Hired help might talk or blackmail. They need someone loyal to the cause."

Rebecca lifted an eyebrow. "The cause? You make it sound like a revolution."

"For them, it is. The men involved are dedicated to finding a cure for syphilis, which is a noble pursuit. Except they've crossed ethical boundaries. *Exitus acta probat.* Finding a cure to the disease could justify anything—even murder."

A somber silence followed her words.

Muldoon broke it by clearing his throat. "Before we went mudlarking, Mr. Kelly sent me a list of names and asked me to research whether any on the list owned property with a basement or an ice house, focusing north of the Thames. Was Dr. Munroe's friend really able to determine where the body had been based on *dirt?*" He sounded amazed.

"Yeah, although that dirt covers a wide area," Kendra replied. "Did you find out anything that could narrow our list of suspects?"

"I'm not sure," he admitted, pulling a notebook from his pocket. He flipped it open. "Most of the gentlemen on the list rent rooms, so no basement or ice house. Sir Preston owns the largest house. Not surprising, I suppose. But I can't imagine him conducting illegal experiments out of it. He has a wife and a rather large staff."

"We were at Sir Preston's last night," Kendra said. "You're right about the staff and lack of privacy."

"And he's too old ter be the man that Bridget saw," Sam added.

Kendra looked at the Bow Street Runner. "Yes, but he could still be involved with the experiments."

"Mr. Beane lives in a small townhouse that he inherited from an uncle," Muldoon continued. "He has a maid-of-all-work and a cook who come in daily. No ice house. I don't know if there's a basement, but I don't think the maid or cook would look kindly on a dead woman being kept there."

"That's assuming they knew a dead woman was in the basement," Kendra commented. "Still, it would be difficult to conduct the experiments without their knowledge."

"Mr. Dawes lives in an impressive manor with a basement, and which may have an ice house—"

"How does an apprentice afford that?" Kendra asked.

"Simple: by living with his stepfather, who happens to be a real estate tycoon." Muldoon grinned at her.

Kendra recalled that it was Dawes's stepfather, Mr. Stevens, who owned the building Goldsten rented for his clinic.

The reporter sighed. "To think I could've been living grand like Mr. Dawes if me mother had met Mr. Stevens before the Widow Dawes. Only one thing that prevented that from happening."

"And what was that, Mr. Muldoon?" Rebecca inquired.

"Me father would have objected."

Rebecca laughed.

Sam snorted. "Like Sir Preston, privacy would be a problem. He'd hardly be able to conduct experiments under his mother and stepfather's noses."

Kendra surveyed the names of the slate board. "What about Burnell and Dandridge?"

"Mr. Dandridge is one of the men who rents rooms. However, Mr. Burnell owns a small cottage in Highgate. He doesn't have a basement or ice house on the property, but he does have privacy. His neighbors said that he doesn't have any servants and he keeps to himself. They don't like him."

"You spoke to the neighbors?"

Muldoon lifted his chin a notch as he met Kendra's gaze. "I spoke to *all* the neighbors of the names on your list, my lady. It's what I do."

"I'm aware. It's why I wanted you on my team." And that was the only compliment she was going to give the man. "Go on."

His mouth twitched as if he were suppressing a smile. "I chatted with the Widow Shaw, who was tending to her garden next to Mr. Burnell's cottage. She told me that he moved in two years ago. When she heard he was a widower, she thought that gave them something in common." Now the twitch became a grin. "Personally, I think she had high hopes of springing the parson's mousetrap on him—"

"We don't need to know about Mrs. Shaw's marital ambitions," Kendra cut in dryly.

The reporter laughed. "Yes, well, she doesn't have any marital ambitions anymore, leastwise with Mr. Burnell. She described him as a cold fish. Stiff-rumped. Mean-spirited—"

"We get the picture."

"Widow Shaw said that the neighborhood was friendly, but Mr. Burnell was disliked by all, and they were grateful that he was never at home."

*Now that was new information.* "Never?"

Muldoon shrugged. "She could've been exaggerating a bit."

Kendra glanced at Sam. "Burnell said he was home alone during both murders."

"I reckon we need ter quiz him about that."

"Yes, we should." She smiled briefly, then shifted her attention back to the slate board. "They're not conducting their experiments out of their homes, so they must have another place. Same criteria—private, with some kind of subterranean chamber, north of the Thames . . ."

She took a breath when it came to her. "Blackfriars."

Muldoon eyed her. "As much as it would help me to narrow down my research, I have to ask, why there, specifically?"

"Because that's where Lady Westford first saw Clarice with Goldsten." God, it was so obvious, she didn't know why she hadn't thought of it before. "She jumped to the conclusion that they had a personal relationship, but what if Clarice was getting treatment nearby?"

"A chance encounter was what started this entire thing?" Rebecca shook her head in amazement.

"This thing—the experiments—was going on before," Kendra said. "But, yes, it was the start of Lady Westford's involvement. Wrong place, wrong time."

Rebecca let out a sigh, then pushed herself to her feet. "I must go. It's one thing to be fashionably late for Lady Chevallier's performance, but to miss most of it would be unforgivably rude."

Muldoon stood as well. "I shall walk you to your carriage, my lady."

The color rose in Rebecca's cheeks. "Thank you, sir," she murmured.

Kendra watched them leave. Apparently, whatever issues there had been between them had been resolved. Or maybe dealing with death made one realize how short life can be.

"I'd best go, as well." Sam drained his whisky, looked regretfully at the empty glass, then put it on the table. "Low tide'll be around four in the morning. I'm gonna get a few winks in before roundin' up the lads. I'll have them positioned around the aqueduct. We can nab the little scamps when they come out of their hole."

"Smart." Kendra nodded her approval as she followed him to the door. "If you get Edwina, bring her here. I don't care what time it is."

Sam met her eyes. "Aye, lass. If we get her, I will."

# FORTY

Kendra woke the next morning to gray light streaming into the bedchamber, an empty space beside her, and a strange restlessness. She rolled off the feather tick mattress and into her yoga routine on the floor. Most of that edginess, she knew, was because there'd been no knock early that morning. Sam hadn't managed to find Edwina—or, if he had, she had evaded him and was in the wind.

*Damn it.*

And the remaining restlessness? She couldn't pinpoint the source. Was it anxiety that she'd missed something, or the sense that they were close to the finish line? She had motive and a list of likely suspects. She just needed to narrow that list down a little more . . .

She just needed a break, and she'd hoped she'd get it from their eyewitness. Without Edwina, she'd plow forward with what she had.

Burnell was number one on her agenda. It might be best to visit the Widow Shaw before she confronted the surgeon about his alibis. Home alone. *Bullshit.*

Kendra finished her yoga routine, and then yanked the bell-pull for Molly. Less than five minutes later, the maid arrived with a tray of coffee, brown bread, and pots of butter and jam.

"Are ye gonna be riskin' yer life mudlarking today?" Molly asked, scowling at Kendra as she ate several slices of bread and gulped down coffee.

Kendra heard the snarky note in the maid's voice. "Are you still angry about the boots?"

"It wasn't about the boots. Although they were fine," Molly

sniffed. "Ye nearly got yerself killed, milady. Ye take too many risks."

Kendra didn't want to argue, so she stuffed the rest of the bread into her mouth.

After Kendra finished the bread and drank another cup of coffee, Molly helped her into a nettle-green, worsted-wool walking dress with gold braiding adorning the hem and cuffs of the long sleeves. She mentally reviewed her notes as she left the bedchamber, hurrying down the hallway to the library.

But a commotion—a shout, a shriek—sent her to the railing. She all but goggled as a red-faced Wakely sprinted after a boy who was currently zigzagging around the foyer like a ricocheting bullet. A maid with a mop in her hand screeched and leapt out of the way when the kid nearly plowed into her. The footman—Hugh?—jumped forward, blocking the pint-sized intruder. The kid swiveled, but Wakely managed to snag his tattered collar. In a move that Kendra had to admire, the boy tried to free himself by stomping on the butler's foot. Wakely yelped in pain, but kept his grip on the child's collar even as the butler grasped the boy's boney arm.

"What the *hell* is going on?" Kendra raised her voice as she sped down the steps.

Wakely tried to assume a dignified posture, but was hampered by the squirming boy. "My apologies, madam—"

"Are ye Lady Sutcliffe?" The boy fixed his furious gaze on her. He was beyond filthy. Brown hair—maybe blonde, if it was washed—stood up in tufts, and his blue eyes seared her like a flame. She estimated him at fourteen or fifteen, but she added decades to those livid eyes. Like most street kids, he was gaunt, all bones and sharp angles that she could see even with the bulky coat covering him.

"Can I help you?"

He jerked away from Wakely. "Aye! It's yer fault! All yer fault!"

"Who are you? And what's my fault?"

"Fish's me name. And it's yer fault that she's gone!" His chin jutted up. "'E came and took 'er. She was safe and now she's gone!"

A chill raced down Kendra's spine. "Who?" she demanded, but she knew.

"Edie. Edwina, We were protectin' 'er, keepin' 'er safe. Then ye came and 'e found her."

"You're one of the mudlarks from yesterday," she said slowly. "What happened?"

Fish crossed his arms, his gaze full of bitter condemnation. "'E must've followed ye."

Christ, the kid knew how to go for the jugular. "Who took her? When?"

"'E was waiting for us on the docks this mornin'. 'E grabbed 'er and took off on 'is 'orse."

"What did he look like, Fish?" She grasped the kid's rigid shoulders and leaned down to look him in the eye. "Hair color, size, age? Anything that stood out to you?"

Fish was silent for a beat. "About 'is age." He pointed to Hugh. "Bigger than 'im, though. Taller. Yellow 'air. I never saw 'im before. 'Is greatcoat was fine quality."

Kendra released Fish and straightened to look at Wakely. "Take him to the kitchen and get him something to eat."

"I don't want food! I want Edie!" The boy glared at her.

"I'm going to find her," Kendra said before she could stop herself. She knew better than to make those kind of promises.

Her chest was tight. She had to take a deep breath and let it out slowly before saying, "Go get something to eat, Fish. You won't be any good to Edwina if you pass out from hunger."

The kid maintained his hostile stance for a moment, then his shoulders slumped, the defiance draining out of him. Wakely put out his hand to guide Fish to the kitchens.

"Wakely?" Kendra said.

The butler paused. "Yes, madam?"

"Please have the carriage brought around. I need to go to St. George's."

He hesitated. "His lordship is on his morning ride. Perhaps you ought to wait until he returns?"

She shook her head and thought, *No time.* "I'm only following up on a few details," she said. "Send word to Mr. Kelly. He'll want to interview Fish about Edwina, then he can join me at the hospital."

"Very well. Good luck, my lady."

She bolted up the stairs, racing to her bedchamber to grab a coat and her reticule, and tried not to wonder if time was running out for Edwina.

Or if it was already too late.

Kendra strode briskly through St. George's lobby, only stopping to flag down a sister carrying a mop and bucket. Given the strong stench of vomit, she guessed the woman was on clean-up duty.

"Is Mr. Burnell working today?"

The woman frowned impatiently. "I saw him . . . somewhere. Maybe surgery?"

"Thanks. Where—" But the woman was already moving away.

Kendra jogged up the steps to the second floor and scanned the hall. People were racing up and down the corridor. *I'm not the only one feeling a sense of urgency*, she reflected.

"Lady Sutcliffe!"

She paused and turned to see Sir Preston coming toward her, his cane tapping out a familiar staccato on the tiled floors.

"Good morning," he said, smiling as he came to a halt. "I didn't expect to see you again so soon. My wife enjoyed your company the other evening. I fear she finds our male conversation quite tiresome."

Kendra had no time for small talk. "Where's Mr. Burnell?"

Sir Preston's eyebrows flew up at her abrupt tone. He peered at her more closely. "Are you all right, my lady?"

"I'm fine. I need to speak with Mr. Burnell."

"Are you certain nothing is amiss?"

*For fuck's sake.* "No. I just need to speak to him. Now."

"He's supervising Mr. Beane with his first amputation. He ought to be finished shortly, and will no doubt wish for a respite. Why don't we wait for him in the lounge, shall we?"

Kendra was forced to slow her impatient stride to match Sir Preston's slower pace as he guided her down the corridor.

"May I ask why you wish to speak to Mr. Burnell?" he asked, shooting her a sideways glance. "You appear . . . overwrought."

"I'm not overwrought." She gritted her teeth. *Next, he'll be bringing out the smelling salts.* "I have a few follow up questions for him."

"I see."

He drew out the words in such a way to imply the opposite. He didn't see, and she could hardly enlighten him that a young girl's life was on the line.

Sir Preston opened the door to the lounge. Dr. Carter was the sole occupant, sitting at the same table as during Kendra's first visit. A cup of tea was cooling next to his elbow as he read a newspaper. At their entrance, he lowered the paper and made a grunting sound that Kendra assumed was a greeting.

"Dr. Carter, do you remember Lady Sutcliffe?" Sir Preston tapped his cane over to the table.

The old man scowled. "I haven't lost my memory. Lady Sutcliffe," he acknowledged with the briefest of nods.

Kendra couldn't stop herself from glancing at the clock on the sideboard. How long did it take to do an amputation? Edwina had been kidnapped, and Burnell was the key to finding her.

She forced herself to look at the cantankerous old man. "Dr. Carter."

"Would you like a cup of tea, my lady?" Sir Preston asked, moving to the sideboard.

"No, thank you."

Sir Preston smiled. "Something stronger? To soothe one's nerves?"

"My nerves are fine, thanks." Still, she took a breath and then let it out slowly. It helped clear her mind a little, and she remembered something. "Actually, I have a few questions for you and Dr. Carter."

Kendra thought it was interesting that each man's eyebrows went in opposite directions—Sir Preston's up in surprise while Dr. Carter's went down in a wary scowl.

"I was told that you both have treated many patients with

syphilis," she continued. "Have either of you ever had patients by the names of Isabella Russo or Clarice Chapman?"

"I can hardly be expected to remember every prostitute with the pox," Dr. Carter groused.

Sir Preston shook his head. "I don't recall them either."

"Clarice was an actress at the Bowden Theater. Isabella Russo worked there, as well, but she dreamed of being a singer. She had a fondness for Vivaldi and had the voice of an angel."

Kendra hoped repeating Mrs. Chirone's words about her sister would help humanize Isabella, get more information about her from the old men.

Dr. Carter's eyes lit up. "Vivaldi!"

"You remember her? Isabella?" Kendra asked.

"Good God, no." His lip curled as he dismissed Isabella with a flick of his wrist. "I remember Vivaldi. I was blessed to attend one of his final performances in Vienna. The man was a genius."

Kendra stared at him and had to wonder exactly how old he was.

He must have read her thoughts, because he glared at her. "I was a child of ten, but I never forgot the magic of *Il Prete Rosso*."

For a moment Kendra's vision wavered, then snapped back into sharp focus. *Oh, my God . . .*

"What did you say?" she managed through numb lips.

"I said that I was blessed to attend one of Vivaldi's final concertos."

Sir Preston eyed her with concern. "Do you feel faint, my lady?"

She barely heard him, keeping her gaze on Dr. Carter. "But what did you call him?"

The old man frowned, clearly bewildered. "*Il Prete Rosso*. It's the nickname given to him after he was ordained as a priest. It means—"

"The Red Priest," Kendra translated. Her pulsed jumped with the surge of adrenalin. *Stupid*, she thought. *I've been so stupid.* "Vivaldi had red hair."

"Yes—"

"Where's Dawes?" She spun to face Sir Preston. She must have looked crazed, because the physician's eyes widened and he took a step back from her. "Dawes. Where is he?"

"Mr. Goldsten's surgery. He's taken it over—where are you going? My lady!"

"Young people—so rude!" Dr. Carter sniffed.

"Lady Sutcliffe—wait!" Sir Preston hurried after her.

"I don't have time to wait." Still, she paused long enough for the old man to catch up. "I have to find Dawes and send a message to my husband," she said as they began walking again.

"Why? What is this about?"

"Dawes is Vivaldi."

"What?"

She blew out an annoyed breath. "I don't have time to explain."

"I shall accompany you, and you can explain on the way." He hailed one of the apprentice's striding down the corridor. "Mr. Quayle, run out to the mews and tell my coachman to bring my carriage around immediately."

Irritation flashed in the young man's face, but he nodded. "Yes, sir."

"I have a carriage," she retorted as they approached the stairs.

"My coachman will instruct yours to deliver the message to your husband. It'll save time, as your man knows your address. Could you please slow your pace a bit, madam? I realize you are in a great hurry to speak to young Dawes, but he's not going anywhere."

Kendra shot him an impatient look. "Sir Preston, this is an emergency—"

"Is someone in risk of imminent death?" He took her arm and smiled at her.

Short of shaking him off, she was forced to slow down.

"Everything is an emergency for the young." He made a tutting noise. "When you reach my age, you begin to—"

"A girl has been kidnapped," she snapped.

Sir Preston's eyes widened. "Good heavens. What does this have to do with Mr. Dawes?"

"He's involved."

"No."

"Yes. Sir Preston—"

"I'm coming with you, my lady." His tone took on a steely edge. "I've known that boy all his life. I went to school with Andrew's father. I'll not let you accuse him falsely."

Kendra was still stunned that Dawes was Vivaldi, but her mind was beginning to clear. Her mistake, she realized, was assuming Isabella's Vivaldi was the leader. There was no way the apprentice was the one spearheading the experiments. He was a follower.

But she was beginning to think she knew who he was following.

# FORTY-ONE

Once the carriages were arranged, Kendra lowered herself into the seat of Sir Preston's, where the old man joined her a moment later. Laying his cane across his lap, he regarded her intently as the carriage jolted forward.

"Now, madam, tell me what this is about, and why you think Andrew is involved in kidnapping a girl."

"The girl is an eyewitness to Lady Westford's murder."

He shook his head in denial. "You are implying that Andrew killed Lady Westford. Why would he do such a thing?"

"For the same reason Dr. Thornton and Jenny had to die. And," she added softly, "Mr. Goldsten."

Surprise flared in the old man's eyes. "Mr. Goldsten killed himself."

"How do you know he committed suicide?"

"This is madness. Everyone saw him do it."

"No, they saw Goldsten go into his office and Dawes follow him in. They *heard* a gunshot. We only have Dawes's word that Goldsten killed himself." She kept her gaze steady on Sir Preston's. "I think Dawes took Goldsten by surprise and shot him pointblank in the head. Then he pretended to save him."

Sir Preston sucked in a breath. "I don't believe it!"

"I actually think Dawes was shocked by his own act of violence." She remembered the apprentice's horror. "It couldn't have been easy for him. To kill his own mentor."

"You are accusing Andrew of being this . . . this vile mastermind."

"No. He's a follower, and was following orders to silence Goldsten before he could talk. He's not the mastermind." She slipped her hand in her reticule, and brought out the pistol, pointing it at the physician. "You, Sir Preston, are the mastermind."

"You are insane, madam!" Sir Preston's hands convulsed around the silver handle of his cane. "Put that weapon down before you hurt someone."

Kendra smiled. "If I shoot you, Sir Preston, it won't be an accident. Where are you taking me, by the way? What message did you give my coachman?"

He blinked. Then, amazingly, he chuckled. "You are quite the Amazon, Lady Sutcliffe. My wife told me not to underestimate you."

That startled Kendra. "Lady Maude is part of this?"

"By this, I assume you're referring to my little research group? No. She was merely making a general observation after meeting you. She's an astute lady." He leaned back in his seat, his hands resting loosely on his walking cane. Kendra thought he looked more comfortable and amused than anyone should be with a gun pointed at them. "I passed on your message to your coachman that we were going to Mr. Goldsten's surgery. I didn't mention your suspicion regarding Andrew, of course."

He tilted his head, regarding her curiously. "You must tell me how you concluded that I was . . . I shan't be so presumptuous and call myself a mastermind." He smiled briefly at her. "Let's just say that I was instrumental in putting the group together."

"You're one of the founders of the Metamorphosis Club, a group to discuss advancement and change in the medical community."

"Is that what gave me away? No," he answered his own question, shaking his head. "Lucien and I founded the club years ago—long before I had the idea to take what was discussed in our meetings and make it a reality."

"Isabella Russo told me."

"Doubtful. The woman was mad even before we finished with her."

"And tossed her aside like trash."

"It was clear that it was too late for her. The pox was already rotting her brain as well as her face. She couldn't be saved, no matter what we did."

"You gave her false hope. She told me she was being cured by Vivaldi and the saints."

He huffed out a laugh. "Andrew and his red hair. How odd to be exposed by the rantings of a madwoman. But why did you suspect me?"

"I knew more than one person was involved. Vivaldi *and the saints*. Every group needs a leader. Someone respected by his peers and followed by his subordinates. You have that kind of reputation, both in your club and at St. George's. My mistake was that I thought Isabella's Vivaldi was the leader."

"Fascinating."

"You were also insistent—too insistent—about accompanying me to see Dawes, and about using your carriage. I assume your coachman was the one watching me down by the river—and the one who took Edwina."

He regarded her intently. "You knew this was a trap, and yet you came anyway."

Kendra wiggled the pistol at him. "I'm not worried."

"Still, why take the risk?"

"You have Edwina," she said simply.

"Ah. You knew—or you hoped—that I'd take you to her."

"I counted on it." She studied him. "You didn't kill Lady Westford." It was a statement of fact. Sir Preston was too old. "Dawes didn't kill her. He's not ruthless or cold-blooded enough."

"Grace's death was unfortunate," he sighed. "She'd learned Clarice was getting treatments, and then . . . well, that went disastrously wrong. Still, we thought she'd listen to reason when she knew what we were attempting to do."

"You thought that because her sister died of typhus, she'd look the other way regarding murder."

"It wasn't murder."

"Excuse me, a 'failed experiment.' If you could have persuaded her to see your point of view, she would have made a valuable ally. She had money, status—and, more importantly, the Queen's ear."

Sir Preston's eyes flashed with annoyance. "As I said, it was unfortunate."

The carriage slowed and turned down a narrow lane. Flicking a quick look out the window, Kendra wasn't surprised to see the seedier buildings of Blackfriars. "Where are we going?"

"Andrew's stepfather owns a considerable amount of property in this area. He was kind enough to lease one of his buildings to Andrew, with the expectation that he'll eventually use it for his own consulting rooms."

"That's right," she said. "He's Goldsten's landlord, as well. I suppose it was convenient for Dawes to go from there to Goldsten's clinic. Unfortunately, you fucked up. Goldsten ran into the girl and Lady Westford saw them together."

Sir Preston's face puckered and turned red. "Language!"

Kendra nearly laughed. The man was responsible for unethical experiments leading to a woman's death and was involved in a conspiracy to commit murder, and yet he was offended by her profanity.

"Why don't you tell me about your experiments," she said. "Why focus on syphilis?"

His mouth compressed. "It's a scourge on humanity. I witnessed its effects firsthand when Andrew's father died of it twenty years ago. Andrew was only four, but it impacted him. I knew he would want to be part of our research. And there's no shortage of test subjects."

"What you really mean is you wanted to experiment on women who held no power."

He gave a derisive snort. "They're hardly productive members of society. Soiled doves. How do you think they became infected in the first place?"

"They're human beings."

"You're missing the point, madam. It's not about *them*. Those women were already dead. They were infected with the pox. We didn't give it to them. They were willing participants in our research." His hands tightened on the silver handle of his cane as he leaned forward, his eyes brightening with excitement. "Put aside the sentimental claptrap, and *think!* What if we are able to cure the pox? And not only the pox, but all illnesses of the blood!"

His hypothesis was flawed at its core. Syphilis wasn't a blood disease; it was a sexually transmitted infection caused by bacteria. But she could hardly tell him that. Instead, she asked, "How do your treatments work?"

"We syphon off the blood and circulate it through an electrical machine, then return it to the body. The electricity acts as a purifier, removing disease from the blood."

Kendra regarded him incredulously. "How do expect the person to stay alive when the blood is removed?"

"Don't be daft! It's a closed loop. We don't remove *all* the blood. We begin the transfusion, passing it through the machine, and the purified blood is returned to the body before the rest of the diseased blood is removed."

"What went wrong with Clarice?"

He blew out a breath. "Andrew and I were scheduled to conduct the treatment, but I was unexpectedly delayed. Foolishly, Andrew proceeded without me. The machine malfunctioned and he couldn't replace her blood in time. She perished." His eyebrows twitched in irritation. "The boy panicked and disposed of the body in the river."

"Why'd you remove the eyes and uterus after you stole the body?"

"Andrew should've removed them before disposing of the body," Sir Preston said, annoyance sharpening his voice. "We can learn from everything. By dissecting organs, we increase our knowledge on how the body operates."

"You crossed a line, Sir Preston. You murdered people—"

"Not I!"

"You were part of it!" she shot back. "Lady Westford, Goldsten, Jenny . . . Dr. Thornton. I thought he was your friend."

"I was with him when his wife died of her blood disease. Of all people, he knew what I was trying to accomplish. And yet he was ready to destroy everything!" He drew in a shaky breath and made a visible effort to compose himself. "It was *you*, my lady. If you hadn't interfered . . . he lost his nerve only when you began your blasted inquisition."

"I guess his conscience got the better of him."

Sir Preston's eyes narrowed. "You still don't understand. What we are doing is beyond the ordinary. Someday, society will understand and fall to their knees in thanks."

*Talk about a God complex.* "They're more likely to hang you for murder."

"It was *one* mistake. One person to save thousands! *Millions!* Society will view us more favorably than you do, Lady Sutcliffe, if the outcome is a cure for the pox. Especially when the girl's death wasn't even intentional."

"You dumped her body in the Thames like she was nothing."

"She *was* nothing, damn your eyes! If we'd been successful, she would've achieved the immortality she'd pursued on stage."

The chance of a cure, the promise of fame. No wonder Clarice and Isabella had been lured in.

"How many?" Kendra asked. "How many women did you experiment on?"

"Only those two. Before them, dogs, sheep, pigs."

"The results?" She saw it in his eyes. "Mixed. And you still moved to human trials."

He frowned. "We've had more successes than failures."

The carriage was slowing.

"How many in your group? Dawes. Thornton—until he lost his nerve." *And then his life.* "You, obviously. How many more?"

His mouth curved in a slow smile. "You'll soon find out."

# FORTY-TWO

Alec swept off his curly beaver hat as he entered the foyer, but something in Wakely's expression made him pause.

"What's happened?" His gut twisted and he added, "Where's her ladyship?"

"Lady Sutcliffe left for St. George's. She was anxious because—"

"Edie's gone because of 'er!"

Alec glanced over at the scruffy boy standing in the hallway. "Who the devil are you?"

"This is . . . Fish," Wakely answered, his tone disapproving. "Her ladyship ordered the scamp fed, but apparently mutton, mashed potatoes, and three tarts have not improved his disposition."

The boy turned his scowl on the butler. "I don't need nothin' improved. I need ter find Edie."

"Are you speaking of Edwina?" Alec asked.

"Aye, Edie. The fiend took 'er. I told 'er ladyship w'ot 'e looked like, and she went off ter the 'ospital."

"She wanted me to inform you when you returned," Wakely said. "I've sent word to Mr. Kelly as well. Her ladyship said she needed to speak to Mr. Burnell."

Alec shoved his hat on his head again. "When did she leave?"

"An hour, no more," the butler replied.

"Oy! Where're ye goin'?" Fish demanded when Alec turned to yank open the door.

Alec lifted an eyebrow at the boy's insolence. "I'm going to find my wife. Does that meet with your approval?"

Fish's chin jutted up. "Aye, gov, but I'm goin' with ye."

Kendra's fingers tightened on the pistol's trigger as the carriage swayed to a stop.

"What's your coachman's name?" she asked Sir Preston.

The carriage rocked as the coachman leapt off his seat. Footsteps crunched outside. Kendra inched backward, making sure she was in a position to cover both Sir Preston and the carriage door.

"Ned," Sir Preston said.

"Either Ned is extremely loyal or you pay him very well."

The old man smiled. "He's loyal. I saved his life when he was a young lad. An emergency appendectomy. You can't buy that kind of allegiance."

"Good to know." Deliberately she shifted the muzzle so it was pointed directly at Sir Preston. "Ned might be willing to take a bullet for you, but he won't risk your life."

The door opened and Kendra ordered, "Don't move, Ned!"

The coachman jerked back, his hand flying to the knife tucked into his belt.

"Freeze, asshole, or I'm going to put a hole in Sir Preston's head!"

Ned froze. His gaze darted from Kendra to Sir Preston.

"Stay calm," Sir Preston murmured, giving a little nod to his coachman. His composure was almost eerie, Kendra thought. But she forced herself to ignore it, keeping her eyes on coachman.

"Here's what you're going to do, Ned," she said. "You're going to place both of your hands on top of your head."

His lips peeled back in a snarl as he complied. "If you harm Sir Preston, I'll kill you."

She ignored the threat. "Lace your fingers together. Now, step back ten paces—no, don't turn around. Face me and step backwards. Keep your hands on your head, fingers laced."

Ned's eyes burned with hatred as he locked his gaze on hers. He stopped after ten paces.

"If you so much as twitch, Ned, I swear to God, you'll be burying Sir Preston." She let that sink in, then, without looking away from Ned, she said, "Your turn, Sir Preston."

"If you're asking me to get out of the carriage with my hands on my head, I have to decline, my lady. I'm old. This cane isn't for show; it's a necessity."

*Shit.* "Fine. Get out of the carriage. *Slowly.*"

He huffed out a laugh. "At my age, that is the only way I can move."

She waited until he was through the door before pressing the pistol's muzzle against the back his skull and then looking to Ned again, she said, "Keep your hands on your head and be very still."

It happened fast. One second, she was following Sir Preston out of the carriage, the next the old man let out a sharp cry and his leg twisted beneath him. She shot a quick look at Sir Preston, then sensed Ned moving. She swung back to the coachman, the bigger threat, and pulled the trigger. Grit exploded out of the brick wall where Ned had been standing a second ago. *Son of a bitch.*

She cut her gaze to where he'd thrown himself and—

Pain screamed through her, stunning her and stealing her breath. She staggered backward and fell against the carriage steps. She heard a clatter as the pistol fell from her numb fingers.

She looked into Sir Preston's eyes. Then she dropped her gaze down to his cane's silver handle that concealed a lethal blade.

A blade that was now embedded in her stomach.

# FORTY-THREE

Alec strode briskly down the corridor of St. George's, Fish at his heels. A sharp-eyed sister told them where to find Burnell, and a moment later, Alec threw open the door to the private lounge.

Kendra wasn't there. But Burnell was at a table with two young men, all three wearing aprons splattered with blood.

"Burnell, I'm looking for my wife," Alec announced.

Burnell raised an amused eyebrow. "You lost her?"

"She came here to speak to you," Alec said coldly.

"I haven't seen her ladyship today. Mr. Beane and I were amputating a leg earlier." He flicked a glance at the apprentice sitting next to him. "Maybe she grew tired of waiting for me and left."

"Lord Sutcliffe."

Alec turned and saw Sam Kelly walk through the door. The Bow Street Runner gave Fish a speculative glance as he said, "Your butler told me that you'd set off after her ladyship. Where is she?"

"I am trying to find that out myself. Mr. Burnell said he never saw her."

Burnell frowned. "I haven't. And I can't imagine why she wanted to speak to me."

Sam's eyes were cool as he surveyed the sawbones. "She wanted ter ask you about your alibis. You said you were home when both Lady Westford and Dr. Thornton and his maid died, Mr. Burnell, but your neighbors say otherwise."

Burnell's mouth tightened. "You went to Highgate?"

"Aye. Do you want ter revise your previous statements?"

"No. I *was* at home—my home in Blackheath. And I find this interrogation damn insulting."

"Blackheath?" Sam's eyebrows popped up. "How many homes do you own, Mr. Burnell?"

The surgeon drew in a breath. "Two—for now. Earlier this year, my maiden aunt passed away and left me the Blackheath house, if you must know. I've been spending most of my free time there as I sort through my aunt's possessions. I didn't feel the need to inform my Highgate neighbors about my inheritance or my activities. It is none of their business."

Sam's eyes narrowed. "Why didn't you tell Lady Sutcliffe this when she asked for your whereabouts for the murders?"

"I told her that I was home alone—and I was. You have my permission to quiz the neighbors in Blackheath. I also suggest going to the local tavern, the Pig and Swan, as I've taken many of my meals there."

Alec shifted impatiently. "I'm less concerned about Mr. Burnell's alibi, Mr. Kelly, than my wife's whereabouts. If she didn't come here, where in blazes did she go?"

"She was here," an old man sitting at the next table spoke up.

"You saw my wife?"

"Yes. She ran off in a most peculiar fashion."

Alec scowled at him. "What do you mean, she ran off? Where did she run off *to*?"

"Well, I don't know *that*," the old man huffed. "I'm only saying that her behavior was strange. We were having a perfectly cordial discussion about Vivaldi. I once saw him perform when I was a young lad—"

Burnell signed heavily. "Dr. Carter—"

"What did she say?" Alec interrupted. He had to curl his fingers into tight fists to prevent himself from dragging the blasted man out of his chair and shaking him.

"That's what I'm trying to tell you!" Dr. Carter snapped. "She behaved oddly when I mentioned that Vivaldi was known as the Red

Priest. She said that Vivaldi was Mr. Dawes. I'm telling you that the woman—"

"My God!" Alec turned abruptly to Sam. "*Dawes.*"

"Where is Mr. Dawes now?" Sam demanded of the assembled men.

Burnell was the one who answered. "He's working at Mr. Goldsten's surgery—"

Alec didn't wait. He ran for the door, with Sam and Fish sprinting behind him.

Dr. Carter sniffed. "How rude."

When Kendra regained consciousness, she was lying on a table. Stale air tickled her nostrils. She forced her eyes to open a fraction and the world spun dizzily. And the pain . . . God, it felt like someone was thrusting a white-hot poker into her side.

*Don't think about it. Focus on something else besides the excruciating throbbing.*

"We don't want her to die yet." Sir Preston's voice sounded far away.

*Yet.* That one word confirmed the fate that Kendra knew awaited her.

Breathing shallowly and keeping her eyes veiled with her lashes, she scanned the room. Rough stone walls, revealed by dozens of lanterns. Metal and glass gleamed on a long wooden counter. Microscopes, beakers, jars with objects floating in murky fluid, and surgical tools—scalpels, needles, forceps, surgical saws and shears.

She heard the drip, drip, drip of water.

"Damnation, why did you bring her *here*?" Kendra recognized the voice. *Dandridge.* "Why didn't you just finish the job?"

"That's the problem with you young people." Sir Preston's tone was light. "You never think anything through. Her blood is too precious to waste."

"She doesn't have the pox."

"That doesn't mean we can't experiment with new techniques.

You need to patch her up, though. We don't want her to bleed out."

"What about Dawes? If she told anyone—"

"She didn't. Still, we can't afford any more mistakes. If Carter tells Lord Sutcliffe, he could go after Andrew. I don't believe Andrew would ever betray us, but it's best to be safe. I've sent Ned to get him, and we will ship the lad to France. Pray tell, does your cousin need an apprentice?"

Kendra opened her eyes a little more, turning her head slightly. Now she could see what looked like a culvert cut into a rough-hewn wall. The water splashed into a shallow creek that extended the length of the room before gurgling into another conduit. An underground portion of the River Fleet, she guessed.

Her heart leapt into her throat when her eyes focused on the two narrow tables next to her, with chains and leather restraints bolted to each side. A table nearby held a large wooden box. Inside the box was glass jars and coiled metal wires.

It was bad. But not as bad as the cages, Kendra decided, when her gaze slid farther down the chamber. There were three. Large enough to hold a Saint Bernard or a mastiff.

*Or a woman.*

Kendra's mouth was as dry as she met the terrified eyes of the girl crouched in the middle cage. *Edwina.*

Then she nearly screamed when a face moved suddenly into her line of vision. Sir Preston smiled down at her. "Ah, good. You're awake," he said. "You're lucky, my lady. The most skilled surgeon in London is on hand to patch you up."

Kendra wasn't surprised when Dandridge stepped up, and she looked into his soulless eyes. "You murdered Lady Westford."

He didn't bother to reply.

Sir Preston was still smiling when he wrapped his hand around the silver cane handle. "I'm afraid this is going to hurt."

She screamed when he wrenched the blade out of her belly, and her vision blurred again. The last thing she saw before darkness swamped her was Dandridge approaching with a needle and thread.

# FORTY-FOUR

Alec brought the curricle to an abrupt stop, his horses' front hooves scraping the air.

"God's teeth," Sam muttered, ashen from the fastest drive Alec had ever done across the city. Fish, crammed in the middle, was grinning, his eyes gleaming in a boyish excitement at having almost crashed at least ten times before arriving at their destination.

Leaping to the ground, Alec tossed the reins to a surprised man loitering on the street outside Goldsten's clinic. "You'll get a guinea if my vehicle is here when I get back," he called before hurtling up the steps. He couldn't explain the sense of urgency he felt as he threw open the clinic's doors. He barely registered the broken and bleeding bodies around the lobby.

Bursting into the operating theater, he saw Dawes on the far side of the room, in deep conversation with a blond-haired man.

"It's 'im!" Fish cried as he skidded into the room. "That's the bastard that took Edie!"

Dawes and the other man glanced at them, and panic flared in Dawes's face. He glanced around wildly, as though looking for an escape route. The other man pulled a pistol from his greatcoat's deep pockets and aimed at Alec.

Grabbing Fish's boney shoulders, Alec threw himself to the side as the man fired. The bullet whizzed past and hit the wall, and all hell broke loose. Patients screamed. Apprentices yelled and dove for cover. Dawes spun and bolted through a doorway.

Ignoring the chaos around him, Alec raced after him. As he

cleared the doorway, another shot blasted behind him. More shouts and sounds of metal clanging and rushing feet, but he didn't look back. He kept his gaze fixed on Dawes's fleeing figure.

The apprentice shot a frantic glance over his shoulder as he shoved open another door in front of him and flew out into the alley. Seconds later, Alec charged through the door.

Dawes was gone.

Ice-cold fear shot through Alec. Heart hammering, he cocked his head and listened, and heard running footsteps to his right. He jogged down the lane, eyes scanning left and right. The pungent odor of refuse rose up all around him. He glimpsed rats the size of small dogs scurrying along the crumbling brick foundations of the tenements.

Still no Dawes.

He was in a labyrinth, now with more people, standing or slumped in doorways, crouched in their makeshift hovels. Staring at him with bleary, brooding eyes. Alec stopped in front of a greasy-haired man with sharp, foxlike features and sly eyes.

"Did you see a man run by?" he asked. "Young. Ginger hair."

"W'ot's in it fer me, if I tell ye?"

Alec pulled his weapon from his pocket. Eyes locked on the other man, he walked forward until his gun was a whisper from the man's soot-smeared forehead.

"I'll let you live."

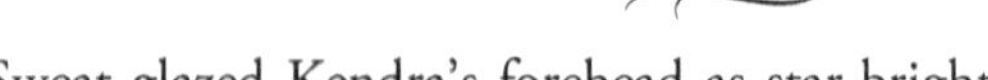

Sweat glazed Kendra's forehead as star-bright pain sizzled through her from both the knife wound and Dandridge's stitching.

"This is a mistake." Dandridge's face was grim as he dressed the wound, wrapping gauzy strips tight around Kendra's waist. "Keeping her alive."

"I don't think so," Sir Preston replied. "We have two perfectly good specimens now for the machine."

They were talking like Kendra wasn't even there. Like she was a rat in a cage.

She released a shuddering breath, watching Dandridge gather and dispose of the blood-soaked rags. If she didn't die of an infection, it would be a miracle.

On the other hand, she doubted they were planning to let her live long enough for that.

She pressed her hands against the bandage as she sat up. Her gaze fell on the scissors. She was as shaky as a newborn colt, but if she could get to them . . .

"You'd only damage yourself and ruin Mr. Dandridge's excellent work, my lady," Sir Preston chided, following her eyes and picking up the scissors. "I'll remove the temptation."

He had the gall to smile at her. *Bastard.*

She took a cautious breath and let it out slowly. "You really think you will be able to cure syphilis with your machine?" she asked, swinging her legs over the table.

"Careful," Sir Preston warned. "If you try to escape, you won't get far."

"I'm not running. I want a closer look at your invention."

Pride flashed in Dandridge's eyes as he stepped over to the large wooden box. She knew how to deal with scientists with massive egos.

Kendra could see the six jars inside the box. About the size of overripe melons, metal foil was wrapped around the bottoms and rod electrodes protruded from their lids. More metal tubes were attached to extra containers and wire coils sprouted from each jar like an avante-garde sculpture.

"It's your invention, Mr. Dandridge?" She remembered how he'd argued about the possible benefits of electricity at St. George's.

"It was my idea, yes." He gave the box a loving stroke. "I came up with it after I saw the electricity experiments. Sir Preston was the one who imagined it could be used to purify the blood, as so many diseases originate there."

Sir Preston said, "You and the girl might not have the pox, but you'll be able to provide us with a unique opportunity of study."

Edwina let out a low, terrified moan.

Kendra slid off the table. Her legs nearly buckled, but she managed to catch herself with a white-knuckle grip on the table.

"Mind yourself!" This time it was Dandridge who snapped out the warning. "The knife missed your vital organs—remarkable, really—but you still lost a lot of blood."

"It's not the first time I've been stabbed," she muttered.

Sir Preston smirked. "I must confess, you are a most unusual female. Still, it will take you a day or two to recover. We want you in top form before we begin our experiments." He paused, his eyes brightening as he looked at Dandridge. "I wonder if a transfusion of purified blood would speed up the recovery process?"

Dandridge looked intrigued. "Yes . . .yes, an excellent idea, Sir Preston. We can't wait too long, of course, if we want to get a true measurement."

Cold fear and fury speared through her as she listened to the rising excitement in the two men as they discussed the idea. A new experiment with her as the lab rat.

"How does it work?" she asked abruptly. A bead of sweat slid down her spine as she forced herself to step toward Dandridge's invention.

"We don't yet know its potential," Dandridge said now. "It works like a Leyden jar, where the rod is charged with static electricity, and the electricity is then stored in the glass container until it's released. But our device is *much* more powerful. It truly is lightening in a bottle."

Kendra nodded, even as she gave a surreptitious glance around the chamber, looking for something she could use as a weapon. There were medical instruments on the counter, sharp and deadly— but too far away. She spotted her reticule and gun on a bench. Closer, but not close enough.

"The machine is fully charged," Dandridge continued. "It can provide an electrical current for six hours. More than enough time to circulate the blood."

"Clever." Kendra glanced at Sir Preston, leaning on his cane, with its silver handle that concealed the blade. Even in her weakened state, she was confident that she could get the weapon from him . . . but that still left Dandridge.

"We remove the infected blood, which is then passed through the machine . . ."

Kendra pretended to listen as her gaze returned to the counter. Her stomach lurched at one object floating in murky liquid. She recognized the orb for what it was: *an eyeball.*

And she knew, absolutely *knew,* she was staring at one of Clarice's eyes.

In a few days or weeks, bits and pieces of her would be in those jars too.

*No fucking way.*

The door suddenly flew open, and a wild-eyed Dawes flung himself into the room.

"Andrew?" Sir Preston asked, startled. "What happened? Where's Ned?"

"He's— I don't—" The apprentice panted, shaking his head. "Lord Sutcliffe came . . ."

*It's now or never.* Sucking in a breath, Kendra launched herself at Sir Preston. Pain exploded in her abdomen as she rammed him with her shoulder, sending the old man wheeling backward. She tried to grab the cane, but Sir Preston was already falling. He yelled as he splashed into the shallow creek.

Kendra turned in time to see Alec, Sam, and Fish barreling through the doorway.

"No! *Damn you!*" Sir Preston cried, drawing Kendra's attention again. He'd managed to get to his feet and his eyes locked on hers as he yanked the silver handle off his cane, revealing the blade. There was only one weapon close enough for Kendra to grab.

She turned and grasped the wooden box, lifting it in one Herculean effort. She felt her stitches rip open as she heaved the machine in a low arc toward the stream. Sir Preston's eyes widened and his mouth opened, but no scream emerged as the box hit the water. His body did a jittery dance as the machine's electrical current was discharged in the creek. Then his eyes rolled up in his head and he collapsed face-down into the water.

Kendra's heart leap into her throat at the sound of a gunshot, and she pivoted to see Dandridge's body sprawled on the floor. Kendra met Alec's eyes as he lowered his gun.

"My God, Kendra . . ." Shoving the weapon into his pocket, Alec raced over to her. "You've been shot," he breathed, his eyes on the bandage and the blood seeping through it.

"Stabbed. Sir Preston's fucking cane hid a knife." She began to shake. "I'm pretty sure I tore out the stitches."

"Damnation." He ran over to the counter and brought back more linen strips. "When we get home, I'll call my physician."

"I'm sort of off doctors right now." She hissed when he wrapped the bandage around her. "Unless it's Dr. Munroe. He's stitched me up before."

Alec muttered something she didn't quite catch.

"You all right, lass?" Sam asked. He pointed his pistol at Dawes, who was on the ground, dazed and defeated, with tears sliding down his cheeks. If he hadn't murdered Goldsten in cold-blood, she could almost feel sorry for him.

"I have to admit, I've had better days," she said. "But this could've been worse. Your timing was perfect."

The Bow Street Runner grinned at her, then his gaze moved beyond her. "Is he . . . ?"

Kendra turned back to Sir Preston's body. "Yes. Water and electricity are a bad combination."

"Stop yer blubbering, Edie!" Fish's exclamation drew their attention. The mudlark was crouched in front of the cage holding Edwina. "I'm gonna get ye out of there, don't ye worry." Scowling, he looked over at Kendra. "Oy! Where's the bloody key?"

*Shit.* "I might have to pick the lock—"

"Not bloody likely," Alec said, and lifted her in his arms. "Mr. Kelly can handle it. We're leaving."

"Aye. Don't you worry, lass," Sam called after them. "I'll find the key once I take care of Mr. Dawes."

Kendra laid her head on Alec's shoulder as he carried her up the stairwell. "They were going to experiment on me and Edwina." The adrenaline rush was gone, leaving only the throbbing pain of her injury.

"I was born an experiment," she whispered, closing her eyes. "I'm never going to be an experiment again."

# FORTY-FIVE

Three days later, Kendra was sitting in the drawing room with Alec and the Duke when Wakely appeared and announced a visitor. The butler ushered in Mr. Boothe, who looked as dapper as he had during their first meeting, now wearing a deep burgundy frock coat with an eye-popping yellow silk vest embroidered with red thread.

Alec and the Duke stood, greeted the royal clerk, then waved him into one of the wingback chairs near the crackling fire.

"Would you like a sherry?" Alec sauntered to the sideboard. "Or something stronger?"

"Thank you, sir. Sherry ought to take the chill off." He flipped open the skirt of his frock coat so as to not crush the fabric when he sat down. "I am quite weary of the rain and cold."

"As is everyone," said the Duke, returning to his seat. "The food shortages and high prices have caused considerable stress on the populace. I've been reading in the newspapers about the riots that have begun to break out around the kingdom."

"'Tis troubling. Thank you, sir," Boothe said as Alec handed him a glass. "But I am not here to discuss the weather. I'm here to thank Lady Sutcliffe for her service. Her Majesty is aware that you were injured, my lady. How are you feeling?"

The clerk scrutinized her so closely that Kendra was sure he could see through her loose blue velvet round gown to the bandages wrapped tightly around her torso.

"Much better, thank you," she replied. She'd had Munroe douse the laceration with whisky before he stitched her up. Whether it was that or Molly's diligent application of herbs and ointments, Kendra had so far avoided the dreaded infection and fever that usually accompanied such injuries.

Mr. Boothe took a sip of his sherry, then sighed. "I confess, this entire series of events has been shocking. I'm not only speaking of the murders of Lady Westford and Dr. Thornton, but of the illegal experiments that Sir Preston and Mr. Dandridge were conducting."

No mention of Jenny and Goldsten, Kendra noticed.

Mr. Boothe continued, "Mr. Dawes said that the women had agreed to participate, though."

The Duke frowned. "What was the alternative? Mercury? 'Tis poison and they knew it. A future filled with sickness, madness, and blindness. They were offered hope and took it. But it was an illusion."

"It's shocking how such brilliant men could be so misguided," Mr. Boothe murmured, shaking his head. "They honestly thought that their electricity machine could cure the pox? That they could use it to purify the blood? Such foolishness."

Not so foolish, Kendra thought. Dandridge's invention could be considered a prototype dialysis machine, or the precursor to advanced therapies like EBOO—extracorporeal blood oxygenation and ozonation—when blood was run through a filtration machine to clean it of toxins, viruses, and bacteria. Supposedly, it helped those suffering from chronic inflammation and autoimmune disorders, and sped up cellular healing.

Like Sir Francis Ronalds, Sir Preston and Dandridge were simply ahead of their time. Of course, Ronalds hadn't experimented on human beings or committed murder to hide his activities or further his cause.

The Duke said, "What they did was inexcusable, and yet I wonder if they would have felt the need to cross those boundaries if the law were less restrictive. Science cannot flourish in darkness. There ought to be research and testing. If guidelines were established and lawful, who knows how far medicine could advance?"

Mr. Boothe exhaled heavily. "Well, it isn't for me to say, thank God."

"What will happen to Mr. Dawes?" Kendra asked. Muldoon had written an article on the illegal experiments that had caused Clarice's death, but he hadn't included names. Looking at Mr. Boothe now, Kendra sensed the hand of the government—or the Palace—in containing the fallout.

*And the cover up begins . . .*

"Mr. Dawes is being transported to Botany Bay," Mr. Boothe said carefully.

"No trial?"

"He pleaded guilty." He shrugged. "A trial would be pointless, obviously."

"He murdered Mr. Goldsten. That's a capital crime. Being sent to Australia seems like he's getting off lightly." Her lips twisted. "I guess it's helpful to have a stepfather who is a wealthy real estate tycoon."

"Many convicts perish on the trip to Australia," the Duke said. "And if they survive the journey, they die at the penal colony."

Mr. Boothe added, "We're aware of his role in this terrible business, but he didn't admit to killing Mr. Goldsten and we can't prove it."

Kendra remembered the tears that Dawes had shed right after Goldsten's death. *It was terrible; more terrible than I could ever have imagined*, he'd said. She'd been dealing with her own guilt in the alleged suicide and had missed the significance of those words. Why would Dawes have imagined Goldsten's death, unless he'd tried to prepare for it prior to shooting his mentor?

Unfortunately, Boothe was right. She couldn't prove it, not with this era's forensics.

She tilted her head as she regarded the royal clerk. "The public will never know about Sir Preston's participation, will they?"

But she knew the answer. *Some things never change.*

"The man is dead, killed by his own electricity machine. Some might call that poetic justice. Either way, Sir Preston's involvement would only cause Lady Maude embarrassment."

"And Mr. Dandridge?"

"The man is a fiend," Mr. Boothe said, snapping Kendra out of her contemplation. "There will be no attempt to hide his responsibility in the murder of Lady Westford and Dr. Thornton."

"And Jenny."

"Yes. Yes, of course." Mr. Boothe cleared his throat. "It's unfortunate that he isn't alive to face his villainy and the hangman's noose, but God will judge him now."

He drained his sherry and then set down the glass. Bracing his hands against his thighs, he pushed himself to his feet. "I must be going. But before I do . . ." He smiled at Kendra as he drew a scroll with the royal seal from his pocket. "Her Majesty is requesting your presence next Friday evening at Buckingham House."

"Uh . . ."

Alec accepted the scroll. "My wife and I shall be pleased to attend."

Mr. Boothe looked at the Duke. "You are invited as well, Your Grace. Her Majesty says that it's been many years since she's had the pleasure of your company, sir."

"The pleasure will be mine." The Duke stood up. "I'm leaving, as well. I shall walk you out, Mr. Boothe."

Kendra scowled at Alec once they were alone. "I can't meet the Queen. I'm injured!"

"When I mentioned your injury this morning and suggested you remain in bed, you insisted that you were in excellent health," he pointed out mildly.

"Then stab me again!"

Alec laughed. "I don't know that I've ever seen you look so panicked—except when I proposed. What are you afraid of?"

"Committing a faux pas that will get you exiled. There are probably a thousand rules I'll need to learn."

"I can invite my aunt to give you instruction."

"Now I really am feeling faint."

He joined her on the sofa. "There aren't that many rules. You curtsy to the Queen, speak only when you're spoken to, and never turn your back on a royal."

"Because they can't be trusted," she muttered.

He smiled. "I mean that literally. When it's time to leave, you are required to walk backward out of the room so that you face the royal at all times."

"That sounds hazardous."

He cupped her chin. "In the time I've known you, you've been shot, stabbed, and brutalized. And you think meeting the Queen is going to be hazardous?" He shook his head and laughed again. "Darling, I adore you."

He lowered his head and kissed her.

"Prove it," she whispered, sliding her arms around his waist. She smiled into his eyes. "Let's go now on that honeymoon you promised . . ."

# AUTHORS NOTE

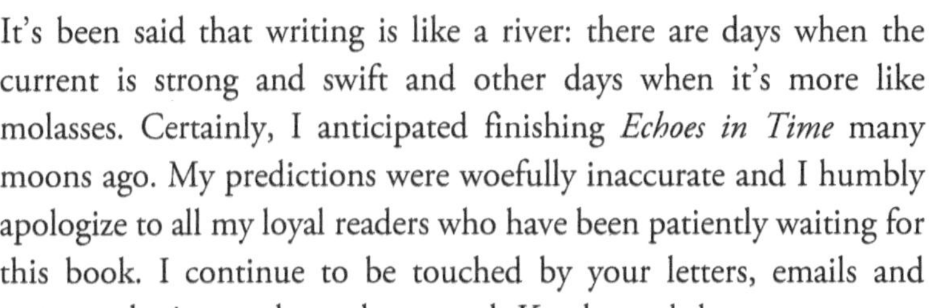

It's been said that writing is like a river: there are days when the current is strong and swift and other days when it's more like molasses. Certainly, I anticipated finishing *Echoes in Time* many moons ago. My predictions were woefully inaccurate and I humbly apologize to all my loyal readers who have been patiently waiting for this book. I continue to be touched by your letters, emails and messages letting me know how much Kendra and the gang mean to you. I am so grateful for your support.

I want to give special recognition to Valérie St-Martin, who inspired me to write the scene where Alec surprises Kendra with flowers; Barbara Toth Federmack, who has been Kendra's most stalwart champion; Ole Bjørsvik, who has given me many interesting ideas to consider, and Brigitte Reinke Chatterton, who continually impresses me with her creativity and positive spirit.

On the professional side, I must give a huge thank you to my editor, Katie McGuire, whose talent and skill have shaped Kendra's world since *A Murder in Time*. Likewise, Derek Thornton of Notch Designs has created each cover, and I continue to be blown away by your artistic brilliance. And I swear that I did not purposefully steal your last name for one of the characters in *Echoes in Time!* Last, but by no means least, I am incredibly grateful to the services of Lorna Reid, who designed the book's interior and who was instrumental in guiding me over the finishing line.

As always, I have my personal circle of friends to whom I owe so much. Karre Jacobs, you are not only one of the best editors I've ever worked with—no misplaced comma or misspelled word is safe from your eagle eye—but you are an amazing friend; Bonnie McCarthy, you are not only a gifted writer and artist, but you always know exactly the right thing to say to encourage me when life gets bumpy; and Lori McAllister, you cheered me on from the very beginning and your personal journey continues to inspire me in ways you'll never know. Thank you to one and all!

History is obviously a big part of the In Time books. For *Echoes in Time*, I delved into medical practices before and during the Regency. Science was advancing, but this was still a period when little was known about blood. Specifically, no one understood that there were different types of blood between humans, much less other species. Transfusions between humans and sheep or dogs, or other animals occurred. Sometimes the patient survived. Sometimes the patient perished. Jean-Baptiste Denis, the personal physician to King Louis XIV of France, found success with such transfusions…until he didn't and was then charged with murder. He was eventually acquitted, but blood transfusions of any kind suffered a huge setback in Europe for centuries. And one can't delve into the history of blood without addressing some pretty macabre practices—yes, a fallen gladiator's blood was drunk as a life-saving elixir—or the mythical tales involving vampires.

While I'm always partial to learning about ghoulish practices, I found myself equally tickled to learn why the stethoscope was invented during this time. It was not created to improve listening to a patient's heartbeat, as one might assume. Prior to the stethoscope, a physician was forced to press his ear directly against his patient's chest. Given the era's sensibilities, this would be highly embarrassing, especially if the patient happened to be female. I can't help but wonder what other inventions were created for the sake of modesty. I strive to be as accurate as possible when it comes to the historical facts that I weave within the fiction of each book. As always, any mistakes are mine and mine alone.